SIXTEEN WAYS TO DEFEND A WALLED CITY

My meteoric rise, from illiterate barbarian serf to commander of an Imperial regiment, is due to the Hus, the Sherden, the Echmen and, last but not least, the Robur, who are proud of the fact that over the last hundred years they've slaughtered in excess of a million of my people. One of those here-today-gone-tomorrow freak cults you get in the City says that the way to virtue is loving your enemies. I have no problem with that. My enemies have always come through for me, and I owe them everything. My friends, on the other hand, have caused me nothing but aggravation and pain. Just as well I've had so very few of them.)

By K. J. Parker

The Fencer trilogy
Colours in the Steel
The Belly of the Bow
The Proof House

The Scavenger trilogy
Shadow
Pattern
Memory

The Engineer trilogy
Devices and Desires
Evil for Evil
The Escapement

The Company
The Folding Knife
The Hammer

Sharps

The Two of
Swords: Volume 1
The Two of
Swords: Volume 2
The Two of
Swords: Volume 3
Sixteen Ways to
Defend a Walled City

By Tom Holt

Expecting
Someone Taller
Who's Afraid
of Beowulf?
Flying Dutch
Ye Gods!
Overtime
Here Comes the Sun
Grailblazers
Faust Among Equals
Odds and Gods
Djinn Rummy
My Hero
Paint Your Dragon
Open Sesame
Wish You Were Here
Only Human
Snow White and the
Seven Samurai
Valhalla
Nothing But Blue Skies
Falling Sideways
Little People
The Portable Door
In Your Dreams

Earth, Air, Fire
and Custard
You Don't Have to be
Evil to Work Here,
But It Helps
Someone Like Me
Barking
The Better Mousetrap
May Contain
Traces of Magic
Blonde Bombshell
Life, Liberty and the
Pursuit of Sausages
Doughnut
When It's A Jar
The Outsorcerer's
Apprentice
The Good, the Bad
and the Smug
The Management
Style of the
Supreme Beings

Dead
Funny: Omnibus 1

Mightier Than
the Sword:
Omnibus 2
The Divine
Comedies: Omnibus 3
For Two Nights
Only: Omnibus 4
Tall Stories:
Omnibus 5
Saints and
Sinners: Omnibus 6
Fishy
Wishes: Omnibus 7

The Walled Orchard
Alexander at the
World's End
Olympiad
A Song for Nero
Meadowland

I, Margaret

Lucia Triumphant
Lucia in Wartime

SIXTEEN WAYS TO DEFEND A WALLED CITY

K. J. Parker

www.orbitbooks.net

ORBIT

First published in Great Britain in 2019 by Orbit

7 9 10 8

ISBN 978-0-356-50673-9

Typeset in Horley by M Rules
Printed in Italy by Elcograf S.p.A.

Papers used by Orbit are from well-managed forests
and other responsible sources.

Orbit
An imprint of
Little, Brown Book Group
Carmelite Houe
50 Victoria Embankment
London EC4Y 0DZ

An Hachette UK Company
www.hachette.co.uk

www.orbitbooks.net

For Constantia and the Stalkers, with thanks

Orhan son of Siyyah Doctus Felix
Praeclarissimus, his history of the Great Siege,
written down so that the deeds and sufferings
of great men may never be forgotten.

1

I was in Classis on business. I needed sixty miles of second-
grade four-inch hemp rope – I build pontoon bridges – and all
the military rope in the empire goes through Classis. What
you're supposed to do is put in a requisition to Divisional
Supply, who send it on to Central Supply, who send it on to
the Treasurer General, who approves it and sends it back to
Divisional Supply, who send it on to Central Supply, who forward it to Classis, where the quartermaster says, sorry, we have
no rope. Or you can hire a clever forger in Herennis to cut you
an exact copy of the treasury seal, which you use to stamp your
requisition, which you then take personally to the office of the
deputy quartermaster in Classis, where there's a senior clerk
who'd have done time in the slate quarries if you hadn't pulled
certain documents out of the file a few years back. Of course,
you burned the documents as soon as you took them, but he
doesn't know that. And that's how you get sixty miles of rope
in this man's army.

I took the overland route from Traiecta to Cirte, across one of my bridges (a rush job I did fifteen years ago, only meant to last a month, still there and still the only way across the Lusen unless you go twenty-six miles out of your way to Pons Jovianis) then down through the pass onto the coastal plain. Fabulous view as you come through the pass, that huge flat green patchwork with the blue of the Bay beyond, and Classis as a geometrically perfect star, three arms on land, three jabbing out into the sea. Analyse the design and it becomes clear that it's purely practical and utilitarian, straight out of the field operations manual. Furthermore, as soon as you drop down onto the plain you can't see the shape, unless you happen to be God. The three seaward arms are tapered jetties, while their landward counterparts are defensive bastions, intended to cover the three main gates with enfilading fire on two sides. Even further more, when Classis was built ninety years ago, there was a dirty great forest in the way (felled for charcoal during the Social War, all stumps, marsh and bramble-fuzz now), so you wouldn't have been able to see it from the pass, and that strikingly beautiful statement of Imperial power must therefore be mere chance and serendipity. By the time I reached the way station at Milestone 2776 I couldn't see Classis at all, though of course it was dead easy to find. Just follow the arrow-straight military road on its six-foot embankment, and, next thing you know, you're there.

Please note I didn't come in on the military mail. As Colonel-in-Chief of the Engineers, I'm entitled; but, as a milkface (not supposed to call us that, everybody does, doesn't bother me, I like milk) it's accepted that I don't, because of the distress I might cause to Imperials finding themselves banged up in a coach with me for sixteen hours a day. Not that they'd say anything, of course. The Robur pride themselves on their good manners, and, besides, calling a milkface a milkface is Conduct

Prejudicial and can get you court-martialled. For the record, nobody's ever faced charges on that score, which proves (doesn't it) that Imperials aren't biased or bigoted in any way. On the other hand, several dozen auxiliary officers have been tried and cashiered for calling an Imperial a blueskin, so you can see just how wicked and deserving of contempt my lot truly are.

No, I made the whole four-day trip on a civilian carrier's cart. The military mail, running non-stop and changing horses at way stations every twenty miles, takes five days and a bit, but my cart was carrying fish; marvellous incentive to get a move on.

The cart rumbled up to the middle gate and I hopped off and hobbled up to the sentry, who scowled at me, then saw the scrambled egg on my collar. For a split second I thought he was going to arrest me for impersonating an officer (wouldn't be the first time). I walked past him, then jumped sideways to avoid being run down by a cart the size of a cathedral. That's Classis.

My pal the clerk's office was in Block 374, Row 42, Street 7. They've heard of sequential numbering in Supply but clearly aren't convinced that it'd work, so Block 374 is wedged in between Blocks 217 and 434. Street 7 leads from Street 4 into Street 32. But it must be all right, because I can find my way about there, and I'm just a bridge builder, nobody.

He wasn't there. Sitting at his desk was a six-foot-six Robur in a milk-white monk's habit. He was bald as an egg, and he looked at me as though I was something the dog had brought in. I mentioned my pal's name. He smiled.

"Reassigned," he said.

Oh. "He never mentioned it."

"It wasn't the sort of reassignment you'd want to talk about." He looked me up and down; I half expected him to roll back my upper lip so he could inspect my teeth. "Can I help you?"

I gave him the big smile. "I need rope."

"Sorry." He looked so happy. "No rope."

"I have a sealed requisition."

He held out his hand. I showed him my piece of paper. I'm pretty sure he spotted the seal was a fake. "Unfortunately, we have no rope at present," he said. "As soon as we get some—"

I nodded. I didn't go to staff college so I know squat about strategy and tactics, but I know when I've lost and it's time to withdraw in good order. "Thank you," I said. "Sorry to have bothered you."

"No bother." His smile said he hadn't finished with me yet. "You can leave that with me."

I was still holding the phony requisition with the highly illegal seal. "Thanks," I said, "but shouldn't I resubmit it through channels? I wouldn't want you thinking I was trying to jump the queue."

"Oh, I think we can bend the rules once in a while." He held out his hand again. Damn, I thought. And then the enemy saved me.

(Which is the story of my life, curiously enough. I've had an amazing number of lucky breaks in my life, far more than my fair share, which is why, when I got the citizenship, I chose Felix as my proper name. Good fortune has smiled on me at practically every crucial turning point in my remarkable career. But the crazy thing is, the agency of my good fortune has always – invariably – been the enemy. Thus: when I was seven years old, the Hus attacked our village, slaughtered my parents, dragged me away by the hair and sold me to a Sherden; who taught me the carpenter's trade – thereby trebling my value – and sold me on to a shipyard. Three years after that, when I was nineteen, the Imperial army mounted a punitive expedition against the Sherden pirates; guess who was among the prisoners carted back to the empire. The Imperial navy is always desperately short of skilled shipwrights. They let me join up, which meant citizenship, and I was a foreman at age twenty-two. Then the Echmen invaded, captured the city where I was stationed; I was one of the survivors and transferred to the Engineers, of whom I now have the honour to be Colonel-in-Chief. I consider my point made. My meteoric rise, from illiterate barbarian serf to commander of an Imperial regiment, is due to the Hus, the Sherden, the Echmen and, last but not least, the Robur, who are proud of the fact that over the last hundred years they've slaughtered in excess of a million of my people. One of those here-today-gone-tomorrow freak cults you get in the City says that the way to virtue is loving your enemies. I have no problem with that. My enemies have always come through for me, and I owe them everything. My friends, on the other hand, have caused me nothing but aggravation and pain. Just as well I've had so very few of them.)

I noticed I no longer had his full attention. He was peering through his little window. After a moment, I shuffled closer and looked over his shoulder.

"Is that smoke?" I said.

He wasn't looking at me. "Yes."

Fire, in a place like Classis, is bad news. Curious how people react. He seemed frozen stiff. I felt jumpy as a cat. I elbowed myself a better view, as the long shed that had been leaking smoke from two windows suddenly went up in flames like a torch.

"What do you keep in there?" I asked.

"Rope," he said. "Three thousand miles of it."

I left him gawping and ran. Milspec rope is heavily tarred, and all the sheds at Classis are thatched. Time to be somewhere else.

I dashed out into the yard. There were people running in every direction. Some of them didn't look like soldiers, or clerks. One of them raced toward me, then stopped.

"Excuse me," I said. "Do you know—?"

He stabbed me. I hadn't seen the sword in his hand. I thought; what the devil are you playing at? He pulled the sword out and swung it at my head. I may not be the most perceptive man you'll ever meet, but I can read between the lines; he didn't like me. I sidestepped, tripped his heels and kicked his face in. That's not in the drill manuals, but you pick up a sort of alternative education when you're brought up by slavers—

Sequence of thoughts; I guess the tripping and kicking thing reminded me of the Sherden who taught it to me (by example), and that made me think of pirates, and then I understood. I trod on his ear for luck till something cracked – not that I hold grudges – and looked round for somewhere to hide.

Really bad things happening all around you take time to sink in. Sherden pirates running amok in Classis? Couldn't be happening. So I found a shady doorway, held perfectly still and used my eyes. Yes, in fact, it was happening, and to judge from the small slice of the action I could see, they were having things very much their own way. The Imperial army didn't seem to be troubling them at all; they were preoccupied with fighting the fire in the rope shed, and the Sherden cut them down and shot them as they dashed about with buckets and ladders and long hooks, and nobody seemed to realise what was going on except me, and I don't count. Pretty soon there were no Imperials left in the yard, and the Sherden were backing up carts to the big sheds and pitching stuff in. Never any shortage of carts at Classis. They were hard workers, I'll give them that. Try and get a gang of dockers or warehousemen to load two hundred size-four carts in forty minutes. I guess that's the difference between hired men and self-employed.

I imagine the fire was an accident, because it rather spoiled things for the Sherden. It spread from one shed to a load of others before they had a chance to loot them, then burned up the main stable block and coach-houses, where most of the carts would have been, before the wind changed direction and sent it roaring through the barracks and the secondary admin blocks. That meant it was coming straight at me. By now, there were no soldiers or clerks to be seen, only the bad guys, and I'd stick out like a sore thumb in my regulation cloak and tunic. So I took off the cloak, noticed a big red stain down my front – oh yes, I'd been stabbed, worry about that later – pulled off the dead pirate's smock and dragged it over my head. Then I pranced away across the yard, looking like I had a job to do.

I got about thirty yards and fell over. I was mildly surprised, then realised: not just a flesh wound. I felt ridiculously weak and terribly sleepy. Then someone was standing over me, a Sherden, with a spear in his hand. Hell, I thought, and then: not that it matters.

"Are you all right?" he said.

Me and good fortune. How lucky I was to have been born a milkface. "I'm fine," I said. "Really."

He grinned. "Bullshit," he said, and hauled me to my feet. I saw him notice my boots – issue beetlecrushers, you can't buy them in stores. Then I saw he was wearing them, too. Pirates. Dead men's shoes. "Come on," he said. "Lean on me, you'll be fine."

He put my arm round his neck, then grabbed me round the waist and walked me across to the nearest cart. The driver helped him haul me up, and they laid me down gently on a huge stack of rolled-up lamellar breastplates. My rescuer took off his smock, rolled it up and put it under my head. "Get him back to the ship, they'll see to him there," he said, and that was the last I saw of him.

Simple as that. The way the looters were going about their business, quickly and efficiently, it was pretty obvious that there were no Imperial personnel left for them to worry about – apart from me, lovingly whisked away from danger by my enemies. The cart rumbled through the camp to the middle jetty. There were a dozen ships tied up on either side. The driver wasn't looking, so I was able to scramble off the cart and bury myself in a big coil of rope, where I stayed until the last ship set sail.

Some time later, a navy cutter showed up. Just in time, I remembered to struggle out of the Sherden smock that had saved my life. It'd have been the death of me if I'd been caught wearing it by our lot.

Which is the reason – one of the reasons – why I've decided to write this history. Under normal circumstances I wouldn't have bothered, wouldn't have presumed – who am I, to take upon myself the recording of the deeds and sufferings of great men, and so on. But I was there; not just all through the siege, but right at the very beginning. As I may already have mentioned, I've had far more good luck in my life than I could possibly have deserved, and when – time after time after time – some unseen hand scoops you up from under the wheels, so to speak, and puts you safely down on the roadside, you have to start wondering, why? And the only capacity in which I figure I'm fit to serve is that of witness. After all, anyone can testify in an Imperial court of law; even children, women, slaves, milkfaces, though of course it's up to the judge to decide what weight to give to the evidence of the likes of me. So; if luck figures I'm good enough to command the Engineers, maybe she reckons I can be a historian, too. Think of that. Immortality. A turf-cutter's son from north of the Bull's Neck living for ever on the spine of a book. Wouldn't that be something.

2

I wasn't the only survivor. A deputy quartermaster's clerk lived just long enough to verify most of what I reported, and a couple of fishermen saw the Sherden sailing out of North Sound and dropping anchor at the quays. They tacked up the channel against the wind to the naval base at Colophon, where nobody believed them until they saw the column of smoke.

The cutter took me back to Colophon, where a navy sawbones patched me up, even though he wasn't supposed to – guess why – before sending me on a supply sloop to Malata, where there's a resident-aliens hospital licensed to treat people with chronic skin conditions, like mine. After a couple of days I was sick to death of doctors, so I discharged myself and requisitioned a lift on a charcoal cart back to the City. Soon as I got there, I was in all sorts of trouble. Commissioners of Enquiry had trekked all the way out to Malata to take my statement, and I hadn't been there. Can't you people do anything right?

Soon as Intelligence were through shouting at me, I tottered down the hill to see Faustinus, the City Prefect. Faustinus is – I won't say a friend, because I don't want to make problems for him. He has rather more time for me than most Robur, and we've worked together on patching up the aqueducts. Faustinus wasn't there, called away, important meeting of the Council. I left him a note, come and see me, and dragged myself back up the hill to Municipal Works, which is sort of my home when I'm in the City.

As a special favour, obtained for me by the personal intercession of Prefect Faustinus, I had a space of my own at Municipal Works. Once upon a time it was a charcoal shed; before that, I think the watchman kept his dog there. And before that, it was part of the Painted Cloister of the Fire temple that Temren the Great built to give thanks for his defeat of the Robur under Marcian III; it's an old city, and wherever you dig, you find things. Anyway, the Clerk of the Works let me leave some stuff there, and letters and so forth pile up in an old box by the door, and I'd made myself a bed out of three packing crates (a carpenter, remember?). I didn't bother looking at the letters. I crawled onto the bed, smothered myself in horse blankets, and fell asleep.

Some fool woke me up. He was enormous, and head to foot in gilded scale armour, like an enormous fish standing on its tail. He wasn't alone. "What?" I yawned.

"Colonel Orhan."

Well, I knew that. "What?"

"General Priscus's compliments, sir, and you're wanted in Council."

That, of course, was a bare-faced lie. General Priscus didn't want me anywhere in his jurisdiction, as he'd made quite clear when I was up for my promotion (but Priscus wasn't in charge back then, praise be). Most particularly he didn't want me on his Council, but sadly for him, he had no choice in the matter. "When?"

"Now, sir."

I groaned. I was still wearing the bloodstained tunic with the hole in it, over the Malata medic's off-white bandages. "I need to get washed and changed," I said. "Give me ten minutes, will you?"

"No, sir."

Among the things I have room for at Municipal Works is a spare grey cloak and regulation red felt pillbox hat. I put them on – it was a hot day, I knew I'd roast in the thick wool cloak, but it was that or go into Council in bloody rags – and shuffled to my feet. The golden-fish men fell in precisely around me. No need for that, but I imagine it was just force of habit.

The War Office is four doors down from the Golden Spire, on the left. It's a small, low door in a bleak brick wall, and once you're through that you're in the most amazing knot garden, all lavender and box and bewilderingly lovely flowers, and then you're looking at the double bronze doors, with two of the toughest soldiers in the army scowling at you, and then you're inside, shading your eyes from the glare off all that white marble. I can see why people get offended when I go in there. I don't half lower the tone.

Still, it's a grand view from the top. Straight down Hill Street, all you see is roofs – red tiles, grey slates, thatch. No green or blue, just the work of men's hands, as far as the eye can see. Nowhere else on earth you can do that. Every time I look at that view, regardless of context, I realise just how lucky I am.

From the window in the Council chamber, however, you can see the sea. General Priscus was sitting with his back to it, while I had the prime lookout position. Over his shoulder, I could see the arms of the harbour, and, beyond that, flat dark blue. Plenty of sails, but none of them the red and white stripes of the Sherden. Not yet, at any rate. If I'd offered to swap places with the general, he'd have thought I was trying to be funny, so I kept my mouth shut.

In terse, concise military language, General Priscus proceeded to tell us everything we already knew; a surprise attack by seaborne aggressors, no survivors, considerable damage to buildings and stores, enquiries continuing to ascertain the identity of the attackers—

"Excuse me," I said.

Out of the corner of my eye, I saw Prefect Faustinus wince. As well he might. He's told me, over and over again, don't make trouble. He's quite right and has my best interests at heart. He keeps asking me, why do you do it? Answer: I have no idea. I know it's going to end badly, and God knows I don't enjoy it. My knees go weak, I get this twisting pain in my stomach and my chest tightens up so I can barely breathe. I hear my own voice speaking and I think: not now, you fool, not again. But by then it's too late.

Everybody was looking at me. Priscus scowled. "What?"

"I know who they were," I said.

I'd done it again. "You do."

"Yes. They're called the Sherden."

When Priscus got angry, he lowered his voice until he practically purred. "Is there any reason why you didn't see fit to mention this earlier?"

"Nobody asked me."

Faustinus had his eyes tight shut. "Well," said the general, "perhaps you'd be good enough to enlighten us now."

When I'm nervous, I talk a lot. And I'm rude to people.

This is ridiculous. Other times – when I'm angry, particularly when people are trying to provoke me, I can control my temper like a charioteer in the Hippodrome manages his horses. But panic makes me cocky; go figure. "Of course," I said. "The Sherden are a loose confederation, mostly exiles and refugees from other nations, based around the estuary of the Schelm in south-eastern Permia. We tend to call them pirates but mostly they trade; we do a lot of business with them, direct or through intermediaries. They have fast, light ships, low tonnage but sturdy. Typically they only go thieving when times are hard, and then they pick off small, easy targets where they can be sure of a good, quick return – monasteries, absentee landlords' villas, occasionally an army payroll or a wagon train of silver ore from the mines. Given the choice, though, they'd rather receive stolen goods than do the actual robbing; they know we could stamp them flat in two minutes if we wanted to. But we never have, because, like I said, we do a lot of business with them. Basically, they're no bother to anyone."

Admiral Zonaras leaned forward and glared up the table at me. "How many ships?"

"No idea," I said, "it's not my area of expertise, all I know about these people is from – well, our paths have crossed, let's say. Naval Intelligence is bound to know. Ask them."

Zonaras never cared for me at the best of times. "I'm asking you. Your best guess."

I shrugged. "At any one time, total number around three fifty, four hundred ships. But you're talking about dozens of small independent companies with no overall control. There's no King of the Sherden or anything like that."

Priscus looked past me down the table. "Do we have any figures for the number of ships at Classis?"

Nobody said anything. A marvellous, once-in-a-lifetime chance for me to keep my mouth shut. "About seventy," I said.

"Hold on." Sostratus, the Lord Chamberlain. If we'd been discussing a civilian issue, he'd have been in the chair instead of Priscus. "How do you know all this?"

I did my shrug. "I was there."

"You what?"

Nobody knew. For crying out loud. "I was there," I repeated. "I was at Classis on business, I saw the whole thing." Muttering up and down the table. I pressed on. "My estimate of seventy is based on a direct view of their ships tied up at the docks. There were a dozen ships each side of each of the three jetties. Six twelves are seventy-two. I don't think there could have been more than that when I looked, because there didn't seem to be room, all the berths were full. They could have had more ships standing by to come in as others finished loading, I don't know. I couldn't see that far from where I was."

Symmachus the Imperial agent said, "Why weren't we told there was an eye witness?"

That didn't improve the general's temper. "The witness hasn't seen fit to mention it until now, apparently. Still, better late than never. You'd better tell us all about it."

I was about to point out that I'd made a full deposition in the naval hospital at Colophon. I think Faustinus can read my mind sometimes. I saw him shake his head, vigorously, like a cow being buzzed by flies. He had a point. So I told them the whole tale, from seeing the smoke to being picked up by the cutter. I stopped. Long silence.

"It all seems fairly straightforward to me," said Admiral Zonaras. "I can have the Fifth Fleet at sea in four days. They'll make sure these Sherden never bother us again."

A general nodding, like the wind swaying a maple hedge. I could feel the blood pounding at the back of my head. Don't say it, I begged myself. "Excuse me," I said.

After the Council broke up, I tried to sneak away down Hillgate, but Faustinus was too quick for me. He headed me off by the Callicrates fountain. "Are you out of your tiny mind?" he said.

"But it's true," I told him.

He rolled his eyes at me. "Of course it's true," he said, "that's not the point. The point is, you've pissed off everyone who matters a damn."

Shrug. "They never liked me anyway."

"Orhan." Nobody calls me that. "You're a clever man and you use your brain, which makes you unique in this man's town, but you've got to do something about your attitude."

"Attitude? Me?"

Why was I annoying the only man in the City who could stand the sight of me? Sorry, don't know. "Orhan, you've got to do something about it, before you get yourself in serious trouble. You know your problem? You're so full of resentment it oozes out of you, like a cow that hasn't been milked. You put people's backs up, and then they'd rather die than do what you tell them, even though it's the right and sensible thing. You know what? If the empire comes crashing down, it could easily be all your fault."

And that was me told. I nodded. "I know," I said. "I fuck up good advice by giving it." That made him grin, in spite of himself. "What I ought to do is get someone else, someone who's not a total liability, to say things for me. Then people would listen."

His face went sort of wooden. "I don't know about that," he said. "If only you could learn not to be so bloody rude."

I sighed. "You look like you could use a drink."

Faustinus always looks that way. This time, though, he shook his head. "Too busy," he said, meaning too busy to risk being seen in public with me for at least a week. "Think about it, for crying out loud. Please. There's too much at stake to risk screwing things up just because of your unfortunate personality."

Fair comment, and I did actually think seriously about it, all the way down Hill Street. The trouble was, I'd been right. All I'd done was point out that the Fifth Fleet wouldn't be going anywhere, not for quite some time. Admiral Zonaras had said that that was news to him; I pointed out that, since all the rope and all the barrel staves – that was what was in the shed next to the rope store, I learned that in the navy hospital, before they threw me out – for the entire navy had gone up in smoke—

Hang on, you're saying, so maybe I should explain. They called it need-to-use stockholding, and they reckoned it saved the navy a fortune each year. The idea being, we had six fleets of three hundred and twenty ships each back then, and a ship on its own is not much use; you need masts, sails, oars, ropes, all manner of stores, of which the most important are barrels, for holding fresh water. Without water barrels, a ship can't go out of sight of land, because of the need to tank up once a day, twice in hot weather. Now, if every single ship in the Fleet had to have its own separate set of gear – you're probably better at sums than me, you work it out – that's a lot of very expensive equipment, and since most of the time only two of the fleets, three in emergencies, are at sea at any given time; and since the navy yards had been to enormous trouble to make sure that everything was interchangeable, ship to ship – it was quite a coup on the part of the government official who thought of it. One fleet – the Home Division, which is on permanent duty guarding the straits – was fully equipped at all times. The other five shared two complete sets of gear, which for convenience and ease of speedy deployment were kept in store at Classis, ready to be issued at a moment's notice when someone needed to use them.

Obviously Zonaras knew all that, at some level. But it's perfectly possible to know something and not think about it. Or maybe the admiral was well aware that he couldn't launch a single ship, now that all his ropes and all his barrel staves were just so much grey ash, but he didn't want the rest of the Council in on the secret. In any event, he called me a damned liar and a bloody fool and various other things, all of them perfectly true but hardly relevant. General Priscus asked him straight out: can you send a fleet to Permia or can't you? So Zonaras did the only thing he could, in the circumstances. He jumped up, gave me a scowl that made my teeth hurt and stalked out of the room without a word.

And that was that, as far as the Council was concerned. From my point of view, probably just as well. I'd already made a world of trouble for myself. If the Council hadn't broken up in confusion at that point, I might easily have gone on to raise various other issues that had occurred to me about the Classis thing, which might well have cost me my neck.

So there I was, in the City, at a loose end. Properly speaking, since my business in town had finished, I should have gone back to Corps headquarters and got on with my paperwork. Somehow, though, I felt that would be a bad idea. It's inconceivable that the general, or the admiral or the Chamberlain or one of the divisional chiefs, or one of their many, many staff, would arrange for a serving officer of the empire to be murdered as he rode home alone along the lonely roads across the moors. But even in an empire as well ordered as ours, there are bandits, discharged soldiers, runaway slaves, disaffected serfs, religious zealots and ordinary loons, all manner of bad people who'd cut your throat for the nails in your boots, and from time to time officers who'd made nuisances of themselves had fallen foul of them, and other hazards of long-distance travel. Give it a day or so, I told myself, then hitch a lift with a merchant caravan or a bunch of pilgrims. I have strong views about not tempting providence and, as a wise man once said, the difference between luck and a wheelbarrow is, luck doesn't work if you push it.

3

Of course, there's no shortage of thieves, crazy people and unfortunate accidents in the City too, but in town you can take steps to reduce the risk they pose. For instance, if you want to stay clear of the displeasure of the properly constituted authorities, who better to help you out than those people who do that sort of thing all the time, for a living?

I'm choosy about the company I keep, so I tend to stay clear of murderers, muggers, housebreakers and the extortion gangs. That still leaves me plenty of people to be friends with. The con men are all right, but they're smarter than me and always on the lookout for business opportunities, so I generally drift towards the forgers, clippers and issuers of false coin. You meet a better class of person.

So I went to the Old Flower Market. If you've never been to the City, take note; you can't buy flowers in the Old Flower Market. Like so many City neighbourhoods, it defines itself in terms of what was done there a long time ago but isn't any more. For the avoidance of doubt, flowers are about the only thing you can't buy there. Life and death, yes, no problem. A simple bunch of roses, no. The Old Flower Market is built on the ruins of a whole district that collapsed and fell into a sinkhole a hundred and fifty odd years ago – turned out it had been built directly over an underground river, which runs down though the middle of the hill on which Hill Street is built and eventually out into the Bay.

I headed straight for the Two Dogs, sat in the corner furthest from the fire and asked for a bowl of tea and a plate of honey-cakes. Nobody orders tea in the Two Dogs.

A minute or so later, she came out and sat down opposite. "You've got a nerve," she said.

"You know about this morning's Council. I'm impressed."

"No idea what you're talking about." She flared her nostrils: warning sign. "People have been in here looking for you."

Her name is Aichma, and I knew her father, years ago, when he was captain of the Greens. He and I served together, before he quit the service and took to the Ring. Like me, he did well in his chosen profession, from tyro to Theme boss in six years. I miss him. When she was fourteen I told her that on his death-bed he made me promise to look after her. I was lying, of course. *Keep away from my daughter or I'll rip your head off* was nearer the mark. And of course he didn't have a deathbed. He bled out into the sand, with seventy thousand people cheering. That must be a strange way to go.

"If they weren't government types, I'm not bothered," I said. "What were they like?"

She shrugged. "Two northerners and a milkface. I told them I hadn't seen you. Which was true."

I relaxed. The milkface was a business colleague. It goes like this. The government sends me the payroll for my men in gold. I pay my men in silver, six tornece a man every month, a hundred and sixty tornece to the gold stamenon. There's no official, legal way to change gold into silver, because of the perpetual shortage of silver coin, which comes about because of the Mint. It's nobody's fault. If you want to be the master of the Mint, you buy the job from the Chancellor for a great deal of money, which you've got to recoup somehow. But that's all right, because your pay is a tenth of a per cent of all the coins struck in the Mint. Now, since it's exactly as much time and work to strike a gold coin as a silver or a bronze one, the Mint strikes lots and lots of gold, silver when it absolutely has to and bronze never; the army regiments take care of the small change, striking their own crude, ghastly coinage on flattened offcuts of copper pipe. So, when I need silver to pay my men, I trade the government gold for somewhat less than official silver, which I get from honest tradesmen like the milkface and the two northerners. Which is how come I know so many people in the Old Flower Market. You can also begin to see how come I've been a success in this man's army. The people who make it possible for me to do my job would run a mile from a blue-blood Imperial straight out of the Academy.

She was looking at me. "Something bad," she said.

I nodded. "Something bloody awful."

She sighed. Her time is not without value, but when I need to talk, she makes time and listens. She nodded to the tapster, who pulled a sad face and went away to fill a kettle. "Politics?"

"Sort of politics."

"I'm not interested in all that. I work for a living."

"You're smart," I said.

She has this sort of wan smile. "This is one of your figure-it-out-from-first principles games, isn't it? Where you make me say what you're thinking."

"Yes, but you're good at it. Because you're smart."

Vanity is her one weakness. She knows she's pretty, because men tell her, over and over again, and it brings her nothing but aggravation. But I'm the only one who tells her she's clever. "Go on," she said.

"You heard about Classis."

She nodded. "Something about pirates stealing a load of stores."

"That's right," I said. "Now, you're the one with the brains, you tell me. Why would that bother me so much?"

When she thinks about something, she has this ritual. She lowers her head, as if in prayer. She stares down at her hands. Don't bother talking to her while she's doing all this, she won't hear a word. You know when she's on the scent because she scowls. When she reckons she's got there, she sits up straight and looks right at you. "Well?" I said.

"What exactly did they take?"

Good girl, I thought. "I don't know for sure," I said. "All I know is what I overheard in the navy hospital, and I wasn't there long. But by the sound of it, mostly basic military supplies."

"Meaning?"

"Boots," I said. "Blankets. Three hundred barrels of scales, for making armour. Two thousand yards of tent fabric. Cartloads of palisade stakes. Seven thousand helmet liners. That sort of thing."

She nodded slowly. "All right," she said. "I'm a businessman. I spend a lot of money on ships and crews, knowing that I'm going to catch it hot from the navy once they've found me, which they're bound to do sooner or later. What do I get for my money? Let's see. Palisade stakes are firewood, which—"

"Grows on trees?"

"Don't interrupt. Tent fabric might do for clothes, but you'd get pennies on the tornece. Helmet liners—" She shrugged. "No use at all. Nobody's going to want to buy all that stuff. Not at a price that'll give you a profit."

"Except?"

She nodded briskly. "An army, a government. But governments don't steal their supplies from other governments, it's too risky. Also it's cheaper to make the stuff yourself, and you've got continuity of supply."

She knows a lot of long words. Gets them from me, I flatter myself. "So?"

"Hang on, I'm still thinking. Pirates steal a load of unlikely stuff, really hard to shift and no real value, and the risk is really horrible. So—" She dipped her head, as if some invisible helper had just fed her the answer. "Stealing to order."

"Stealing to order. But not a government, we already decided that."

She rubbed her thumb against her palm. Her father did that when he was angry, or confused. "Not a government. Maybe someone who isn't a government right now but—"

"Wants to be one." I snapped my fingers and pointed at her. "Your father always said you were sharp."

That got me a scowl. "Hang on, though," she said. "Still doesn't make sense. Just suppose there really is someone who wants to set up an army, from scratch. I don't know, someone founding a colony up in the Armpit, or down south somewhere, or a free company. You can buy all that stuff at the surplus auctions. Cheap."

I smiled at her. "Yes," I said, "you can. Or you could buy a thousand skilled men and set up a factory. But they didn't. So?"

She went back into thinking mode, and while she was in conference the tea arrived. I poured a bowl and put it aside to cool down.

"Money," she said. "Actual cash money. Whoever he is, he hasn't got any."

"But the Sherden – the pirates," I said, a bit too late. Her eyes flicker just a little when she learns something she doesn't already know.

"It must be a long-term partnership," she said slowly. "No money now, working on spec, and a really big payout some time later. Which doesn't sound like the Sherden," she added. "Too organised, if you see what I mean. The long term for a Sherden is tomorrow afternoon."

"I thought so too. So?"

Frown. "So it must be a really good deal, for them to be interested. A really big payout, at some point."

She's like her father in many ways. Brave, loyal, kind-hearted, sharp as a knife and slippery as an eel. But he had charm. "Out of interest," I said, "the first thing they did, before they set to thieving, was set fire to the ropes and the barrel staves."

"Chandler's stores. For which there'd be a ready market."

"Or they could have used them themselves. But no, up in smoke; and *before* they started looting, it's as though they'd been told, first things first."

"To make sure the Fleet couldn't follow them."

"Only temporarily."

"Someone told them to do that," she said firmly. "First, stop the Fleet, then take the stuff." She looked at me. "Now that's interesting."

"Keeps me interested all night, when I'd rather be sleeping. Only temporary, but maybe temporary's long enough. If whoever it is plans to make his move very soon."

"And he's got all our stuff, and we haven't got anything."

I nodded. "Because of centralised supply. Two birds, one

stone. In the short term we're paralysed, army and navy. He's ready, we're not. But that begs the question. Who's *he*?"

"Not the Echmen, or the Auxenes, they'd never hire pirates. And besides, why would they want a war with us? They've got their hands full with their own savages." She shook her head. "Sorry," she said. "No idea."

"You're just stupid, you are."

She gave me that look; you're a clown, but I forgive you. I sipped my tea. They make it just right at the Dogs – remarkable, since they don't use the stuff themselves and I'm the only customer for it. Weak and refreshing at the top of the pot, strong and soothing at the bottom. Great stuff. The only good thing ever to come out of Echman; therefore (it's only just occurred to me) yet another blessing conferred upon me by the enemy.

"What's all this in aid of, anyway?" she asked me. "You're scared."

"You bet," I replied.

She gave me a scornful look. "Not your business," she said. "You're just a glorified carpenter."

"Hardly glorified." She was watching one of the tapsters. She can spot someone palming a coin at twenty paces. "And, yes, it's none of my concern."

"Good."

I grinned. "I'm concerned," I said, "because the people whose concern it is don't seem concerned. If that makes any—"

She sighed. "I like talking to you," she said, "but basically you're a pest. My dad said, don't let him get started, he'll make your head spin."

"Bless him."

She was giving me her full attention now. "Why do you do it?" she said. "Why do you come in here and make me think about a whole load of stuff that's got nothing to do with me? I don't like it."

"You do. It's like playing chess to you."

"Why do you do it? You knew all that, but you made me figure it out."

"Because your father isn't here any more," I said, "and he was the cleverest man I ever met. But he's gone, so I have to make do with you."

She smiled at me, not unkindly. "You know what," she said, "when he was sick one time, he made me promise him something. Look after Orhan, he said, make sure he doesn't come to any harm. Weird thing to say. I was only twelve."

"Did you promise?"

Nod. "Had my fingers crossed behind my back. So." She parked her elbows on the table. "What are you going to do?"

"Me? Nothing. Not my place. We agreed on that."

"Never stopped you in the past."

"Nothing," I repeated. "Not unless they want a bridge built. In which case, I'll be on it like a snake."

She loves it really. I know her too well. She likes to use her brain, just occasionally. Women aren't allowed to be officers in the Themes, but a lot of clever men in the Greens spent a lot of time in the Dogs, chatting up the landlady, and, by a strange coincidence, the Greens were on top for the first time in a century—

It's just occurred to me that maybe you don't know very much about the Themes. It's possible, if you're from out of town. Maybe all you know is that there are two rival groups of supporters in the Hippodrome, one lot with blue favours, one lot with green, and they cheer for their side in the swordfighting and the chariot races. Which is true. It started that way, certainly. Then, about two hundred and fifty years ago, the Blues took up a collection for the fighters' widows and orphans. Naturally, the Greens did the same. A bit later, they extended the fund to look after the dependants of Theme members; you pay a few trachy every week into the pot, and if you fall on hard times you get a bit of help till you're on your feet again. Well, an idea that good was bound to catch on; just as bound to go wrong. Before long, the Theme treasuries controlled huge assets, invested in shipping and manufacturing since commoners can't own land. Money brought power, which wasn't always used wisely or honestly. Then the Greens started organising the labour at the docks, the Blues did the same in haulage and the civil service, lower grades. Wasn't long before the government got scared and tried to interfere, which got us the Victory riots – twenty thousand dead in the Hippodrome, when the City Prefect sent in Hus auxiliaries. Since then, the Themes have kept a low profile. What they do, the funds and all the activities that go with them, is strictly illegal, but since when did that stop anybody from doing anything? Besides, if you get sick or break a leg in this man's town, it's the Themes you turn to, or starve to death. Her father was a trustee of the Greens fund, and quite a big man in the movement; did a lot of bad things and a lot of good ones, until he neglected to sidestep in the Hippodrome and got skewered. I'd assumed he'd creamed off enough to set his daughter up for life, but it turned out he gambled it away as fast as he embezzled it. As far as she knows, there was enough left to buy her the Dogs. Actually, there wasn't, and regimental funds had to come to the rescue. Well, it was that or three thousand regulation shovels, and we have plenty of shovels. I was always a Blue, incidentally, until I met her father. So, you see, people can change their minds, on even the most fundamental issues of conscience.

4

The false coin people caught up with me the next day, and we did good business. There's an advantage in changing your gold with the Old Flower Market crowd rather than the Mint; they do deals. The government says it's a hundred and sixty tornece to the stamenon, but in the real world their opinion doesn't carry a lot of weight, and government gold is ninety-seven pure, which gives me a lot of leverage in negotiations. My friends were a bit on edge that day, probably because the Classis thing was worrying the shipping people, and gold does a lot to calm the nerves. I closed with them at two hundred and sixteen of their excellent, in many ways better than the real thing silver-ish tornese to one of my official gold cartwheels, thereby clearing a substantial profit for my regimental rainy-day fund, which nobody knows about except me. That's how come I can outbid other units for supplies, pay my boys when the treasury screws up, splash out on proper boots with seams that don't split whenever Supply's on an economy binge. That's how you get ahead in this man's army when you're not someone's nephew and you have a chronic skin condition, and, since it's a game I'm rather good at, I'm all for it.

Admiral Zonaras would rather have bitten off one of his own ears than admit he'd listened to me, so it must have been coincidence that the First Fleet was pulled off guarding the straits and bundled off to the Schelm estuary. When they got there, nobody was home. All the little fishing villages were deserted, boats and nets gone, livestock pens empty, not a dog barking. They set fire to a few wattle-and-daub sheds, which I suppose is as good a way as any of persuading the unenlightened savages of the superiority of our culture and way of life, then came home. It was sheer bad luck that they ran into a filthy storm off the Pillars, which sank three ships and scattered the rest. It took a week for the Fleet to regroup, another week to patch up the damage, and then they hauled up the home straight into the Bay. I spoke to a midshipman on one of the ships in the lead squadron, and he told me they saw the smoke rising as soon as they rounded Cape Suidas.

Note smoke rising; indicating still air, no wind. It was really bad luck that they got well and truly becalmed just inside the Cape; it happens, from time to time, and nobody knows why. There was nothing they could do. The First Fleet is mostly galleots and dromons, massive great things with acres of sail, fast and beautifully nimble, but only when the wind is blowing. The Sherden, by contrast, use skinny little galleys, twenty oars a side, with one big square-rigged sail, so when there's no wind they can row. Which is what they did, right past the Fleet, which was powerless to stop or chase them. The man I spoke to said he counted eighty-seven ships, all riding low in the water, on their way back from looting and burning Salpynx.

What a bloody fool I am. It's no consolation that Admiral Zonaras didn't see it coming either. Salpynx is – sorry, was – a single-purpose facility. It's where the big charcoal barges from the Armpit put in to land their cargoes, thousands of tons of the stuff every month to supply the forges and foundries of the Arsenal. No wonder the smoke was easy to see a long way off. Apparently the Sherden took their time, loaded their little ships until there was barely room to move, then set light to what was left and ran for it. Luck was on their side. If it hadn't been for the storm and the calm, they'd have run into the Fleet off the Pillars and that would've been that. I assume that whoever planned the operation reckoned on Zonaras's boys putting a bit more effort into finding someone to kill up in the estuary. Still, fortune favours the brave.

By this point I'd had enough of the City to last me a good long time. I hired three big carts to lug my dodgy silver back to regimental headquarters at Cacodemon – normally I'd have sent it by fast ship, but somehow that didn't seem sensible. I was in a hurry to get out of town before Priscus called another Council, so I hitched a ride with Eynar the scrap metal king as far as Louso and hired a horse at the Unicorn. I hate riding – it's not the day after, it's the day after that – but something told me I needed to get back to my own people and find something to do for a while, preferably a long way away, where communications would take some time.

I save up rainy-day jobs for just such occasions. About nine months earlier, some Academy brat had sent for us to build him a bridge up in the Teeth mountains, halfway to the Armpit. I have better things to do than trudge up mountain tracks, carrying my establishment with me like a snail, so I wrote back saying

I'd try and get around to it when I had five minutes. Those five minutes had now become available. The lads weren't exactly overjoyed to be leaving the refined delights of Cacodemon for an extended trip to the middle of nowhere, but I had one of my sporadic bouts of deafness, and off we went.

I won't bore you with an account of our adventures building a pontoon bridge across a river in spate between two sides of a steep ravine in the mist and the driving rain, just so that our Academy boy didn't have to take a ten-mile detour when he wanted to go skirt-chasing in the nearest town. Actually, it was a lovely piece of engineering, though I say it myself, and we did it with salvaged or scrounged materials, so it didn't cost Division a bent trachy, and the casualty list was two broken arms and a few bumps and bruises – that, with a seventy-foot drop into frothing white water for the view that greeted us when we started work each morning, isn't bad going, trust me. But it was a waste of time and energy, and I reckon the lads began to suspect that something funny was going on. There were a lot of conversations that went quiet when I walked up to the campfire, and I had to fend off a lot of artful questions, which isn't something I'm used to doing. Just as well the boys trusted me, or it could've been awkward.

News doesn't get that far up the map; the only form of it they have up there is coins, which tell the few of them who can read when there's a new emperor. The soldiers we were building the bridge for hadn't heard from Division for three years; hadn't been paid, either, so they spent most of their time herding sheep and hoeing cabbages. The young officer had scars on his left wrist, where he'd tried to open his veins out of sheer boredom. Therefore, I didn't get any hard data about the goings-on at Salpynx until we finished the bridge and withdrew, in a leisurely fashion, to Maudura, where we stopped off to mend a leaky aqueduct. There I ran into a man I knew slightly. He told me the lighthouse keeper saw the pirate ships sneak out from under the blanket of fog, trace their way through the truly horrendous shoals and come down on Salpynx from the north-west. They rounded up the longshoremen, had them load the ships till they couldn't carry any more, then herded everyone into the main storage shed, nailed the doors shut and set fire to the roof. Amazingly, a couple of men made it out alive, and lived long enough to make sworn depositions to the magistrates. No question that the raiders were Sherden. All this was more or less what I'd already heard, but news to me was that they'd stopped off on their way out, loaded to the gunwales as they were, to smash up the other lighthouse, the one on Stair Point. Curious thing to do, unless you wanted to make sure that the Second Fleet, due back any day now from a routine cruise to the Friendly Sea ports, wouldn't be able to clear the shoals until the light got fixed and would therefore be trapped for weeks, possibly months, on the wrong side of the straits.

I tend to keep my thoughts to myself, which is why I scowl a lot, but sometimes it's nice to have someone to think out loud at, and when I'm with the Corps it's generally Captain Bautzes who draws the short straw. I have a lot of time for him, though I'd never dream of saying so. As far as he's concerned, I regard him as an inoffensive halfwit who can be trained, with patience, to perform simple tasks. He's not, of course. Nicephorus Bautzes is an off-relation of the incredibly ancient and illustrious Phocas family. His sideshoot or tendril – you couldn't in all honesty call it a branch – of the family fell on hard times about seventy years ago; they've still got a little village and a falling-down old manor house in the Paralia, with discoloured patches on the walls where the priceless icons and tapestries used to hang before they got sold off, and a library of fine old books which make your hands all sticky, because of the mould, because of the damp. Nico makes you realise what the Phocas must've been like five hundred years ago, in their heyday, because he's – well, if you'd never met an Imperial but had read all the romances, Nico is what you'd expect. He's six feet nine, shoulders like an ox, bald as an egg apart from a silly little beard (but no moustache, naturally); he can lift the back wheels of a Type Six supply cart off the ground, jump his own height from a standstill, all that sort of stuff, makes me feel tired just watching him. He's read all the best books and understood about a fifth of them, which isn't bad going at all. He's hard-working, conscientious, respectful, orthodox, eager to learn, beautiful manners, brave as a lion – everything I'm not, in other words – and one of these days he might turn out to be a competent engineer. He'd be a typical example of his race and class, except that he seems to like me and has problems with his vision (can't always distinguish between brown and pink) – I don't know what to make of him, really, but until I see evidence to the contrary I'm forced to the conclusion that he's all right.

Nico has this knack of knowing when something's bugging me. Naturally he's too polite to say anything, but he takes to standing around looking down at his feet. Since he takes up a lot of space, it's hard to ignore or work round him, so we talk.

On this occasion, we'd just finished packing up all the gear after fixing the busted aqueduct. It's Nico's job to traipse round all the wagons, make sure everything's tied down safely and properly stowed, and then he reports to me. Bugging out after a job is always a stressful business, and while he's doing the final checks I like to sneak off to my tent, put my feet up, close my eyes and not think about anything for at least an hour, on my own, no interruptions. The one thing I really don't like about my job is having people all round me all the time, from the moment I wake up until I close my eyes and fall asleep. It's not natural. So, on bugging-out days, Nico puts his head round the tent flap, says All done, or just nods, and goes away. This time, though, he came in and stood there like one of those ornamental pillars in the desert; if he'd been wearing an ascetic philosopher on top of his head instead of a hat, he'd have looked just right. I sighed. "What?" I said.

He gave me his cow-eyed look. "Something's the matter," he said. Statement of fact, not a question.

"What makes you say that?"

"Oh, things. Like the jobs we've just been doing. All this low-priority stuff, bridges and aqueducts. We've had generals howling at us for months to do work round the City, and you drag us off to the middle of nowhere to build a bridge for a damn subaltern."

I rested my cheek on my fist and gazed at him. "Is that right?"

He nodded. "How bad is it?" he said.

Nico is huge; when we're together I look like his kid brother or his pet monkey. Regardless, there are times when I feel an overpowering urge to protect him, from all the bad things that are perfectly capable of happening to the innocent and well-meaning. But he's a captain in the Imperial army, therefore deemed to be tough enough to cope with most things. "Not wonderful," I said.

"You went to a Council meeting in town."

I nodded. "General Priscus and the full dog show."

"And then we do this job a long way away."

"Possibly not far enough," I said. "Tell me," I went on, "when you were at the Academy, did they teach you about General Allectus?"

He nodded. "Seventh-century AUC. When the empire was invaded by the Bel Semplan, Allectus commanded the Third Army in Bessagene. He proclaimed himself emperor and ran Bessagene as an independent state for twenty-six years until the empire recovered and drove out the Semplan, whereupon he surrendered, handed back control of his province and was executed for treason. Why?"

"Interesting man," I said. "One theory is, Allectus figured that the empire had had it, and he took over Bessagene so that a little bit of Robur civilisation would be preserved somewhere, albeit in the arsehole of the universe, while everywhere else all the lights slowly went out. It's not true, of course, but it would be nice to think it was."

He looked at me. "That bad."

From where I was sitting I had a view out over the bleak, wind-scoured moor towards the horrible pointy mountains. I hated it because it reminded me of home. "We could stay here," I said. "You saw those men back at the fort, where we built the bridge. They're not soldiers any more, they're farmers. We could join them. There's, what, three thousand of us. We could buy or steal three thousand women, build a bloody great big wall across the Odontis Pass. Farming can't be hard, or farmers couldn't do it. And then we wouldn't have to get involved, and if something really bad is just about to happen, then at least there'll be one corner of a foreign field that'll be forever Robur. Which would be nice," I added, "I'm sure you'd agree. Well?"

He grabbed the spare camp stool and sat down. It creaked under his weight. "That bad," he repeated.

"If we go back," I said, "there's a good chance we'll be pulled back to the City to repair the walls. Once we're there, I don't suppose we'll get another chance to slip away. If something bad is coming, we'll be right there in the bullseye."

Typical of Nico not to ask me what the bad thing might be. I believed in it, therefore it existed. "On balance," he said, after a moment's solemn thought, "I'd rather be Gennaeus than Allectus."

I smiled. Gennaeus, of course, founded the Robur nation after fleeing with one ship from the burning ruins of Moa; he stayed on the wall until the very last moment, and even then stopped to scoop up his elderly parents and the holy icons. Myself, I read the myth slightly differently. I think Gennaeus only got out alive because he saw that Moa was doomed, and spent his evenings digging an escape tunnel, the existence of which he neglected to share with anyone outside his family and immediate friends. But that's not the version Nico heard at his grandmother's knee. Duty and hope. Oh dear.

"Would your answer be different," I said, "if this place wasn't the arsehole of the universe?"

He grinned. "Possibly yes. But it is, isn't it?"

I sighed. "Nobody wanted a bridge built in Baionia," I said. "Fair enough. Let's go home and be brave. Dismissed."

He gave me a vague smile, picked up his helmet (very bright and shiny, but he bought it second hand from the Colias brothers), saluted and slung his hook. I suppose I'd wanted his permission. I hadn't for one moment expected him to say yes. He is, after all, a friend, and remember what I told you about my friends.

Here's a case in point. My best friend when I was growing up, Ogus. Marvellous boy Ogus was. He could run the fastest, throw the furthest, he could shear a sheep all on his own when he was six, and everybody liked him, but he chose to hang about with me, small, scruffy, generally held to be good for nothing much. But I've always had a tendency towards the quiet life and the avoidance of trouble. Not so Ogus. He loved to make a fuss. Also, he's what they call a born leader – learned a lot from him in that regard. Even now when I don't know how I'm going to get people to do what I want, I ask myself, what would Ogus do? Anyway, there was this exceptionally fine apple tree, growing on its own in what I guess was once a garden, though the house was long since rotted away. It was exactly on the boundary between his dad's place and their neighbour's, and that neighbour was a miserable bugger. There had been many a falling-out over the fruit of that tree. They even got the village council involved, to decide whose tree it was; and the council, being a political body, reached a decision that pleased nobody and made everything worse; the tree should be cut down and burned, to prevent further discord. So then Ogus's dad and the neighbour had a fresh falling-out over who was going to do the felling, and come apple season there the tree still was. Magnificent crop that year; actually the apples were sour and only fit for cooking, but Ogus resolved to have the lot and decide what to do with them later. He planned a neatly coordinated commando operation, which of course involved me. No, Ogus, I said, I've been in enough trouble lately and I don't want to come between your old man and that bastard. Absolutely not. So, long story short, off we went with his mother's big wicker basket to rob the apple tree. I was to be lookout while he climbed up and did the robbing. We'd half filled the basket when the miserable old neighbour showed up, with his three horribly savage dogs. Ogus was down out of the tree and three fields away before you could say *strategic withdrawal*. I, of course, got my sleeve caught up in a patch of evil briars, and by the time I'd got it free the dogs had got me surrounded, softly growling, with their hackles up; if I so much as blinked, they'd have me. And then up came the neighbour, and he had a curious look on his face. He whistled, and the dogs fell back, clearly feeling that they should've been allowed to finish the job and make the world a better place.

"You Orhan?" he said.

"That's right."

"Everyone's out looking for you, son. You want to get back home, right now. Your sister's had an accident."

Have I mentioned my sister? Probably not, since she's of no importance to the story; she died when I was six, fell off a wall and smashed her head when I was out scrumping apples when I should have been keeping an eye on her. Anyhow, Ogus's dad's miserable neighbour walked back with me to our place; didn't say anything until we were almost at the door, then he looked me in the eye, said, "Don't blame yourself, son, these things happen", and walked away. I found out later his kid brother had fallen through the ice, many years ago, when they were fishing for eels, and he hadn't been able to do anything. Friends and enemies.

5

We returned to Cacodemon after seven weeks away. During our absence, the situation had changed.

I underestimated Admiral Zonaras. I never thought he'd manage to find the pirates. But he did. He scraped together enough stores to launch three out of the five squadrons of the Third Fleet and headed for the Pillars. Slight amendment; he didn't find the pirates, they found him. They must've gathered every ship in the north; even so, Zonaras outnumbered them two to one, and his galleots should have smashed through them like a fist through a biscuit. Instead, they turned and ran like hares, and Zonaras sailed after them straight into the narrows between the Pillars, where his ships were bunched up so close you could've walked from one side of the Fleet to the other – at which point, the pirates set fire to a dozen worthless old hulks, loaded with cotton waste, lamp oil and flour, and launched them directly at them. The wind was behind them, so there was no way to stop them, and that same wind spread the flames back through the Fleet faster than a man could run. The flagship and three others managed to pull out and get clear. The rest were burned down to the waterline in just under half an hour. The currents are nasty round the Pillars, not a good place to go swimming. The pirates picked up a couple of hundred survivors, but that was all.

Very bad. We still had plenty of ships, but no sails, no ropes, anchors, nothing. The greatest sea power the world has ever seen was now in the position where it couldn't launch anything bigger than a dinghy until the Stair Point light was mended and the First Fleet could be brought back from the wrong side of the straits. Talking of which: the Sherden had been back to Stair Point, slaughtered the repair crew and broken up the enormous wrought-iron cradle that supports the light, making it possible to swivel it and illuminate the safe passage through the straits. An interesting development – barely enough charcoal left in the City depots to build the monstrous fire needed to found a new cradle; not enough skilled engineers to install it and get it lined up and calibrated, on account of some fool of a colonel-in-chief leading the entire Corps off into the wilderness to build some fatuous bridge.

Yes, I did feel bad about that. Also, it didn't feel right, somehow. We set off as soon as we could, but since we didn't dare go by sea, we had a very long march ahead of us, Stair Point being on the far side of the straits . . . I was starting to feel the way I do when I play chess against someone who actually knows the game. Genuine intelligence was at work here, and that's simply not something you're accustomed to facing when dealing with—

Milkfaces. Quite.

So off we went to fix the lighthouse. Needless to say, we never got there.

We were trailing up the long climb to Melias Beacon when we saw a horseman charging down the slope towards us. I could see him swaying about in the saddle; I thought he must be drunk. He was wearing a navy pillbox felt hat, but you can buy one in any bar. When he came close, I saw that his right hand was clamped to his stomach.

He was navy all right, and he was clutching his guts to keep them from falling out. He had that grey look. We tried to help him off his horse, but he yelled, keep away, get away from me. Calm down, I said to him, we can help you, we've got doctors. He shook his head; no time, he said. So we let him talk.

There had been a storm brewing, so the Fleet put in at Ricasa and the captains sent the men ashore, since they'd been at sea for weeks. Just after sun-up, our man was woken up by loud yells and people running. He opened the door of whatever grog-shop he'd passed out in, and looked out at the harbour. It was driving rain and the sky was red. The Fleet was burning. He had no idea who'd done it and didn't have a chance to find out; someone whose face he didn't see stabbed him and left him for dead. He passed out, and when he came round there were dead bodies everywhere. Somehow he scrambled to his feet and got moving, and by some weird stroke of luck walked straight into a horse, saddled and bridled, nibbling moss off the low eaves of a house. The strain of getting on the horse made bits of his insides pop out, but he thought, the hell with it, and headed out of town as fast as he could get the horse to go. He had no idea how long he'd been riding – And then he died.

Brave man. Not sure I'd have bothered, in his shoes. We were all stunned, as you can imagine. Nobody spoke for a long time, then Nico started babbling about fire ships. I told him to shut up and act like nothing had happened – the boys were watching us, and one thing you don't want is men under your command hearing bad news from anyone except you.

We buried the navy man under a pile of stones, and then I sent a couple of my brighter young lieutenants ahead on horses. Find out what you can, I told them, but whatever you do, don't be seen. Then I ordered full stop, fall out and a kit inspection, to take everyone's mind off anything anyone might have heard.

The two boys came back in the middle of the night. They looked scared stiff. They'd gone along the coast road as far as – I forget where, exactly, but they had a good view down into the valley and there was a hell of a lot of smoke coming up from the direction of Ricasa. They were trying to decide the best way to get down there when they saw a party of horsemen break the skyline about seventy yards away. So they got off the road double quick, leading their horses through the gorse and bracken, picked the road up about half a mile down and rode like lunatics back to the column. They didn't get much of a look at the horsemen, they said, but they both agreed on two points. They were milkfaces, and they were wearing armour.

The Corps of Engineers is part of the Imperial army, but we don't kid ourselves, we aren't soldiers, not in the fighting-people sense. We carry weapons, which we mostly use for prying open crates and frightening civilians, but it's widely accepted in the Corps that we aren't paid enough to stand around and let men of violence try and hurt us. We packed up and hit the road so fast you'd have blinked and missed us, back the way we came.

When Engineers do it, it isn't running away; it's withdrawing in good order, or simply relocating. We relocated like hares, down the long straight and back up to the lip of the Spendone escarpment, at which point I had one of my bright ideas.

"Tell you what," I said to Nico, who'd just come back from

hurrying up the rearguard, "let's take a short cut through the woods. We can knock fifteen miles off."

He gave me that look. "That's illegal."

Well, of course it was. The Spendone forest was the emperor's private hunting reserve. "Fine," I said. "Let's break the law. Better still, we can lure the enemy in after us, and then arrest them for trespassing."

He doesn't like it when I make fun of him. "You're the one who'll get in trouble," he said. "Besides, tactically speaking—"

I sighed. Spendone forest, for crying out loud. It's practically the suburbs. "We go through the woods," I told him. "Pass it along."

He nodded stiffly. "In that case, permission to form the men into defended column and send out scouts."

I ask you. Still, I imagine you tend to think like that when your head's two yards off the ground. "No," I said. He clicked his tongue at me and got on with it.

There is no Spendone forest now, so you have no way of knowing if I'm telling the truth; but it was a lovely place, if you like nature and stuff. It covered a gently sloping valley down to the river; spindly old twisted holm oaks with a canopy so dense it cut out the top light, so apart from occasional clumps of thick holly where a tree had blown down (good cover for wild boar), no underbrush, you could move about fairly freely. The road followed the river, naturally. It was paved with roadstone, like the military highways, wide enough for two carriages to pass, and tolerably flat all the way, and where it crossed the Spen – which is pretty wide and deep at that point – there was a proper pile-and-plank bridge, which one of my predecessors built, and a very nice job he made of it. We sauntered down one of His Majesty's huntsmen's neatly trimmed rides and picked up the road easily enough. Nice and cool under the shade, with the dappled sunlight slanting down between the crooked branches—"Someone's been along here recently," Nico said.

"His Majesty persecuting the deer," I said.

"A lot of people."

"You ever seen one of those hunting parties? Auges had fewer cavalry when he conquered Bessagene."

I mention that because I'm an honest witness, especially for the prosecution. I was still thinking, Nico, what a clown, he fusses about every damn thing, when we came round a corner and saw dead bodies.

I talked to Nico about it afterwards and he admits he had the same thought as me; bandits, because the bodies had all been stripped naked, every last manufactured object removed. We knew they were Imperials because of the skin colour. Nico's first thought was; oh God, the emperor – ambushed out hunting by thieves or a free company. Mine was merchants, a caravan taking an unauthorised short cut and paying an exorbitantly high toll.

"We'll have to report this when we get back," Nico said. "We ought to bury them, only maybe we shouldn't move anything, they'll want to send investigators—"

A third possibility had occurred to me. I put my hand on his shoulder. "Keep your voice down," I said, "there's a good lad."

"You think there's a chance we can catch whoever did this?"

I looked at him. "I bloody well hope not," I said.

His eyes opened very wide; then he nodded, and headed back to pass along the word; dead quiet, keep together. I was thinking, maybe it would be sensible to get off the stupid road. But we had big carts and pack animals, and all that heavy equipment. And maybe it really was bandits, after all.

I liked that theory and I was sad when it died. Which happened when we came into the long, straight bit of road that leads to the bridge, which wasn't there any more. That was where they'd sprung their main attack, hiding up in the dense holly brakes on either side of the road and taking the column in both flanks and rear. Most of the killing was done there; first a couple of point-blank volleys of arrows, then javelins, then closing with spears and axes. At least some of the men at the front of the column had tried to swim the river; we found their bodies still in full armour, caught up in reed beds and branches fallen across the river. The rest may have made a fight of it, I don't know; if they did, it made not the slightest difference. All the bodies were stripped bare. We didn't count them, it would've taken all day, so it's just my best estimate: between six and seven thousand. We didn't find a single milkface among the piles of dead, so they must have retrieved them and buried them somewhere else. I don't suppose it took them long.

Fighting soldiers get used to that sort of thing. I'm not a fighting soldier, I build bridges. So I sneaked off when Nico's attention was elsewhere, looking for somewhere I could throw up in modest seclusion. I saw a thicket of holly clustered round a stand of tall ash trees and made a beeline for it. And came face to face with General Priscus and most of his senior staff.

Face to face literally. They'd flayed the faces off the bone and nailed them to the ash trunks at head height, like squirrel skins put up to dry.

I'm not a brave man. But Nico is, and when he came running to see what I was screaming and yelling about, it hit him like a hammer, I could tell; his knees folded up and he sat down on his aristocratic arse, thump. Which made me feel a bit better, some time later.

At the time, though, I was so terrified I couldn't even puke. Felt like there wasn't a single bone in my body. I grabbed Nico's arm, pulled him to his feet and dragged him out of there, back onto the road. "Not a word," I hissed in his ear, "to anyone." He nodded, he couldn't speak. First time I'd ever seen him go all to pieces. Couldn't find it in my heart to blame him.

I got the column moving, somehow. Double defensive, scouts, word perfect by the book. But we weren't going anywhere in a hurry, of course, because the bridge was broken down. Could've fixed it, needless to say, that's what we do, but it simply didn't occur to me. Then some junior lieutenant who'd somehow managed to keep his brain working pointed out a track where a large number of men had gone off in a hurry.

My mind had frozen, but I made it get going again. I had the lads unload everything we could carry off the carts and turn the pack mules loose; tens of thousands of stamena's worth of good military equipment dumped in what we now had to consider enemy territory, but to be honest I couldn't give a damn. Then we headed off down the beaten track, hoping and praying that the men who'd made that track were our lot, and still alive.

One out of two isn't so bad. The track led uphill for maybe a mile, then down into a little dip, and there the remainder of the army, about six thousand men, made their last stand. They can't have done much of a job of it. Once again, the dip was fringed all round with thick holly, out of which came arrows, then javelins, then the final rush. They'd have been surrounded on all sides, and it would have been over very quickly. I knew straight away that it must've been the last stand, because once it was over, the enemy found time to celebrate, let off steam. They cut off the dead men's heads, hands and dicks, heaped them up in three tall, neat stacks. About a dozen poor souls – prisoners,

I assume – they'd nailed up on trees and used for a spear-throwing contest. They'd stripped the dead bodies clean, as before, and a few they'd flayed, and they'd stuck up the head of a milk-white horse on a pike. Whatever lights your candle, I suppose. I have to admit, they'd earned the right.

Among his many talents, Nico can do arithmetic. "Thirteen thousand," he said. "What's the strength of the City garrison?"

I didn't reply, because he knew the answer as well as I did. Somehow, the bastards had managed to lure General Priscus and the entire home army into this abattoir. Which meant there was nobody in town minding the store.

6

Nobody said much on the way to the City, which suited me fine. I needed to think.

Not only had they disposed of the entire Imperial army in the home province, they'd also acquired thirteen thousand suits of regulation lamellar armour – the finest in the world, goes without saying – ditto helmets, shields; something in the order of a quarter of a million arrows, all precision-made and meticulously quality controlled; twenty-six thousand high-class boots; thirteen thousand all-wool tunics, ditto cloaks, ditto trousers, knapsacks, round felt hats, cotton scarves to stop the shoulder straps of the cuirass chafing the neck; cooking pots, portable tripods for hanging cooking pots off, tools for cooks, carpenters, cobblers, surgeons, farriers, armourers, smiths – nothing but the best for our brave lads in the Imperial service, and, though that can be a bit theoretical out on the frontiers, back in the home provinces they really mean it. Pampered isn't too strong a word. I don't suppose the new owners of all that kit had ever seen so many *things* all together in one place in their entire lives, and none of it junk. All real quality stuff you'd be proud to own.

What's this, thinking about material objects at a time like this? Shame on me; well, yes. But those material objects would have a direct bearing on what happened next. Not just a horde of victorious savages. A horde of savages with the best arms and equipment money could buy. And if they weren't headed straight for Town, they needed their heads examined. Town; where we were going. Think about that.

We thought about it. "There's no guarantee," said one of my captains, who I'd never had much time for, "that the City's still standing. If they could do that to the Guards—"

"That's stupid," interrupted Menas; he's in charge of supply. "They'd never get past the wall. People have been trying for a thousand years. You'd need a siege train, sappers—"

"Which they may well have," the captain snapped back. "Don't you get it? We can't assume anything about these people. For all we know—"

"I think Menas is right," Nico said quietly. "The wall stopped the Echmen seventy years ago, and they had all the artillery in the world. Nothing's been invented that could put a dent in the wall."

"Fine," said a lieutenant, career specialist; he'd been badly rattled by what he'd seen. "So there they are, sitting down all round the wall, making sure nobody gets in or out. And then we show up. How long do you think we'd last?"

I cleared my throat. I usually keep quiet until my mind's made up, let them all talk themselves out. "We have to go back," I said.

The captain was furious with me. "With respect—"

I held up my hand. "You may well be right," I said. "It could easily be too late. There would be no reason for the gates to be shut. If they sent an advance party dressed like civilians, they could walk straight in, right past the sentries. And you could be right, too," I added, looking at the lieutenant. "If they're sat down in front of the walls, there's no way we could get past them and into the City. Nevertheless, we've got to go. There's nobody else."

"What about the Fleet? The crews, the marines. At least some of them must've got away."

I shook my head. "They've got no reason to think anything's wrong, beyond their own disaster. I wouldn't be in any hurry to get back to the City if I was in their shoes. And by the time the news reaches them, it'll probably all be over, one way or the other."

Nico looked at me. "If General Priscus took the whole Guards, then all that's left inside the walls is the Watch."

"That's right," I said. "Six hundred bent coppers. Which is why we're going, soon as it's light." I paused, looked round, to signify that I didn't want to hear anything else from anyone. "So I suggest we all use our imagination and pretend we're soldiers."

Nobody said anything. They stood up and drifted away. God help me, I couldn't blame them for their lack of enthusiasm. From their perspective, the world was about to end. Not mine, of course, because I'm not Robur, I have only a tenuous professional attachment to the City, I can envisage a world getting along reasonably well without it – men and women on small farms in places that don't merit a mention on any map, but where the sun rises and sets, summer follows winter, wheat and barley somehow manage to grow, calves are born and cows give milk, all without the help or permission of the emperor. Now Nico and his compatriots couldn't get their heads around an idea like that. They couldn't imagine a world without the City any more than they could imagine a world without a sun; it would be dark and cold and silent, and you might as well be six feet under for all the good being alive would do you.

I wanted a good night's sleep, in anticipation of a long and trying day ahead of me, but I wasn't going to get it. Around midnight, when I'd finally finished all the planning and figuring out I had to do and was just about to lie down and close my eyes, I heard a gentle tap on the tent post. I sighed. "What?" I said.

In came Nico, and three other officers. My guess is, they couldn't sleep, and they had the kind of generous nature that reckons insomnia isn't something you hoard all for yourself, you share it with you friends and loved ones. I beckoned them in and fumbled with a tinder box. The lamp was still warm. "What?" I repeated.

They looked at each other. Then Stilico – captain, very good engineer, twenty years' service but no chance of promotion – did one of those dying-sheep coughs. "We didn't want to talk in front of the others," he said.

"Of course. What's on your mind?"

"Seriously." He looked at me. "How bad do you think it is? Really."

"Really?" I closed my weary eyes and rubbed my eyelids. "I honestly don't know. It could be that Priscus wasn't stupid enough to leave the City undefended while he went off chasing phantoms in the woods. Maybe he was able to call in another unit, and when we get there we'll find the walls bristling with spearpoints and the granaries full to bursting. Or maybe not. Maybe we'll get there and find a pile of split stone blocks and ashes. Or maybe we'll be the only Imperial forces who can get inside the walls before whoever it is brings up his siege ladders.

Talking of which," I added, "has anyone else realised that we left behind all our tools and equipment? Exactly what you'd need if you wanted to build catapults, siege towers, battering rams—" I saw Nico's jaw drop. I forgave him. Usually he's quite bright. "A hundred and thirty barrels of nails," I said. "Twenty-seven five-ton winches. If by some miracle I get out of this alive, remind me to execute myself for gross negligence."

I realised I wasn't helping matters, so I shut up. Silence, for a long time. Then Artavasdus (only nineteen and his dad paid cash for his commission, but he's sharp as a tack) said, "So let's think the unthinkable, shall we? How would it be if we didn't go home?"

Ah, I thought, so that's why they're here. "Good idea," I said. "In which case, we turn around and head back to the coast, where I suggest we split up. What we've got is an amazing advantage; we're all skilled men. We're carpenters, masons, smiths, the world loves us, there's never enough of us to go round. Look at me. Even when I didn't belong to myself, I was valuable. It's your actual philosopher's stone. Being able to saw a straight line turned me into solid silver in someone's pocket, which is how I got to be colonel of a fucking regiment. We split up, we melt away, we have long, happy lives making ourselves useful. Believe me, you can get away with anything if you've got a trade. You can even be the wrong colour, so you blueskins will get along just fine when the rest of your kind are feeding the crows." I smiled at him; at that moment, he hated me so much I don't know why he didn't go for my throat. "Or we can go back and try and save *your* city, your people and your blue skins. It's up to you. I'll go along with what the rest of you boys want."

Nico was breathing through his nose, like a bull. Stilico looked as though I'd just put my hand down his trousers. That left Genseric. His blood is as blue as bilberry juice, but he was a bad boy about eight years ago and ended up with me. Actually, I like him, he's all right. And he was looking like he'd just trodden in quicksand. "Well?" I asked him.

"Actually," he said, "we had a talk and decided that whatever you decide is fine by us."

I nodded. "You want it to be my fault," I said, "that's perfectly reasonable. After all, it's what I'm for. All right, I'm going back. You lads can do what you see fit."

"And why would you do that?" Artavasdus said; he was still burning angry. "After all, you said it yourself. It's not your city and we're not your people. Your people will be the other side of the wall. Makes no sense."

I raised my hand. "Artavasdus, I'm sorry I called you a blueskin. I only did it to make sure you were listening. I'm going back because it's my duty. You don't have to, because duty is a very bad reason for committing suicide. More to the point, I'm guessing there's four thousand terrified men outside this tent having this same conversation. Whatever we decide, we've got to sell it to them, so I suggest we make our decision and then clarify our thinking." I put my hand down. "Over to you."

Nico looked round; he was now the spokesman. "The men want to stay together," he said. "They reckon that if we split up, the savages will pick them off and they won't have a chance. After all, we do rather stand out in a crowd."

I made a show of thinking for a moment. "All right," I said. "In that case, if we stick together, wherever we go we're under siege. So, makes sense to head for somewhere with high walls. You have my permission to tell them that from me," I added.

"We tell them you're going home."

I shrugged. "If you want."

"The men will follow you anywhere. You know that."

Actually I didn't, not until he said it, and for a moment I felt like I couldn't breathe. That's one thing about human beings I don't see the point in: love. It does nobody any good. You love someone, and either they let you down or they die. Either way, you end up crucified. What the hell is the point in that? See above, about enemies helping and friends being the source of all bad things.

But I meant what I'd said. My job is for it all to be my fault. So, if the men followed me out of love (you can use a different word, but that's what it amounts to) and I got them all killed – my fault. My responsibility. That's why they pay me the big money, slightly less than you'd get for playing the flute in the Court orchestra.

"If you think it'll help, you tell them anything you like," I said. "Me, I'm going to go to sleep now."

They trooped out, properly solemn, and left me feeling a bit guilty. Why? Because I had one card up my sleeve, and I'd neglected to mention it. Not a marvellous card; maybe a jack or a ten. But if I'd mentioned it, they'd have built their hopes up, and as far as I'm concerned, hope is also on the major-pests list, about two down from love. Therefore I entertained hope, so they wouldn't have to.

7

Almost certainly you're smarter than me, so you've already figured it out. I hadn't, and neither did Nico and his three buddies, or if they did they didn't mention it. Bear in mind that we were bone-tired and shit scared, not at our best; and give me some credit, because I woke up about an hour later, and it was blindingly obvious.

Thirteen thousand dead men stripped bare. Therefore, imagine you're the sentry on the City wall. In the distance you see the sunlight flashing on helmets and spearpoints. Splendid, you say to yourself, here's General Priscus, back already from teaching those savages a lesson. And you yell down to the duty sergeant to open the gates.

How close would they get before someone saw that their faces and hands were the wrong colour? What I'd have done, of course, was get my men in their captured armour to rub dirt on their exposed skin. Just how smart was the very smart man who was doing all this? And who the hell could he possibly be?

It was that special time of night when you wake up, start

fretting and know you won't be getting any more sleep. I got the lamp lit and went over my notes for the morning.

Before we set off, I did something I rarely do. I ordered the men on parade.

I think it must've frightened them, made them realise they were now fighting soldiers; they lined up, stone-cold quiet and still as death. I walked up and down looking at them. God help us, I thought.

In the green corner, a minimum of thirteen thousand superbly equipped warriors, fresh from slaughtering an entire Imperial army in a flawlessly executed ambush. In the blue corner, four thousand terrified carpenters. Nearly everyone had a sword, because you've got to have one. The quartermaster hands it to you, wrapped in oily cloth, with the inspector's seal holding the string together. What's that for, you inevitably ask, and the quartermaster makes one of five tradition-hallowed replies, like he's done a thousand times. Later you break the seal, because it's your responsibility to clean off all the packing grease, sharpen and polish the bugger, ready for inspection – so that's what it's really for, to be inspected. Marvellous. What you get if you're an engineer is a Type Thirteen A. Not a Fifteen, that masterpiece of ergonomic design. Not a Fourteen, honest, dependable workhorse of the Imperial military for forty years. You get a Thirteen A; parallel sides, point heavy, lozenge-shaped pommel that rubs your wrist raw, rounded point, steel quality and temper not all it might be, because the Thirteen A was made to a price, found to be no good and withdrawn from service seventy years ago. But they made a quarter of a million of the things, and waste not, want not. They'll do for cooks, bandsmen, clerks, stretcher-bearers, engineers; anyone who's never going to use the useless thing but needs to have a sword for inspections.

I said nearly all, because there's always the clown who loses it, breaks it, trades it for a quart of cider. To them I'd issued axes. We had plenty of axes, three-pound head, straight ash shaft, very well suited for cutting and shaping timber, lethally useless for fighting with. About a hundred men had bows, non-regulation, not supposed to bring privately owned kit with you, but a bit of fresh meat makes a change from rations. You could kill a deer with one, at twenty paces. No chance whatsoever of piercing armour.

Talking of which; no, we didn't have any of that. No call for it. What we do get given is the issue jack; twenty thicknesses of linen quilted together around cotton waste. Actually, it'll turn any sword, most spears, some arrows; it's hot as hell and hinders your movements, but it's considerably better than nothing. Real soldiers wear them under their armour. We all had them. We'd left them, goes without saying, at home. No helmets or shields, no body armour, no greaves, cuisses, rerebraces or vambraces, gauntlets, gorgets or knee or elbow cops. Wonderful.

An old man I met in the slave camp told me once, always be positive. He died of gangrene, something it's hard to be positive about, and he spent his last week on earth whimpering, but I've always tried to follow his advice, even so. Accordingly: we know what we haven't got, we don't need reminding about what we haven't got, but what *do* we have? Think about that.

I thought, or tried to, only some fool kept interrupting me. "Artavasdus is still livid," Nico told me mournfully, as we trudged up the fells at Tarent Cross. "He's talking about bringing you up on charges."

"And why not?" I said. "He's got every right. And if we

get home and there's someone to bring me up on charges to, nobody will be happier than me, believe it. Meanwhile, I'd like your opinion."

Nico did his wise face. "Fire away."

"Who do you think these bastards are?"

Oh dear. Picture of a big man trying to think. "The Sherden?"

I shook my head. "All told," I said, "in the incredibly unlikely event you could get them all in one place without them murdering each other, there's maybe eighteen thousand adult Sherden males, total. And they're thieves, not soldiers."

"But they attacked Classis. And the other stuff."

Walking uphill and talking leaves me short of breath. "They're good with ships," I said. "They're like us, specialists."

He sighed. "I'm sorry," he said, "geography's not my thing. What about those people you told me about? The Hus?"

Nico, of course, can walk uphill all day long while singing arias from Teudel's oratorios. Nevertheless, given the choice, I'd still rather be smart than fit. "The Hus are shepherds," I said. "They herd huge flocks of sheep on the high downs, always on the move. They wouldn't go anywhere without their sheep and their women and kids. The most you tend to see is a hundred or so crazy young braves looking to steal enough valuable stuff to raise a bride-price. And most of the time they thieve off each other. They only go bothering other people when times are very hard. Also, they're petrified of the Robur. They cremate their dead, so they think you're ghosts, charred brown by the flames. Not the Hus."

I was getting on his nerves. He doesn't like to be reminded that he doesn't know everything. "I don't know," he said. "There's hundreds of tribes up away north and east, always moving about and beating up on each other. Could be some lot we've never even heard of."

"Indeed," I said. "Like the Alba or the Maldit or the Sanc Fui or the Sebelot Alliance or the Flos de Glaya or the Prezadha." He gave me a blank, worried stare. I shouldn't tease him. "But then it'd be like waves on the seashore. There's a big storm out in the middle of the ocean, and you get tidal waves at the coast. The Alba drive out the Maldit, the Maldit drive out the Sanc Fui, and, at the very end of the line, the Seventh Army has to cope with hordes of marauding Bassanegs trying to cross the frozen Astar. And these things don't happen overnight. We'd have heard about it." I remembered a few Council meetings and amended; "I'd have heard about it."

He looked at me. "Nothing like that?"

I shook my head. "We go to a lot of places and I meet a lot of people. Not the sort you'd be seen dead with. They tell me things. Anything as big as a mass migration, someone would have heard something."

"Nobody has."

"Nobody's told me anything."

I was bothering him. Nobody's happy out of their depth. "So who do you think it is?"

I'd done enough harm for one conversation, so I didn't reply.

From Phainomai Einai to the City is prime growing country. It's where the deer and wild pigs from His Majesty's inviolable forest come out to graze on honest men's cabbages, safe in the knowledge that it's five years' hard labour for anyone not born in the purple to shoot them. Stand on top of any of the plump little hills and you won't see less than a dozen farms, whitewashed and golden-thatched, rich green fields quilted with arrow-straight hedges. In my wildest dreams, I've quit the service and bought one of those farms. Away to the north the land gradually rises, and that's where you get the wonderful vineyards. The point being, a lot of people live there, and they're out and about all day, they notice things. They noticed us. They stopped working and stared.

One old boy came to his yard gate and scowled at us as we tramped past down the road. I stopped and gave him a friendly smile. "Excuse me," I said. "Did the army pass this way, a few days back?"

"Who wants to know?"

I gave Nico a gentle shove. He's good with people. "Captain Bautzes, Imperial Engineers," he said.

Oh, that accent of his. It impressed the farmer. "Three days ago, sir." Sir, mark you. "In a right old hurry. Came through in the middle of the night."

I remember a friend of mine, got himself gutshot in a bit of a scrimmage. We hauled him to the surgeon, who pulled the arrow out and looked at it; all rusty. Oh dear. A bit like that.

"Forced marches," Nico said, keeping his voice down as we moved on. "We've been stopping every night. They're not even bothering to forage."

"No need," I told him. "They'll have plenty of food, courtesy of General Priscus. And the last thing they want is to raise the alarm."

Nico went all quiet after that. Splendid. I was able to think.

So, at the White Bear crossroads, we turned right. Left is the main road, to the City. Right takes you down beside the Silverlight to the coast. It's a deep valley, wooded – a bit like the road through Spendone forest, a resemblance that wasn't lost on my brave men – and it comes out at Bel Semplan. Just before Bel, of course, is Watersmeet, where the Isnel joins the Silverlight.

Maybe you don't think a lot about shit. Why should you? But

it's an interesting subject. Let me take you back five centuries, to the Great Plague. After it was over, His Majesty Euric III got it into his head that it had been caused by dirt, and nobody had the nerve to contradict him. So he founded the shit patrol, which still operates to this day. They're the band of miserable-looking souls who go round the streets in the still, small hours before dawn emptying the shit-pans and piss-pots and scarfing up all the stinking food and mouldy bedlinen, dead dogs, broken junk, all the rubbish that Euric was convinced brought on the Great Death. The shit goes out on carts to the farms to grow delicious cabbages, the fullers get the piss, but the rest of it is loaded onto big, flat barges and punted out of the Watergate down the Isnel to Watersmeet, then via the Silverlight to Bel. Then they row it out about four miles, past the point where the currents would sweep it all back into the City harbour, and dump it. Then they sail the barges back up the coast to the City. They do it that way so the river has all the hard work of moving the fully laden barges downstream, and the tide does the same for the empty barges on the return trip. Smart. I believe it was a colonel of Engineers who thought of it, though nobody remembers his name.

It was a gamble, or do I mean an augury? I think that's the word; where you basically give God a choice – if you're on my side, let this happen, if not, do what you like. If we figured in His plans, the shit fleet would be on the river or in dock at Bel. If it was on its way back to town, He clearly didn't want us to save the City, and we'd be free to take whatever shipping we could lay our hands on and sail away – up to the Armpit was my favourite option, because everybody knows the Robur founded a mighty colony at Olbia, though whether it's still there and where the hell Olbia might be are open to conjecture.

I still believe in Olbia, at least I believe in it rather more than I believe in Him, but I never got the chance to find out. The barges were tied up at the quay at Bel. No crews; because they'd done the daily run and were three-quarters of the way home when they met a gaggle of small boats, rowing like hell up the coast. The people in these boats yelled at them to turn back. Don't go to the City, they said, it's under siege. There's about a million savages all round the Land Walls and no soldiers to fight them off. We got out in time. Whatever you do, don't go back. You'll be killed.

So the barge crews turned round and rowed to Bel, held a quick meeting and melted away. Most of them were in the bars, drinking what was left of their money, on the grounds that since there would be no tomorrow, why the hell not? I had my boys round them up, and gave them a talking to.

We, I told them, were proper soldiers, and we'd come to relieve the City and defend it until the rest of the army showed up. Guessing we wouldn't be able to get past the siege lines in time, we'd come to Bel hoping to commandeer the shit fleet and sail it into the City harbour. The question was, had they seen any warships when they were there? No, they hadn't. Fine. My biggest fear was that the Sherden had been brought in to give naval support to the land forces – it's what I'd have done, or anyone with half a brain; if they hadn't done it, there had to be a compelling reason (and there was, as I found out later: big storm off the Needle, Sherden fleet scattered in all directions; probably an augury, though I still don't believe in Him). Anyhow, we could sail into the harbour and there'd be no pirates to sink us.

Being, in my own small way, a part of Authority, it never ceases to amaze me how much people believe in it and trust it. I see it from the inside, of course – inefficiencies, stupidities, corruption, bloody-minded ignorance and simple lack of resources to cope with the magnitude of the endless, ever-multiplying problems. But other people see it from the outside. They see the Land Walls. They see the emperor's head on the coins, with Victory on the reverse. They see the temples. They see soldiers in shining armour. They see, and they believe, that the empire is big, strong, wise, unbeatable. They know they can't fight it or outsmart it (though some of my friends in the Old Flower Market have spent a lifetime trying and haven't been caught yet) so they assume nobody else can, either. As witness those poor fools of barge crews. When I told them we were the army, it was as though they'd just woken up and discovered it was all a bad dream. Here we were, so everything was going to be all right after all. The fact that we were wearing felt hats, tunics and Type Thirteen As and there weren't actually very many of us seemed to escape their notice. That's all right, then, they said to themselves, and set about doing as they'd been told. It probably helped that they were drunk, but even if they'd been sober I don't suppose it'd have made much difference. A man in a uniform gave them an order, and they rejoiced. I felt bad about that, of course, but I was on a schedule.

One stroke of entirely unexpected luck. While Stilico's men were rousting drunken sailors out of the dockside bars, he happened to find out that one of the big lumber freighters that make the run from Weal Eleis to Naufragia had been forced into Bel by bad weather. It was carrying two hundred and seventy tons of seasoned Elymaean cedar.

"We're having that," I told him. "Bound to come in useful."

Stilico went away, came back a bit later. The captain, he said, refused to allow our men to commandeer the ship or its cargo without compensation. I sighed, tore a page out of my notebook, and wrote a draft on the treasury for ten thousand stamena—

"You can't do that." Stilico was shocked to the core. "That's ten times what it's worth."

"So?"

"It's public money."

I considered explaining, but there wasn't time and I didn't have the energy. "Do as you're told," I said and gave him the bit of paper. He walked away, looking deeply offended. I called him back.

"Better put a couple of dozen of the lads on the ship," I said. "Just in case."

8

For the record, I'm not at my best on boats. I tell myself it's because I'm an engineer. I live in a world of straight lines, fixed points, things that stay where they're put, the exact opposite of the sea. She reckons it's because of where I was born, two weeks' painful trudge inland, up mountains and across rivers. Nico smiles indulgently and points out that the Robur have always been a seafaring nation, and that's the source of their superiority. In any event, I spent the short trip from Bel to the City hanging over the side regretting everything I'd eaten for the past week, which was very good; I was too preoccupied to think about anything else. If I hadn't been, I'd have scared myself to death imagining what we'd find when we arrived.

Once you're in the Bay, the wind and the currents calm down a lot, and I realised that I was going to live after all. On this occasion, once we were past the Spearhead, we sort of glided home, as smooth as a bolt down the slide of a crossbow. Small mercies. I stopped groaning and started panicking. But there wasn't a ship to be seen in all of that vast blue semicircle.

One good thing about the shit barges – they're distinctive, no other boats like them on the water. Even so, I was a bit worried about the reception we'd get. For one thing, we didn't look like Imperial soldiers. For another, whoever was in charge in the City had probably figured out by now that appearances can be deceptive. Further or in the alternative, the shit fleet isn't exactly a state secret, so our mysterious genius enemy could easily have heard about it, commandeered it and packed it to the gunwales with armed men. They'd only know it was us when we were close enough for the watchmen on shore to see the brown of our faces; seventy yards, say. Effective archery range is a hundred and fifty yards. But if I told everyone to get their heads down, our reception committee wouldn't see brown faces and would have every reason to start shooting.

Awkward; except there was no reception committee. The quays were deserted; no ships tied up, no dockers, nobody lounging about or selling things. I felt like I'd swallowed a block of ice.

I was in the lead barge. We nosed up against the quay, someone jumped across with a rope and tied up. The gangplank hit the stone with a clatter. I'm not a brave man. "Nico," I said, "just run ahead and see if you can find anybody."

He gave me that look, but off he went, and nobody was in any hurry to follow him. He walked up the quay about a hundred yards, stopped, looked round; then I saw him wave at someone we couldn't see. Then he yelled to whoever it was, and we heard a voice calling back. Beside me on the barge, the sailors were all on edge, ready to cast off and jump to the oars in a heartbeat. Then Nico nodded, and trotted back to us.

"Harbourmaster," he said. "He's barricaded himself in his office. But he's coming down now we're here."

Oh well, I thought, and gave the order to disembark. The other barges, which had been hanging back, drew in. The freighter was still standing off, like a fat girl at a dance. Just as well I'd put men aboard, or they'd have spooked and bolted.

Up came the harbourmaster. He had a mailshirt on, and a helmet, a hundred years old and two sizes too small. He looked straight past me until Nico did the introductions.

"Where is everybody?" I asked.

"Gone." The harbourmaster didn't sound happy. "Soon as they heard what was going on, everybody was down here, trying to get on a ship. They were fighting like animals, you never saw anything like it."

Gone. "There's no ships?"

He laughed. "Cleared out, the lot of 'em. Nobody cared where they were going, so long as it was away from here. Them as couldn't get on board went back up the hill to the temples, fat lot of good it'll do them." He peered at me, as if trying to see in through my eyes. "Wherever you're headed, take me with you. I've got money."

"We're not going anywhere," I said.

He rolled his eyes and words evidently failed him. He tottered back the way he'd just come, leaving the harbour to us. Fair enough.

I stood there, trying to think, until Nico said, "Well, it's still standing. What do we do now?"

I dragged myself back from wherever I'd wandered off to. "Someone," I said, "has got to be in charge. Who would that be?"

Nico knows these things. "In the absence of a ranking military officer," he said, "that would be the City Prefect."

My pal Faustinus. Oh God. Still, if you need to knock in a

nail and you don't have a hammer, use the heel of your broken-down old boot. "Fetch him," I said.

"Shouldn't we—?"

"We're busy. No, you go, you're polite." He stood there, looking gormless. "Go on. Move."

He shrugged, and ran. I turned round, so I wouldn't have to look at the City, and started ordering people about. It calms me down, and there was a lot to do.

First things first. We got the barges up out of the water onto the quay and knocked holes in the bottoms; nothing we couldn't fix later, enough to stop desperate citizens rushing us and taking them. We brought in the freighter, unloaded the cargo, then sent her out again, too far for anyone to swim, with five of my best sergeants on board. Then I split the men up into eight units, five hundred each. By the time I'd done that, Nico was back, with poor old Faustinus.

He was drunk. He has a problem that way at the best of times. It's no big deal. He waved at me and gave me a big, crazy grin. I pulled him away so nobody could see him, into some shed where they kept tackle and stuff. I sat him down on a big coil of rope and said, "What happened?"

He just grinned at me, so I hit him. Then I helped him up off the floor and asked him again. "What happened?"

He was fingering his jaw. "You bastard," he said. "What's the matter with you?"

"Tell me," I said, "what happened."

So he told me. It started with reports that a gang of about five thousand savages had appeared out of nowhere and were burning farms on the far side of the Spendone escarpment. There was a Council meeting. General Priscus decided that the only thing to do was come down on that sort of behaviour like a ton of bricks. He mobilised the Guards – all of them – and marched out. He wouldn't be gone long, he said, it'd be a piece of cake.

A few days later, the watchmen on the towers saw what looked like the army coming back. Faustinus sent word to open the gates, get people out into the streets, put garlands up all round the Hippodrome, make sure there was plenty of food and drink for the victory street parties. Then, he told me, our luck must have turned, just a tiny bit. Some clerk from the War Office had some bit of urgent business he needed Priscus's seal on. Rather than wait until the army got home (and then they'd all be busy making whoopee, and no chance of getting any work done or days) he grabbed a chaise from the messenger service and rode out to meet them. He was right up close when he realised something wasn't right; the men in the soldiers' uniforms were the wrong colour.

He turned the chaise round and dashed back to the gate hell for leather; a hundred or so cavalry set off after him, but those chaises are fast. Faustinus was at the gate when this clerk came racing through, screaming and yelling like a lunatic, shut the gates, shut the gates. Just as well Faustinus knew the man and knew he was the most unimaginative, boring creature who ever drew breath. They got the gates shut and the bars down a few heartbeats before the cavalry outriders reached it. By then, of course, the men on the wall could see milk-white faces under their helmets. Two Watch sergeants went sprinting off down the ramparts to the other gates. It was a horribly close shave, but all the gates were shut in time.

Pretty desperate, even so. Faustinus had at his disposal the two hundred Watch who were on shift – dispersed, it goes without saying, right across the City. That was all. Quite by chance, he had forty or so within the range of his voice. He got them up on the wall, but he knew he was in dire trouble.

The bare statistics aren't widely known, but they're in books where anyone can read them. The Land Walls are thirty-eight feet high, eighteen feet thick at the base. All the gates are ten plies of oak laid crosswise, so they can't be split down the grain, and each of the eight hinges weighs a quarter of a ton; if nobody disturbs you, you could hack and bash your way through them in half an hour (given unlimited manpower and the proper kit) or pile up brushwood and burn them through in a day. Get through them and you're into the Olive Press, a strip twenty-five yards wide between the Land Walls and the Inner Curtain, twenty-six feet high, fifteen feet thick; the idea being that anyone who makes it that far will be shot to pieces in seconds by the siege engines and massed archers on the Curtain ramparts, with no cover and nowhere to run to. It's an unbeatable defensive setup so long as you've got even a handful of men, which of course Faustinus hadn't.

In theory, the Prefect has at his disposal all the ten thousand or so able-bodied citizens who get their pay from the government; the Watch, the Board of Works, the Fire Brigade, the Inspectorate of Weights and Measures, all that. But they weren't where they were supposed to be. They were down at the harbour, fighting for deck room on a ship. The only outfit who were prepared to do as he told them were the hundred or so operatives from Parks and Gardens, and then only when he offered to pay them triple time.

(That I could understand. When I'm out of uniform in the City, I'm often mistaken for a gardener. A senator explained it, a few years ago. Milkfaces are shorter than Robur, therefore closer to the ground, therefore naturally suited to stoop labour, like planting and weeding.)

So up onto the ramparts they went, holding hoes and brooms

like they were spears. You don't have to do anything, Faustinus told them, just stand there, give the impression there's somebody home. Amazingly, it worked. The enemy stopped and drew up three hundred yards from the wall, sent out scouts to ride up and down and take a good look. Which they were still doing.

According to the books (there's an extensive literature on the subject) there are fifteen ways to defend a walled city. You can try one of them, and if that doesn't work—

Indeed. But the books were written for generals, kings, emperors; better luck next time, and we have plenty more cities where that one came from. And, to be fair, each of the fifteen ways is practical and sensible, provided you've got an adequate garrison, and sufficient supplies and materiel, and a competent staff of trained officers making up a properly constituted chain of command.

What the books don't tell you is, there's a sixteenth way. You can use it when you've got nothing; no stuff, no men and nobody to lead them. Apart from that, it's got nothing to recommend it whatsoever.

Fine, I thought. Let's give it a go.

"All right," I said. "Here's what you need to do."

Of all the crazy ideas I've ever had, that had to be the craziest. But, Faustinus had said three hundred yards, which could only mean one thing. A Type 16 torsion engine (that's a catapult to you) has an extreme range of two hundred and seventy-five yards. Of course there were no Type 16s, no engines of any sort. They'd all been in storage at Classis, dismantled and crated up, ready for deployment in the unlikely event that they'd be needed somewhere. Plainly, the enemy didn't know that.

Luckily, I knew exactly where to find what I needed. I sent

two of my eight companies down the quay to the West Dock, where they unload the grain ships. They requisitioned all the big cranes, dragged them all the way up that steep hill to the wall, broke them down into their four main pieces and hauled them up onto the towers, where they put them back together again and draped them with tarpaulins. From a distance, if you don't really know what you're looking at, a freight crane covered in a tarp looks a little bit like a catapult. At any rate, it looks like a big, powerful machine, or it did to the enemy scouts, which is why I'm still alive and you're reading this. Like I said, crazy.

Meanwhile, Three Company was ransacking the factory quarter for anything they could find; drop hammers, wine presses, looms, the mechanism out of the Blue Temple clock, anything that would look scary under a dust sheet. By then, word had got about that the Prefect was handing out silly money to anyone prepared to haul on a rope; we scraped together about four hundred of the market-square crowd who reckoned that if they were going to die they might as well die rich. Bless them, they put in a bloody good hour's work, and we got two-thirds of the artillery niches filled. The scouts stopped cruising up and down, and the enemy settled down and started putting up tents. And that, my children, is how Colonel Orhan saved the City.

For now, anyway. The trouble with now is, it's over in a heartbeat, and then you've got to think of something else.

9

I'd been putting it off, but it had to be done. But I was damned if I was going to walk. I was shattered, and it's a steep hill. I sent Stilico to find me a horse and he was confoundedly efficient about it. I hate horse riding.

Never seen the City like it; deserted. Nobody on the streets, windows shuttered, doors closed, dead quiet. Even in the dead of night, during curfew, there's always a drunk singing or a woman yelling or the Watch beating up a tramp. In fact, night is a busy time, because that's when all the heavy carts come rumbling in from the country – too many people got squashed when they used to let them in by daylight; you put your foot down one of the knee-deep ruts and you're a dead man, you'd be mad to try and cross the street between sundown and third watch. Then, fourth watch, the carters come out from cutting the dust in the market-quarter bars, which is always lively and entertaining to see from a distance; fifth watch there's generally a murder or a gang fight somewhere, Blues and Greens finding a healthy outlet for pent-up aggression. Sixth watch, you get the country people coming in and setting up stalls, the shit patrol, bakers lighting their fires, respectable men sneaking home after a night in the cathouse. Empty, quiet streets are, therefore, a truly terrifying thing to see, especially in the mid- to late afternoon.

I passed a gang of my lads hauling something – my best guess was the drive-shaft assembly from a waterwheel – on a handcart; I gave them a wave, they waved back. Apart from them, didn't see a soul until I reached the wall, where a drunken Watchman tried to arrest me. I took my foot out of the stirrup and kicked him in the mouth. Always wanted to do that.

To get up onto the rampart, you go up one of those horrible screwthread spiral staircases inside a watchtower. There's supposed to be a rope on the outer side to hold on to, but there wasn't, and the steps were worn smooth as glass. I was shaking when I came out into the fierce white daylight, where some clown shoved the blade of a hoe under my nose and said, "Who the hell are you?"

"Take it easy," I said to him in Alauzet – I knew he was from the Old Country by the colour of his hair. "I'm Orhan, colonel of the Engineers. And you could put an eye out with that thing."

He grinned and put it down. He'd heard of me; the only Alauz to have made good in the big city, I'm famous. *Sold out* is the term they generally use, but I'm sure they mean it kindly. "Pass," he said.

I slid by him and put my hands on the parapet. Never been keen on heights, which is a problem in my line of work. I looked out over the plain, and saw the enemy.

At first, my brain didn't register anything wrong. I was looking at an Imperial army, all shiny and neat in cornrows, a reassuring sight on any battlefield if you happen to be on their side. Then I remembered and I got this lump in my throat and my knees went weak. There were ever such a lot of them, and they looked the way they're meant to look: terrifying.

Except they weren't doing very much. Five ranks were standing to arms, shields rested on the ground, spears pointing skywards. Too hot to do much except stand still if you're wearing all that ironmongery. Behind them, a lot of men in jacks but no metalwork were moving about – setting up tents, carrying things from here to there, digging latrines, grinding corn, sitting round fires. I could hear the tick-tick of distant hammers – farriers shoeing horses, smiths peening rivets. Quite evidently they were in no hurry. I took another look round, watching out for signs of my counterparts working on big baulks of lumber; because if I was down there, you can bet I'd have been building scaling ladders or siege towers or a battering ram. Nothing like that as far as I could see. Or I'd be binding up thick sheaves of brushwood – fascines, we call them – or handing out picks and shovels to the sappers, who'd be getting ready to move the million tons of earth it takes to drive a sap underground to undermine a wall. And there'd be flat-bed wagons laden with pit props, handcarts to shift the spoil, men leading pit ponies. Not something you can easily hide. Nothing like that, either.

They're waiting for something, I thought. Or somebody.

But I didn't know that for sure; and I knew what had to be done next. Properly speaking, it wasn't my job, but I had a nasty feeling I'd be doing it. Hope, however, springs eternal; maybe I could shuffle off responsibility onto somebody else. In which case –

In which case, God help me, my next move would have to be, go and see the emperor.

*

Clemens IV, brother of the Invincible Sun, regent of Heaven and Earth, Undefeated, Father of His Country, King of Kings, whatever. He'd been on the throne seventeen years, which is not bad going – the average is around twelve, but that includes the dozen or so who lasted a matter of months, and who ended up with their heads on pikes and a splendid view up Hill Street – and he was born in the purple, which means a lot to the Robur. It's next best thing to impossible to know whether the man on the big chair during your lifetime is going to go down in history as The Great or The Wise or The Cruel or Old Coppernose or The Mad; the government boys would have you believe he never puts a foot wrong and we're living in a golden age, your friends in the market or the Two Dogs tell you he's a drunken, perverted halfwit and the empire's going to hell in a handcart, and what you see with your own eyes (shining new temples, mighty armies parading at New Year and Ascension, over-grown fields, starving kids in the street) is almost certainly atypical or isolated incidents or the exception that proves the rule. If you'd asked me, I'd have said that Clemens was prob-ably all right, if a bit misguided in his choice of advisers. I'd have wanted to believe that. Besides, what possible business was it of mine?

Certain facts were readily available to anybody who could read, or hear things read to them. Clemens was forty-six years old; he had two sons, Audax and Roburtinus, nineteen and fifteen respectively, so the succession was well and truly secure. His wife, Volumnia of Molossus – a cold woman, by all accounts, head in a prayer book most of the time – had been dead for ten years, and there was talk – when wasn't there talk? – about a diplomatic marriage with one of the Echmen princesses, either for Clemens or Audax – one princess was fifty-six and the other one was twelve, but they don't worry about things like that in those circles. It must be funny being an emperor.

I needed to see him (I explained to Prefect Faustinus) in order to get the position straight. If, as I was horribly afraid, I was the senior military officer in the City, I needed confirmation or a warrant or something. If there was someone higher up than me, I desperately wanted to hear about him and ask him for orders. So, how do you go about it?

Faustinus looked petrified. "How the hell should I know?" He'd sobered up, just about, and wasn't feeling his best. "I've never met him."

"You haven't."

"Of course not, talk sense. I go through channels, naturally."

I nodded. "Fine. What channels?"

"The Chamberlain."

"Right. Take me to him."

The crazy grin was back. "He skipped out on the first ship to leave. Also the Grand Logothete, the Chief Domestic, the Master of the Wardrobe, the Leader of the House and the Count of the Stables. There are no channels. They left."

My head was starting to hurt. "That's not possible," I said. "There must be—"

"No." He'd raised his voice. He doesn't do that. "You know what it's like in this town, there's a hierarchy, a system, protocols. Only now there's a hole in all that you could drive a horse and cart through. We're cut off, stranded. He might as well be on a desert island. We've got no way of contacting him."

Poor devil, he believed it. Years of conditioning. The only way to do things is through the chain of command, and if the chain breaks you're stuck. I shoved my hand under his chin and tilted his head up. "Pull yourself together," I suggested. "Now, who's next after the Count of the Stables?"

He was staring at me as though I'd gone mad. "Me," he said. "I guess."

"Fine," I said. "You'll do. We can go together."

So we went to the Palace. This is madness, Faustinus said, we'll never get past the guards. But there weren't any guards. We simply walked in through a half-open door into a very big, empty entrance hall.

Faustinus wanted to leave. I reasoned with him by twisting his arm behind his back. We carried on into another huge, empty chamber. It had the most amazing painted ceiling, and twice-life-size statues all down one wall. At the end of it was a green marble staircase flanked by gilded bronze lions the size of oxen. We went up it, making the most horrible noise – actually, that was me, hobnail boots. At the top of the stairs, we met a bald man in a white tunic. He was sitting on the top step, with his head in his hands.

"We want to see the emperor," I said.

He stared at us. Faustinus repeated what I'd just said. The bald man looked over the top of his head. So I hit him.

That livened him up. "Where is he?" I asked. The man pointed; right, down a long, high passage with a mosaic floor. At the end of the passage was a bronze door, twelve feet high. I gave it a shove. It swung open.

"This is all wrong," Faustinus said. "We could be executed for this."

I smiled. "Who by?"

"We can't go in there. That's the Purple. Nobody goes in there."

I proved him wrong. The Purple is this enormous square room, so called because its walls, floor and ceiling are polished porphyry. I gather it's a sort of dressing room, only without a single stick of furniture. The next door looked worryingly like solid gold. I knew people in the Old Flower Market who'd have something like that off its hinges and vanished without trace in five minutes flat.

"The Bedroom," Faustinus whispered. "We can't—"

I'd had enough of him. "Stay there," I said. "I shouldn't be long."

I gave the door a gentle nudge and it opened.

It was dark. I could just make out an enormous bed, hung round with curtains. Sitting in front of it on a low stool was an old man.

He turned and looked at me. I guess there was enough light for him to see my face. He gave me a sad look. I knew what he was thinking.

"I'm Colonel Orhan," I said, "Engineers. I need to see the emperor."

He laughed. "Be my guest."

He pointed to the bed. I didn't like that, but I couldn't see what else to do. I walked over, quiet as I could, and pulled back the curtain.

In the bed lay a man. Ordinary looking; bald, with wisps of hair combed forward. He was dressed in a plain white nightshirt. His eyes were open and he was breathing. He didn't move.

"He's been like that for nine months," the old man said behind my shoulder. "He had a massive stroke, the day they told him his sons had been killed. He hasn't moved since. I'm his doctor, by the way."

I remember once riding straight into a low branch. I didn't fall off, but I was completely out of it. Like that. "The emperor," I said, or something equally intelligent.

"The emperor," the doctor repeated. "Needless to say, we kept it quiet. Nobody knew, outside of this room. I haven't left it since they brought him here."

"Will he—?"

"No," the doctor said. "No chance at all. He'll be like that until he dies."

Made no sense. "The princes."

I heard the doctor draw a deep breath. "Audax and Roburtinus took a boat out into the Bay," he said. "They were drunk, I guess it seemed like a good idea at the time. Audax fell overboard. He couldn't swim. Neither could his brother, but he tried to save him nonetheless. The old man was genuinely fond of them, God only knows how. Anyway, there's your emperor. Ask him anything you like."

Faustinus pounced on me like a cat when I came out. "Well?"

"All done," I said.

"What?"

I walked away. Faustinus had to trot to catch up with me. "I asked him for total authority," I said.

"You did what? What did he say?"

"I got it. I'm now in charge." I stopped for a moment. I felt dizzy and sick. "You're my deputy," I said. "That's official too. You and me are running the fucking empire."

He looked as though I'd just cut off his ear. I felt sorry for him. "How are we going to prove it?"

I opened my clenched fist and showed him the Great Seal. It had been on a table beside the bed. No idea how it came to be in my hand. It must've fallen off and I caught it without thinking. "Come on," I said, "we've got work to do."

The Purple, still empty. Likewise the two echoing marble halls and the courtyard. We passed through the wide-open main gate into the Golden Mile. "Where are we going?" Faustinus asked me.

"The Old Flower Market," I said. "Don't suppose you've ever been there."

He caught my sleeve. "Orhan," he said. "This is hardly the time."

I pulled my arm free. "Yes it is," I said. "Now keep up or piss off."

Nobody in the Old Flower Market. Faustinus had the creeps quite badly. He kept telling me how many unsolved murders and stabbings and muggings there'd been down there in the last six months, which surprised me. I didn't think anyone bothered counting. You'll be fine, I told him, you're with me. I don't think he believed me.

The Dogs was all shut up, shutters on the windows. I banged and kicked the door a few times, to no effect. "That would suggest there's nobody home," Faustinus said. I ignored him. There had to be somebody home, or the City would fall. Therefore, there must be someone home. I looked around for something to use as a jemmy. Some hope; things like that aren't left lying about in that neighbourhood. I tried shoulder-charging the door a few times, but had the wit to stop before I hurt myself. Stupid. Supreme ruler of the empire, couldn't even get a door open.

Fortunately, before I burst into tears, a window opened. "What the hell do you think you're doing?" she said.

I looked up and grinned joyfully. "Open the stupid door."

"Go away, Orhan," she said. "I haven't got time for you right now."

"Open the door. Please."

She called me a name she must've learned from her father, and the shutter slammed. A short time later, I heard about a dozen bolts being drawn, and the door opened. "I'm sorry," she said, "but I don't want any soldiers here. You understand."

I pushed her out of the way; she took a swing at me, but I ducked. "I need to talk to the Theme bosses," I said. "Urgently."

"Who's he?"

"What? Oh, him. That's Faustinus, the City Prefect. The Theme bosses, Aichma, where do I find them? It's really important. I need to talk to them right now."

She looked at me. "Is it true? Are there really savages—?"

"Yes. That's why I have to see the Theme bosses. Now."

"But the army—"

"All dead," I told her, and her eyes opened wide. "There's no army and no fleet, there's just me. Which is why it's essential I see the Theme bosses, straight away. Do you know where they are or not?"

"They can't be," she said. "Not all of them."

"Aichma."

Known her since she was small enough to lie on the palm of my hand. Aichmalotus, her father, thought she was the most amazing thing in the history of the world; my kid, Orhan, he said to me, like it was some kind of miracle. And before that, he was the last man you'd ever expect to turn out to be the proud-father type. It takes some people that way. Aichmalotus wasn't his actual name, of course. It means 'prisoner of war' in Aelian, and that was what was written on the label round his neck. The recruiting sergeant couldn't pronounce his real name, so he was

Aichmalotus for the rest of his life. Aichma means 'spear'. He chose it because she was the better half of him, and sharp as a nail. But she looks just like her mother.

"What do you want them for?"

"*Aichma.*" Mustn't shout. Getting her to do what you want is like getting a pig into a cart. If you push it, it backs up the other way with all its considerable strength. You've got to make it *want* to go into the cart, or it just won't happen. "Use your head. There's no army, and there's about a million savages the other side of the Land Wall. Why would I want to see the Theme bosses?"

She looked at me. "They won't—"

"Fine, But I'll ask them anyway. That's if you'll bloody well tell me where to find them."

"I can't do that," she said. "But I can fetch them here."

"Wonderful," I said. "Do it now."

She hesitated for a moment, then pulled her shawl over her head and walked straight past me through the yard and out into the street. "What was all that about?" Faustinus said.

I'd forgotten about him. "It's something you just don't do," I said, "tell the likes of us where to find someone. Especially the Theme bosses. You understand that, surely."

He was getting all het up again. "Oh, sure," he said. "What I don't understand is what you want with a bunch of gangsters. Most particularly at a time like this."

I ask you. City Prefect; he's got the job of running the capital city of the empire, and to him the Themes are just gangsters. "Go back to the prefecture," I told him. "I need to know exactly how much money we've got. Not money of account, not credit reserves, actual gold coins. Don't tell anyone else and come straight back here. And if you see Captain Bautzes, tell him I want full armour and weapons for all my lads, and then I want them on the wall."

"Who's—?"

"Forget it. Just go and find out about the money. Please?"

And then I was all alone, in front of the open door of the Two Dogs. I decided it was time for some unilateral executive action. I went inside and requisitioned a bottle of brandy. I had the authority, after all; but I left thirty trachy on the bar, even so.

You'll have noticed that I used the term 'Theme bosses', rather than their actual names. That's because I didn't know the names. Very few people do. You don't become boss of the Blues or the Greens for the glory. Holding office in a Theme carries the death sentence, mandatory. In fact, if anyone really wanted to find out, it wouldn't be all that hard. The Themes choose their leaders from working gladiators, if not the colour's current champion then one of the top ten at the very least. Luckily, the government has always taken the view that someone qualified to be Theme boss won't be around for very long by the very nature of his trade. Why make a big fuss arresting a man and putting him on trial and hanging him when, sooner or later, a business associate will do the job for you, with people paying to watch? For my part, I was sure I knew who the Blue boss was, and had a pretty shrewd idea who led the Greens. I was wrong, of course, on both counts. I should be used to it by now.

Turned out the Blue boss was Hierascus – he always refused to answer to that, said his name was Arrasc and if the blueskins couldn't pronounce it, tough. He was number four in the Blue rankings, fought forty-seven, won forty-four, drawn three. His father was Sanc Fui; by the look of him, his mother was Robur. They tell you that never happens, but it does. I'd seen him fight a dozen times, admired his footwork and his controlled aggression, knew nothing else about him at all. He was a long, lean man, about thirty-five, so old for a Hippodrome fighter. He looked like your typical arena bruiser, except that he had sad, clever eyes.

His opposite number was Longinus, ranked Green number two. It's always good to see a friendly face in a stressful situation. He and I went way back, to when he was the most blatantly dishonest quartermaster's clerk in the history of the Supply Corps. He once sold me two thousand of my own regulation pickaxes, issued to me under sealed requisition. He gave me a big smile, which cheered me up enormously. He was a big, wide man with arms the size of legs. There were two different versions of his story. One version was that his mother worked in the leisure and entertainment sector and he grew up in the Old Flower Market, a bit like the trees you see growing high up in the cracks in walls. The other was his mother was a chambermaid in a very grand house; from her he got his cheerful disposition, while his physique and intelligence came from his father. He had the most beautiful voice; he could have been an actor, he told me once, but he got carried away in a fight scene and broke the leading man's jaw, and after that nobody would work with him. I'd say he was maybe an inch taller than Nico and about the same as him across the shoulders, and he was only number two in the Greens because he hadn't fought often enough to get the ranking points. He'd gone thirty bouts in the Hippodrome undefeated, and he was twenty-eight years old.

There they stood, with Aichma between them like the barriers in the lists, as though if they happened to collide there'd be an explosion. I felt a tiny bit uncomfortable, I have to confess. Hippodrome fighters have that effect on people; like big dogs, you can't really be sure they won't suddenly bite. I reminded myself that I was a soldier. "Gentlemen," I said, "thank you for coming. Sit down and have a drink."

So they sat down, on opposite sides of the table, with me at the north end and Aichma at the south. I hadn't asked her to stay. I hadn't asked her to leave, either. While I was waiting I'd raided her private stock for two bottles of date wine and four horn shot cups. I proposed the old Hippodrome toast: the losers, God save them. The date wine made my eyes water. I'm not a drinking man.

"You'll have heard the news," I said. They nodded. "Now, we all know who runs this town. The other side of the wall, there's a bunch of savages who just wiped out the Guards. You boys are in the trade, I'd like you to think about that for a moment."

Arrasc scowled at me. "We're screwed," he said.

"No," I replied. "Not yet. I have no idea who these jokers are, but they're smart, which is lucky for us. They're smart enough to know that the wall is too strong for them, and they're smart enough to stay out of catapult shot. Now, between us four, there aren't any catapults, but they don't know that. Last I looked, they were sitting down, making themselves comfortable. I don't know if they're waiting for their heavy kit to arrive, or whether they're planning on building it on site. In any event, we seem to have a bit of a breathing space. We aren't dead yet, gentlemen. We still have a chance."

Longinus refilled his cup and sipped it, very refined and genteel. "I saw some of your boys wheeling a load of junk on barrows," he said. "What's all that about?"

I told him and he laughed. "Give my lads a few days and a couple of barrels of nails and they'll be real machines up there, not pretend ones," I went on. "But there's only four thousand of us, plus six hundred Watch, who I wouldn't trust as far as I

could fart them out of my arse—" smiles from both of them "—
and the massed hoes of the Parks and Gardens boys, and that's
it. I need willing hands and strong backs, gentlemen. You have
plenty of both. We need to make a deal."

Dead silence. Aichma was getting fidgety, which meant she
was nervous. For my part, I felt like I was standing in a pen with
two bulls. Stupid, really. Aichmalotus was a Theme boss, and
he was my friend.

"Here's what's in it for you," I said. "First, the City doesn't
fall and we don't all get slaughtered like sheep. In case you were
thinking of getting out by sea, you can forget that. There's no
ships. There's the shit barges and one freighter. No way you
could get even a fraction of your people out on them. If you want
to stay alive, we have to hold the City. I think it can be done. No
promises, no guarantees, but I reckon it's possible."

I took the Great Seal out of my pocket and put it down in
the middle of the table. Longinus raised his eyebrows and said
nothing. Arrasc said, "Is that—?" I nodded.

"Mine," I said, "so I can do what I damn well like. And
what I'd like to do is legalise the Themes. Legal to join, legal to
wear the colours, legal to hold office. You'll each have a charter,
like the Knights of Allectus or the Hospitals. You'll be able to
buy and own land, raise money by subscription, sue for debts
in the courts instead of breaking kneecaps. We all know that
all the government in this City that's worth doing is done by
you boys. Now you'll be able to do it openly, with the Prefect
helping instead of making your lives difficult. If you want, you
can even come to civic dinners and march in the Ascension Day
parade." That made Longinus laugh. "That's what I'd like to
do," I said. "You ask Aichma here, I've been saying it for years,
it's time the Themes are recognised for what they really are in

this town. And I can do all that. All I need is a bit of paper and some hot wax."

They were looking at me. Arena fighters look at you in a special way, dead still, taking it all in, actually watching. Comes of all that swordfighting. Terrifies the life out of you until you get used to it, and you really shouldn't. Hippodrome men are dangerous, at all times.

"What do you want?" Arrasc said.

"All the men you can give me," I said. "And women, and children. I want fighting men on the walls. I want fetchers and carriers, men to dig trenches and saps, build walls, knock down houses, find all the stuff I need, get it from A to B. I need people I can trust to gather up all the food in the City and hand it out, strict rationing, no cheating. If I left that to the Prefect, first thing you know, you boys'd be running a black market, and you're so much smarter than he is. So I want you two to do it, and anyone who cheats gets his legs broken. I want—" I searched for the right word, but all I could think of was "—co-operation. I think, as you do, that this is your city every bit as much as it's the emperor's. Fine. You want it, you're going to have to fight to keep it. And if we win, I promise you, you'll have what's rightfully yours. And if we lose – well, it's not going to matter a shit, is it? Well? What do you think?"

Another long silence. I was worried. Then Longinus said, "Is anybody going to be paying us for all this work?"

"Yes," I said. "Rations and cash money. Now I'll be straight with you, there's only so much coin in the City and we can't very well send out for some more when that's gone, so if this goes on for very long, sooner or later it'll have to be paper. But there will be money, and you will get what's fair. You can trust me on that."

They looked at Aichma, who nodded. Big risk for her, but

she didn't hesitate. Then Arrasc reached out his big bony paw. "Deal," he said.

I shook it. He had a grip like a dog bite. I looked at Longinus. He was thinking about it. That was when I realised I'd neglected to consider a vital factor. The Blues and the Greens are enemies, they hate each other. Hell, I thought.

"I should have mentioned," I said, "nobody's expecting Blues and Greens to work shoulder to shoulder. Perish the thought. But that's all right, there's no need. We'll sort out who does what, and it'll either be a Green job or a Blue one."

"And the Blues get all the easy jobs and we get all the shit," Longinus said. He was looking at Arrasc when he said it, trying to provoke him. "Do I look like I'm stupid?"

If you've ever cut down a tree, you'll know about the first soft little creak that means it's about to go, and unless you get out of the way really fast, it'll quash you flat. Like that. But I hadn't anticipated the problem, so I hadn't figured out what I was going to say. "Fine," I said. "If the Greens won't work with me and the Blues will, I have no choice, it's not up to me. But I'd rather have both of you."

Longinus gave me a look that would've scared a tiger. But then I thought of all those men on the other side of the wall, and you know what, he wasn't as terrifying as them. "Well?" I said.

Longinus hesitated. "No shit jobs," he said.

"Plenty of shit jobs," I said. "But shared equally."

That made him laugh. "Deal," he said, and reached out his hand.

"You did what?"

Faustinus is one of those handsome men; so handsome, you think he must be an idiot. He's also shorter than me, so tiny for an Imperial. He's, what, forty-five, hard to tell his age because he'll look more or less the same when he's seventy. His wife died the year before the siege. He was devoted to her.

"Calm down," I said. "We got them cheap. We need manpower."

Arrasc and Longinus had gone away with long lists of things to do. I'd hung on at the Dogs because I'd told Faustinus to meet me there. He'd taken longer than I'd expected, and it was nearly dark. Aichma had made me a big kettle of tea, and we'd been talking about old times.

Faustinus was beside himself with fury. "You've promised a *charter* to two criminal gangs, plus pay at double what the Guards get, and you expect me to—"

"Faustinus," I said, "shut up. You're not helping."

He stared at me as if I'd slapped him. Then he looked away for a moment, then back at me. "You've gone too far," he said. "You'll never get it past the House. Then you'll have to go back to your gladiator friends and tell them it's all off, and then we'll have riots. What in God's name were you thinking of?"

I let him run on. It was easier. Meanwhile, I was doing mental arithmetic. According to Faustinus, in actual cash money we had three million, two hundred and seventy-six thousand stamena, plus gold and silver in hand to strike maybe a million more. Not a great deal, in other words.

"Faustinus," I interrupted him. "Who's boss of the Mint these days?"

He stopped and looked at me. "Segimerus," he said. "You know him?"

"Not any more," I said. "Find me someone who'll do what he's told. Then we melt down three million stamena."

"What?"

"Devaluation," I said. "We won't have enough money, so we need to bulk the gold out with copper. We can use water-pipe, there's plenty of that."

"Orhan, what are you talking about? You know the stamenon's nine hundred parts pure. It has been for centuries."

I shook my head. "While we're at it," I said, "we need smaller coins. We'll be paying the Theme workers, it'll take too long for them to earn a stamenon. So when we restrike, we'll issue a new coin, a quarter of the weight. That way, we have a more useful denomination, and people won't notice there's less gold in it."

He shook his head. "This is all getting out of hand," he said. "I think you've lost your grip. I'm sorry, but I can't be part of this."

I yawned. It had been a very long day. "Let's see," I said, "a hundred and sixty tornese to the stamenon, so a quarter would be forty. Oh, and we'll need to water down the silver a bit. Don't worry about the technicalities. I have friends who're good at this stuff."

Meaningful glare. "I know you do."

"But that's all right, it can wait till the morning. Right now, I need an inventory of the armouries. I don't suppose you've done that yet."

He gave me a tragic look. "What's got into you, Orhan? I'd say you were drunk, except you don't touch the stuff. You're behaving very strangely."

"Go and see to that inventory," I said. "Please."

And off he went; and Aichma, who'd been sort of hovering, came and sat down opposite. "He's right, though," she said. "What has got into you?"

I didn't want to talk about it. So instead, I asked her, "How would you like to be Minister of Supply?"

10

I'd have preferred to crash out at the Dogs – a nice heap of straw in the stables would've suited me just fine – but sadly I couldn't afford such luxuries. It was dark by now, and I still had so much to do. I left my new minister still swearing blind she wasn't going to do it, and set off through the Lanes.

I was thinking about various issues, mostly military equipment, and so maybe I wasn't paying as much attention as I usually do. No excuse. A man walks in the Lanes after dark at his own risk, and his safety is his own responsibility.

They hit me over the head, probably with an axe handle. I remember it hurting, and then nothing until I woke up. First light in the City is a sort of sea-blue. I had a splitting headache and I was cold and wet. They'd taken my coat, my trousers and my boots. I put my hand to my head and felt caked blood. I guess they thought they'd killed me, which explained why they hadn't cut my throat. Lucky old me.

I tried to stand up, several times. Then I realised I was much better sitting with my back to the wall, at least until the world stopped spinning. It was while everything was going round and round that it occurred to me that the Great Seal had been in my coat pocket.

"You again," she said; and then, "God almighty, what have you been doing to yourself?"

I resented that. I sat down on the front step of the Dogs and let my head bump against the door. "You remember Thrasso," I said.

"Is that blood? You're all covered in blood. Have you been *fighting*?"

"Thrasso," I said. "I need him now. It's really, really important."

"Hold still while I get some water and a sponge."

"No," I said. "Thrasso. Now."

So she got water and a sponge and washed away the blood, then scolded me for making a fuss, because it was only a scalp wound. "Thrasso," I said. "It's life and death."

"Who's Thrasso?"

I sighed. "Thrasso from Lower Town," I told her. "You remember him. He's Cordouli, about my age. Big nose and really bad breath."

"Oh, him. What do you want him for?"

"Find him," I said. "Bring him here. It's incredibly important."

It was so important, she sent the odd-job boy, an evil little toad who hung around the Dogs in the hope of stealing food. By then, I'd more or less given up. I felt dizzy and sick and I wanted to go to sleep, which wasn't good. Just as well that Nico came barging in looking for me.

"Where the hell have you been?" he said, as soon as he saw me. "We've been looking everywhere. They said you might be here. I said, no, he wouldn't be so irresponsible—" He broke off and gazed at me. "My God," he said. "What happened? Have you been in a fight?"

I swallowed a couple of times, to keep from vomiting. "Has Faustinus done that inventory yet?"

"What? No, I don't think so, I haven't seen him. Are you all right?"

I grabbed his wrist. "Get that inventory," I said. "While you're talking to him, get him to tell you about the Themes."

"What have the Themes got to do with anything?"

"He'll tell you. What have we got on the wall, right now?"

"Two hundred of our boys, three hundred Watch and fifty or so gardeners. No developments. The enemy are just sitting there."

"Waiting for someone." I hadn't meant to say that out loud. "Allow me to introduce our new Minister of Supply." I looked round. She wasn't there. "Oh, for God's sake. Aichma, get out here."

She put her head round the door. "What?"

"This is Aichma," I said. "She's in charge of sniffing out all the stocks of food in the City, impounding them and setting up rationing. Aichma, this is General Bautzes." The fool took off his hat, like he always does when there's a female present. "He's my second-in-command. If you need soldiers, he'll give them to you."

"Hang on," Nico said. "Did you say general?"

She scowled at me. "First, I won't do it, it's ridiculous. Second, why would I want soldiers?"

"In case anyone gives you any trouble," I told her. "And will you stop pissing around with dusters and get to work? This is *important*."

She was about to argue when the boy came back, with Thrasso the Cordouli trailing along behind him like a sheep to slaughter. I gave him a huge smile. "There he is," I said. "Nico, Aichma, give us a moment, would you? I need to talk to this man."

I poured him a drink. My hand shook so much I spilled most of it on the table. He sat down opposite, watching me like a cat.

Thrasso is one of the most evil, unpleasant people I've ever met. When he's drunk he's violent, when he's sober he's slippery as an eel. But he's the best unofficial die-cutter in the City. "I need you," I said, "to make me a copy of the Great Seal."

He gawped at me, then burst out laughing. "Fuck you," he said, and stood up to go.

"Sit down." I can do it, sometimes. I'd have made a good bully if I'd had the chance. I've learned the craft from masters, like an apprentice. "The fee is five hundred stamena, a free pardon and a job cutting dies for the Mint. I need it now. Straight away."

He shook his head. "It can't be done," he said. "Everyone knows that."

Yes, everyone does. The Great Seal was cut four hundred years ago by Strymon of Leucas, the greatest sculptor of the age. Strymon's work is unique, which is why he was given the job. Over the centuries, God knows how many clever craftsmen have tried to copy the damn thing, but none of them has ever managed to get it right, so that it'll fool anybody; not even when they've had imprints of the Seal in front of their noses, to copy from. Strymon's style simply can't be reproduced. They've given up trying. Can't be done.

I called Nico. "Arrest this man," I said. "He's a forger. Cut off his head and stick it on an arch somewhere."

Thrasso jumped up but Nico was too quick for him. He got him in an arm lock that made him scream.

"General Bautzes will see to it that you have prints of the real thing to work from," I said. "Now, have you got the materials, or do you need us to get them for you?"

No sooner had Nico and Thrasso left us but Faustinus showed up. We had a reprise of the where-have-you-been-what-happened-to-you routine, and then he handed me a bronze tube with a sheet of paper rolled up inside. "You'd better read it to me," I said. "My eyes are a bit funny."

It was worse than I'd thought. Basically, there were no military supplies in the City. Why should there be, after all? We have places like Classis for all that. However, Faustinus surprised me. He'd used his head. In the cellars of the Guards barracks were twenty crates of the miserable Type Thirteen A swords, still in their grease, dumped there and forgotten about. The Speuthes brothers, dealers in scrap metal, had recently bought off the government one thousand suits of regulation armour, classified as unfit for service; luckily, they hadn't been cut up yet, and we could have them at practically cost. Meanwhile, the Imperial treasury's list of gifts received by the emperor from foreign dignitaries over the past six centuries included five hundred swords, six hundred helmets, seven hundred and forty suits of armour of various types and patterns – all enamelled and inlaid with gold and garnets and engraved with mythological scenes by artists of world importance; but never mind, at the end of the day, a helmet's still a helmet. All told, we had swords for seven thousand, armour for two thousand; no spears, no bows, no arrows. To all intents and purposes, we were defenceless.

My head was splitting. I'll worry about that later, I decided. "Faustinus," I said, "I'd like you to meet our new Minister of Supply."

*

"For crying out loud answer the question," she said, when finally we were alone for a few minutes. "Why me?"

I sighed. I'd have thought it was obvious. "Because," I said, "first, it's a job that calls for brains, resourcefulness, clear thinking and imagination. Second, there's the opportunities. You'll have total control over food supplies in a city of a quarter of a million people. Anyone else, I don't care how noble and selfless and idealistic, sooner or later the temptation would get to him, or else it'd be blackmail, or the faces of the starving kids. But if this is going to work, there can be no exceptions, no special cases, no little favours, no compassion, no graft. It's got to be done right, by the book. I need someone I can trust absolutely."

She looked at me. "You're crazy," she said.

11

I'd managed to put it off this far, but the horrible job still had to be done. I packed Nico off on an errand to the ropemakers' quarter, and sent for Artavasdus and Stilico. For two pins I'd have set up my office right there, in the front parlour of the Dogs. But it made Nico and Faustinus uncomfortable, and the Palace is handier for the walls. They had to carry me in a sedan chair, which was embarrassing.

"I want a square of white cloth," I said, "about so wide and so long. And a stick to tie it to."

Stilico's eyes went wide. "We're going to negotiate."

I nodded. "I'm not getting my hopes up," I said, "but I've got to try. You two are coming with me."

By this point I was back on my feet, and we walked the last hundred yards to the North Gate. As the gate opened and we passed through, a guard in gloriously shiny golden armour gave me a grin and a cheery wave: Longinus, pulling a shift on sentry duty. I felt a surge of relief that nearly knocked me over. I hadn't had time to ask if any Theme men had showed up for duty yet.

Stilico was holding the white flag, on the left. Then me, then Artavasdus. The plain in front of us looked impossibly wide, and, in the distance, the sun flashing on five endless ranks of grounded shields. As I have said, I'm not a brave man. I really didn't want to be doing this incredibly stupid thing.

"Our offer is," I told them, "if they'll let us evacuate the City, they can have it. Maybe they'll let us take some stuff with us, but if not, so be it."

Stilico was shocked. "Give them the City?"

I shrugged. "We can't defend it."

"But where would we go? All those people—"

"We'll cross that bridge when we come to it."

They'd seen us; men were running about. When we were a hundred and fifty yards from the front line, a gap opened. I saw a row of men kneel down. "Run," I said.

They shot at us. Of course, I tripped and went flat on my face. Stilico and Artavasdus grabbed my arms and dragged me back to the gate. They told me afterwards they thought I'd been shot. So much for negotiations.

When I got back to my new headquarters at the Palace, there was a deputation waiting to see me. They were standing about in the entrance hall, very unhappy to have been kept waiting.

I was all covered in dust, with one boot missing. "I can't possibly see you all at once," I said, raising my voice to make myself heard. "Senator Fronto, if you'll follow me. The rest of you gentlemen, wait here."

Fronto was Leader of the House. He was ready to explode. A big man in every sense of the word. You could walk a thousand miles, from Rupilia to the Sea, over land he or his family owned.

Breeding tells, you know. I felt like if I got within six feet of him, I'd get burned. "Sit down," I said. "You'll have to excuse me, I've been rather busy."

He stayed standing up. People who know about these things reckon he was the finest public speaker since Androcles, whose stuff I've never got around to reading. He had soft, thin white hair and a chin you could've broken rocks with.

It was intolerable, he said. Not only had I assumed command without even notifying the House, let alone receiving its confirmation, I had proceeded to make appointments to posts that were and always had been the prerogative of the House, attempted to negotiate with a foreign power, granted pardons to criminals, appropriated buildings and stores—

I hit him.

I'm not a big puncher. I don't favour the full swing to the jaw, the powerhouse right-hand cross. I find a short jab just below the ribcage works just as well, and you don't waste your strength or skin your knuckles. He sat down, like I'd asked him to. For a moment, he was lost for words.

"I'm sorry about that," I said, looking past him at a spot on the wall. I'd just knocked all the breath out of him, but I still couldn't bring myself to look straight at him, like the sun. "For what it's worth, I respect the Robur principle of government, I think it works well. I like the way absolute power is diluted and naturally tempered by delegation to successive levels of command and bureaucracy. I admire the way the House has always stood up for its right to be consulted. As an outsider, coming from a country that has no central government or overall authority, I think I can appreciate the merits of the Imperial system rather more than most Robur." I paused for breath. I still wasn't feeling right. "Now, though, is not the time. I've got a lot to do, and you aren't helping. So, please, go home and stay out from under my feet. Is that clear?"

He looked up at me. He still couldn't speak. I should have been ashamed of myself, hitting a man of his age.

"The City," I said, "is under martial law. I have the emperor's commission and the Great Seal. You're just going to have to trust me, that's all."

I stood up, helped him to his feet, held his elbow as we walked to the door, which I opened for him politely. Then I shut it, bolted it and sat down. I was shaking like a leaf.

"You can't do things like that," Faustinus told me. "You just can't."

We were standing on the wall. The enemy were still there, five ranks of shields in front of a bustling community going about their business. I'd given up trying to count them, but somewhere in the order of forty thousand. And they were waiting for someone. I just knew it.

"I can, though," I said. "Well done with that scrap armour, by the way. Any more where that came from?"

He shook his head. "I tried all the scrapyards in town," he said. "They don't usually keep bulk stock here, warehouse space is too expensive. Don't change the subject. I know it's tempting, but you can't just trample all over the government and you can't just ignore it and do things your own way. You've got to work with these people."

I hadn't told him about losing the Seal. No need for him to know, not yet. "First thing in the morning," I said, "we'll need to pull the roof off the Guildhall. You'd better find somewhere else for all your clerks for a day or so."

"What? You can't—"

"I need the rafters," I told him. "Really big, solid oak beams. Private houses, the beams just aren't big enough. Besides, nobody lives in the Guildhall."

He gave me his words-fail-me look.

"Artillery," I said. "Fifty long-range spoon onagers, at least a hundred ballistas, and I'd like to put some scorpions in those corner towers there, for enfilading the approaches to the gates. For which we need a great deal of seasoned timber, something we don't have enough of. Later we'll need reinforcing beams for propping the gates and the walls, and after that I expect we'll want about a hundred thousand pit props, for when they start sapping under the walls and we start countermining."

"The Guildhall is the administrative centre of the City," he said. "You can't—" Wisely, he stopped and started again. "There's a hundred acres of lumber yards in Lower Town," he said. "They must have all the timber you want, surely."

I shook my head. "Softwood, small-section. Oh, we'll need all that, but for other things. I've asked Longinus and the Greens to see to stripping the Guildhall roof. I've told them they can have the lead." I grinned, before he could say anything. "We'll be needing that, too, but we can buy it back from them."

He drew in a deep breath. "Is it because they've always bullied you?" he said. "Payback time. Is that what this is all about?"

He deserved an honest answer. "I thought about that," I said. "And the answer is probably no. I say probably," I added, "I'm not sure."

"Don't pretend you didn't enjoy it. Punching out the Leader of the House."

I shook my head. "I needed to get his attention," I said. "I need to be taken seriously. We're that far—" I pointed to the gap between the walls and the flashing shields "—from being slaughtered. If they were to come for us now, right this minute, we'd hold them up for maybe half an hour. That's all."

His face changed. I guess he hadn't really grasped it before. I felt sorry for him.

"They're waiting for something," I said. "Or someone. Someone, I'm inclined to think, because they've got all the things they need, and all the manpower. No, I think their orders are, don't start the party without me." I turned my head so I couldn't see the look on his face. There are times when you don't intrude on other people's despair; it'd be indecent. "With the rafters from the Guildhall roof made into artillery, I can possibly extend that half-hour into half a day. With all the pine planks from the Lower Town yards split and planed into arrows, assuming I can conjure up bows and someone to shoot them, thirty-six hours. You see what I'm getting at? Every stupid, bloody desperate little thing I can think of buys us a tiny scrap more time, once *he* gets here. It's all ridiculous and pointless, of course, but I've got to *try*." I looked at him. "Everyone keeps telling me what I can't do, but they're wrong. The only thing I can't do is nothing."

He shook his head and walked away.

"I can't," she told me. "I'm sorry."

Late evening on the second day. I'd had about enough. Thrasso had brought me his attempt at the Great Seal. It was a beautiful piece of work. Someone told me once, a really great fake can't just be as good as the original, it's got to be better. Thrasso's seal was better. I stamped it in hot wax and was stunned by the beauty of the thing. He looked at me and knew what I was going to say. I tried, he protested, God knows I tried, I got my calipers and measured every distance, to within a hair. I smoked the die over a candle and put it over a genuine imprint and there wasn't a single smudge. It ought to be perfect, he said. I punched his face, hard. Do it again, I said. I can't, he said, that's as good as it gets. I put the thing of beauty he'd made under the heel of my boot and ground it into bits of gravel. Do it again, I told him.

"What do you mean, can't?" I said.

She was close to tears. "I can't do this job," she said. "They won't do what I tell them. I have to scream and shout to get anything done, and they're so slow, and they make me feel like I don't know what I'm doing." She paused and looked straight at me. "And they're right. I don't."

There are times when you just don't want to hear it. "Be firm with them," I said. "You know how to do that."

"You're not listening. They're right. I don't know how to do this stuff. I'm making it up as I go along, but that's not good enough. You need a proper clerk, who knows about ward registers and where to look up property tax records and how to roster duty shifts. Maybe I could do it if I spent a year figuring out a system. All I'm doing is wasting time. You need people who know what to do."

"The Theme district mobilisers—"

"No," she said, "they're no good. They know where people live, in Poor Town, and how much money they make, but it's all in their heads, not down on paper. Finding things out from them takes too long. You need the written records. You need the clerks." She was quiet for a moment. "You can't bypass the system," she said. "I know it's the enemy, but you can't do anything without it."

I could feel myself getting angry. The truth does that to me, when I'm in the wrong. "They're just a bunch of—"

She shook her head. "You need them," she said. "I know what you're trying to do. The empire failed, so you think it's up to the rest of us to save the City. The other empire. The soldiers all got themselves killed, so we won't use soldiers. The City magistrates all ran away, so we'll use the Themes. Let's have a milkface stomping around like he's the emperor. Let's have a woman running Supply. What's the old proverb, the worms of the earth against the lions? Let's try that. Orhan, I'm sorry but it's not going to work. You need the clerks *as well*. And you need a clerk doing this job. I'm sorry. I'm on your side, but I can't do it."

"Fine," I said. "Go back to the Dogs and wash some dishes."

She left without a word.

Faustinus had a big pile of papers for me, all needing the Seal. I told him I was too busy. Fine, he said, lend me the Seal and I'll get them done for you. It's in the pocket of my other coat, I said. I'll send for it directly, soon as I've got a minute.

Nico came back from the ropewalk. There's only one in Town these days, where there used to be a dozen, but the noble family who owned the freeholds closed them down and sold the land to builders. Not to worry; the Pausa brothers were still very much in business and they had plenty of rope. Something going right for a change.

"We'll need about a mile of the good stuff, horsehair for choice, for the catapult springs," I told him, "and get them to send three miles of best hemp over to the Blue lodge. Tell you about it later," I explained. "Just see to it, will you?"

He's used to me. "Right away," he said. "Look, can I ask you something?"

"If you're quick."

"What's going to happen when they cut the aqueduct?"

I know my faults. One of them is, every time I go away on a job or a visit, I forget something. Spare pair of boots, pen nibs, keys, the present I promised to bring someone from the City, always something. However hard I try, however many lists I make, there's always one damn thing, and it always makes me feel unbearably stupid. Like that. "The aqueduct."

"Yes, the Aqueduct of Jovian. It supplies all the water to Lower Town and the mills."

I shook my head. "They'd need the proper tools."

"Yes, which we left behind in Spendone forest, remember? Chisels, wedges, screwjacks, lifting gear, everything they need. If you recall, I did say at the time—"

Dear God. "Leave it with me," I said, "I'll think of something. Right now, I need that rope."

12

The aqueduct. How could I have been so colossally stupid?

You say things like that – out loud, inside your head – trusting on some level that someone will contradict you – you can't think of everything, you've had so much else on your mind, there's nothing anybody could have done. You exaggerate, taking on yourself more blame than you deserve. Truth was, I hadn't thought that far ahead. We were still alive because they were waiting for someone, and when he eventually got here, it'd be a matter of time and how much of a nuisance we could make of ourselves before we all died. But every little step I took – real siege engines instead of olive presses under tarpaulins in the artillery niches on the wall, Theme button-men bulking out my tiny garrison, decommissioned substandard swords and armour instead of empty hands and bare bodies, each pointless flare-up of ingenuity, each minuscule triumph in the face of impossible odds pushed the final fall of the curtain just a bit further back; we might last days instead of hours, thanks to me, and apparently my reward for all that hard slog and brainwork would be getting shown up as the halfwit who hadn't arranged for an alternative water supply when they cut the aqueduct. So, fine, I wasn't really expecting a laurel crown and a chariot drawn by white horses to carry me under a triumphal arch with my name on it. But would it be too much to ask that one of those minuscule triumphs made things easier, instead of crushingly more and more difficult?

I appointed a clerk by the name of Hrabanus Geticus as Minister of Supply. He was a short, hairless, shrivelled little man, looked eighty but according to the file he was sixty-two, started in the Cartulary at age fifteen, been there or thereabouts ever since. In six hours he designed a collection, storage and distribution network that was a miracle of elegantly simple efficiency, while his ten under-clerks, who were obviously petrified of him, divided the City up into search-and-enter zones for the collection squads. He wasn't the least bit bothered at the idea of using Theme officers to do the actual collecting. Good idea, he said, not looking up from the schedule he was working on, they know the people and the districts, and who's got false ceilings and hidden cellars, and who's been buying more than they can possibly eat. I left him to get on with it, feeling guilty and defeated, even though I'd clearly just made a brilliant appointment.

"Linen," I said. "Lots and lots of linen, and glue. But glue's easy, you can make it out of practically anything." I looked down my nose at them. "You do know how to make glue, don't you?"

Yes, they knew just fine, so I condescended to explain. In Chorroe, six months' journey to the east, where no Robur had ever gone, they make very fine armour out of linen and rope. They do this because there's no iron ore in those parts; they have to import all the iron they use, at ruinous cost. So they take fifteen layers of linen and glue them together, and the result is light, cool in summer and warm in winter, easy to repair and maintain, and it'll keep you safe when people are trying to hurt you just as well as a mailshirt or a coat of scales. Furthermore, in Chorroe the manufacture of armour is exclusively the province of women, of whom we had an ample supply.

Silence – they found me embarrassing; then one of them (big fat man, ran the Blue Swallow mill) stood up and bowed politely. "With respect," he said.

I rolled my eyes. "What?"

From his sleeve he took out what looked like a small tile. "My grandfather probably heard the same travellers' tales as you did," he said. "We looked into linen armour about forty years ago." He rapped the tile with his knuckle; sounded like a man knocking on a door. "This is seventeen thicknesses of unbleached coarse linen. The glue's just basic gesso – rabbit skins," he explained (you do know how to make glue, don't you?). "And, yes, it works very well, according to my grandfather's notes. He bashed it with swords and axes and shot arrows at it, and the Quartermaster General was most impressed, he recommended it for an extended trial, which it passed. But the emperor said he wasn't sending his men out to fight in bits of botched-up rag, he'd be a laughing stock, and that was the end of that." He handed me the tile. "You're quite right," he said. "It would do admirably."

"Well, then."

He nodded. "In hot weather," he said, "it takes a minimum of thirty days for the glue to dry." Smile. "A bit like planting acorns, don't you think, in the circumstances."

Indeed. Plant oak for the very finest timber, but you'll never live to use it. "Thank you," I said. "I'd be grateful if you'd share your research with the rest of these gentlemen. In light of what you've just told me I don't think we'll bother with prototypes and all that stuff. Crack on and make me as many suits as you can, and I'll see you all in a month."

Awkward moment. "About the money side of things," someone said.

I did a vague hand wave. "You tell me how much you want," I said. "Believe me, that's the least of our problems."

Acorns and oaks. It's the tradition, where I come from, that on the day you're born your father plants an apple tree. It grows with you, and when you die they dig your grave in its shade. Nice idea; it's all about stability and continuity and the pretty notion that things, left to themselves, will get stronger and bigger, and that when you go to bed at night there's a better than even chance that the world will still be there in the morning.

Maybe my tree's still standing, I have no idea. I know from personal experience that things end suddenly, that the axe achieves more in ten minutes than the tree does in twenty years. First time I saw the City, I remember thinking, here's a tree nobody can cut down. I liked the idea of the emperor, as represented on the back of the money. The emperor's face never changes, only the name; the portrait is that of Mezentius III (though I bet you he didn't look like that) who died four centuries ago, after a reign of nine months. So: names and bodies come and go, like leaves on a tree, but the emperor stays the same, always, imperishable, like the wall. Meanwhile, on my watch, it's generally understood that thirty days is so wildly optimistic, it's probably not worth bothering. Planting acorns.

*

"What are they up to?" Stilico asked me.

He's a better man than me, but I have better eyesight. It was one of those needle-sharp mornings, when the sea-mist clears at dawn and you can see for miles. "They do say," I said, "that in Chorroe they have these brass tubes with bits of glass in them—"

He grinned. "You've been reading a book," he said.

"Fascinating place, by all accounts. Anyway, with one of these tubes you can see things a mile away as though they're right in front of your nose."

"And they make armour out of bits of rag, I heard about that. It was a good idea."

The moment anybody starts to bleed, there's Stilico with a pinch of salt between his fingers. "Not much, is the answer to your question," I said. "They're building something over there, look, between that stand of ash trees and the old gravel pit, but there's tents in the way and I can't make out anything except scaffolding. You'd probably get a better view from the North Gatehouse."

"It's a siege tower," Stilico said. "A bloody great big one. I had my sergeant take a look."

Bad news, like the cough that won't go away. "We know what to do about siege towers," I said.

Stilico nodded. "I've got the Greens requisitioning cooking oil," he said. "It'd help if we knew which gate they were planning to use it on."

"Doesn't have to be a gate," I told him. "How's the artillery coming on?"

"Surprisingly well. Maybe the day after tomorrow, if we're lucky."

I took a deep breath. The view from the wall was like looking up, at the stars, as though the world was besieged by the sky. "Stilico," I said, "you're a bright boy. Is there anything we could be doing that we haven't already done?"

He didn't need to think long. "No," he said. "Me personally, I'd have built boats, not catapults. By now we could've thrown together a bunch of rafts, enough to save maybe a thousand people. But that's just my opinion."

I nodded. "Which thousand?"

"Ah." He smiled. "That's why I'm glad I'm not in charge."

"I considered that. But then we'd never have got the Themes on our side. They'd have known they wouldn't be on those rafts. And without them, we couldn't have done anything."

"True." He turned away, breaking eye contact with the enemy, like you're not supposed to do when you're facing down a lion or an angry bull. "We've been ingenious, resourceful and inventive, and we haven't let ourselves be hindered by outmoded or irrelevant ways of thinking. It's a shame, really, because nobody will ever know how clever we were."

So I made a decision. We were going to wreck their siege tower.

Amazingly, and worryingly, nobody yelled at me or told me I must be out of my tiny mind when I announced it at that evening's staff meeting. Instead, there was a long silence, and then Artavasdus said, "Well, I guess we've got to do *something*," and Nico made that grunting-pig noise that means he wishes you weren't right but you are, and Arrasc of the Blues said, "Finally," or something like that, and I think the only person round that table who reckoned it was a truly terrible idea was me.

"Fine," I said. "So, how do we go about it?"

I rarely ask for suggestions, because, when I do, people tend to make them; in this case, all at once and very loudly. Nico was all for a head-on frontal assault; the element of surprise, do the thing they least expect you to. Arrasc agreed with him before he'd even stopped talking, so, naturally, Longinus of the Greens had to disagree; Arrasc called him a coward, Longinus said the Greens wouldn't be taking part, and for a moment I thought I'd been let off the hook. Then Artavasdus lost his rag with both of them and – I really don't understand people, give me inanimate objects any day – they both said yes, you're right, we really do need to do it, and suddenly it was all on again. And then they turned and looked at me.

My head was completely empty. No ideas, not a clue. And then I heard myself say, "What we're going to do is this."

13

Allow me to introduce Aelia Zenonis, universally known as Sawdust.

She was born, thirty-two years before the Great Siege, somewhere in the Poor Town district, a Blues neighbourhood. Her mother was indentured in a button factory. Sawdust worked in the factory until she was nine, and would probably have stayed there if her mother's foreman hadn't lost her in a game of knucklebones. The winner was a freelance carpenter by the name of Zeno, a Green, who spent most of his time in and around the Hippodrome, earning money building and fixing bleachers, rails, fittings, you name it, and then losing it betting on the fights and the chariot races. The carpenter had no son and his daughter, a superior creature, stood an excellent chance of being taken on as a lady's maid in a good house, so Sawdust became a carpenter's monkey – carry the tools, hold this, pass me that; unusual for a female but not unheard of where a man's too poor to afford an apprentice. The life must have suited her, because she shot up, filled out, picked up the trade like other people get mud on their boots; by age fifteen she could cut a dead square mortice, taper a barrel stave, dovetail a joint, as well as old Zeno or better. Most men would be embarrassed, but Zeno didn't mind; she earned him good money, her mind was almost always on the job and she had a cheerful, uncomplaining disposition which made a very pleasant change from what he was used to at home. She genuinely enjoyed the work – she liked being good at something, she explained – and, most of all, she positively relished constructing the props and gadgets for the masques and stage shows that they put on to mark the opening of the big events: the Championship, the Gold Crown, the Wooden Sword and so forth. Now that sort of thing doesn't just mean careful, precise work (and always on an impossibly tight schedule); it also calls for a degree of imagination and ingenuity, designing the clever little mechanisms for trapdoor latches, rising flats, revolves, all manner of tricky stuff that hasn't been done before and for which no guild-approved pattern exists. Needless to say, it's also horrendously competitive; the Greens want their Grand Entrance to be a hundred times better than what the Blues did last year, and vice versa. You have to be very, very good to be entrusted with the commission, but if you prove you can do it you've got the respect and admiration of your Theme sewn up in a little silk bag, regardless of who or what you are; even if you're some indentured fatherless brat from Poor Town; even if you're a milkface; even if you're a *girl*.

When Sawdust was nineteen – the name, of course, referred to her skin, the colour of freshly sawn pine, and her hair, ditto oak; brush the sawdust off, the other kids would jeer, knowing that she couldn't – Zeno celebrated a lucky win at the track with a boisterous night at the Two Dogs, and next morning stood on a scaffolding plank that wasn't there, ninety feet above the Prefect's Box. By now his wife was dead, his daughter had married and he had no other dependants; his property, therefore, passed by custom and tradition to the Green treasury – including, needless to say, Sawdust's indentures. Custom and tradition likewise ordained that all such legacies be put up for public auction. Whose bright idea it was for the Blues to buy Sawdust, at a ridiculously high price after a furious bidding war, we'll probably never know, but it was a masterstroke of tactical malice, leading to street fights and bloodletting, all to no avail. Come the next Prefect's Trophy, the Blue fighters made their entrance into the arena on a three-quarter-size replica of an Imperial warship. I was there, and I saw it; most amazing thing. There were no ropes or levers, not that anyone could see. The sails filled out and billowed, and the ship suddenly moved forward – out of the tunnel under the stands, mark you, so not a breath of actual wind, the billowing effect must all have been done with wires sewn into the sailcloth, and how they got the ship to move, let alone glide along smoothly just exactly as if on the water, I'm not ashamed to confess I still don't know to this day. It was the biggest coup the Blues had pulled off for about a decade, and they made no bones about who deserved all the credit. Sawdust, the little chippie girl, sold by the idiot Greens, bought, freed and elevated to her rightful rank of Master Carpenter by the intelligent and perceptive Blues.

Anyway, that was Sawdust. So, when I wanted someone who'd be able not just to copy the Pattern 68 stationary catapult but tweak it up to add an extra fifty yards' range, I knew exactly who I needed.

Most carpenters are Green, most stonemasons are Blue. I sent for the big man in the masons' guild and told him what I wanted. Can't be done, he said. I told him where he could find the specialist equipment he'd need, in yards staffed and controlled by his guild members. That's not nearly enough, he said. I told him who to see about getting the machines copied, and how many he'd need to build, and how long it'd take. He told me I was being wildly optimistic. So I showed him the warrant for the arrest of him, his entire family and forty-six leading members of his guild. I had my hand over where the Seal should have been. He gave me a terrified look and said he'd do his best. No, I said, do what you're told. He went away, hating me to bits. Can't say I blamed him.

Then I sent for my general staff – Nico, Stilico, Artavasdus, Menas, Arrasc and Longinus. While I waited for them to show up, I amused myself throwing stones and little wooden balls at a flower pot, which cheered me up no end. I wish it hadn't, because – you'll have to take my word on this – I really don't enjoy the thought of bloodshed, or damage to human bodies. You spend your life trying to fix it so that the people doing dangerous jobs under your command don't get all smashed up, and then you find yourself figuring out ways to hurt people on purpose. It just doesn't feel right, somehow. Probably why archery instructors make such poor soldiers.

The next day was busy, busy, busy – for everyone else, not for me. I had my men patching up the holes they'd knocked in the shit barges. I had Theme hands working back-to-back shifts, the masons and Sawdust's carpenters. I had Parks and Gardens men drilling with swords on the parade grounds, Hippodrome wranglers sawing and banging away in the coachworks sheds out back of the Blue Portico, and that was just the hands I'd assigned to special duties. Everywhere else, everyone else (except me) was skittering about executing the orders I'd given yesterday, or the day before, or the day before that. Hrabanus's clerks and the Theme ward bosses were counting the stores, which were now all safely lodged in secure warehouses, with savage-looking gladiators guarding the door; inside, you couldn't move for sacks of wheat and barrels of bacon and jars and jars of that horrible pickled cabbage. Three and a half thousand Green women were glueing strips of linen. Four thousand Blues were pulling down public buildings – the Mansion House, the Arch of Valerian, the Chamber of Deputies – and hauling away the salvage; stone to the masons' yards, timber to the lumber mills, even the nails, shipped off in barrels to the smiths for forge-welding into spearblades and arrowheads. Without realising it, or intending to, I'd changed the City out of all recognition. The market squares were empty. No stalls, no shoppers, no beggars or clusters of surplus manpower lounging in the shade of the porticos spoiling for a fight. No surplus manpower anywhere. Thanks to the Great Seal (or the illusion thereof) and my friends from the Old Flower Market, there was money for everyone who cared to show up and do a job of work. We'd reopened the old clay seam in Poor Town, closed down seventy years ago because it was cheaper to ship in clay from Proxima, and nine hundred Greens were making bricks again – we'd be needing bricks by the million once siege engines started pounding the walls. On the waterfront, the last two shipyards to close down were back in business. Glory be, they'd never managed to find buyers for the real estate, so when we smashed down the gates (the padlocks were too rusty to open) we found everything more or less as it had been when the last shift moved out: saw benches, cradles, cranes, tools still in their racks, still with an edge on them. Four hundred Blues who'd worked there before the closure were turning Guildhall rafters and Mansion House floorboards into warships, using the grey-with-age patterns they'd found hanging on the walls, where they'd left them ten years earlier. Five thousand women were splitting cedar planks and planing them down into arrowshafts in Watchbell Yard; another two thousand were glueing on feathers. And two hundred and seventy Greens who'd drifted unasked into the City when the copper mines at Dauris shut down had formed the new Miners' Guild, with the Haymarket Watch House for their guildhall. We chose it because a lot of people can queue up outside it without obstructing the traffic. The Miners' Guild was recruiting: half a tornece a day for trainees, a full tornece once you'd got your ticket. We'd be needing every sapper we could get once the enemy started undermining the walls. All told, it was as close as you'd ever dream of getting to the Great Society. A well-paid job for everyone, working together in harmony for the greater good; no fights, no muggings, because anyone caught doing that stuff would be thrown out of his Theme, and no Theme, no food, simple as that. Besides, why bother when you could earn silly money doing a proper job? Indeed.

And of course it was built, like all Great Societies, on lies. Lie One: there was no Great Seal. Lie Two: the silver tornece flowing like water out of the Paymaster's were three parts copper, lovingly made for the government by professional forgers. Lie Three: everyone had plenty of money in their pockets but nothing to spend it on, with food and booze centrally issued and strictly rationed, all the markets and shops shut, even the brothels and gambling halls closed down by order of the Themes (and since the Themes ran them all, we had a unique example of prohibition that actually worked). Oh, and Lie Four: the happy dream that if we all pulled together and did our bit, we'd still be alive in a month, or three months, or a year; that we'd live to lay the bricks and man the ships and shoot the arrows; that we weren't all just waiting for him to arrive, take command and issue the order to storm the City and stamp it into the ground.

Lies; so what? Many years ago we were building a bridge in Monouchis. We had to dig down deep to find hard rock to rest on, and we turned up the ruins of a city. Whoever they were, they'd built to last, and they dressed their massive ashlar blocks immaculately, every corner a dead square, every line unimpeachably straight, every block lettered and numbered, in letters and numbers none of us recognised – I don't give a damn, but one of my junior officers was a scholar's son, and he copied down examples to show his father, who said he'd never seen them before. So there was a city, for all I know every bit as big and brave and strong as ours, and no doubt they had their emperors and their first families and their guilds and Blues and Greens; all gone now, as though they'd never existed, and if we hadn't been building a bridge we'd never have guessed that the green-topped hummocks had once been a glorious living city, teeming with vitality and action, and determination to survive, and hope. Their lies didn't save them in the end, did they?

Still; so what? At least we had work to do, and work fills in the time, and time is the enemy. Personally I've never had a problem with lies, so long as they serve a useful purpose. Lies have consistently and reliably done me far more good than the truth. The way I see it, the truth is just barren moorland, all useless bog and heather. It's only when you break it up and turn it over with the ploughshare of the Good Lie that you can screw a livelihood out of it. Isn't that what humans do? They take a dead landscape and reshape it into what they need, and want, and can use. I've never hesitated to adapt the world to suit me, when I can get away with it.

*

Forgive me, I'm drivelling on. The next day; busy, for everyone but me. The day after that, some clown dragged me out of sleep while the sky was still dark blue with a message from Sawdust; come and see, we've finished.

So down I went to the artillery yard, only to find it deserted. Eventually, I found an old man cooking porridge; for when they get back, he told me. They're all up on the wall, didn't you know? So I dragged myself up onto the wall, where Sawdust's Greens had just finished installing forty-six newly built Pattern 68-As.

I'd granted her the glory and privilege of that -A as a special reward, in recognition of her outstanding effort and achievement; the highest honour I ever paid anyone, as a matter of fact. The emperor can make you a duke or a prince, the priests can declare you a saint, you can make a million stamena buying and selling and the House can ennoble your swineherding family back fifteen generations, but these are trivial distinctions, meaningless, because nobody can possibly know if you've really earned them or not. But to be the one who establishes a new class in the Imperial military nomenclature; that's something else. Take me. Fifteen years ago I designed a revolutionary new pontoon, one that actually works. There must be thousands of the things out there in service right now, all across the empire, from sunrise to sunset. But look in the inventories and the pontoons are still listed as Type 17, like they were before I was born. Not 17-A, or 17*, definitely not Pontoon (Orhan's). Actually, I resent that like hell. But so what?

I looked at the things, and saw the pitch glistening on the newly sawn timbers, and smelled the tar on the ropes, and suddenly I was terribly afraid. A wise man once said, it's not the despair that destroys you, it's the hope. Forty-six state-of-the-art artillery pieces, pointing at the enemy. Sawdust's foremen told me there'd be sixty-nine more in place by the end of the day. Suddenly we had artillery; suddenly, the big lie I'd managed to pull off that first day when we blew in on the shit fleet had turned into the truth.

Artillery, but nothing to shoot out of it. Which was, of course, my fault. Tell you about that later.

A perceptive soul like you will have noticed the strong hint of whining that's crept into this story. Forgive me. I never intended to be a commander, a giver of orders, though I don't exactly object. At heart, though, I still think of myself as a carpenter; and all around me there were wood shavings curling up off the plane, and not me making them. All I'd done was tell people to do things, which I can never bring myself to think of as work. Truth is, I felt left out, useless, lazy. So I went and found Sawdust. She was down on her hands and knees, trueing up the lie of a catapult cradle with a straight edge and a protractor. I stood over her and got in her light. "Go away," she said, not looking up.

"Nice job," I said.

She jumped up, banged her head on a thwart, made a sort of whimpering noise, wriggled round and scowled at me. "Are they all right?" she said.

I shrugged. "I don't know, do I? You tell me."

She got up and flicked a tiny proportion of the dust off her smock. "Well," she said, "I think we sorted out the problem with impact stress on the crossbar with an extra three turns of rope, and the creep in the joints is probably no big deal so long as we keep an eye on it, and the ratchets—"

"I'll take that as a yes," I said. "You've tested them, haven't you?"

She gave me the filthy look such a stupid question deserved. "Yes, at a quarter power. You said we can't wind them up to full."

I nodded. My fault, like everything else. The enhanced performance of the new pattern was part of the element of surprise, which was really the only thing I had going for me. Therefore, we couldn't test the bloody things, therefore we had no idea if they'd work or tear themselves to pieces, not until we started actually using them in anger against people dead set on killing us. Bloody stupid way of going about things, and entirely my decision.

I asked her some detail of the calibration system, to which she answered (as I knew she would) that without a chance to zero the engines at full power, any attempt at calibration was at best an educated guess. Completely irrelevant, in any case, but all I wanted to do was keep the conversation going.

"I'll need them ready to go by sunset," I said.

"Can't be done," she said. "We need the trestles, for raising the front ends. Otherwise I can't give you that trajectory you asked for."

I gave her a big smile. "No such word as can't," I told her, and walked away, giving her plenty of back to swear at.

Ready by sunset. As I said it, I felt my insides turn to ice. At sunset, we'd be doing a bloody stupid thing, on my orders, and if it went disastrously wrong it'd all be my fault.

So I went to the Blues' masonry yard, where they'd somehow managed to do what I'd so unreasonably asked of them. The results were being loaded on huge wagons with the biggest crane in the City. No chance of testing that theory, either. It would work, or it wouldn't; and if it didn't, four hundred Blues and Greens and three hundred Parks and Gardens men would be slaughtered in about a minute and a half, all to no purpose. No pressure, then.

So I went to the Hippodrome workshops, basically three

enormously long sheds, where generations of skilled craftsmen have lovingly built and maintained the most carefully designed and crafted artefacts in human history: the racing chariots.

To give you an idea. It costs five thousand stamena to build a warship for the Imperial fleet. A racing chariot costs three times that. Every inch, every ounce, has been pondered over, fiddled with, improved, reimproved, rethought from scratch. There are two hundred and seven nails in a racer, and some of the brightest, most brilliant minds that ever lived have thought with terrible intensity about every aspect of each of those nails; could it be longer, shorter, thinner, thicker, slightly more tapered at the front end, made out of a slightly different alloy? Could we do away with just one of those nails and get away with two hundred and six? Could we do away with all of them and use hickory dowels instead? Crazy. If we could breed people the way they build racing chariots in those sheds, a man would be eight feet tall, weigh ninety pounds, run ten miles in twenty minutes, live to be two hundred and never catch a cold. When I walked through the shed door, fifty faces turned and scowled at me. Quite right, too. What I'd told them to do was far worse than murder.

14

"We don't have to go through with this," Nico said. His teeth were chattering, I assume because of the cold. Actually, it was quite warm. "We could go back."

Nico is as brave as a lion. I'm the coward. "No," I said.

He was standing on the gangplank. "It's a good idea," he said, "on paper. But we're not soldiers. You're always telling us that. And everything depends on the timing, and things we haven't really tested properly."

"Move," I told him.

The plank bowed slightly under his weight. Actually, there was no need for him to go, and the sensible thing would've been to leave him behind, in case something bad happened to me. Come to that, there was no need for me to go. In fact, both of us were likely to be more of a hindrance than a help. But there. I shuffled along the plank and someone helped me aboard the barge, like I was somebody's old aunt. It was dark as a bag. I could hear the barges creaking but all I could see was vague dark shapes.

Stilico was there to see us off. If we bought it, he was in

charge. I couldn't see his face. "Remember," I told him, "red flag means start, green flag means—"

"Good luck," he said. Then I heard the rope splash in the water, and the barge began to move.

"Ah well," Nico said. I sat down. The bottom of a barge isn't comfortable for sitting. "You've got the flags?"

I held them up, but of course it was too dark for him to see them. "Yes, of course," I said. "Now shut your face and settle down."

We'd timed it so that the ebb tide would take us out; no need for oars or flapping sails, anything at all that might be seen by the watchmen I knew the enemy had posted on the promontories either side of the Bay. We'd be out of their sight and earshot by the time we needed to set the sails or start rowing. Nothing to do but keep absolutely quiet for a couple of hours. Sheer torture.

No need whatsoever for me to go on this escapade. Artavasdus, who didn't even like me, had begged me not to go. He said something embarrassing about how I was the heart of the defence; if anything happened to me, everything would fall apart and they might as well unlock the gates and let the bastards just walk in. I knew he was right – at least about the pointlessness of me going along – but you know how it is when you simply can't bring yourself to do the right thing. So we compromised. Instead of leading the attack proper – where I'd be sure to get in the way, almost certainly get myself killed and everyone else with me – I was going to be the signalman, perched on the top of the old watchtower on Beacon Hill. Since there was a better than even chance there'd be enemy sentries up there, Nico was coming with me as half of my bodyguard, the other half being Lysimachus of the Greens, currently ranked Number One in the summer League, therefore by definition the most dangerous man in the world. With Lysimachus along, Nico was obviously superfluous, but I made him come with me anyway. To protect me from Lysimachus, I rather suspect. That man can't help looking villainous, it's his job, but I really didn't want to be alone with him if I could help it.

The captain of our shit barge had never been out in the Bay at night, needless to say. Nobody in the City had, or at least nobody admitted to it, for fear of being appointed Lord High Admiral and forced to take part in this damnfool caper. Since none of the barges had lights, we had no way of knowing where the other six were, and all seven of us had only a vague idea of where presumably deserted Bel Semplan was, and that was where we were headed. The idea was, we'd drift out until the tide stopped drawing us, then bear sort of right until first light, at which point we'd know where we were. Bloody stupid idea. Guess whose.

I'd talked airily of getting some sleep on the barges, but I was deluding myself. There we all were, twenty men and ten horses to a barge, all wide awake, scared stiff, bobbing about in the pitch black. Faustinus had suggested, very sensibly, that we leave in the middle of the night, or better still three hours before dawn; we'd be there in plenty of time and no pointless hanging about on the dark sea. I'd overruled him, blathering about catching the ebb tide – a slight advantage, to be fair, but hardly a game-changer, we had oars, for God's sake, and it wasn't far. No, I'd known that if I'd had to wait around in the City until third watch, my nerve would've gone and I'd have called the whole thing off. Hardly a good reason, but realistic.

"Artavasdus was right," Nico said. We were well away from shore by now, so I had no excuse for shutting him up. I really didn't want to talk, though. "He often is," I said.

"About you being the heart of the defence."

"Oh, that. No, that's bullshit."

"No it isn't. Just think what you've achieved. When we got here, we were an hour or so away from the savages storming the gates. You—"

"Bullshit," I repeated, slightly louder than I should've. "They haven't attacked the City because they're not ready. That's all there is to it."

"You keep saying that. I'm not sure I believe it."

"Suit yourself."

Poor sod, he was trying to be nice; and he's one of those people who thinks that if you've got something on your mind, you ought to put it into words. All that expensive education, probably. Me, I talk about the job in hand, problems to be dealt with, possible solutions; technical issues, properties of materials, the defects and qualities of things. Of course I do, I'm an engineer.

What I can do, though, is put together a schedule, a sequence of events. Thus: first light, and we could just make out a dark blue blur on the skyline. We altered course and headed for the coast; just shy of where the captain guessed the shoals were, they lowered a horrible little boat and Nico, Lysimachus and I got into it. I had my arms full of flags; they rowed. By the time we hit the beach, we could see the Beacon quite clearly. I hadn't appreciated just how steep that bloody hill is. Halfway up it, Lysimachus the bruiser gave us professional soldiers a look of utter contempt and suggested that we wait there and rest while he went ahead; if there were sentries up there, he pointed out, they'd hear us gasping and panting a quarter of a mile off.

He was gone for a long time and I was getting worried. Timing was crucially important. Either he'd been killed by the sentries, in which case the whole thing was off but we had no way of telling the main party, or by the time he got back from the top and then we'd dragged ourselves up there, we'd be ages behind the clock and everything would unravel into a tangle. But back he came, eventually, with a gash on his right shoulder and blood on his hands that I assume wasn't his. "All done," he said. That man scares me.

No dead bodies when we got up there, so he must've got rid of them somehow. The sun was now well and truly up – in fact, we were exactly on time, entirely by luck rather than judgement. I scrambled up the semi-derelict stone steps to the top of the tower, then rested my arms on the parapet and caught my breath.

Amazing view from up there. I could see the North Gate guardhouse, where Stilico would be waiting. I could see the scaffolding all round the enemy siege tower, which must be nearly finished. I could see the back lines of their camp, which we'd had to guess at when we were planning this nonsense. By the look of it, we'd slightly overestimated the extent of their rear defences. There were three rows of tents, housing the rear-guard; I'd anticipated four. No big deal, either way. They simply weren't expecting an attack from that direction, knowing full well there was nobody out there to attack them. And I could see the little round ash spinney that marked the furthest extent of the Citomer forest, another of His Majesty's deer parks, which stretches up from the sea to within a half mile of the North Gate. What I didn't know was whether a man sitting in the topmost branches of one of those tall ash trees would be able to see me. If he couldn't, we were all screwed. I'd gambled on that, and there was no way of testing it beforehand. Stupid, stupid idea.

Still, here we were, and it was time. I went to raise the flag—

"Not the green one," Nico hissed at me. "The red."

Just as well he'd come along, wasn't it? I raised the red flag and gave it a waggle. Then I waited, to see if my big idea was actually going to work.

All started many years ago, when I was a sergeant. We'd just finished a job and the boys were relaxing, taking their boots off, pulling corks. Come and play Bollocks, someone said. What's Bollocks, I asked.

Answer: the typically elegant and tasteful name the Imperial army gives to the universal game of throwing a stone and then seeing who can roll a wooden ball closest to it. Everyone everywhere in the world plays this game or a variant thereof. Turned out I was quite good at it; good enough to be popular with the men, not good enough to win and show myself up for a smartarse. But it set me thinking, all those years ago; and this is what I thought.

You start with a stone, any old stone. You pitch it up high in the air; it comes down thump, lands, stays put. Then you take your smooth, perfectly round wooden ball and you gently pitch it, on a low trajectory. It lands, bounces once or twice, then rolls implacably toward the mark. All in fun, of course, and it's a good game, especially when you've been drinking.

Now think about artillery. Your Pattern 68 hurls a two hundredweight slab of rough-hewn asymmetrical rock up in the air at an angle of forty-five degrees, which science and experience have concluded is the optimum angle for distance. It goes up, it peaks, stalls and goes down, it hits the deck and half buries itself. Extreme range, from a perfectly tuned catapult with new horsehair ropes, all the joints tight to reduce vibration, etcetera: two hundred yards. Which was why the enemy had drawn up their triple line two hundred and seventy-five yards from the wall.

Let the catapult shot be the mark; now think of the game. The round wooden ball cruises easily up to it, often as not goes past it. Now picture me, walking up Hill Street one evening, pausing to admire the perfect stone balls, about twice the size of my head, stuck up by some rich man to decorate his gateposts.

It's the way my mind works, and I'm not proud of it. I went down to a masons' yard I know, made out I wanted to buy a pair of stone balls, like the ones I'd seen. No problem. Out of interest, I say, how do you make them so perfectly round? Is that some poor sod chipping away with a chisel? I get a smile for my naivety. We've got a machine for that; and he shows me, a stone lathe, bloody great big thing powered by six donkeys turning a mill, though the bigger yards downtown use water power. Turns out a perfect seventy-pound stone ball every hour, each one identical; yours for the ridiculously cheap sum of—

Told him I'd think about it; that was no lie. Thought about it a lot. But, having thought it over for about fifteen years, came to the conclusion that I wasn't put on this earth to make trouble for people. I build bridges. True, from time to time people cross those bridges on their way to slaughter the enemies of the empire, or to take food and supplies to the slaughterers, or carry messages backwards and forwards to and from them – you spin it out, like flax, and after a while it gets thin and vague, and you're not really doing anyone any harm, you're just making it easier to get from one side of a river to another, nothing bad about that. So, I thought about it, decided I'd think some more, got on with something else. Until now.

Until I waved the red flag.

For a count of maybe three, nothing happened, and I thought, that halfwit Stilico, he's screwed everything up. Then something caught my eye, something a long way away, a curved line in the air more than an object, a flat arc. I didn't hear the distant slam of the catapult arm against the frame until some time later, because for some reason sound is much slower than seeing.

The soldiers drawn up in triple line, two hundred and seventy-five yards down the gentle slope, saw it, too. They laughed when the shot pitched woefully short. They laughed when it bounced the first time, and the second. The third time they didn't laugh at all, as a hundred and fifteen seventy-pound balls bounced a third time and smashed into them at head height, snapping necks, pulping bones in the first, second, third ranks; bounced a fourth time in the open space between the back rank and the tents; then carried on rolling along the ground, actually picking up pace thanks to the damned slope; seventy pounds rolling just faster than a man can run is a lot of momentum, takes a hell of a lot of stopping. Bone can't stop it, neither can tent poles, wagons, tethered horses, flesh, blood. Nothing can stop it until the ground levels off and starts to slope upward, and by then—

By then, of course, Stilico's men had loosed another volley.

I heard Nico swearing fluently beside me. Lysimachus was staring as though he'd just seen the Ascension, the most wonderful thing he could possibly imagine in his most profound yearnings, bloodthirsty savage. Me, I felt – You couldn't possibly understand. But I'm an engineer, I work with massive weights in motion and suspension. When I was a captain they made me safety officer, it was my job, my responsibility, to make sure that those massive weights didn't get loose to smash bone and crush flesh. And most of the time they didn't, but sometimes they did – my fault, I freely confess, my bloody stupid fault. I've seen men squashed like fruit until their guts burst, I've seen sharp ends of bone sticking out through pulped skin and muscle, I've seen men decapitated by flying ropes, legs and arms ripped off by runaway rollers and timbers, men with their spines crunched up like the veins of a dry leaf and still just about alive – I was safety officer, my responsibility, you can't blame the wood or the stone or the rope. There was nothing you could've done, they told me, and even when I believed them it didn't make any difference. It's not something you let happen. It's definitely not something you do deliberately—

"The flag," Nico was yelling. "The green flag, for crying out loud."

I'd forgotten all about it. He snatched it from my hand and waggled it about above his head. Stupid green flag. All I could think about was what I'd done. More stone balls in the air; the whole plain in front of me was moving, men running like lunatics, a lot of men, a *lot* of men not moving at all. And I couldn't remember the flag for ceasefire (because there wasn't one, of course; we *wanted* this to happen) so I couldn't make the ghastly accident stop, only it wasn't an accident. And Nico was waving a flag, which made no sense until I remembered. Phase Two.

Out of the little round ash spinney the chariots came racing. Aboard each chariot, designed with infinite skill and care for one man, were two men, one driving. The other had charge of fifteen road pins, a pottery jar of lamp oil with a bit of cloth stuffed in the mouth instead of a stopper, and a storm lantern.

Road pins – bit of iron rod about four feet long, half-inch diameter, with a point on one end and a wiggle like a shepherd's crook on the other. Bet you you've seen them, just never knew what they were called. We mostly use them for surveying, but they come in handy for all manner of things; including the traditional Engineers' game of Throwing the Road Pin; closest to the mark wins a beer. You can't chuck them much more than fifteen yards because they're so heavy, but you can get quite accurate with them, and they'll go through sixteen-gauge steel plate. Or armour.

I knew there'd be trouble, because the chariots were so light and flimsy. I saw three turn over before they got anywhere near the line of tents. But the rest made it, and just as they got there, men started spilling out from under the tent flaps, and got road pins in them just for being in the way. Past the tents – another two chariots went out of control and crashed – and they were where I'd wanted them to be, right up close to the siege tower, magnificent under its covering of hides. I saw little flares of yellow light, the pots of oil with lit wicks sailing through the air to shatter against the frame of the tower. The surviving chariots turned and went back the way they'd come. For a while I was sure the flames on the siege tower had gone out or hadn't caught; then a fat orange bloom, then thick black smoke. Was that it? Had we won?

"Come on," Nico said. "Time we weren't here."

I let him lead me down the hill. I felt stupid, like the time a beam got loose on a rope, swung round and hit me right between the eyes. Had it worked or hadn't it? I didn't know. No idea what victory's supposed to look like.

Halfway down, Nico said to me, "You do realise what you've done, don't you?"

Last thing I needed to hear. "Enlighten me."

"You've only revolutionised battlefield infantry tactics for a generation," that idiot said. "From now on, field artillery's going to rule the battlefield. Close-order heavy infantry and phalanx formation have just been made obsolete at a stroke. Sheer genius. It's probably the greatest single leap forward in tactical—"

"Nico," I said. "Shut the fuck up."

15

Had it worked or hadn't it? I remember talking to a man once, a captain in the regular cavalry, who was in some battle. He'd been given his orders – ride over to that hill there, cut out their light cavalry, turn round, come back here. So he did that, and (according to him) did it supremely well. The enemy didn't see him coming until it was far too late, so he was able to roll them up like a carpet and slaughter pretty nigh the lot of them, with none of his boys killed, two or three with minor scratches. So, done that, collected up his men and trotted back over the hill, which of course had masked his view of the rest of the battle. Whereupon he found his general dead, the infantry massacred, the light cavalry running like deer across the skyline, the enemy in possession of the field. He did the only thing he could: crept back over the brow of the hill and got the hell out of there.

The general feeling in the City seemed to be that, yes, we'd won. At least, we'd killed a lot of the enemy, forced them to pull back a quarter of a mile, burned their siege tower and made them look very, very stupid. People were out on the streets like they hadn't been since it all started, cheering, shouting, as though it was League Final day in the Hippodrome. The sight of them made me feel angry, and if Nico hadn't bustled me inside the Palace I'd probably have started yelling at them.

Artavasdus and Longinus of the Greens came busting in to congratulate me; brilliant, magnificent, we really showed them, didn't we? Showed them what, I didn't ask. I told them to go away and get on with some work – Longinus laughed, Artavasdus was offended and stomped out in a huff. Then Faustinus came in and told me he'd always known I had what it takes, and surely now they'd realise they stood no chance, and go away.

I cleared everyone else out of the room. "We're in deep trouble," I said.

Not what he'd been expecting to hear. "What? What trouble?"

"The bloody Seal," I said. "That clown of a forger can't copy it. We need the real thing. I've got a stack of requisitions and warrants a foot thick, and no seal. Any minute now, people are going to realise there's a problem, and then we're screwed. No money. No authority. Probably they'll hang us."

He looked as though I'd just hit him. "That's terrible," he said, usefully.

"Isn't it? Listen, we need to find the real thing. Someone in this town knows where it is."

He looked at me. "If I'd stolen the Great Seal," he said, "I'd get rid of it, damn quick. I'd throw it down a well or a garderobe, before I got caught with it. Everyone knows it can't be sold. It'll be long gone by now, I'm sure of it."

"It can't be," I said. "We need it."

He had that dazed look, as though he couldn't believe this was happening to him. "Well, you'd better get your Green and Blue friends to find it," he said. "They control all the thieves in this city."

"Don't be so stupid." I hadn't meant to shout. "I can't let them know that all the paper I've been paying them with is worthless, or that all the promises I've made them are just bullshit. That'd be the end. We won't need the enemy to trash the City, the Themes'll do it for us."

He was silent for a while, letting me get a grip. "You'll have to tell them," he said. "Otherwise, it can't be found. Only they can find it."

I drew in the breath to tell him he was crazy, out of his mind, but I knew he was right. "Get Arrasc and Longinus," I said. "Right now."

Credit where it's due, they took it quite well. There was a deadly silence. Longinus was looking murder at me; God knows how anyone ever had the guts to face him in the arena. Then Arrasc sort of shook himself, like a wet dog.

"Right," he said. "What are we going to do about it?"

Longinus gave him a horrified look. I ignored him. "Find the Seal," I said.

But Arrasc shook his head. "Don't hold your breath," he said. "It'll be in the Bay by now."

Didn't want to hear that, so I looked at Longinus instead. I could see him forcing himself to think about something other than ripping my head off. "Who have we got to fool?" he asked, quite quietly.

Arrasc didn't understand; I did, after a couple of heartbeats. "Everyone who has to authorise payments on government scrip," I said.

"Meaning?"

The man was a genius. Actually, there weren't that many of them. "Paymaster's office," I said. "Treasury department.

Works and Ways and Means." I paused, hardly able to believe my luck. "That's about it."

Longinus nodded. "Most of the clerks will be Greens," he said. "Get rid of the ones who aren't and replace them. Then let me handle it."

Time for Arrasc to look daggers, but I couldn't be bothered with him right then. "You can square them."

He nodded. "No problem. I'll tell them it's our scam, they'll believe that."

Now that woke me up, like a smack round the face. Call me an innocent; it hadn't occurred to me that, at a time like this, the Themes would even contemplate ripping off the desperately cash-strapped government. The way Longinus said it, I got the impression that it wasn't just a matter of contemplation. Still, I told myself, it's all pretend money anyway. Either we were all going to die, in which case it didn't matter, or else we'd survive, and some other poor fool would be left to deal with the apocalyptic mess I'd made of the Imperial finances, in which a little mild peculation by the Greens would be neither here nor there. The labourer is worthy of his hire, after all.

I looked away from him and turned to Arrasc. "You have to be all right with this," I told him.

I could feel the weight on his shoulders. Nothing in it for him, apart from the survival of the City. He took a long time to find his words. Then he said, "We've got a forger, a good one."

"I've tried that. Can't be done."

Arrasc shook his head. "Our forger is very good."

"You can't copy the Seal."

It's nice when you give people opportunities to enjoy themselves. I'd done just that. "We already have," he said.

The things you learn. "You're kidding me."

He grinned at me, not a kind smile. Then he told me what to look up, in which archive. Copies that had already passed muster and been accepted. "We don't use it very often," he said. "It's sort of a last resort."

Longinus was half out of his chair by now; one of the documents Arrasc had just referred to was a death warrant, that of a leading Green. Then he sat down again.

"We'll do both," I said. "I'll replace all the honest clerks with Greens, and I'll pay you a million stamena for your Seal. Agreed?"

That stunned both of them. Then Arrasc said, "You'll pay us a million stamena for a fake seal we could have used to write warrants for ten million."

"Yes."

"And you'll seal it with the fake."

My turn to smile. "It won't be the fake by then," I said. "It'll be the real thing."

"Oh look," she said. "The conquering hero."

My belief is, either you understand things or you understand people. Nobody can do both. Frankly, I'm happier with things. I understand stuff like tensile strength, shearing force, ductility, work hardening, stress, fatigue. I know the same sort of things happen with people, but the rules are subtly different. And nobody's ever paid for my time to get to know about people.

"Get me a pot of tea, would you?" I said. "I'm gasping."

Aichma gave me a look that would've stripped rust. "Coming right up," she said.

I'd seriously considered going somewhere else – the Blue Posts, or the Victory; but all the good bars are Blue or Green, and if I went to a Blue bar I'd have the Greens imagining treachery, and vice versa. The Dogs was the only neutral ground in Lower Town. Also, nowhere else did tea. As it was, as soon as I walked through the door the whole place went quiet. I didn't like that at all. I'm used to walking into the Dogs and everyone there knows who I am. This was different. You remember the old parable about the holy prophet who got thrown into the lions' den. I felt like a lone lion in a den of prophets.

She slammed the pot down in front of me. "Fifteen trachy," she said.

"You what?"

"Fifteen trachy."

Never ever, in my entire life, have I paid for a drink in the Two Dogs. I stared at her, shocked half to death, then dug around in my pocket and found a single tornece. A good one, too, government-made. "Keep the change," I said.

She breathed out through her nose. "Thank you," she said, and walked away.

The hell with this, I thought. But I'd arranged to meet some Theme bosses, two Blue and two Green; it had to be either the Dogs or the Palace, and they were nervous about going Uptown, so I had no choice but to sit there until they showed up.

Hapax, the Green, turned up early. I knew him from way back, and he'd known Aichma's father. He gave me a funny look as he sat down.

"What's got into her?" I asked.

I knew he wasn't going to tell me, though he knew what it was. "Women," he said.

Fine, I thought. I wasn't going to embarrass myself by pressing the issue. "You'd better buy your own drink," I said. That made him grin.

Then the others showed up, and we conducted our business

in a reasonably civilised manner, made a deal and went away. I was headed down to the sawmills. I was nearly there when someone I didn't know ran up to me, waving his arms. He was out of breath and looked terrified.

"You'd better come quick," he said.

"Slow down," I said. "Who are you and what do you want?"

"There's been a stabbing," he said. "At the Two Dogs."

I went cold all over. I just knew. The message itself was like – well, suppose someone stopped you, all wild-eyed and breathless, and told you the sun had risen that morning. There's always a stabbing at the Two Dogs. To make it newsworthy, therefore –

"Is she——?"

"I don't know, do I?"

Sometimes I wonder why they made me an officer. Other times – like this – I knew they made the right decision. It's all to do with how your brain works.

I grabbed his left hand and stuck a gold five-stamena in it. "You know Cartgate?"

"Yes."

"Sixteen, Cartgate," I said. "Doctor Falx. If he's not there, they'll know where he is. There's another one of them when you've got him to the Dogs. Run."

He stared at the coin in his hand, then at me. Then he ran. I've seen men running for their lives, but he was faster. Incentive is everything.

He'd gone, and I needed support staff. I ran down Temple Court. There were two sentries, Parks and Gardens men, outside the Admiralty building. "You two," I panted at them. "Know who I am?"

"Sir."

"You," I told the one on the left. "Get me a horse and cart, or a chair. Anything that moves, the first one you see. Bring it back here. You have absolute authority, understand?"

The look on his face. But he jumped to it; he had no choice, because of the look on mine, and that's why they made me an officer. "You," I told the other one, "I want ten sheets of parchment, pens, ink and the Admiralty seal. Move."

Temple Court's a good place for hijacking vehicles. Even with all the restrictions I'd imposed, there's always some senator or permanent secretary paying a call. The sentry came back a minute or so later with a chair and four porters. I recognised the livery painted on the door; under any other circumstances, I've have pissed myself at the thought of the enemy I'd just made. I fished in my pocket and found four half-stamena, one in each of their big, damp hands. They looked at them; like the Ascension. You believe it exists, at some level you hope one day you might get to see it in the distance, as one of a crowd of blessed pilgrims; you never imagine it might actually happen to you.

Then the other sentry came out. There was a clerk behind him, dragging on his sleeve, being towed along like a small, inefficient plough. "Stop him," the clerk was yelling. "He's stealing the Seal."

Of course the clerk hadn't been on the wall, didn't know who I was, so I hit him. He went down hard, which I regretted, but there just wasn't time. I grabbed the Seal, the bits of paper and the pens and hauled myself into the chair. "Know the Two Dogs?"

"Sure," said one of the chairmen.

"Quick as you like," I said, and they were off. I only just had time to beckon the two sentries to follow me before we were out of sight round the corner into Salt Street.

*

My enemies have always done best for me, but complete strangers come a fairly close second. The chairmen ran their hearts out, and all for a few bits of metal. That's magic. Reminds me of a story. A man sets up a stall in the market. For five dollars, he says, I'll sell you a magic token which will make anyone give you anything you want. Fine, says a passing merchant, here's five dollars, prove it. So the showman leads him to a baker's. He pulls out a penny. Give me, he says to the baker, a loaf of bread. Indeed. That's real magic.

Bloody doctor hadn't got there yet; if he'd been there, I'd have smashed his face in for not being there yet – which is how your mind works when you're in that sort of a state. I jumped out of the chair – the sentries hove in sight behind me, panting like tired dogs – and grabbed the first man I saw. "Where is she?" I yelled at him, like it was all his fault.

He gave me a terrified look and pointed. I spared his life, ran inside.

They'd got her lying on a table. Blood everywhere. She was wearing the smock I'd seen her in an hour before, except that there was a gleaming red patch the size of a ham. There were men and women standing round her, not doing anything, gawping. Get out, I told them. I looked round for water and a cloth, couldn't see anything like that. I had no idea what to do.

Enter Doctor Falx. Ex-service, retired before they threw him out, some nonsense about embezzling from regimental funds. Since then, he's been the patcher-up in residence at the Hippodrome, except when he's in the Watch House for practising medicine while disqualified, and nobody on God's earth knows more about puncture wounds. He doesn't like me one bit, possibly because it was the Engineers' funds he was caught thieving from, and it was me who did the catching. He looked at the thing on the table, then at me.

"Friend of yours?" he said.

"Doesn't matter."

"I assume that means she is."

I think that if he could have let her die, he would have. But he didn't, of course, any more than a savage dog can help biting if you tease him. I watched his face as he worked. I'd seen him in action before, notably when he pulled a splinter of wood ten inches long out of the side of my neck. He looked worried. That wasn't good.

"Why have you stopped?" I yelled at him. He didn't answer. He stood there, his hands red to the wrists, doing nothing. "Look, if it's money, you can have what you want. Or your licence back. Both. Just for God's sake—"

He looked at me. "I've finished," he said.

Oh. "Will she—?"

He shrugged. "It's a deep cut from a long, thin knife. She's lost a lot of blood. It could go either way from here." He plunged his hands into a basin of water, which turned pink. "Absolutely no way of knowing."

"What else can we do?"

"Nothing."

I turned away, sat down, wrote him a draft on the Admiralty for fifty thousand stamena and sealed it with the Admiralty seal and beeswax from a candle. I handed it to him. He glanced at it, dropped it on the floor. I can never understand people who bear grudges.

"Thank you," I said.

He wiped his hands on the only clean towel in the place. "Drop dead," he said. "After I've gone," he added, and walked out.

16

I wanted to stay but I couldn't. Some fool came looking for me. The enemy had brought up trebuchets.

Trebuchets, for crying out loud. We knew about them, because about forty years ago someone smuggled a copy of a book out of Echmen. There's a description, which makes no sense (problems with translation, I assume), and a highly improbable picture; and ever since we've been trying to build one, only it can't be done.

The idea's quite simple. You have a lever, balanced round a fulcrum, mounted on a massive frame. The lever has a short end and a long end. On the short end, you hang a heavy weight – crate full of rocks does just as well as anything. At the end of the long end you fix a sling. Pull on the long end with a rope to raise the counterweight, then let it go; the short end drops, the long end whips up and the sling hurls a stone a very long way. In theory.

Can't be done, was the conclusion reached by the standing committee. The stress on the long, thin end of the arm is too great; it snaps like a carrot as soon as it reaches peak load. Also, you can't get the sling to release; and the stone gets trapped in the net, whirls round, breaks the arm and falls on the heads of the crew. Also, the cradle shifts so much it tips over, assuming the arm doesn't break around the axis pin under the weight of the raised counterweight. Therefore, the whole thing had to be wishful thinking by some armchair theoretician, and the reports of trebuchets actually being used in sieges in the far eastern provinces of Echmen were just misinformation and fake news. There's no such thing as trebuchets; likewise dragons, elves and magic swords.

I plodded up onto the wall. It was starting to get dark. I said, "Some fool's been spreading stupid rumours about—" One of my officers, his name slips my mind, put a hand on my shoulder and pointed.

Oh, I thought.

Five hundred yards is too far to see details, but plenty close enough for shapes. I'd seen the pictures – copies of them, anyway. At rest, the throwing arm leans slightly back, like a tall, spindly tree blown by a wind coming straight from behind you. The cradles were massive; probably oaks from one of His Majesty's insufferable deer parks, where the shipwrights aren't allowed to fell and trees grow huge. They'd built them on a small hillock, safe from our bouncing, trundling artillery balls. I counted seven.

No guarantee they actually work, I told myself. They could only just have finished building them, prefabricating the parts offsite and only carting them up here for assembly, so chances were they hadn't tested them. Untried, unproven, untroubleshot; just like our artillery, which snapped men in half and smeared them like squashed beetles. And meanwhile, Aichma was lying on a table at the Two Dogs, possibly dying, and I wasn't there with her.

I heard Menas' voice in my left ear. "Now what?" he said.

I tried to think. While I was trying, I said, "Get our artillery down off the wall, right now. If those things work and they open up on us, we can't afford to lose a single one. And get masons up here. I want a reinforced redoubt round every catapult emplacement. Then get the catapults back up."

Oh, is that all? "Right," he said. "How thick?"

"What?"

"How many courses of brick should be emplacements be?"

My head was starting to hurt. "I don't know, do I? Enough to withstand a direct hit from one of *them*. If they work."

Just then, I heard a noise; a creak, and a whistle. It didn't sound sinister, but it made me look up. Nothing to see; then, with a shock that made the stonework I was standing on quiver, something hit the wall. Menas stumbled, grabbed hold of me, nearly pulled me over. I hauled him up. Another impact. No idea where, whether it was close or far away; we were both on our knees. What the hell's going on, I asked myself. Then something different. Not the same bone-jarring thump, but the air was full of flying stone. A chunk missed me by an inch. Menas was a foot away from me, no more than that, and the left side of his head was gone. I had a glimpse of bone, and brains, and the right side of his face wearing a puzzled expression; then the rampart three feet to my left disintegrated. Something brushed my face, like a bird's wing or a cow's tongue licking me, the same rough feel, only very quick. I put my hand up and saw blood on it. Dust, I realised; grit, moving incredibly fast, had scoured the skin off my cheek.

"Get down!" someone was yelling. I didn't move. My brain was still trying to catch up, because nothing seemed to be making sense. Then someone, no idea who, charged up behind me and dragged me down. He was on top of me when the next stone hit, and I felt his blood soaking into my clothes and trickling in fat streams, like melted ice only very warm, over my face and down my neck. I realised why I couldn't move. You say scared stiff, not really thinking about what it means or whether it means anything. Believe me, that's exactly what it's like. You go stiff, like you're frozen, like your arms and legs are splinted, like you've been dipped in something melted that's cooled off and set rock hard. The way a dead body stiffens, and if you try and straighten it you're more likely to break the bone than overcome the locked joints and sinews. Like that. And my eyes were full of dust, and I couldn't move my hands to rub them clear, and my mouth was full of blood, and I'd shat myself for the first time since I was a little boy. And then the next impact, and the next, and the one after that.

(And in the back of my mind, sounding quite calm and faintly reproachful: was this what it was like for the men who happened to be in the way of your damned ever-so-clever bouncing stone balls? Did they freeze so they couldn't run? Which is worse, objectively speaking: half your face sliced off by a flying splinter, or all your bones and guts crushed until you burst like a sausage skin?)

Some fool, some brainless idiot with absolutely no imagination whatsoever, was standing over me, dragging me by one foot. Any second now, there'd be another impact and the flying gravel would shred him into bloody tatters, my fault, because it was me he was trying to save. If my leg had been working I'd have kicked him in the face. Then the halfwit slipped, my head banged against something, I felt the most intense pain of my whole life and the light closed in around me like the mouth of a sack.

*

I opened my eyes. They felt gritty and sore; I rubbed them, but it didn't help. I could see a face looking down at me, a great golden face, oval, with big sad eyes and a small, faint mouth. I recognised it as the Mother of Sorrows. I was in the Palace chapel, where they have those old mosaics that people bang on about all the time.

Then two other faces, closer, leaned in on me. One was that idiot Faustinus, and the other was Sawdust, the carpenter. And a voice I didn't recognise was saying, "He'll be fine now" in a tone suggesting he was in a hurry to be somewhere else, doing something important.

"Thank you," Faustinus said. Then he gazed earnestly at me. "How are you feeling?" he said.

Then I remembered. It was like looking down and realising you're just about to step over a cliff. "How is she?" I whispered – voice none too good. "Is she still alive?"

Faustinus frowned, didn't know what I was on about. "I'll go and find out," Sawdust said, and then she wasn't there any more.

"You've had a nasty bump on the head," Faustinus said, like I was eight years old, except people didn't talk to me like that when I was eight. "You're going to be fine, but you've got to stay still and quiet for a bit. It's all right," he added quickly, as I tried to get my mouth working properly, "the bombardment's been stopped and we're seeing to the damage right now. Everything's fine."

Oh, that. I couldn't talk, but I could raise my left hand. I grabbed his ear between the nails of my thumb and forefinger and dragged his head down so he could hear me. "Is she still alive?"

He forced my fingers apart. Dear God, he was stronger than me; obviously I was in a hell of a state. "I'm sorry," he said, "you're not making any sense. That's perfectly natural when you've had a bit of a bump. You'll be fine soon, I promise."

Sawdust had understood and gone to find out. That was the best I could hope for. I sighed, let my arm fall and closed my eyes. "Go away," I said, and pretended to go to sleep.

(And then I guess I was asleep, because I distinctly remember being left alone with the Holy Mother, who gave me a reproachful look out of that vast, golden, unchanging face. I was a great disappointment to her, she said; she'd always hoped I'd make something of myself, but here I was, been fighting again, and look what that had led to. I tried to explain, but my words came out in Alauzet, which obviously she couldn't understand. So then she took a hammer and drove a nail into my head, and—)

I woke up, with a pounding headache. There was a great crowd of faces round me, most of whom I didn't know. But I recognised Faustinus, and Lieutenant Genseric, and Longinus of the Greens. I blinked at them. It felt like someone had made a lot of money selling tickets to watch me sleep.

Someone yelled, "Doctor, he's awake", and the crowd parted, and that miserable old fart Falx loomed over me, stuck out his hand and peeled my eyelid back. I hate that. I lifted my arm and knocked his hand away.

"He'll do," Falx said.

I grabbed his wrist. "What are you doing here?" I shouted at him. "Why aren't you at the Two Dogs?"

He grinned. "She made it," he said. "More or less. Nearly lost both of you. And what a real shame that would've been."

Then he twisted his wrist and my fingers were broken free, and he stepped neatly back out of range before I could get at him again. "Who gets the bill?" he said.

Faustinus opened his mouth but Longinus was quicker. That surprised me a lot. Falx withdrew. I turned to Longinus. "Aichma," I said.

"She's fine," he said. "Don't worry about her."

"I want him back there now," I said, and then I felt dizzy. It was as though someone had got hold of my feet and was pulling, almost as though I was back on the wall again. Then someone said, "Orhan" loud and clear, and I sort of broke free. "What?" I said.

"You nearly died," Faustinus said. "You've been asleep for five days."

My head twanged like a cable. I winced, couldn't help it. "For crying out loud," I said, "don't shout. What do you mean, five days?"

"I mean you've been lying here nearly dead for five days," Faustinus said. "And things are a real mess, believe me. It's been one nightmare after another."

Then I remembered. "The wall," I shouted. "The trebuchets. What's happening? Have they broken in?"

"He needs to rest now," said a voice behind me somewhere. "Please leave, all of you. Come back in four hours."

"Don't you dare," I yelled. "Tell me what's happening, I've got to know."

"Everything's fine," said Faustinus, who'd just told me it was a real mess and a nightmare. "Soon as you're better, I'll tell you all about it. Don't worry. Everything's under control."

"Did they break in? Where's Nico?"

"Get some rest," Faustinus said, retreating out of my field of vision. "Try and get some sleep. The sooner you're back on your feet, the better, believe me. Everything's just fine."

*

So I got some rest, about half an hour's worth, as long as it took for everyone to go away. Then I got up, snooped around for some clothes, found an old workman's tunic hanging up on a hook in a corridor and a pair of cracked old boots with half of one sole missing in a heap of trash in a small yard. My head felt like it was full of nails. Time to go and rule the empire.

Where to start? What I wanted to do was get straight down to the Dogs. But Longinus had said she was fine, whereas Faustinus had said everything was a mess, one nightmare after another. So I set course for the wall, wondering how far I'd get before an arrow or a lump of rock stopped me.

The streets were quiet but not empty. I saw a man I recognised, had to think for a moment who he was, remembered he was one of my lance corporals. He was bustling along with a big canvas toolbag over his shoulder. I had to break into a trot to catch up with him, which half killed me.

"Colonel." He gave me a scared look. "They said you were—"

"What's been happening?"

He blinked, then set down his toolbag and stood to sort-of-attention, which is about as close as we get in the Engineers. "We stopped 'em, sir," he said. "Sorted 'em out pretty good."

He seemed to think that constituted a report. The hell with it. I suddenly felt shattered and we were about a hundred yards from the King of Beasts, from which I'd been banned about ten years ago for antisocial behaviour. "I know," I said. "I'll buy you a drink. No, I haven't got any money. You buy me a drink, and you can tell me all about it."

He gave me a startled look, as if I'd just kissed him on the mouth. "Very good, sir," he said, and led the way.

I always miss all the fun, and the last five days had been no exception. Apparently, according to Lance Corporal Scevola and his fellow historians in D Company, it was the bruiser Lysimachus – you remember, the Green champion, my bodyguard when we burned the siege tower – who saved my life on the wall, dragging me out of the line of fire, when the tower we were on was pounded into gravel, and Menas was killed. He hauled me to the top of the stair, which was great; then he tripped, and I went down the staircase on my back, head-first, which wasn't so good, though I'd lived to hear the tale, so no real harm done.

I think I may have mentioned that this Lysimachus scared the life out of me, and I never felt comfortable in his company. Fine. But when he saw me lying in the rubble at the foot of the tower, dead (as he thought) – I'm not sure how to account for it, really. True, he was an arena champion who carved people up for a living; a pretty straightforward sort of man, in other words, with one instinctive response to all contingencies; and he was my bodyguard and (he thought) he'd failed and I'd been killed on his watch, and arena men actually do believe in honour and shame, up to a point. Anyhow, for whatever reason, when he thought I was dead he went a bit berserk. He sprinted down to the Hippodrome, liberated one of the chariots that had made it back from our jaunt outside the walls, grabbed a half-dozen lanterns and told the North Gate guards to open the gates. They were Greens, so an order from the Green champion was like a command from God. While they were at it, Sawdust the carpenter, who'd been on the wall prepping the catapults – (You will recall that I'd ordered Menas to pull the catapults off the wall, just a moment or so before his head was cut in half. Talk about your silver linings. My spectacularly stupid order never got carried out, which saved the City. All thanks to the enemy; as usual.)

17

Sawdust came running down the stairs, saying what the hell do you think you're doing, and the guards told her, Lysimachus told us to open the gates. So there's Sawdust, standing directly in front of Lysimachus and four foaming-mouthed Hippodrome horses, demanding to know what he thought he was playing at. I'm going to burn those catapult things, he told her. They killed Orhan, and I'm going to kill them.

I like that girl. She can think. Fine, she said. In that case, take a direct line straight at them, don't go a foot right or left, and I'll see what I can do to help.

Don't suppose Lysimachus had a clue what she was on about, but he had the wit to believe she knew what she was doing. He lashed on the horses and they shot out through the gate like an arrow from a bow. Sawdust, meanwhile, was back up on the wall, where her catapults were all spanned and ready to loose. She made a few quick adjustments to the lie of a few of them, then gave the order. Off went a hundred of those horrible stone balls, bouncing and rolling – but leaving a clear channel for

Lysimachus' lunatic one-man cavalry charge. Needless to say, as soon as the balls were in the air, the enemy dropped whatever they were doing and ran like deer for the high ground; all except the crews on the seven trebuchets, up on that bloody hillock.

Of the seven, two had broken down after the first couple of shots. One had bust its beam as soon as they tripped the sear, just like all the theoreticians said it would. The other one, the sling didn't release and the net wrapped itself round the beam and snapped it off. That left five, all working just fine. My guess is, the trebuchet crews were too busy to notice Lysimachus until he was right up close, and by then it was too late. In his hurry he'd neglected to bring any weapons with him, but in the event that hardly seemed to matter. Besides, the crews would have been engineers, and everybody knows they can't fight worth spit; he tore apart two or three of them with his bare hands and the rest of them hopped it – straight into the path of Sawdust's stone balls, worse luck, but that's war for you. With them out of the way, Lysimachus got busy with the lantern oil, waited just long enough to make sure the trebuchets were burning prettily, and set off back to the City. He walked; the chariot had bust its axle in the home straight, so to speak, and a man like Lysimachus wouldn't run, it'd look bad. He *strolled*, probably with a bit of a swagger, back to the North Gate, with the man-slaying stone balls bouncing on either side of him, pausing only to pick up the snapped-off end of the second busted trebuchet and hoist it on his shoulder, as the only convenient thing he could find for a trophy.

(And, in so doing, did more good to the cause than practically anyone in this story. Tell you about that later.)

Anyhow, I wasn't dead after all, and all seven trebuchets were out of action, and when Nico and my lads came to look at the damage – I'm getting ahead of myself; to the point where the corporal and I had finished our drink, and I asked him, rather nervous about the reply I'd get, what had happened to Nico. Oh, he wasn't there, Corporal Scaevola told me, he was downtown at the sawmills; of course he was, because I'd sent him there with a job to see to, only I'd forgotten.

He was on the wall when I finally managed to drag myself up there. He was horrified to see me. Why wasn't I in bed?

"Shut up," I explained. "What's the position?"

What follows is what Nico got from Artavasdus, who was on the wall when the bombardment started. He was five towers down from where I was, but as soon as the trebuchet stones started to hit, he sprinted up the battlement catwalk, only stopping when a stone took out the walkway a yard in front of his feet. So, being Artavasdus, instead of diving for cover and shitting himself like any normal human being, or me, he stood there, watched carefully and took notes. He quickly figured out that the enemy were trying to pound a breach in the wall big enough to get in through. But the stones that hit the lower wall just bounced off, doing some damage but not much. It was only the ones that hit the rampart that had any significant effect, because the rampart was only supported from below, therefore more liable to fracture and shatter. In real terms, therefore, the trebuchets could smash up the ramparts and battlements, but they couldn't easily breach the wall itself. Once Artavasdus realised this, he quit worrying. Smashing up battlements was all very well, but with only seven machines it'd take a very long time for them to do enough damage to compromise the defence in any meaningful way, and the only position the enemy had where trebuchets would be safe from our catapults and still in range of the wall was that confounded hill. Long story short; if the trebuchets couldn't breach the wall enough to let soldiers get in, the most they'd be able to achieve would be to make life a bit miserable for some of our people, some of the time.

Anyway, that was Artavasdus's story, as told to me by Nico, who didn't seem to think there was anything remarkable about a man standing rock-still and straight as a die with trebuchet stones thundering down all round him, provided there were useful observations to be made and valid conclusions to be drawn. That's Imperials for you, and it's why I can't really find it in my heart to loathe them, even though they rape and plunder the earth, and regard the likes of me as so much garbage. The worms of the earth against the lions; the old rebel rallying cry, all through the Social Wars and the slave revolts and the provincial rebellions. And, yes, the Robur are predators, who kill and maim as of right, and if they give anything in return it's unintentional, just as lions are the carrion eaters' most bountiful benefactors. Still, and even so; if it's a choice between lions and wolves and jackals and foxes, give me lions any day. You can't ever justify what they do, but they've got style.

So, where were we? The panic was over. The trebuchets had been stopped, the wall was still in one piece, I wasn't dead, Faustinus was in charge of the City until I got better. A disaster, in other words, poised hovering, waiting to happen.

And he was trying to do the right thing, bless him. He wanted to see the grateful, admiring look on my face when I came round and the first thing I heard was, the villain who'd knifed my Aichma was in jail awaiting trial and execution. So he had the Watch – can you believe that, the *Watch* – go down to the Two Dogs and find out who did it. Needless to say, when they got there the place was deserted, apart from Aichma and the doctors and nurses the Blues had sent to look after her. So the

Watch started pushing the doctors around – they hadn't arrived on the scene until six hours after the event, had seen and heard nothing, never mind – and when that didn't work, they woke Aichma out of the first proper sleep she'd had since it happened and asked her. Goes without saying, she told them nothing, so they threatened her with jail for obstructing justice, whereupon she told them to go away, in that special way of hers; they left. Then they went to Blue headquarters and started arresting people at random on suspicion. Of course, of *course*, that led to a riot, and it was only the incredible forbearance and public spirit of the Blues and the personal intervention of Arrasc himself that got them out of there alive, though naturally a bit worse for wear.

Faustinus realised he'd probably been going about things the wrong way. How he'd got it wrong he honestly didn't know, but he could read between the lines. So he tried another tack; five thousand stamena reward for the name of the perpetrator. Could've told him he was making trouble for himself. Within an hour he had a list of a hundred names, all with witnesses who swore blind etc., even though they hadn't been there at the time. While he was busy getting rid of these idiots, a Green who had actually been there walked up and gave him the genuine name: Solisper.

Remember, this is Faustinus we're talking about. Immediately he has the roll checked; there's only one Solisper in the City, so he sends twenty Watch to arrest him. What he should have done, what any fool would've done, what any fool's pet rat would've done, was ask Longinus of the Blues (remember, a Green laid the information) if the name Solisper rang a bell. Whereupon Longinus would have told him, yes, that's my father.

It's been a long time since the Victory riots, and maybe people in Upper Town have forgotten just how grumpy the Themes can get when someone does something really stupid to annoy them, such as arresting the father of a Theme boss. Arrasc had managed to rein in the righteous indignation of the Blues, out of patriotic spirit and, I rather suspect, personal regard for me. But it wasn't his old man who was sitting in the Watch House with chains on his wrists. To do him justice, I think Longinus did make at least a show of trying to calm his people down; they weren't having it, and he quickly gave up and let them have their heads. Fair enough. If he'd made a genuine attempt to stop them, he wouldn't have been Green boss for very much longer. Also, quite reasonably, he was mad as mustard. When it's family, the hell with the City and doing your best for the public weal. And quite right, too.

I maybe ought to mention that Solisper was indeed guilty. He was drunk, and he wanted to stab someone who'd insulted him, and Aichma tried to stop him, and he'd stabbed her instead. These things happen. The rights and wrongs of the matter were entirely beside the point. I imagine that, left to himself, as soon as Aichma was up to seeing visitors, Solisper would have crawled in there looking pathetic and sad, apologised profusely, meekly taken his tongue-lashing and lifetime ban from the Dogs and gone away. Then a substantial sum of money would have changed hands, honour would have been satisfied and everyone would have been happy; which is how things go in Poor Town, so long as the law keeps its sticky paws out of other people's business.

So; we have the Greens in arms, ready to loot and burn and smash the Watch House to rubble. It was therefore predictable and inevitable that Arrasc should have led the Blues out in full force to bar the way. That's the very essence of the Themes. If the Greens want to do something – anything – it's the bounden

duty of the Blues to stop them. So there's Arrasc, piously spout-
ing the truce and the accords while his men gear up for a real
good rumble; how, you ask, could Faustinus possibly make this
atrocious situation worse? Good question. But he managed it.
He called up the Corps of Engineers – my lads, who had important work to be getting on with, patching up the damage the
trebuchets had done; my lads, who weren't involved and who
most definitely aren't soldiers – to go and stand between the
Themes and stop them butchering each other.

Goes without saying, no normal Engineer officer would've
stood for it. But who's in charge of the regiment while I'm sleeping peacefully in the Temple infirmary? Nico. Nico the Imperial
gentleman, Nico the Slave of Duty. Of course he told Faustinus
he was being a bloody fool and fifty times more dangerous than
the enemy on the other side of the wall. But Faustinus had given
him a direct order, so he had to obey it.

From time to time I say harsh things about Nico, all of them
true to some extent. But when he hasn't got me breathing down
his neck he's no fool. He has his own way of doing things, and
from time to time I find myself wondering if perhaps he might
be safe out on his own without a nursemaid one of these days.

I want you to imagine you're coming up Fish Street with the
Greens. You're mad as hell because the authorities, with whom
you've been collaborating like mad, against a lifetime of instinct
and experience, because we're all supposed to make nice to save
the City, have arrested Longinus's dad and thrown him in jail.
Now you're coming up to the crossroads with Horsefair; on the
other side of which are the Blues, taking this opportunity to stab
your Theme in the back, well, we'll see about that. And once
we've dealt with them—

Well, there are the Blues. They've come to a dead stop and

they're all bunched together on the north side of the Horsefair junction. So, this is where it's going to happen. Fine. But as you get closer, you get the impression that they aren't lined up to fight. It's like there's something in the way; a sinkhole's opened up in the street, or angels with fiery swords are blocking their way. So you crane your neck for a better view; and there, in the middle of Horsefair, is this man sitting in a chair.

He's in ordinary clothes – well, ordinary Rich Town clothes, not a uniform is the point – and he's clearly unarmed but the chair he's sitting in is an army folding camp chair, and you recognise him as Nicephorus Bautzes, the milkface Engineer's top sidekick. You've seen him often enough, rushing about telling people what to do. You have no opinion about him one way or another. But there he's sitting, in his chair, wine jug on the ground next to him, reading a book.

The Blue front rank opens and a man comes forward. You know him, of course, it's Arrasc, the Blue boss. He walks up to General Bautzes, who appears not to have noticed him. He stands there for a moment, clears his throat, but it must be a really good book because Bautzes doesn't seem to have heard him.

As a Green, you naturally find this amusing, which makes Arrasc look a fool. You can practically smell him struggling to keep his temper. He takes a step forward and says something; Bautzes suddenly notices that he's there, puts a bookmark in the book to keep his place, gives him a friendly greeting. There's a short conversation, which you can't hear, though I imagine you get the gist of it. Then Arrasc stomps back to his line with a face like thunder. Cue raucous Green laughter.

Then you notice that Longinus, in the Green front rank, has got that look on his face. He's not happy at all; but he steps up, and Bautzes greets him politely, and they talk. You can see Longinus getting angry; he's waving his arms about, but Bautzes just shakes his head. Nothing doing. Longinus comes back to the Green lines. The Blues are hooting and sniggering, which is pretty hard to bear, considering that their man got humiliated in exactly the same way a moment ago.

And while all this has been going on – first the curiosity, then laughing at the Blues, then sort of laughing inside where nobody can see at Longinus getting the same treatment; somehow, the burning rage that made you want to kill people and break things has sort of gone off the boil a little. You can figure out what's happened. Bautzes has told both of them, politely but firmly, that if they want to have a bloodbath followed by mass looting and storming the Watch House – fine, there's nothing he can do to stop them, obviously. But first, they're going to have to walk all over him, which is basically the same thing as walking all over Colonel Orhan and everything we've all been doing for the City; and he's so quiet and calm and so unfazed by it all, because he *knows* that deep down we're all sensible people who want to save the City, and the only way to do that is to stop fighting each other, pull ourselves together and start acting like grown-ups. In other words, the moment has passed. We're not a mob any more, we're six hundred or so responsible adults who can see painfully clearly what a bloody stupid thing we were on the point of doing, and probably the best thing would be to go home and never mention all this again—

"I was scared shitless," Nico told me. "Naturally. But I just couldn't think of anything else to do."

So I went to see Longinus, and handed him his father's release order, so he could be the one to deliver it to the Watch. Thank you, I told him, for not killing my boy Nico, and thank you for not trashing the City. Don't mention it, he said, and I'm really sorry about what happened to your girl. He meant it, too. He's a decent enough man, apart from the duplicity and that vicious streak.

18

And then, finally, I was free to go down to the Dogs and see if she was still alive.

"Oh," she said, "it's you. I was wondering if you were ever going to bother to show up."

"I'm sorry," I said. "I got sidetracked."

She looked awful, sort of grey and brittle, as though if she fell on the floor she'd shatter. "You look like death," she said. "I gather you got a bump on the head or something."

"Something like that." I took a deep breath. "I let Solisper go. I had to. Longinus was foaming at the mouth."

"Arsehole," she said. "Still, it's more that lunatic of a Prefect's fault than yours. You ought to put a muzzle on him. He's a menace."

"I intend to have words with him," I said, "when I've got five minutes. How are you feeling?"

"Awful," she said. "Oh, and I've got a bone to pick with you. Your bloody Supply Commissioners have been here saying I can't have any more booze for my customers. How am I supposed to run a bar with no alcohol?"

My Supply Commissioners. "I'm sorry," I said, "but it's got to be the same for everyone, you know that. Damn it, you were doing the job yourself, you should know better than anyone—"

"Oh, shut your face," she said. "What's the point of being friends with the top man if nobody's going to make a few small exceptions?"

"Aichma—"

"And another thing. There's no black market in this town. Really. You just can't *get* anything. And you know why?"

"Listen—"

"Because you've got the bloody Themes, who should be running the stupid black market, going round telling anyone that if they sell so much as a cashew nut off ticket, they'll get their legs broken. That's just not right. It's *tyranny.*"

"Aichma, shut up and listen." She gave me that shocked look, as though I'd just kicked a kitten. "Aichma, you were in charge of it, you know perfectly well why it's got to be that way. Just a minute," I added, as the penny finally dropped. "Have you been trying to buy stuff off ration?"

"Yes, only there isn't any. I've tried the Corason brothers, I've tried Lampadas and Streuthes, but they're all petrified. It's barbaric. You simply can't do that sort of thing, you're the government."

"For crying out loud," I didn't shout, not quite. "Have you the faintest idea how it would look if it came out that my – a personal friend of the Colonel's been trying to trade on the black market? How could you be so irresponsible—?"

"Fuck you," she said. "I've got a business to run, it's my living. I can't run a bar with no booze."

My head was hurting, and I don't think it was the concussion. "All right," I said, "fair enough. You figure out how much money you're losing, and I'll make it up to you. Now I can't say fairer than—"

"You're missing the *point*." She yelled so loud she scared me; I didn't want her busting stitches. "I don't want charity, I want to run my bar, and you're stopping me. You know what those bastards did? They came round here with a handcart and took away all my flour, all my dried meat, all my figs and raisins and olives—"

"Well, of course they did. And you got paid, didn't you?"

"Oh, right. They gave me a stupid bit of paper, like that's worth anything. And they weren't Watch or Town Hall, they were bloody *Greens*. My own Theme, marching in here and stealing my stuff. I ask you, Orhan, what's the point of fighting those savages out there? They aren't going to do anything much worse to us than that."

She was starting to get on my nerves. So I thought what Faustinus would say at this point, or Nico, and I said it. "Fortuitously," I said, "it doesn't actually matter. After all, you won't be running the bar for a good long time, not till you're all healed up. So really, it makes no odds."

"You're barred."

"You what?"

"You can't come in here any more. Take your horrible stupid tea and get someone else to make it for you."

19

"I think you may have been right," Nico said.

He startled me. It was the way he'd said it, the very reluctant respect. "About what?"

We were on the wall, inspecting the repairs. The masons' guild had rebuilt the ramparts in soft, half-baked brick. Theory was, if it copped another direct hit it'd crumble, not shatter into a million razor-edged flying shards. We were talking about facing the whole length of the battlements with the stuff, as and when we had five minutes.

"About them waiting for someone," he said. "I didn't believe you, but now I do, I think you may have something."

I felt like I'd just been handed a golden crown. "Thank you," I said.

"I think," he went on, "that the trebuchets were meant to be ready for when he gets here, but not used till then. But when we launched our sortie it made them lose their temper, or else they felt they had to do something to restore morale. So they did something, but it didn't work."

On that damned hillock they were hard at work, building seven new trebuchets. It seemed to be taking them a long time, and I guessed they didn't have the same calibre of carpenters as us. Fair enough; it's easy to forget when you live here, but this is, after all, the heart of the world. Naturally we have the best.

"I think," Nico went on, "that *he*, whoever he is, won't be happy when he gets here and finds out they've blown their principal advantage. If they'd had seventy trebuchets instead of seven—"

"We'd have smashed them to bits with bouncing balls," I said. "He wasn't expecting that, either. The idea was to pound us to dust from four hundred yards, when our maximum range is two-fifty. And he believed the trebuchets could crack the base of the wall, and they can't. Probably we've saved him lives and embarrassment."

Nico smiled. "Maybe," he said.

I heard footsteps behind me; someone slipping on the smooth stone of the staircase and catching their balance by grabbing the wall. Sawdust; she's one of the clumsiest people I've ever met. "Excuse me, but have you got a moment?"

Something was bothering Nico. He looked panic-stricken. "If you'll excuse me," he said. "Things to do." And he bolted off down the stairs, nearly knocking the poor girl over. Hello, I thought. But I could be wrong. I usually am.

Sawdust, with something under her arm wrapped in a blanket. "What've you got there?" I asked.

She unwrapped it. A sort of iron hook thing, and a ring for it to go in, and a catch of some sort, and the frayed end of a rope. "It's the release mechanism from one of the trebuchets," she said. "Lysimachus brought it back, did they tell you?"

Vaguely remembered something of the sort. "Let's see," I said, and she handed it over.

Refined, aesthetic types like you would get that sort of a thrill from seeing a Monomachus altarpiece, or hearing the monks at the Silver Star singing the Absolution. I'm an engineer. "It's amazing," I said. "So simple."

She smiled at me. "You just pull on the rope, and the slider falls back, and that drops the sear, and you're away."

I pressed the catch and the hook fell into my hand; no fuss, no hesitation. So simple; but you could see how difficult the problem was, to which this was the perfect solution. Whoever made it did good work. But we had good workers, too. "That still leaves a whole lot of problems," I said. "The beam snapping under impact. The shear force on the axis pins."

"I've been thinking about that," she said, and from the sleeve of her tunic she pulled a brass tube, out of which she poked a scrap of paper.

I have this flaw in my otherwise godlike character. I can't help finding fault, if there's any to be found. So I tried. I was silent for a long time, trying.

"Have I missed something?" she said.

I looked at her. "No."

She beamed at me. Not one of those women who's always grinning all the damn time. She looked quite different, somehow.

"I want a prototype," I said. "And we're going to test it, somewhere they can't see us. Set it up on the docks and chuck stones in the sea. I want this to be a surprise for them."

The next three days were solid, torrential rain, the sort we get in the City every five years or so. It turned the streets into swamps, so we couldn't move carts, there was flooding in Lower

Town and about thirty tons of irreplaceable charcoal got soaked and ruined. And I was so happy I could hardly look out of the window without bursting into song. Why? First, because we had houses with roofs, they had tents. Second, because all that rainwater poured down off the slates and tiles into drainpipes and gutters, and eventually found its way into the storm drains, which I'd ordered to be diverted into cisterns.

Excuse me for a moment, I'm going to boast about something. I designed the whole system, and it worked. I'm particularly proud of the banks of gravel through which the drainwater passed; filtered out all the crap and litter, leaving stuff fit to drink, provided you boiled it first. I can't remember where I first heard about that trick, but it works.

The fourth day, I was down at the docks. It's a strange place when there's no ships, like a hill covered in stumps when all the trees have been felled. Actually, that's not a bad comparison, because it reminds me of a young plantation in winter, when all the leaves are off; rows of tall, bare poles sticking up at the sky. But there wasn't a mast in sight that day, and the only pole was the beam of the Trebuchet, Experimental, Mark One. Got to hand it to that girl, she works quickly and well. I'd hate to work for her. You'd kill yourself trying to keep up, so as not to be humiliated by a woman.

You can tell when someone hasn't slept or eaten much lately, let alone washed. She had cuts all over her hands, just the normal nicks and gashes that can't be helped when you're handling chisels and rasps and planes. I think she'd reached the stage where she was past tired and out the other side, moving slow but steady, ignoring the inconvenient fact that everything hurts.

"You've changed the beam taper," I said.

She nodded. "I found a piece of hickory just the right size," she said. "So I've gone slimmer and gentler in the taper, for more spring."

"That's not a very good idea," I said. "We've got to build hundreds of these things. Where are we going to get hundreds of straight hickory beams?"

"We'll use ash and the original spec." She yawned so much she nearly tore her face. "Ash is lighter, so it's broad as it's long."

I hated doing it, but I said, "Did you make an ash beam? To spec?"

"Got one rough-hewed, but then we found the hickory."

"Fine. Finish it, take off the hickory, shift the fittings over to the ash and use that. A one-off proves nothing."

She gave me a pitiful look, then nodded. "You're right," she said, "I'm sorry. I just thought, well, hickory's better."

"It would be. A buffalo horn thirty feet long and backed with dragon sinew would be better still. But we haven't got any of those, either."

She stifled another yawn, then tottered away to tell the crew to take down the beam they'd just bust a gut winching into place. I heard raised voices; they weren't happy, and who can blame them? They were my lads, so I went over and gave them a filthy look. No more trouble.

It took the rest of the morning to finish the ash beam, drill it for the ironwork, fit it out, get it mounted. I hung around, itching to grab a plane and join in, but I couldn't quite trust myself to do good enough work, in front of everyone. Stupid, really. It's not something you forget, and I was a skilled man, once upon a time. So I hung around getting under people's feet, occasionally dealing with some nonsense or other brought down by runners from Upper Town. I could've gone back and got on with my own job, but the temptation was too great, so I told myself I was still sick and needed the fresh air. I guess that's what it's like for retired athletes or arena men. They can't do it any more, so they watch.

Typical of me, I was looking the other way when the beam eventually dropped into place and they slid the axis pin home; job done. I was reading some idiotic supply report; I looked up and there it was, finished, towering over me like a monster crane fly with a broken wing. I looked at Sawdust; she was swaying slightly. She caught my eye, grinned and said, "Give us something to shoot at."

Hadn't thought about that, had I? "See that marker buoy?" I pointed. "A hundred stamena if you hit it."

They didn't, of course. It was five hundred yards away, and very small, just a floating log with a flag stuck in it. But they weren't all that short and they weren't all that wide, and most of all, the bloody machine didn't break. There was a cheer the enemy must've heard, and then they were winching the counterweight back down. "Now do it again," I said.

Sawdust was giving orders; two minutes up, three minutes left. Missed again, but a fraction closer. "All right," I said, "try something easier."

So we launched a shit barge and I had them row it out four hundred and fifty yards, then row back in the dinghy. Just as well Sawdust didn't manage to hit it, though she came unpleasantly close. What really impressed me was that she overshot it a couple of times – four-fifty yards *plus*, so a good fifty yards further than even the mythical trebuchets of Echmen were supposed to be able to shoot. I decided I'd save up that extra fifty yards for a rainy day and make sure nobody mentioned it to anyone.

20

Thanks to Nico, we'd got away without a full-scale Green-and-Blue war, but things like that don't just melt away like the snow in spring. There were a lot of people going around muttering things like *we should've given those Greens/Blues a proper seeing-to while we had the chance*, and I couldn't help noticing that the two Themes weren't getting along as well as they had been. Only natural, I suppose. They'd been working flat out side by side with their worst enemy for weeks on end, on the strict understanding that if they didn't the world was going to end; but it hadn't ended, and now we'd beaten the savages in the sortie and seen off their secret weapon, so obviously the so-called emergency had been blown up out of all proportion; in fact, more than likely the whole thing was a scam put up by the government to break up the Themes and kid people into working their guts out for rubbish money. And what were the Theme bosses doing about it?

I think Arrasc had his people on a pretty tight rein, but that wasn't Longinus's style. He got into leading the Greens because he liked to be popular, and suddenly he wasn't. His view, if he ever thought it through to such an extent, was that he'd been elected to look after his people and get them what they wanted. Obviously looking after them came first, and when we'd been defenceless with the enemy at the gates, he'd done his deal with the Devil and it had worked, no regrets on that score. But that was some time ago, and it was now clear enough that the savages weren't actually up to much. The bouncing balls had sent them running for cover, their siege towers and trebuchets were now so much firewood, and all they did was sit there; we could take them if only we had a proper soldier leading us, and as soon as the Fleet came home the marines and the navy boys would make short work of them, and that would be that. So, all a lot of fuss over nothing. Meanwhile, what the Greens wanted was a showdown with the real enemy, and as Green leader it was his duty to give it to them.

So now we recognise (as they say in the House) yet another unsung hero who saved the City single-handed, although that wasn't what he intended to do, and I don't suppose he knew he was doing it. Said hero is one Antigonus Vorraeus, no fixed abode, occupation a dealer in stolen property and illegal merchandise. Vorraeus was a Scaurene, been in the City about five years – he jumped ship off a freighter – and didn't belong to a Theme. What he was really good at was being invisible, and neither the Blues nor the Greens knew much about him. He was very hard to find unless he wanted to be found, and having no affiliations he was uniquely positioned to start up a one-man black market, if only he could lay his hands on some stuff to sell. He also had a broad, uninhibited imagination, and a small boat he'd neglected to hand over to the authorities.

At great personal risk, therefore, he sneaked out of the

harbour in the middle of the night and rowed all the way down to Chirra, against the tide, in the hopes of finding something to buy. He got lucky. He fetched up in Chirra about seventy-two hours later, half dead with exhaustion, and immediately ran into a Scaurene freighter, which had turned back with its cargo hold full of wine and strong cider because there were no buyers from the City in town. They hadn't heard about the siege in Scauroe yet.

Vorraeus and his countrymen did a deal. In return for a sum of money – a small fortune to the Scaurenes – they gave him their ship's longboat, loaded with barrels until it was barely afloat. The longboat had a sail, and fortunately there was a handy following wind all the way back to the City. Vorraeus hung about on the other side of the Cape till nightfall, then drifted in nice and easy on the midnight tide. He had a hell of a job unloading all that booze single-handed, but he managed it somehow, got it off the boat, into a handcart, then about two dozen trips to the broken-down shed he used as a warehouse. He had just enough strength left to stow the boat away in a corner of a friend's boathouse, and crawled away a little before daybreak for a well-earned rest. Next afternoon, when he'd recovered enough to move, he went down to the Two Dogs, where he knew the management was offering stupid money for off-ticket booze.

And that's how Vorraeus saved the City. Thanks to him, the Dogs had wine and cider again, so the bar was open, so the Green war council had somewhere to meet and be overheard when they planned the big rumble.

It was the middle of the night. Actually it was later, about the time when bakers light their ovens and the fullers do their rounds, and everyone else is fast asleep. Everyone but me; I had financial reconciliations to finish, though my head weighed a ton and kept drooping on my neck like a dead flower. Didn't help that we had absolutely no money at all left, and I had to think of some way to disguise that fact before morning, when I was meeting the Paymaster. I was adding up a column of figures for, I think, the fifth time, and some fool came banging on my door.

"Go away," I said.

Silence. Good. I started again at the top of the column. About a third of the way down, more banging.

I may have said something uncouth. But the tiny part of my brain devoted to the exercise of common sense was insisting that nobody who knew me would come bothering me at that hour if it wasn't lethally important. "Come in," I said.

Enter Pamphilus. He's all right, actually, even though he's one of Faustinus's clerks. I'd had dealings with him before the emergency, back when I was nobody, and he'd been helpful and not too fastidious about interacting with dross like me. Accordingly he was now my assistant personal secretary. And, yes, he knew better than to hassle me in the wee small hours for anything less than the Second Coming.

"Someone to see you," he said.

I yawned. "You're serious, aren't you? For crying out loud, Pamphilus—"

He had that worried look. "You gave orders," he said. "She's to be admitted any hour of the day or night."

Which could only refer to one person. Only she was supposed to be half a mile away, under the zealous care of tyrannical nurses. "She's here?"

"Downstairs. She can't manage stairs, she said."

I jumped up, spilling the ink over my night's work. I winced, cursed. "See if you can clear that up, will you?" I said, ever the optimist. I was pulling on my slippers. "Is she alone, or—?"

"There's two women with her, and a man. I think he's a doctor."

I left him dabbing at a sea of ink with the corner of his sleeve. Down the stupid marble stairs, three insufferable flights of them. She was in the lobby. For idiotic aesthetic reasons, there's no chairs in the lobby, so she was standing, her arms round the necks of two nurses. A Theme doctor whose name I couldn't remember was hovering, looking anxious. "What the hell are you doing here?" I yelled at her. "You should be in bed."

That's what we told her, said the nurses' faces. They had my sympathy. "In there," I said, pointing at the nearest door. It was one of sixteen ante-rooms, all the size of a good hay meadow, but there were chairs in there, and couches. "Get her comfortable."

In the Palace they have bells in every room, which you ring by yanking on a silk rope. Damn thing came away in my hand. Then I remembered I'd fired – I mean reassigned – ninety-five per cent of the Palace staff.

"Stop fussing, I'm fine," she said, then squealed like a pig.

"What is it?" I snapped at the doctor. "Is it the stitches?"

He was rolling up her dress to have a look. She smacked his face so hard, it echoed off the ceiling. He carried on as if nothing had happened. "They're fine," he said.

"I'm holding you responsible," I said. "What the hell were you thinking of, letting her come here in her state?"

He didn't say anything, just looked at me. Quite right, too.

"You three, get out."

That was her, not me. Remember me telling you, on the subject of my old pal Ogus, about the concept of the natural-born leader? That makes two I've known in my lifetime. The doctor looked at me and I nodded. The poor man had suffered enough. He left, and the nurses followed.

"No," she said, "shut up and listen. In just over an hour, when the bell rings for Matins at the Silver Star, the Greens are going to burn down the Blue clubhouse."

I have my faults. But when I hear bad news that's palpably true, I don't argue or ask for proof. I took one look at her face and knew she was serious. Then I was in the lobby yelling out names at the top of my voice: Nico, Artavasdus, Menas – no, wait, he's dead. Genseric. Dead silence; then I heard their boots on the marble.

During that dead silence I knew what we were going to do, as though someone had told me and I was just passing on the message. Genseric to the Blues, warn them, full permission to take all steps necessary for their defence. Artavasdus to the Watch – fat lot of good they'd be – and the Parks and Gardens. Nico to send for Faustinus, then downtown to fetch our boys. I stopped him just long enough to scrawl the order of battle and basic moves in the dust on a small mahogany table. He grasped it instantly, nodded once – meaning he understood and approved, and, boy, did that make me feel better – and then he swept the dust away with his elbow and was off like a chariot in the Hippodrome, and I was alone again.

I went back into the ante-room. She was sitting up on the couch. "Am I really barred?"

"What?"

"From the Dogs. You said, don't come round here any more."

"*What?* No, of course not, I didn't mean it." She looked straight through me and out the other side. So what? I'm nobody special. "What are you going to do?"

"Stop it, of course," I said. "Look, will you be all right? I'd better go."

"Take care."

Useless advice for a man heading for a combat zone, but nice to hear. "You, too," I said.

I put on my armour. Complete waste of time. Yes, it protects you when you're on your feet, up to a point, but not if you're down on the ground. Also, it really slows you up when you're running away. But it's expected of you if you're in command, so I tied myself in knots squeezing into the scale cuirass on my own – it's a two-man job, you just can't reach the straps, let alone tease them into the stupid buckles – snapped the greaves round my legs and whimpered as the bottom front edge dug into the top of my instep; the helmet came down over my eyes, so I fiddled with the liner laces, and then it just about balanced on the top of my head, and fell off as soon as I moved. Fine, I decided, I can carry it under my arm. Then down two flights of stairs, realised I'd forgotten my sword, trudged up the stairs again (it's misery walking upstairs in armour that doesn't fit; the neck of the cuirass crushes your windpipe and the greaves shred the skin all round your ankles), couldn't find it, found it, back down the stairs – exhausted, like I'd done a day's work, and I hadn't even left the house yet.

Lurking by the door was an ominous dark shape. Lysimachus. You'll recall he's a Green.

"Clear off," I told him. "Won't be needing you tonight."

He gave me a grave look. "Reckon you will."

"You do know—"

"Yes. You can trust me."

God, I thought. Just when you think it can't get worse. For some reason, though, I believed him. "Fine," I said. "Though I'm not going anywhere near the fighting."

He grinned. "Suits me."

There was a two-porter chair waiting for me in the courtyard. The porters would be Themesmen, of course. Everyone is, in this town. But it was that or walk in those crippling greaves. We set off at the run, with Lysimachus loping alongside like a horrible dog, the sort that won't go away even if you throw stones at it. I tried to think serious tactical thoughts, but my mind was a complete blank.

Everything depended on the element of surprise, which I was convinced – treachery, or just blundering about like fools in the dark – we wouldn't have. But the chair stopped three blocks short of Goosefair, and Lysimachus and I walked smartly up as far as South Parade, where I hoped to God Artavasdus would be waiting, his men all neatly hidden in the shadows. No sign of anyone, until I was nearly skewered by a Parks and Gardens man who jumped out of nowhere with a bloody great pike. Lysimachus took it away from him before he could hurt anybody, and then he recognised me, so that was all right. He led me into a building, in the back and out the front. In the porch, Artavasdus was crouched down, gazing at the front door of the Blue House, directly opposite.

"Nothing yet," he whispered.

"Is Nico—?"

He shrugged. "Let's hope so."

The Blue House door was shut, all the windows were shuttered. Inside there, I hoped, Genseric and the Blues were ready to repel the first assault. Of course, the mission statement as I'd heard it had been to burn the place down, not bust it open and sack it. But it's much easier to torch a building from inside, and, as far as Lysimachus knew, there was nobody home apart from a senile old caretaker.

I've never been much of a one for waiting around. I fidget,

I can't get comfortable crouching in doorways. "Keep *still*," Artavasdus had to hiss at me more than once (me, the supreme commander, like I was twelve years old.) I'd made up my mind that the whole thing had been a mistake, trick, diversion because the real attack was happening right now on the other side of town, when I heard a familiar noise, the creaking of handcart wheels. I looked up, and suddenly it was a whole lot lighter – I'd been staring at the ground, and missed the sunrise, typical. Nothing to see, just creaking wheels. Then they came round the corner of Rose Street; about twenty-five, thirty abreast, with carts in the middle of the line, loaded down with timber. I recognised it as rafters we'd stripped out of the chapel in the Gardens of Pacatian; absolutely prime seasoned timber we desperately needed for catapult crossbars, and they were proposing to use it as firewood. I think that made me angrier than anything else.

Longinus wasn't hard to identify; taller than everyone else, middle of the front rank, leading in every sense of the word. He had his very best arena armour on, so he sort of glowed gold in the dawn sunbeams. On either side of him, men with whom I'd been doing a lot of business lately, men I trusted, convinced they'd got the message and were on our side. I admit it, I was shocked, let down, like I'd just caught my wife with my best friend. Stupid of me; because I'd really been kidding myself I understood the Themes and what they mean to people – me, from out of town, the milkface, presuming. I'd been filling my head with worms and lions to the point where I'd forgotten what the Themes are for, and what they came out of. Not us against them but us against us, because that's what people are really like, that's what they actually want.

Well, it was out of my hands now. I wished I hadn't come.

Remember me telling you about the old Engineers' game of

Throwing the Road Pin? Nico kicked off with a volley, from the balconies of the houses on either side. First the poor devils knew about it was men dropping to their knees, slumping backwards, dead men's heads banging the heads of their friends in the rank behind; yelling and screaming, and nobody knowing where it was coming from or what was happening. Then up jumped the Watch and the Parks and Gardens, yelling, clashing swords against shields, not moving an inch. Somewhere out back where I couldn't see, Nico and fifty of my best lads would be creeping into position, to cut off their retreat. Now the door of the Blue House swings open, and the Blues inside launch their volley – arrows, slingshots, javelins, road pins. Longinus is standing there perfectly stunned, realising he's surrounded out in the open, not knowing who's against him or how many. He's exactly where I want him, where he's supposed to be.

A shrill voice, a woman's voice, behind the rear of the Green column. I'm ashamed of myself. I closed my eyes.

The woman was Sawdust, up on the wall, and what she yelled was the order to loose. Twelve catapults, trajectories racked right down; twelve bouncing stone balls, looping over the roofs of the buildings of Horsefair and Rosemount, pitching in the back two ranks of the Greens, bouncing and rolling through solidly packed ranks of my fellow citizens, whose fragile bodies took so much way off those obscenities that they rolled up to the Blue House wall, sort of nuzzled the stonework like friendly sheep, and came to a gentle stop.

I'd ordered just one volley, but you know what it's like, at night, with inexperienced crews and everyone a bit on edge. For the second volley they shifted the point of aim two minutes left, so the balls wouldn't waste their mayhem on dead bodies. Standard procedure, the two-minute shift had become, as

Sawdust had noticed the tendency of a formation under bombardment to bunch up out of the way of the fall of shot, like the furrow cast up by the plough, thereby presenting an even juicier target if you came over just a tad . . .

And that was that. The clattering of dropped weapons was like rain on a roof. They were all howling, we surrender, don't shoot, hands in the air like the canopy of a birch forest grabbing at the light. And up close, the bodies, the crushed, squashed, smeared, popped, every-bone-broken bags of seeping mince; what had Nico called it, the greatest single advance in the science of land warfare, or something like that?

There were several things I wanted to do at that moment. Standing up and talking wasn't one of them. But it had to be done. Had to be me, nobody else. A natural-born leader would've been on his feet and shooting off well-chosen phrases like a rat up a pipe. Me? Standing up was like being a tooth pulled from a jaw.

So I stood up, and I don't suppose anybody saw me, and I was wondering how the hell I was going to make myself heard above all that screaming and yelling. I tried shouting, but I couldn't hear myself, it was as though my mouth was working but nothing was coming out. Ludicrous.

Just as well that thug Lysimachus was with me; he knew what to do. He jumped up, grabbed a couple of Parks and Gardens men – literally, by the scruff, lifted them single-handed off the ground, brought them over to me like a cat with a kitten in its mouth. He told them something, I couldn't hear what it was. They took hold of a shield between them; then Lysimachus put his arm under my shoulders and hoisted me like I was five years old onto the shield, and the two Parks men lifted it shoulder high.

A moment later, you could've heard a pin drop. Explanation, if you don't happen to be Robur: lifting a man on a shield is an incredibly symbolic, meaningful thing. Back in the distant heroic past, it was basically an act of coronation. After the battle, the winner's soldiers lifted him on a shield, and that's how everybody knew he was now the king. Things have blurred a bit since then, of course, and we've got two thousand years' worth of the most arcane and impenetrable court ritual the world has ever seen. Even so; couldn't say who was more shocked and stunned, me or everybody else – Greens, Blues, Watch, my lads, the artillery crews on the wall. It was one of those moments that change everything, a man standing on a shield, something that grabs and monopolises your attention even if you've just had your leg ripped off by a bouncing stone ball.

(I asked Lysimachus later; why did you do it, what the hell were you thinking of? To which he replied; you wanted them to look at you. His mind works that way. Achieve the objective, and the hell with collateral damage.)

And then I felt myself wobble a bit. Note: the shields we'd issued to the Parks crowd were slightly curved, not the easiest thing to keep your footing on. I swear to you, if the shield had been flat and I'd felt just a tad more secure, I'd have jumped off, believe me. But I couldn't, not without slipping and coming down on my nose or my arse, the worst possible omen, as various would-be emperors found out the hard way over the centuries; fall off the shield and, trust me, you don't live long afterwards. No, the moment had passed, there was no way off that shield, I was stuck, as surely as if I was cut off by the tide. And everybody was dead quiet, staring at me as though I had three heads.

A voice in my head said, *can't be helped*. Why do I listen to those voices? Common sense dictates that any voice you hear inside your head must be just you, thinking; so, if you know it's just you and you know you're basically an idiot, what possesses you to do what the stupid voice tells you?

Anyway. I opened my face and this is what came out. "Wounded," I said, "stay where you are, don't try and move, we'll get doctors to you as soon as we can. Greens, go home, right now. Longinus is dead, this never happened. Be at work as usual first thing in the morning if you know what's good for you. Blues, go home. Soldiers, to me."

21

That was it. Oratory's not my thing. It worked, though.

Goes without saying, there weren't enough doctors. Faustinus had managed to rustle up a dozen, and the Blues had fifteen or so in the Blue House; not enough to do very much, though most of the bloody messes on the ground there were past help anyhow. Nobody said anything out loud, but the ones who were too badly smashed up had their veins opened, and what else could you do? But there were a couple of hundred we did manage to save, which under the circumstances wasn't bad at all.

'Soldiers, to me' was the only way I could think of to get down off that fucking shield. Once my lads were crowded round me, screening me from sight, I hopped, not giving a stuff about how I landed. As it happens, Nico caught me and lowered me gently until my feet touched the ground. "Are you out of your mind?" he asked me.

"Not my idea," I told him. "Really."

He didn't believe me. Nor did Artavasdus, Genseric, or any of the others. I could read them like the golden letters on the Arch of Maxentius; you planned this, and you didn't tell us because you knew we'd try and stop you. Fuck them, I thought. Then Artavasdus said, "Orders?" I looked round for Lysimachus; I wanted to stick a knife under his chin and make him tell them, it was his idea, not mine. But he wasn't there, the bastard. Always there when not wanted, but when I actually needed him, nowhere to be found. Typical.

What's done is done, said the stupid little voice. "Right," I said, trying to do an impersonation of me and making a hash of it. "What's happening? I can't see."

"They're going home," someone said. "Greens and Blues."

Success. The disaster averted, albeit at unspeakable cost. You could almost say, triumph. Except that, at the crucial moment, some idiot gladiator had done one small thing that made that unthinkable triumph barely relevant, a sideshow, a footnote. "I want discreet patrols," I said. "Make sure they don't hang about anywhere. And I want the names of any Greens who don't show up for work."

Someone pointed out that there were about three hundred dead Greens who'd never clock in ever again, but since we didn't know their names yet, my order would be hard to put into effect. I hadn't thought of that, naturally. Do it anyway, I said, and get those bodies identified.

Nico was looking at me, like I was some sort of monster. "What do we do about the Greens?" he said.

"Nothing," I told him. "But I want you to go to the Green House later today, find out who's in charge, tell them I want a new Green boss elected and in place in the next forty-eight hours. Tell them it's their business entirely who they choose, so long as they choose someone. And then I want to see him, whoever he is. Got that?"

Nico hesitated. I knew why. He wasn't sure how to talk to me, now I'd proclaimed myself emperor. To someone like Nico, formalities *matter*. So, was I Sir or Your Majesty or Your Imperial Highness, or what the fuck? "Nico," I said, "don't stand there goggling, move." He gave me a startled look, then the faintest, most perfunctory of salutes (he's never ever saluted me, only once, when I forbade him ever to do it again) and marched stiffly away, back as straight as a set square.

"You did the right thing," Aichma told me.

I don't like swearing at women, so I didn't reply.

"You did," she said. "If the Greens had burned down the Blue House, the whole city'd be a war zone right now. Thousands of people would be dead, and the savages—"

"Leave it," I said. "Please."

"You had to stop it," she continued. "And you simply didn't have enough men to do it any other way. Actually, it was quite brilliant."

She was feeling better, I could tell. I'd flatly refused to let her go back to the Dogs. So far, no reports of any trouble in the streets, but it was too early to be sure; besides, there was a real risk that someone might figure out how I'd learned about the Greens' plans, in which case she couldn't go back to the Dogs ever again. No point trying to explain that to her, of course. She wouldn't listen.

"Also the coronation thing," she said. "Now that was smart."

I shut my eyes. She wasn't being ironic. You know when Aichma deploys irony, just as you know when a volcano erupts. "It wasn't my idea," I told her.

"Of course it wasn't." Now that *was* irony; red streams of lava tumbling down the shattered mountainside. "Stroke of genius.

No, really, I mean it. Suddenly, nobody's going to be talking about anything else. You actually managed to upstage a major riot. That's class."

"It was Lysimachus," I said. "And when I lay my hands on him—"

"Risky, of course," she went on, over me, like a cartwheel over a hedgehog, "but you judged it just right. It's what everybody wanted, though I don't suppose they knew it till it happened. No, I take my hat off to you, it was exactly what was needed. Of course, it changes everything."

"Aichma," I said. "Will you please shut the fuck up?"

Nico was still speaking to me, though he was jumpy as a cat. Artavasdus kept looking sideways at me, as if expecting me to turn back into a dragon at any moment. Faustinus took me to one side and said he'd thought long and hard about it and he was on my side, no matter what, but even so, he felt he ought to protest, in the strongest possible terms. Oh, and crowds started cheering me in the street, which was just bizarre.

The Green committee came to see me. It was all a bit awkward to start with; they stood there, with their hats in their hands and imaginary invisible nooses round their necks, until I offered them a beer. Then they all sort of shuffled backwards, leaving one Bronellus sort of stranded, like a beached whale.

I looked at him. "You're it, then."

Bronellus isn't someone you look at if you can help it. He's got this scar, cheekbone to cheekbone, no tip to his nose. He didn't say anything, which I took to be a confirmation.

"Congratulations," I said, and stuck out my hand. He shied back, then took it and shook it. "Right, we need to get you up to speed. Basically, these are the areas the Greens are responsible for."

I don't suppose he took half of it in, though I came to realise he was an intelligent man; rather more so than Longinus, rest his soul. Later I heard that nobody wanted the job at any price; there was a deathly silence in the Green chapter-house, everybody holding his breath and trying to be invisible. Eventually Bronellus stuck his paw in the air and said, "I'll do it," like the fifth man cast away in the open boat with water enough for four. Apparently he was the life and soul of the party when he was younger. But when he got the scar he went all quiet, and had stayed that way ever since.

I prattled about his duties and responsibilities until I couldn't think of anything else to say, and then I smiled at him. He looked at me. "What's going to happen to the Greens?" he said.

"How do you mean?"

"After the other night. What are you going to do?"

"Oh, that," I said. "All right, tell you what. When you can think of some punishment that won't make matters a whole lot worse, come and tell me and we'll see what we can do. Otherwise, put it right out of your mind, as far as it'll go."

He considered me as though I was an equation, then nodded. "No more trouble," he said.

"Plenty of trouble," I replied. "Everyone seems to have forgotten, but we're under siege. If they attack, and if they can stomach the losses they'll take getting as far as the gate, I don't think there's very much we can do to stop them. I'd like you to think about that."

His eyes went wide. "As bad as that."

I nodded. "But that doesn't leave this room. What we've got to do," I went on, "you and me and Arrasc and a few others, is make sure they don't attack. Not till the Fleet gets here."

"You've heard from them."

"No," I said. "But out there somewhere we've got six hundred warships, with a full complement of marines. Sooner or later they'll come sailing up the Bay, and then things will be easier. Then we'll have a chance. Meanwhile, we hold the fort. All right?"

He nodded. "No more trouble," he said. "I promise."

"Good enough for me." And I meant it. In the course of a long (feels that way, anyhow) and eventful life, I've learned that nothing encourages good faith, loyalty and a desire to work tirelessly for the common good like blind terror. If he was scared enough, who knows?

22

Unless you've spent your entire life in a cave under a mountain somewhere, you know all about the volcano that buried the mighty city of Perennis under a million tons of ash in about five minutes, roughly a thousand years ago. What you may not know is that Eugenes IV, the scholar-emperor and philosopher-king who lost half the eastern provinces and presided over plague and famine, and is therefore referred to in the histories as The Wise, sent three regiments of Guards to the site of Perennis to dig it all up. Which they duly did; it took three years and cost more than the Fifth Fleet, or enough corn to feed two provinces, but they managed it, in spite of Eugenes insisting that they remove the hardened ash with trowels and little brushes, to avoid damaging the remains.

About a hundred years before my time, of course, but I read the official report, which ended up in the Engineers' archive, presumably because the project involved digging. What they found was weird enough to jangle the brains of the career Guards officer who wrote it all up; you can tell how deeply it got to him by the way his style deteriorates, from textbook military reportage to barely coherent ramblings. It takes something special to do that.

What they found was human shapes; not bodies, but a sort of eggshell of hardened ash enclosing where the body had once been – a bit like the lost-wax process the bronze-casters use. One smart tap and the outer shell crumbles away and there's nothing inside, flesh and bone having long since rotted and seeped away through the porous shell. There was no chance of making out fine detail, faces and so on, because all of that information would've been on the inside of the shell. Instead, what remained was a sort of generic human shape; Everyman, if you like, frozen in a few minutes of crucial action, going about his supremely ordinary life just as the world exploded around him.

Because the ash came down so damn fast, the report said, there was no time to panic. Most of the dead clearly hadn't really understood what was going on. They found people asleep in bed, sitting on stools writing up ledgers, squatting on potties, one couple at it like knives in an alleyway, completely oblivious of everything except each other – touching, or bloody stupid; what they didn't find was people panicking, running through the streets, kneeling before altars in prayer, writhing on the ground in agony. So quick, they never knew it was happening. Vague human shapes, no faces. You and me. Everyman.

I mention this because that's how the world changes. It's either so quick that we never know what hit us, or so gradual that we don't notice. It's only later, when books are written and scholars decide what mattered and what didn't, that red lines are drawn – before this point, the world was this way, after this point, everything was different. You could be there and not have a clue. You could be asleep, or looking the other way, having a quiet shit or screwing in an alley, and an unseen pen draws a line. Here the Empire ended. Here the Dark Ages began.

I *was* there, as it happens. And I was awake, and taking notice; possibly the only man alive who was looking out for it, expecting it to happen. I was lying in bed, unable to sleep, going over the minutiae of trebuchet design in my head. I know Faustinus was at home, fast asleep; Nico was officer of the day, so he was in his lair at Headquarters, probably drawing up duty rosters. Aichma was playing checkers with one of the cleaners. Probably I asked Artavasdus where he was – later, of course – and presumably he told me, but if so I've forgotten what he said. Anyway, that's us accounted for when the ash of History started to fall. None of us were looking up, so of course we never saw it.

Not that there was anything much to see. A junior button-man of the Blues who was on sentry-go on the North Gate tower reckons he saw torches, about seven, eight hundred yards away. He says he wondered who was riding into the enemy camp at that time of night, made a mental note to report it when he came off shift but forgot to do so. Who knows? Maybe what he saw was the moment that changed everything, or maybe it was someone else riding into camp in the middle of the night, and when the real event happened he was looking the other way, or having a crafty piss in a dark corner.

Like it matters. There was, of course, nothing we could have done about it, any more than the poor fools at Perennis could've stopped the ash.

No, the first we knew about something having changed was when a column of soldiers appeared on top of the Hog's Back ridge, heading down the valley on the old West Road. And, because people are idiots who will insist on hoping for the best, we honestly believed that they were our boys, Imperial troops marching to relieve the City. Suddenly everyone was up on the wall, trying to see. People with especially good eyesight were hustled to the front, and they said, whoever they are, they're wearing red cloaks, they've got regulation shields, they look like our boys; and we'd all filled our lungs to start cheering when the column turned sharp left down the Toll Road – heading not for the gates but the enemy camp. Fine, we all said, they're going to attack. But horsemen were riding out to meet them. A brief conference of leaders; then the new army marched into camp, and they lit fires to cook them breakfast.

All morning and half the afternoon they filed in, regiment after regiment; they pitched their tents, stacked their shields and spears, unloaded their carts, lined up for beans and bacon. We put the total at about twenty thousand, give or take a few hundred. That was the first day.

The next day, eight thousand more. Two days later, twelve thousand. The day after that, nine thousand, mostly cavalry. Five days after that, twenty-one thousand. The whole of the flat plain between Nine Springs and Old Castle was filled with their supply carts, and the meadows where the City women used to do their washing beside the river became a corral for their draught oxen.

Seventy plus forty is a hundred and ten. A hundred and ten thousand men; almost as many outside the walls as inside.

"You were right," Nico said to me. "They were waiting for something. I think we can guess what it was."

Yes, I didn't say, but it makes no sense. Something was missing. Or something else had happened (more important than the arrival of seventy thousand enemies), and at the time we'd been looking the other way.

"Imperial issue stuff," Artavasdus repeated. "Everything they've got is Imperial issue. They must have taken Classis."

I reminded him; Classis was ashes. "Well, obviously it isn't," he replied. "Because all the gear for the whole empire is stored and issued there. So, obviously, that's where it's all come from."

"It could be surplus," someone suggested. "We sell off a lot of equipment."

"Not that much," Artavasdus snapped. "Not current pattern."

"Then maybe they're copying our stuff," said Glycerius, a young second lieutenant I'd recently promoted. "You can't tell if it's genuine or copies. They're too far away to see details."

"I think the supply clerks at Classis must've been selling stores on the quiet," Genseric said. "They were always a bunch of crooks. Isn't that right, Chief?"

"Quite true," I said. "But the scale of it. Seventy thousand sets of full kit."

"Drop in the ocean," Genseric assured me. "You've been to Classis, you know the vast amount of stock they carried. And the stories I've heard, about wastage. You went into the stores with a chit for twenty Size Three bolts, they'd say, sorry, you can't have just twenty, they come in barrels of a thousand or not at all. I imagine it was the same for breastplate scales, mail rings—"

"It's possible," I said. "Not sure I'm convinced, but it could have happened. A lot of our stuff came to us that way, I know that for a fact."

I like to let them talk things out, but fact isn't a democratic process; if a thing isn't true it isn't true, even if everybody votes that it is. I was fairly sure I knew how the enemy had come by all that equipment. But this wasn't the time for saying that sort of thing out loud.

Aichma, however, likes to brandish the truth in your face. "It's obvious, isn't it?" she said. "They got it where the first lot got their stuff from. Off dead bodies."

"The thought had crossed my mind," I said.

"Of course it did. That's why nobody's come to relieve us. They're all dead."

"Keep your voice down."

Her eyes went wide, and she lowered her voice. "It explains everything. That's what they've been waiting for. They didn't want to start the assault until the rest of our armies had been accounted for."

She was feeling better, evidently. "I'm not sure," I said.

"You mean you're deluding yourself."

"Maybe," I said. "But seventy thousand is a lot of men. Where did they all come from? And it'd be more than seventy thousand," I added quickly, before she could interrupt. "If they've really wiped out all the armies in the provinces, inevitably they'll have taken heavy losses. Say fifty thousand, and that's as low as I'm prepared to go. A hundred and twenty thousand competent fighting men, good enough to beat Imperial regulars? Where did they come from?"

She frowned. "Search me," she said. "Where the forty thousand who wiped out General Priscus came from, presumably. Nobody's ever explained that, but we know it happened. The mystery just got a bit bigger, that's all."

Sometimes she can be so annoying. "You can't leave it at that," I said. "They must have come from somewhere. They must be something. Unless someone got hold of a box of dragons' teeth and neglected to read the warning on the lid."

She gave me that look. "Of course," she said patiently. "But we don't know and we've no way of finding out, unless there's stuff you haven't told me. Is there?"

"No."

"Fine. Saloninus the philosopher reckoned he could deduce the nature and origin of the whole universe from a single grain of sand. I work for a living, so I haven't got the time or the patience. When you get some more facts, tell me and I'll see what I can do."

23

I was in a meeting with the Blue and Green bosses. Nobody had told me that, back end of last season, Arrasc and Bronellus had met in the arena, one of those mock battles the punters like so much; ten men on each side, and it's over when there's only one man standing. That had been Bronellus. Everyone thought Arrasc was dead, but Doctor Falx pulled him round and sewed him up and he survived; than which there's no greater disgrace, apparently. The rule is, no grudges. More honoured in the breach, as the saying goes.

So, it was a sticky meeting. Neither of them took their eyes off me for a second, for fear of having to look at the other man. Actually, we got a lot done, since each of them was trying to be more reasonable than the other. Still, it's hard to feel at ease when you're in the same room as a combined mass of nearly six hundred pounds of top-flight killer and you just know that one wrong word –

A clerk came in, I didn't know his name. Strict orders not to be disturbed, and the poor man looked petrified. "What?" I snapped at him, mostly because I was so nervous.

"There's an embassy," he said.

Made no sense. "Sailed into the Bay?"

"No, sir. From the enemy. They're flying a white flag."

You may recall that, when I tried to negotiate, they shot at me. "You're kidding."

"No, sir."

I jumped up. "Gentlemen, I suggest we adjourn. Thank you for your time." I left them sitting there – crazy thing to do, but luckily no harm came of it – and followed the poor clerk out into the courtyard, where Nico was waiting for me, looking worried.

"They want to talk," I said.

"Apparently."

"How many?"

"Twelve horsemen, one white flag. They've stopped about three-fifty yards from their lines."

Well within shot from the catapults, in other words. For a moment, I had my hands full just breathing.

"Fine," I said. "I guess we'd better go and see what they want."

Lysimachus came, too. I think Nico would've had to fight him to make him go away, and I'm not sure who'd have won. So, the three of us, on horseback, rode out of the North Gate, feeling very strange indeed. It had been so long since the gate had been opened, and since we'd any of us done something as normal as riding down a paved road. Lysimachus, by the way, was no horseman. He was clinging to the pommel of the saddle with both hands, the reins knotted on the nape of the horse's neck, the way kids ride.

Fifty yards between them and us, and someone called out, "That's far enough. Leave your blue friends there and come on alone."

I thought about it, and came to the conclusion that if they wanted to kill me they could do it perfectly easily with or without Nico and Lysimachus. "It's all right," I told them, "I'll be fine. Stay here, and don't interfere."

I rode forward. So did one of the twelve; a dazzling figure head to toe in actual gold armour – not polished bronze, not even gold plate, the real deal. Nothing else shines quite like it. The clown, I thought; but he was the size of a house and he seemed to be controlling the horse by sheer willpower; bareback, no reins. I only ever knew one man who could do that, and I knew for a fact he was dead.

Leave your blue friends. Odd way to start a negotiation.

He stopped his horse about fifteen yards from me, slid off easily, walked towards me. I dismounted; rather a performance, as I got my foot stuck in the stirrup; grace isn't my strong suit. My back hurt, and I was crouching like an old man.

Golden Man was wearing one of those parade helmets, where the visor's a mask that covers your face. His was the face of the Eternal Sun. He undid the buckle and lifted it off. I stared.

I know him, I thought. Only—

"Caltepec," I said. Couldn't stop myself. The name burst out, like the evil sheep that won't stay in the pen.

"Don't be silly," he said. "It's me."

Caltepec; I'd know him anywhere. He taught me to tickle trout and flip a flat stone across a river, when I was five years old. But it couldn't be Caltepec, because that was over forty years ago, and he'd have changed. Also, he was dead.

He was looking at me. Overjoyed to see me, exasperated because I was being so dense. "Who are you?" I said.

"Orhan, for crying out loud." Caltepec, the blacksmith in our village. Tallest, strongest man in the district, also the gentlest and the kindest. The father of my best mate. The Sherden killed him. "Orhan, you halfwit, it's *me*."

And then, just as the penny dropped and I realised, he lunged forward, threw his arms round me and gave me a hug that forced all the air out of my lungs. He never did know his own strength, my pal Ogus.

"Let go of me," I whispered. "I can't breathe."

"Say what? Oh, sorry." He let go and I staggered back, gasping for breath. He really did look the spit and image of his old man. "You know what, Orhan, you haven't changed a bit. God, it's good to see you."

"Ogus? What the *hell* are you doing here?"

He gave me that grin; like looking straight into the sun, which you aren't really supposed to do. "Long story," he said. "Come on, let's have a drink."

I was still short of breath. "I can't," I said. "They'll think—"

"Oh, screw them," said Ogus cheerfully. "Tell 'em you'll be back directly."

Crazy. But I turned round to face my escort. They were on foot. Nico had Lysimachus's arms behind his back, to restrain him from charging up and pulling Ogus's head off, for touching me. "It's all right," I called out to them. "I'm going to their camp, to talk. I'll be fine, I promise."

The way the wind was blowing, I didn't catch what Nico said. Didn't need to. Are you out of your tiny mind, or words to that effect. But what the hell. It's not every day you meet an old friend. "I'll be fine," I repeated. "Go back. Take the horse." Then I turned my back on them and walked back to Ogus, my pal.

24

"I knew you were here, of course," Ogus was saying, as we walked back to the enemy lines. "Counting on it, if truth be known. Of course, you being in charge of the whole shooting match is the most amazing stroke of luck. I never anticipated *that*."

His legs are so much longer than mine, so I always have to trot to keep up. All my life I've walked really fast, habit I got into, keeping up with Ogus when we were kids. "Ogus," I said, "what are you talking about?"

"This is my tent," he said, pointing at something the size of the Capitol, only made of cloth-of-gold rather than basalt. "I managed to get some of that tea you like, the black stuff with the dried yellow flowers." He stopped and gave me another terrifying hug. "You have no idea how good it is to see you again, my dear old friend. Tea!" he thundered. And there it suddenly was, on a silver tray.

I lowered myself awkwardly into a sort of seething bog of cushions. Ogus wasn't drinking tea, of course. He knocked the top off a bottle and took three enormous glugs. "How long's it been?" he said. "Thirty years?"

"Thirty-seven," I said. "I thought you were dead."

"Me? God, no." He was grinning. "Oh, of course, you were sold on when I was down with that nasty go of fever. Actually, that was a real stroke of luck. By the time it cleared up the buyers from Lepcis were in town. That's where I went. Marvellous place. Been there?"

I shook my head.

"I was seventeen years in Lepcis," he said. "Worked my ticket in six, set up on my own, made a go of it. Then, of course, I came back. I know all about you, of course. You've made a real go of it, I'll give you that. I always knew you'd do well."

It was the tea I especially like. You can't always get it, even in the City. No idea where it comes from. "Thanks," I said. "Ogus, what are you doing here?"

He gave me a blank look. "How do you mean?" he said.

"With these—" Couldn't think of the right word. Probably just as well.

"What? Oh come on, Orhan, you never used to be stupid. This is my army."

Now I looked at him, I could see the differences. Caltepec was a bit rounder in the face. And, of course, his eyes were grey, not blue.

"I always knew this was what I was born for," Ogus was saying. "Ever since – well, you know. I remember sitting by that miserable fire in the rain, that day we reached the sea. I thought to myself, this is all wrong, it's got to stop. And then it sort of came to me, out of the blue. Someone's got to stop it, and that someone is me."

I waited for him to continue, but he didn't. "Excuse me," I said. "Stop what, exactly?"

"The Robur, of course." He was still beaming at me. "Wipe every single one of those bastards off the face of the earth. It's the only way, you know that, a smart fellow like you."

"It was the Sherden—"

He raised his hand, and I couldn't have said anything even if I'd wanted to. "They don't matter," he said. "The Sherden only steal children because the Robur pay money for them. I don't hold a grudge against the Sherden. Actually, they've been bloody useful. Well, you know that, obviously."

I looked at him. He's the sort of man everybody's eyes naturally turn to, like sunflowers. "You did all this."

"Took me a while," he said. "It's been a real game, I'm telling you. There were times when I thought, the hell with it, why me, why should I bother? And then I thought of you."

It could have been worse. The sky could have fallen on my head, with nail-studded clouds. "You what?"

"Don't you remember? My God. You must remember."

"Remember what, for crying out loud?"

At which point, I remembered.

Picture me, nine years old, huddled by a dying fire, wet through, beside a road somewhere between what used to be home and the coast. Ten days' forced march in the Sherden slave caravan; we'd had a couple of bowls of filthy porridge and a few slurps of muddy water out of puddles, our feet were bare and raw, the ropes round our necks and wrists had chafed the skin off – to be honest, all that hardly registered. Nine days' march, I'd been so numb I wasn't taking it in. Just numb, that was all. I hadn't shed a single tear – not sure I ever got round to it, now I come to think of it. Too wrapped up in my strange, confused thoughts, which were basically: this can't be happening, none of this is true, sooner or later they'll let us in on the joke and we can all go home. Tenth day, the penny dropped. My life was going to be different from now on. I wasn't angry or frightened. I'm not sure I gave a damn. As an experiment, I tried to remember what my father and mother looked like. Is that them, I asked myself, and I wasn't sure. The pictures in my head were like the portraits on the coins; exaggerated, idealised, crude, could be more or less anybody, and you only know who it's supposed to be by the letters round the edge; Siyyah, father, or Erstam, mother. I remember thinking what a callous, worthless little shit I must be, to feel so very little.

But Ogus, next to me, was crying his eyes out. Now that was really weird. Ogus didn't cry; not when he fell and cut himself to the bone, not when he was caught stealing and whipped, not when his sister was carried away by the river and drowned. Not that he was callous and unfeeling, like me (apparently). If anyone else was sad or frightened, Ogus would be there, saying exactly the right thing or not saying anything at all, strong, wise, dependable, master of every situation and vicissitude, invincible. Never could figure out why someone like him chose to hang out with someone like me; but that was Ogus for you. He didn't need a reason to be your friend, he didn't need anything in return – what could anybody give him that he hadn't already got?

And there he was, broken at last; it shocked me more than I could believe possible. And, goes without saying, I hadn't the faintest idea what to do or say. All I knew was, I had to stop those tears, before I lost all faith in everything. It was like seeing your father cry, or God. So I said the first thing that came into my head, something like, "Don't worry, it'll be all right, we're better than them, one day we'll get them for this, you'll see." I think I said that because Ogus was a great one for honour, in those days; if someone got you, you had to get them back, or the balance of nature would be disturbed. And once he'd exacted vengeance a few times, nobody wanted to mess with him, and so of course he was proved right. Not that I ever doubted him for a minute.

Well, he stopped crying, at any rate, but he went all quiet, not like him at all. Then, the next day or the day after that, he stumbled and fell on the march, stood up and got back in line, and he had something crushed in his hand, a mushroom. I whispered to him, you don't want to eat that, it's poisonous. He looked straight ahead and hissed back, I know. And the day after that, when it was our turn to take the guards their food, I think (couldn't swear to it) I saw him drop something in one of the bowls; and that night one of the guards woke us up with his screaming, and was dead by morning.

I didn't say anything. But, as we walked past the body, he sort of nudged me and said, Thanks. I pretended I hadn't heard.

"Oh, that," I said. "What's that got to do with anything?"

"I thought about it," he said, offering me a plate of honey-cakes; my favourite. "Years later, when I was in Lepcis. I realised, it wasn't the Sherden's fault. Might as well blame the arrow for the archer. And I thought of what you said to me, and how it had given me the strength to go on, to *prevail*—" He smiled. Just like his old man when he smiles. "You know that saying, may the best man win? It doesn't make sense, when you stop and think about it, it's nonsense. The best man always wins, because the winner's always the better man. By defini-tion. It's that simple. If you beat me, you're the better man. If I come out on top, I am. That night, on the road, I proved it. I was just a little kid, no weapons, all trussed up with ropes and kicked around, but I beat that bastard, I won, I was better than him. That was what you meant, when you pulled me through my bad patch."

"Actually—" I said. He wasn't listening.

"Then," he went on, "when I was settled nicely in Lepcis I heard about you. You'd just been made a captain, and you'd come up with some clever improvement for building pontoon bridges, and some trader or other had got wind of it and brought the idea to Lepcis and was trying to sell it to some people I knew. Youngest ever captain in the Engineers, he said, and him a milk-face; only goes to show what a man can do if he sets his mind to it. And I remember thinking, Orhan would be so ashamed of me if he could see me now, all comfortable and settled, making money, not getting on with the job. So that night I got talking to some people, and between us we figured the whole thing out." He beamed at me. "And now, here we are, you and me, and it's all about to happen. Isn't that grand?"

I took a deep breath. He was – is – my oldest friend, and I don't suppose anyone's ever known me better. "Ogus," I said, "I'm on the other side."

He laughed. Good joke. "Doesn't that just make it perfect?" he said. "Almost like it was meant. All along I figured, when things start happening, you'd be called back to the City for the defence, there'll be someone there on the inside I can count on, so long as I can figure a crafty way of getting in touch. But to find you in charge of the whole thing – I ask you. Can you think of any better proof that this was meant to happen? You, of all people. You and me, in at the kill."

I needed time to think, so I said, "Who are all those men out there? Where did they come from?"

"My army, I just said." He snapped his fingers. More honey-cakes came, just like that. "About two-thirds of it, anyway. The rest are busy right now, but they'll be along directly."

"Was it you?" I said. "At Classis. The Sherden."

He looked troubled, not exactly guilty, but I think he felt he owed me an explanation. "The way I see it," he said, "they're like a weapon. When the fight starts, the other man's got it. So you knock it out of his hand, and then it's your knife, it's gone from bad to good, just like that. The Sherden are victims every bit as much as we are, Orhan. It took me a long time to understand that, but once I'd got it, everything just sort of fell into place. It's us against them now. You remember that old saying back home, the worms of the earth against the lions, who would win? It's our turn now."

My breath caught in my throat and it took me a moment before I could say anything. "I was at Classis," I said. "They nearly killed me."

That bothered him. "I'm sorry," he said. "Obviously, if I'd known—" He shrugged. "But you're all right, so that's fine. Have another cake. You haven't been eating properly."

That made me laugh. Then I realised, it was supposed to. "Let's talk peace," I said.

25

I'd said the wrong thing.

"Sorry," he said, "I don't quite follow."

Suddenly I was desperate for a way back. "Surrender," I said. "Terms. I'm sure between us we can sort something—"

"Terms?" He was staring at me, as if he'd realised he'd been talking to a stranger under the misapprehension that he was an old friend. "What are you suggesting?"

"Oh, come on," I said, with a sort of ghastly forced cheerfulness I feel ashamed of to this day. "Whatever you want, to lift the siege. You name it."

You know those silences where you find yourself saying any damn stupid thing, just to fill them. I managed to keep my face shut, but only just.

"All right," he said, as if he could barely keep his temper. "Pile up all your weapons and open the gates."

"And then?"

"We march in and slaughter the lot of them." A long pause, and then he added, "Not you, of course. We're friends."

He'd said them, not you. But he was looking at me in a way I didn't like at all. He always had a bit of a temper, Ogus. And he hated anything he could possibly manage to construe as disloyalty. "Why?" I asked.

"Because they've got to go, that's why," he snapped. Then he realised he'd been shouting. "You understand, don't you? You of all people. We can't just let them go, *forgive* them. It's got to be done properly or not at all."

My turn to be silent. He stuck it out for a couple of heartbeats, then went on; "Besides, it's out of my hands now. I promised them, every last Robur. If I tried to go back on that now, they'd tear me to pieces. For God's sake, Orhan, what's the matter with you? You haven't grown attached to these people?"

"A bit," I said.

"You can't," he said, hard as stone. "It's not like trapping a spider under a cup and putting it outside instead of squashing it. They're blueskins. We've got to start the world all over again without them."

I took a deep breath and let it go slowly. "What exactly do you mean, " I said, "they won't let you?"

He stared at me, then broke into a big wide grin. "Haven't you figured it out yet? Who my men are? They're two-thirds of the bloody Imperial army. Not the blueskins, of course. Auxiliaries. Poor fools from the conquered nations, given the alternative; come and fight for us or we'll burn down your villages. It's how the empire garrisons its territories, now they're so big there's not enough Robur to go round. Well, it worked for a long time, until some clever soul – I think it was me – realised that these days there's a lot more milkfaces than blueskins in the Imperial army. Trained by the Robur, supplied and kitted out from the same stores, every bit as good at soldiering, and when there's actual fighting, who gets stuck in harm's way in the front line while your precious Robur stand by in reserve? So, once it was explained to them— Doesn't apply to the navy, worse luck, they never could quite bring themselves to trust savages with their beloved ships, so I had to do a deal with the fucking Sherden. Worth it, though. Right now, all that's left of the blueskin regulars are cooped up in fortified cities all across the empire, with my boys sitting under their walls making sure they don't get out. So, that's one third of the army kettled up safe, another third keeping them there, and the third third is right here, to stamp on the snake's head. So that's what I was talking about. Do you really think those men are going to let the Robur walk out of here alive? Of course not. They want blood. And so, come to think of it, do I."

I drank some of the excellent tea. I'd let it go cold. "You've given me a lot to think about," I said.

He gazed at me as though I'd gone mad. Then he burst out laughing. "There's nothing to think about," he said. "Dear God. This isn't a situation where you carefully weigh up the pros and cons. You just *know*. Or don't you? What's come over you, Orhan? You've changed."

It suddenly struck me that he was right. I remembered the boy he'd known. That wasn't me any more. Curious thing. You don't notice yourself changing, because it's so gradual. Then one day you catch sight of your reflection in a pool or a puddle, and you wonder, who's that? But talking to Ogus again – I'd mistaken him for his father. Easy mistake to make, he'd grown into his father's image. Maybe I had, too, don't know, can't honestly say I remember what my old man looked like. I have a lot of memories with him in them, but his face is always turned away, or he's in shadow; like the icons and triptychs, where the artist's been paid to add in his patron as a minor saint or a bystander, but the convention demands that he's somehow obscured, barely noticeable. They say that if you can smuggle yourself that way into a great icon, by a truly inspired master, all your sins are forgiven. That's cheating. Robur thinking.

Now the question: had I changed for the better?

Well, not for me to say. Ogus clearly thought not. "I build bridges," I heard myself say, thinking aloud. "I'm not a soldier. All I ever wanted to prevail over was a few rivers."

"It's not about what you want," he said. "And we're all soldiers. We didn't start the war, but we're all in it."

"If it wasn't for the Robur—"

"Sure." He spat the word at me. "They found you useful. And it's good business to look after your tools, and your livestock. After all, they cost money. Be honest with yourself, Orhan. Are you really grateful to them because they sharpened you, and gave you your own hook on the rack?"

"I'm my own man. I'm the colonel of the fucking regiment."

He nodded. "Yes, that's true. You're so good at your trade and you've done such good, valuable work for them, sometimes they actually condescend to treat you like a human being. Some of them even pretend not to notice there's something wrong with your skin. Such good manners. And for that you love them. Good dog. Well-trained dog." He knew he was getting on my nerves. He knows me so well. "Come on, Orhan. It wouldn't hurt if you hadn't already thought it yourself."

"Getting your own back," I said. "It was always so important to you."

"Yes."

I waited. He took his time. "And to you, too," he said.

*

Which was true. Is true. I get my own back on the empire, the army, the established institutions, the arrogant blueskin masters of the earth, by cheating. I forge seals, I embezzle money, I pay with false coin. I keep my self-respect with countless small acts of dishonesty. I do it to get my own way in spite of them, and to prove to myself that I'm so much cleverer than they are. The worms declared war on the lions, and all the animals in the forest were sure the lions would win. But the lions couldn't catch the worms, because they dug down into the ground and wouldn't come out and fight. But at night, when the lions were asleep, the worms crawled in through their ears and ate their brains and killed them, every one. It's a popular story where I come from, though the Robur have never heard of it. And when I tell it to my Imperial friends, I always ask them first, which would you rather be, a worm or a lion? And they all say, lion, of course – except Artavasdus, of all people. Why? Because, he said, I'm an engineer, and worms dig really good tunnels. Mind you, he only said that because he knew it was a trick question.

"I know what you do," he said. "You cheat them, every chance you get. You steal from them because you want to get back at them, and you make it all right with your conscience by lavishing the spoils on your engineers. You prey on them. You wouldn't do that if you loved them."

"I never said I—"

"Good. You didn't tell a lie." He looked at me, straight in the eye, point-blank range. "I can understand why you fought for them when you thought it was just nameless savages. I can understand why you invented those horrible bouncing stones and slaughtered the enemy. But we're not the enemy. We're your people. We're me. Do you want to crush me to death with one of your bouncing stones, Orhan? Do you?"

"No, of course not."

"Every one of those boys you kill is me. Can't you see that? Your own kind. People just like you. More like you than those blue monkeys can ever be."

Blue monkeys. I don't let my friends, my milkface friends, talk about the Robur like that. Maybe because I'm afraid that if they do, I might catch myself agreeing with them.

He looked at me with his head on one side, like dogs do when they can't figure out what you're doing. "Maybe you're sorry for them," he said. "Is that it?"

"Maybe."

"Fine. There was a doctor like you once. He had a chance to wipe out the plague, once and for all. But he didn't. He felt sorry for it." He pursed his lips. "Three guesses what he died of."

"Maybe I think that what you're planning to do to them isn't much better than what they did to us."

Fake yawn. "I don't know about better," he said. "I'd say it was the same thing, more or less. You've been around these people too long, Orhan, you're starting to think like them."

"Maybe."

"*Maybe*", in a mock-childish voice. "Definitely. You know how the Robur think? If they win, it's manifest destiny; spare the conquered, grind down the proud with war. Recognise that?"

"I do read books."

"Delighted to hear it. So, if they win, it's that. If they lose, it's *fighting is wrong*. It's *there has to be a better way for rational human beings to settle their differences*. No, trust me, Orhan, there's nothing wrong with fighting, nothing at all. It's how you tell the better man from the worse."

I cracked a grin. "But the Robur always win."

He wasn't smiling. "Not this time."

"That still doesn't make it right. You know that, don't you?"

And then Ogus turned his head to the side and cupped his hand round his right ear. "Sorry," he said. "Didn't quite catch that."

Now I think of it, there's one thing I neglected to mention.

Don't know if you remember the story I told you, about Ogus poisoning the Sherden slave-driver. Well, it was a few days after that. There was one of those Sherden who'd made up his mind he didn't like me. Don't know why; it happens, people take a dislike to you, doesn't have to be a reason. This man couldn't stand me, never missed an opportunity to kick me or smack me round the head. Well, I thought about what Ogus had done; but I'm no killer. My talents lie in other directions. So, when we stopped that night I worked away like fun to get the rope round my wrists and ankles loose. Then, when the guards were asleep, I sneaked over to where my enemy was lying. I'd noticed he had a little whalebone carving of a dolphin that he wore round his neck on a bit of leather string for a lucky-piece; a dolphin, presumably, as a charm against drowning. Nice and slow and easy, I took the knife from his belt, cut the string, took the dolphin, put the knife back where I'd got it from – razor-sharp edge about an eighth of an inch from his throat while I was doing it, never even crossed my mind to do anything except rob him. A nice thing like that, I told myself, will be worth something to someone at some point in the future, and in the meantime I've got my own back on the bully, I've prevailed, I've won.

Some lessons you learn the hard way. For example, don't go robbing people, even in the middle of the night, when the ground's sodden wet, because you'll leave footprints. Hadn't seen them, of course, it being dark. Come morning, plain as anything.

The guard woke me up with a kick to the collarbone, which is one of the most painful places you can hit someone. I think he was planning on killing me, because he'd dragged a senior colleague along, to bear witness that I'd robbed him and he was within his rights. Didn't take them long to find the dolphin, tucked away between my belt and my tunic.

"Fair enough," the other guard said. "He's all yours. Do what you like."

"It wasn't him."

They both looked round. There was Ogus, sitting up, wrists and ankles unbound. "It wasn't him," he said. "I stole the dolphin. It was me."

My special friend the guard roared at him, bullshit, but the senior man made Ogus say it again.

"I did it," Ogus said. "And I hid it on my friend, so if we got found out it'd look like he did it, because everybody knows the fat guard doesn't like him. But I was stupid, I forgot about the footprints."

The senior man looked at him for a long time, and I do believe I could read what he was thinking. I'm pretty sure he didn't believe him, but there was no way of proving it one way or another; also, I reckon, he was thinking: if this kid's got the guts to take a beating for his pal, fair play to him, let him. So he nodded, then lashed out with his boot and caught Ogus the most terrible blow on the side of the head.

I was sure he'd killed him; there was blood trickling out of his ear, and he wasn't moving. "That's how we deal with thieves," the senior man said. "Think on." He walked away. The bully gave me a long look, then followed him; and the odd thing was, he didn't give me a hard time after that.

Ogus was all right, more or less, eventually. But he was deaf in his right ear ever after, until we were parted. Still is.

I didn't reply. No answer to that, is there?

"Besides," he went on, "you're overlooking one important thing. The City can't be defended, not against an army this size, there's no way on earth it can be done. Sure, you're so clever and resourceful and imaginative, and your men love you so much, you'll put up one hell of a fight. Probably you'll make a real mess of parts of my army, with your bouncing balls and your trebuchets and God knows what else you've thought up and not told anyone else about yet. But it won't make the slightest difference, in the long run. The City will fall. The people in it are dead already."

He paused and I looked at him. "So?" I said.

"So." He met me, look for look. Bit like a mirror, really. "If there was the faintest chance you could beat me, then fine, yes, absolutely, fight your damnedest and bloody good luck to you. But there is no chance. Your blue pals are dead. There's nothing anybody can do."

"Except?"

Mild grin. "Except," he said. "Because you're my best pal and I could never hurt you, I'll let you save – what, let's say a dozen of your pet blueskins: Nicephorus Bautzes, your man Faustinus the Prefect, Artavasdus, Gaiseric—"

"Genseric."

"You're quite right, Genseric. Lysimachus, your loyal bodyguard. And of course there's Aichma, your old pal's daughter, and Aelia, the little carpenter girl. She likes you, by the way."

Where did that come from? "Bullshit."

"She does, you know. Trouble brewing in that quarter if you're not careful, because Captain Nicephorus likes her, and she likes you. Anyway, that makes seven, leaving you five more. Or we can make it two dozen, if you'd prefer. Simple fact: if you decide to defend the City against me, they're all going to die. Well, maybe not the carpenter girl, because she's a milkface, my boys won't hurt a milkface, she won't come to any harm. But the rest of them——" He drew the tip of his finger across his throat. "But if you join me, they're safe. Your friends. The people you care for. That's not a threat, by the way, do what I tell you or your pals get it. When the time comes, I'll give orders, find these people and spare them if you can. But Nicephorus and Artavasdus will die before they surrender, stupid blueface honour, and only a few of my officers know the others by sight; with the best will in the world, I can't help them. Only you can do that. Or are you the sort of man who'd watch your friends die just because of your stupid principles and your stupid pride?"

You're not meeting Ogus at his best. That said—

People change, sure, but not that much; besides, I hadn't observed anything about him that was inconsistent with the boy I once knew, loved, worshipped. And worshipped why? Because he was strong.

I guess you can only understand the significance of that if you were a small, weak kid, like I was. At that age, human beings are animals. The biggest and strongest rule over the small and the weak; no justification needed or sought, it's instinctively recognised as the way things are – and should be; the small, weak kid doesn't doubt the validity of the system, he just thinks it's unfair he was born little. Later, we learn to talk, to talk our way out of trouble, into what we want; charm, deception and lies take the place of height and muscle, and that's what we call being grown-up, being intelligent, rational humans, being civilised. Same difference, if you ask me, where justice is concerned, but that's beside the point. When we're kids, grown-ups govern and command us because they're bigger and stronger than us and can hit harder. Naturally, we use the same system of values among ourselves. For a start, it makes sense – so much more so than the things they try and kid you into believing later, morality, right and wrong, good and evil. Can't say I've ever really got the hang of any of that stuff. Can't honestly say I've really tried.

Ogus was a big, strong kid; I wasn't. But Ogus, who could have been friends with anyone he chose, chose me. He defended me, let me bask in his glory – there's a little fish, they tell me, that lives by battening onto the hide of a shark, and the other fish never give it a hard time, and it feeds on the scraps the shark doesn't want. That was me. Never anything asked in return, not even flattery, praise or adulation, the sort of thing the gods want, apparently, but not Ogus. I never asked him why but I know what he'd have said if I had; because we're friends. Simple as that.

Now reflect on what I've told you about my life. When Ogus wasn't there any more to keep me safe, I did the obvious thing and looked around for another big, strong bully to look after me; I found the empire. Of course, they wanted something in return. They wanted bridges, put up fast, guaranteed not to fall down. Hardly selling my soul to the Evil One. Sure, they weren't particularly nice to me, but they weren't utterly horrible either. I was useful, so they put up with me, even though I persisted in going around the wrong colour, knowing how distressing that must be to people of refinement.

People like Nico don't approve of me hanging round places

like Poor Town and the Old Flower Market. They don't hold with the company I keep: thieves, cheats, deceivers and prostitutes; especially the latter. Me, I've never had any problem with whores. I'm one myself.

I hadn't said anything for a bit. Ogus smiled at me.

"I know you're not like that," he said. "I know you'd do anything for a pal. For me, and your new City friends. Lucky, isn't it, that the interests of all your friends coincide."

"You've changed," I said.

"No," he said, stating a fact, "I haven't. Neither have you. Think about it, will you? What have you been doing, ever since you suddenly found yourself in charge?"

I gave him a grin. "The best I can."

"A bit more than that, I think you'll find. Soon as you had the opportunity, you started trying to build the Great Society. The poor people were shut out and exploited, so what do you do? You sideline the House and all the rich bastards, you legalise and recognise the Themes, you find every excuse you can to pay good wages; you even try and get a woman to run a major department of state, because it's not right that women are excluded just because of what's between their legs. It's the worms of the earth against the lions, and you couldn't resist. Soon as you had the chance."

I had nothing to say to that.

"And look what happened," he went on. "Aichma does the job for a few days and resigns. The Themes work together for a bit, and then there's a riot, you have to turn your amazing new artillery on your own people, just to stop them butchering each other. Orhan, it can't be done – not in there, in the City, the Great Society won't work there. And you know why? It's because they're who they are, Robur. It's not the worms against the lions, it's just stronger lions and weaker lions. And you think they love you for it, but they don't. Read this."

He took a small brass tube from his sleeve and tossed it to me. I caught it, poked out the slip of paper and read it. Then I looked at him.

"Perfectly genuine," he said. "You recognise the writing?"

"Yes."

"And the seal?"

"Yes."

"All right. Now tell me what it says."

I didn't want to, but Ogus is hard to disobey. "Senator Fronto, who I punched in the face, and half a dozen other leading members of the House have arranged to have me killed. Once I'm dead they plan to take over the City and crown Fronto as emperor. They've recruited five hundred Greens who don't like Bronellus and hate me because I killed their fellow Themesmen. They're also going to kill Nico, Artavasdus, Faustinus and Aichma, because they're afraid they'd make trouble after I'm gone. The plot is set for the day after tomorrow." I rolled it up and tried to put it back in its tube, but my hands were shaking; Ogus took it and did it for me, then handed it back. "You might want to hang on to that," he said. "Oh, and this, too." He handed me something, wrapped in a scrap of blue silk. The Great Seal. "Now then, look at me."

I didn't want to do that, either, but I did.

"All right," I said. "What do you want me to do?"

26

Ogus offered me a horse but I said no, thanks, and walked back to the North Gate. Nico was waiting for me. "What the *hell*—?"

"Long story," I said. "Tell you later."

"For crying out loud, Orhan—"

"Later." Didn't mean to shout; a bit overwrought, if truth be known. Anyway, it shut Nico up. No small achievement.

"You were gone a long time," Faustinus said. "What did he want?"

"Total surrender," I told him. "No guarantees. I told him no."

"Thank God for that." He looked at me, nervous, as though he expected me to bite him. "Who is he?"

"Good question," I said. "As far as I can make out, he's some sort of lunatic crusader. He wants to overthrow the empire. Not take it for himself. Get rid of it."

That got me a stare. "Why?"

"Because it's evil and tyrannical and mankind can never be free until it's been disposed of. Go figure."

"That makes no sense. The empire is the greatest force for civilisation in the history of—"

"Tell him that," I said. "Though I think you'd be wasting your breath. The bad news is, he's turned the auxiliaries against us."

"Oh God." Faustinus's eyes went wide. "Which unit?"

"All of them."

I thought he was going to pass out. "But what about—?"

"The Robur troops? Cooped up in the garrisons, under siege. No hope whatsoever of them coming to the rescue. They're waiting for us to rescue them."

"He's just saying that."

I shook my head. "It's true," I said. "He introduced me to about a dozen auxiliary officers. They confirmed it. They've bought into his crusade. The conquered nations don't like us any more."

"Oh my God, Orhan. What are we going to do?"

I gave him my calm, steady look. "Hang on," I said. "One thing he did let slip, the navy's rock solid. Well, they would be, they're all Robur. And they're still out there somewhere. And sooner or later they'll come, and it won't just be us any more. We'll survive."

"What, just the marines against all those savages? We can't beat them off like that."

"That's not what I said," I told him. "I said we'll survive. If we have the Fleet, and they can't breach the walls, they can sit there for a thousand years and we'll survive. We control the sea. We have ships to bring in food, we have thousands of skilled workers, the best in the world; we can make goods to trade for food, which is what we do anyway. The Fleet can raid the rebel homelands, make their lives miserable. Eventually it'll dawn on those idiots out there that they're wasting their time, and then we can make peace. A sensible settlement, negotiated by rational human beings. Meanwhile, we have to hold on. We can do it, Faustinus. We're better than them."

He gave me a curious look. "What aren't you telling me?"

"What sort of a damnfool remark is that?" I snapped at him.

"I'm sorry. Only you sounded like you were trying to convince yourself of something. I worry when you do that."

"You're an old woman, Faustinus. You worry about everything." I felt in the sleeve of my tunic and took out the silk bundle. "Meanwhile," I said, "guess what turned up."

I threw it to him. He muffed the catch, stooped and picked it up. "My God," he said, "that's not the real—"

"Keep your voice down, there's a good lad. Yes, the one and only. It's back."

"Where did you—?"

"Trust me," I said. "You don't want to know."

That startled fawn look. "No, I imagine I don't. Still, this is a stroke of luck. It's marvellous."

I nodded. "I would've told you earlier, but I got sidetracked. That's the good news. The bad news." I found the brass tube. "See for yourself."

He read it and whimpered. "Why me, for God's sake?"

I like a man with priorities. "Because you're my right-hand man, of course."

"We've got to do something about this," he said. "Right now."

I laughed. "Such as what?"

"Arrest them. Straight away."

"Right. I send soldiers into the House and have seven respected senators dragged out by the hair."

"You've got the Seal, you can do anything."

"They've got five hundred armed men. What they don't have, but what you seem hell bent on giving them, is justification for their actions. No, first I talk to Bronellus. You don't say anything to anyone. And keep inside, don't go anywhere without a guard, Blues or my boys. Leave the whole thing to me."

I found Bronellus at the Green House. He was shocked and saddened – well, he would be; his own people thought he was no good. I told him what to do.

Then I went to the State Cartulary, which is a mouldy old tower sticking up out of the spine of the Resurgence temple, which used to be a monastery, years ago. They never got around to shifting all the mountains of old government papers stored there; reports from the Prefect's office, mostly. I found an old clerk who reckoned he knew where to find what I was looking for. It took him a while, but he pulled out a big brass tube as thick as my leg and handed it to me with a beam of satisfaction.

It wasn't what I needed, but at least it told me where to look; in the Clerk of the Works' archive, on Needle Street. Down in the vaults there's a wall covered floor to roof with shelves, each shelf crammed with brass tubes, all numbered. Took me four minutes to find the tube I wanted. Simple as that.

Interesting stuff; a report on the collapse of a street of houses in Poor Town about a hundred and seventy years ago, and a map showing the affected area before it fell down, and a couple of other maps from a century before, and one very old map indeed.

"Can I borrow these?" I asked the archivist.

"It's strictly forbidden to remove any document from the premises," he said.

"I'll take that as a yes," I said, and went back to the Palace.

*

Bronellus showed his five hundred dissidents the error of their ways. One in ten were killed; the other suffered various injuries. Wherever possible I don't ask questions about how work I delegate to others gets done.

The planned coup never took place. Senator Fronto fell ill after eating something that didn't agree with him and died howling. The other six senators found themselves shuffled onto a subcommittee; lots of work, no spare time. They were no bother after that.

I didn't tell Nico or the others. I did tell Aichma. Everything. Nearly everything.

"So," she said, "what are you going to do?"

Aichma takes after her father, but she looks like her mother; both of them were half milkface, but with Aichma you have to look quite hard to see it, though it's there. Her mother was the daughter of an immigrant tent-maker who fell on hard times, ended up having to sell his kids on a ten-year indenture.

(Marvellous system, indentures. In theory, once you've done your time, you're free as air, so it's not slavery, which is uncivilised and barbaric. But while your indentures are still running, your master's perfectly entitled to bill you for food, clothes, lodging, training in any trade he may require you to learn; and of course there's interest running on all that, fixed by statute at fifteen per cent compound. Goes without saying, by the time your indentures are through, you've run up a hefty tab, which you can only clear by labour, for which you're paid a wage, also fixed by statute, illegal to pay more. And while you're working off your debt, naturally, you're still eating and wearing clothes and taking up bedspace. It isn't slavery, because slavery's an abomination which the Robur have vowed to put and end to. It just amounts to the same thing.)

Anyway; Aichma looks like a diluted version of her mother. There are savages out east who mix their tea with milk; a bit like that. Adulterated is the word I'm groping for. But her mother was a sweet, gentle soul, kind to everybody, never a harsh word, with a sort of serenity about her. Aichma takes after her father.

"Tell me," I said. "If you were in my shoes."

Her eyes gleamed. "Are you kidding?"

"Tell me."

"Take the deal, obviously. You just told me what he said. If you don't, you're dead and so are all of us. I don't want to die out of solidarity to the empire. It'd serve no useful purpose, and, besides, they're arseholes."

"You're Robur."

"Not quite Robur enough, so I've been given to understand. Also, I'm rubbish. It's not my empire, I just live in it. More to the point, we can't win. Therefore I'm going to die, unless you do the deal. Don't tell me you had to stop and think about it."

"I thought about it very hard."

"Why? What the hell was there to mull over, for crying out loud?" She had that oh-for-God's-sake look on her face. "It's like – all right, supposing there's a fire. What do you do? You grab everyone and everything you can and you get the hell out of there. You don't agonise about letting the fire win. Staying alive doesn't make you the fire's accomplice. Orhan, you've had the most amazing stroke of luck. Just for once in your life, being who you are's worked out in your favour, not against you. And if you're still not convinced, think about your friends. Trust me, this isn't a grey area. This one's pretty bloody straightforward."

"You think so."

"Idiot," she said. "Stupid fool. You just told me, Fronto and the senators were going to murder you. Five hundred Greens were going to help them do it. If you want to know what a representative cross-section of Robur society think of you, there's your answer. Fuck them. Fuck the lot of them. Take the deal."

It annoys her like nothing else when she gets all forceful and I stand there stone-faced. "What do you think your father would have said?"

"Him? Take the deal. Save my little girl's life. You promised, remember?"

"That's true," I said. "I did promise."

She frowned. "You have made your mind up already, haven't you? You never ask my advice unless you've already decided."

"I'm not sure," I told her.

"Not sure? What kind of an idiotic answer is that? Pull yourself together, Orhan, this is *important*." She made a visible effort, lowered and softened her voice. She can do it if she has to. "Listen, you did your best. You did amazingly well. When you got here, we were an hour or so from being slaughtered like sheep. You held them off, you gave them a bloody nose, and while you were at it you shook up this stupid city like nobody's ever done before, you tried to make it into something that might conceivably be worth saving. But it couldn't be done. The Themes are still at each other's throats, even with Death banging on the front door, and the boss Robur want to knife you in the back. How many times have you got to hear it before it finally sinks in? Don't bother trying to save the City, it can't be done. Save us instead. We're your friends. Everybody else hates you."

I let her see that I was still thinking. Then I nodded. "So on balance," I said, "you think I should take the deal."

"On balance," she said, "yes."

27

Opening the gates of a besieged city to the enemy isn't as easy as you might think. It takes a lot of thought and planning, involves a great many people and calls for careful timing and excruciating attention to detail.

You don't think so. You think, all you have to do is wait till the middle of the night, sneak down to Foregate, pull back a few bolts, job done. In which case, I'd like to live in your city. With citizens like you, it has nothing to fear from treachery.

I knew how the gates were guarded, because I'd set up the system myself. With the people split into two warring factions, an aristocracy that hated me and what I'd done, not to mention a substantial criminal element perfectly capable of betraying the City for money, I wanted to make the system as traitor-proof as possible. So; each gate was guarded by not one but two contingents, one Theme and one official. Thus, one night it'd be Greens and Engineers, the next Blues and Parks and Gardens, then Greens and Watch, Blues and Engineers: you get the idea. Each guard unit was fifty men, ten of whom would be standing directly in front of the gate, in full kit. Each pair of gates was fitted with five bolts, thick as your leg. To reach the fifth one, you needed a long ladder and someone to hold it for you; if you tried to shoot the top bolt without someone at the bottom, you'd fall and break your neck. Also, each bolt was fitted with a padlock, and for these padlocks there were only two sets of keys: one for the gatehouse, one in a safe in my room at the Palace. Just to make life interesting, custody of the keys was split between the two details – if it was Greens and Engineers that shift, the Greens would have the keys to bolts one, three and five, the Engineers would have two and four. That wouldn't be a problem for me, of course, since I had the master set.

So what? I'm in charge of the City, everybody has to do what I tell them. No problem for me to walk down at a time I've agreed with the enemy outside and issue a direct order: open the gates. No, I'd thought of that. The idea was, what if I'm killed or otherwise indisposed? Command passes to Nico, or Faustinus, or the Theme bosses, whoever happens to still be alive. The men on the gates probably won't know what's going on; they have to take someone's word for it that I'm dead and so-and-so is legitimately in command, and you can see the potential for deception there. Also, the City is simply crawling with actors – the Hippodrome, the Opera, the Comedy and Tragedy, probably the finest theatrical tradition in the world – and one of our favourite genres is impressions. Never saw much to it myself, but you'd be amazed how many people will pay good money to watch a man dressed up to look like someone else. Bear in mind that a good number of the men on duty on the gates at any given time will only have seen me once or twice, in passing, at a distance. Since I'd become a public figure, I'd earned the dubious honour of being impersonated, and I have to say, some of them were very good indeed at being me, rather better than I am myself. Therefore, insufferable smartarse that I am, I'd taken precautions. Nobody, not even me, could give the command to open the gates on his own. There had to be two authorised officers, out of a small and select pool – me, Nico, Artavasdus, Faustinus, Arrasc and Bronellus (both together, not one on his own) – together with the duty officer for that particular gate on that particular shift, who had to have seen a written order bearing the Great Seal.

I'd explained all this to Ogus, who rolled his eyes and said something about too clever by half, with which I found it hard to disagree. But that's all right, he went on, you set up this cockamamy system, you can replace it with another one. Not really, I told him, it'd look a bit suspicious, and, as you just demonstrated, I'm not exactly popular with a lot of the key players right now. But not to worry, I assured him. There are other ways into the City besides the gates.

"So you're the little bird," I said.

He stared at me. Someone more unlike a little bird it'd be hard to imagine. His name was Nausolus and he was an Honour Sergeant in the Blues. That's a responsible job. An Honour Sergeant – there's a dozen in each Theme – sees to it that Themesmen who commit honour violations (passing on information to the authorities or the other Theme, disobeying the orders of the Theme bosses, murder, rape or aggravated theft against a fellow Themesman, that sort of thing) come to a bad and well-publicised end. Honour Sergeants are handy with small knives, poisonous chemicals and dangerous objects and processes. They know everybody and have very few friends. They're paid well, direct from Theme funds. No Honour

234 K. J. Parker

Sergeant has ever gone to the bad, because of what would happen to him if he did.

When he wasn't doing all that, Nausolus kept poultry, in five long, stinking sheds down by the North dock: chickens, ducks, geese, doves and pigeons. He was particularly good with the pigeons, and before the siege he'd trained about a dozen of them to carry messages, to his cousin Vossus in the Paralia. When the savages came, he sent a pigeon to his cousin with a suggestion: go and find the enemy leader, ask him how much it would be worth to him to have regular detailed news from inside the City, from a very well-placed source indeed. A deal was quickly made, and the pigeons had been busy ever since. Mailing the Great Seal by pigeon post had been a particular triumph; he'd hung it round the bird's neck on a short strap, and tied it down with string under the armpits, for want of a better word, to keep it from coming loose and bobbing about. Can't be done, the wiseacres on Ogus's staff had declared, but Nausolus and his champion bird had proved them wrong.

"The mine of information," I clarified. "The bringer of glad tidings."

Nausolus was quick, I'll say that for him. He was on his feet, past the guards and halfway through the door before Lysimachus brought him down with a beautifully thrown chair, to which we tied him thoroughly before resuming the interview.

"Now I don't want to make you do anything you don't want to," I told him. "If you don't want to co-operate with me, that's fine, I quite understand. I'll just hand you over to Arrasc and tell him what you've been doing."

He didn't seem to like that idea very much.

"Glad to have you on board," I told him. "Now, I'm quite happy for you to carry on sending messages to the enemy, provided I see them first. The sort of stuff you've been giving him so far will do fine. If your stuff suddenly turns useless, he'll get suspicious, and then you'll be no good to me at all. Very occasionally, I'll get you to send something I've written. Now, that's not a problem, is it?"

He assured me it wasn't.

"Fine," I said. "Nice to have met you."

I don't hold with codes, ciphers, all that rubbish. Clever men can figure them out. If you've got the code and someone sends you a message, you find yourself spending hours compiling charts and diagrams and writing things out in rows and columns until your fingers ache, just so you can read: *nothing much happening at this end,we had fish with parsley sauce again, how about you?* Life's too short.

Much easier to use normal, regular words, provided they're in a language nobody but you and your pal can understand. Alauzet, for example, my and Ogus's native tongue. There may have been three dozen other Alauzet speakers in the City, maybe a couple of hundred in Ogus's massive army; we don't get around much, unless we have no choice. The only slight drawback is that Alauzet has never been a written language, since none of us can read or write. Still, there's a first time for everything. I found I could write Alauzet more or less acceptably using the Jazygite alphabet – no *y*, and you have to use *uu* for *w*; otherwise, no big deal. I happen to know Jazygite – long story, not important – and there was bound to be someone in Ogus's polyglot multitudes who knew it, too, but Jazygites are even thinner on the ground that Alauz in these parts. Now that's what I call cryptography.

"What's all this?" Nausolus asked, when I gave him the message to send. "It looks like gibberish."

"It is gibberish," I told him. "Completely meaningless. Think how much time and energy they'll waste before they figure that out."

The other way into the City, I'd told my oldest and best friend, calls for a bit of work on your part, but you won't mind that. Then I asked for paper and something to draw with. I sketched out the course of the main drain, which naturally empties out into the Bay, on the southern side, so the current washes all the crap out to sea. What my scruffy hand-drawn map showed, and all the up-to-date official ones don't, is the old spur drain, which was closed down and sealed off after the sinkhole incident in Poor Town. This spur originally led out to a soakaway outside the walls, I told him, in what was then marshland; it was drained about seventy years ago, and now it's lush green grass. Now then, I said, if someone were to dig a sap, precisely fifty-seven feet down below the surface, starting from the derelict tannery and driving directly towards the belltower of the Golden Hope monastery, pretty soon he'd find himself cutting into the side of the abandoned spur drain, which would lead him to the bricked-up junction with the main drain, and once he was there he could take his pick of a dozen or so wide, well-maintained access tunnels leading to the surface. Nobody would hear him digging, not that far down, and if he chose to emerge in, say, Cutlers Fields in the middle of the night with a thousand or so of his very best men, he could overwhelm the guards on the East Gate before they had a chance to raise the alarm and have the gates open before anybody could do anything about it.

The only problem he'd encounter (I went on) was about thirty feet of solid rock, which he'd bump into about a hundred yards from the junction with the main drain. Originally, I explained, the spur drain had bypassed this obstacle, going round it in a long, wide loop. But the loop section had caved in, taking several streets of houses with it, and was now comprehensively blocked. It would therefore be quicker and easier to cut through the original obstacle than muck about trying to clear the caved-in bypass, assuming you could even find it. Yes, I pre-empted him, cutting through thirty feet of rock is no small undertaking; but in an army of a hundred and twenty thousand men, surely he had skilled and experienced sappers who'd breeze through something like that as though it wasn't there. Yes, he admitted, he had, at that. There you are, then, I told him. And if you start your sap at the old tannery, under cover of the walls, and make sure you're discreet about it, anyone watching from the walls won't be able to see that you've got mining operations under way, and I won't be obliged to make life hell for you with catapults and trebuchets.

I wasn't there, having work to do, so I didn't see what happened. My guess is, something like this.

Soldiers, or Watchmen, banging on people's doors in the middle of the day. This is never good. Eventually, someone, probably the woman of the house (men are by nature very brave, except when it comes to opening doors to strangers) answers and says, What do you want? The soldiers tell her.

What the hell do you want that for, she says, not unreasonably.

The soldiers, with whom the reason has not been shared, shrug and say, Don't know, don't care, orders is orders. You got any or not? The woman says No. The soldiers say, You sure about that? Only, anyone says no, we got orders to search their place from top to bottom.

Come to think of it, the woman says. Wait there.

And she comes back a minute or so later with a pudding basin, a preserving pan, a jerry. The soldiers take them and put them carefully on their handcart. Will I get them back? the woman asks. The soldiers say thank you and move on to the next house.

An hour or so of foraging, and now we have about a thousand bowls, buckets, pans, basins, chamber pots. These are unloaded off the handcarts and placed carefully on the ground, a foot or so apart, all the way up Masons Alley, Portway, Key Street, Monksgate, Shambles, Potters Ground and halfway up Shepherds Walk. A bunch of Blues follow on with a two-wheeled bowser and buckets, filling each one two-thirds full with water. When they've finished they move on; their places are taken by Engineers, one man to a hundred buckets. For the next six hours, they walk up and down the line, staring at the buckets as though their lives depended on it.

It's a bit of a performance, but it works. Mining operations deep underground can't be seen or even heard, but they can be felt; the vibrations make the ground shake, ever so slightly. You may not be able to feel it, even kneeling down with the palms of your hands pressed flat on the deck, but water can. A very slight ripple on the surface of a wide enough pan will tell you where the tunnel is, and how fast the sappers are progressing. It's an old dodge – I got it out of a thousand-year-old book, tried it out just for curiosity's sake many years ago, tucked it away under the lining of my mind in case it ever came in useful. For some reason, people don't bother with the old books these days. More fool them.

About midday I went down to Poor Town to find out for myself. I'd put Genseric in charge of co-ordinating and correlating. He started me at Porters Yard, where the water was trembling like anything, then led me down New Alley, across the Old Flower Market and up Key Street, where I saw the faintest trace of ripples just starting to form.

Genseric was with me when I did my experiment, back when I was still a captain and he was a freshly minted second lieutenant. He could read the signs as well as I could. "It's massive," he said. "There must be hundreds of them down there."

"About a thousand, I'm guessing," I said.

"What the hell are they up to?"

I shrugged. "Don't ask me," I said.

I got the impression he couldn't understand why I was taking it all so calmly. "We'd better do something," he said.

I nodded. "Like what?"

Good question. "Countermine?"

I shook my head. "First you tell me where to start digging, and how far down you want me to go. No, we'll never find them."

"We can't just wait for them to come up somewhere."

"Actually," I said, "that's what I had in mind."

He gave me a bewildered look, then pulled a brass tube out of his sleeve. "Look at this," he said. "It's an old map, I found it in with some other junk in the Surveyor-General's office."

"That's a very old map."

"Here." He jabbed with his forefinger. "It's colour-coded, see. The red's all heavy clay, the blue's porous limestone and shale, the green is that crumbly yellow muck and the grey is your actual hard sandstone."

I made a show of orienting myself, though of course the map hadn't told me anything I didn't already know. "So right now we're standing on the grey."

He nodded. "One big solid blob of it," he said.

"Which they'll be running into," I said, "any minute now. That'll spoil their day, for sure."

I think he may have guessed that his map hadn't come as a complete surprise. "That's why you're not worried," he said.

"I admit, I knew that lot was there."

He gave me the might-have-told-me look, then prodded the map again. "What I can't make out," he said, "is what this line here means."

"Oh, that."

28

Some people have a talent for treachery. I'm not one of them, which surprises me, given how dishonest I fundamentally am. I think nothing of cheating, stealing, forgery, lies and deception. As I think I've already pointed out, I owed my promotion in the Imperial service almost entirely to my gift for getting hold of stores and supplies by any means necessary. Let's not beat about the bush: I'm as crooked as a mountain path. But treachery, no. I draw the line. Loyalty matters to me.

Which raises the question: loyal, but who to?

My emperor, my city, my people or my friend? What a choice to have to make.

The emperor was a vegetable; to all intents and purposes, practically speaking, I was the emperor. That is, I had his Seal. So we can forget about him, for now.

My city; not mine at all. There are substantial parts of it which I'm not allowed to go to; no milkfaces allowed. There are temples I can't go in, parks I can't enter, drinking fountains that would be polluted by the touch of my lips. I wasn't born here, and I'm not allowed to own a house or any real estate.

My people. My people are the Alauz, and if the truth be told I can barely remember them. Redefine people, therefore. My people are the Corps of Engineers and a few select friends, most of them blueskins. Or my people are those I have most in common with: the excluded, the oppressed, the have-nots and the not-allowed-to-haves, the worms of the earth (diggers, as Artavasdus pointed out, of exceptionally fine tunnels). But the Blues and the Greens resent me because I won't let them rip each other to shreds, and, besides, they don't care much for milkfaces either. Which leaves the other earthworms, such as the ones fifty feet under the soles of my boots, right now hacking into a massive ridge of sandstone with tools and resources I didn't have.

My friend. Well. That's my business.

"That," I told him, "is the River Tace."

"The what?"

"The River Tace. It's all right, you won't have heard of it. It's, what's the word, subterranean. It rises in the mountains on the east coast, runs directly through the middle of the hill under Hill Street, down across here, look, and eventually drains into Lake Patera, away down there somewhere. A hundred years or so back, it ate through all this clay here, flooded one of the subsidiary drains and undermined a large chunk of this part of town. The only thing holding it back, in fact, is that big lump of sandstone we're standing on. If it wasn't for that—"

He stared at me, then burst out laughing. I didn't laugh with him.

*

I saw it all happen, in the bowls of water.

First, a frantic shuddering, which I could feel through my boots, and water actually slopped out of the bowls onto the ground. Then steady rippling, all the way from Key Street to Porters Yard. Then nothing. Still, flat, motionless. All over.

If you're obliged to do something unpleasant, such as betray your people and your friend, you might as well get any collateral benefits that happen to be going while you're at it. So; when Ogus's men broke through the sandstone and unleashed the river, and it flooded their sap and drowned them all in probably less than a minute, the following good things came about.

One, I'd killed off my enemy's best sappers – skilled men, rare as hens' teeth among the less favoured races, because the Robur don't teach savages key skills like deep-level mining. The only way he'd be able to take the City would be by undermining the walls, for which he'd need trained, experienced miners, which he no longer had. No doubt he'd be able to replace them, but not quickly.

Two, an unlimited supply of fresh water, previously inaccessible because it was too far down, was now ours for the well-sinking. I'd known practically from the moment I took command that when, not if, the enemy broke down the aqueduct, we'd be in desperate trouble unless an alternative could be found. The Tace would do admirably, except that there was this impenetrable mass of sandstone in the way. To clear solid rock underground you need skills and equipment that we hadn't got. Wasn't it lucky that Ogus had both.

Goes to show, doesn't it, how clever I am – and how worthless. Oh, and let's not forget stupid. Nothing had changed. There were still a hundred and nineteen thousand enemy soldiers outside the wall; they wouldn't be digging their way in any time soon, but inevitably they would come, and they would win, and we would all die. I'd achieved precisely nothing. That's me all over.

"Right," I said, "there's nothing more for us here. Pack up all the crockery, I'm going back to the Palace."

Genseric looked at me. "I don't understand," he said. "What just happened?"

I looked at him, as if at a mirror. "Put it somewhere safe," I told him, "we'll be needing it again."

I was right about one thing. Next morning, all the pumps and fountains in the City ran dry. The enemy had cut the aqueduct. Panic.

Fortunately, the Corps of Engineers was on hand to save the day. Miraculously, the colonel of the regiment happened to have by him a map of the City showing where and how deep to sink wells; no trial boreholes or fooling about with hazel twigs, probably just as well since I can't ever remember seeing a hazel tree anywhere inside the walls. Eighteen hours after the pumps ran dry, the first bucket of water was winched up out of a well in Monksgate. It was an offputting sort of brown colour, but I gather they're used to that in Poor Town.

Goes without saying, wells in that part of the City weren't much use to respectable people. So it was handy that I'd recently made good use of an idle hour or so figuring out the shortest route for a pipe to connect up the new water to the main system, using the existing pumping stations. Took three days, during which time the honest citizens of Upper Town had to collect their water in jugs from bowsers and water carts. They took it in good part, even though they (or, rather, their servants) had to queue up in the midday heat. Look at us doing our bit, they said to each other, we're all in this together, and you don't smell too bad if you splash on plenty of scent.

Complicated feelings of guilt on my part. I've found over the years that I don't brood nearly so much if I'm occupied – not paperwork or supervising or marching around the place giving orders, but actually doing something with my hands – so I joined the work detail digging the trench for the new pipe. Nico didn't approve but Faustinus said that, actually, it was a good idea, leading by example, not afraid to get his hands dirty, all that; I tried to put that out of my mind in case it ruined the whole thing for me. I never was much of a one for digging, but someone had to cut and fit the timbers to prop up the sides. It was nice to find I could still saw a straight line and cut a mortice square by eye. Needless to say it came on to rain, and my clothes and boots got caked with mud. Somehow the miracle of water isn't quite so miraculous when you're standing up to your ankles in it, and it's running down the back of your neck.

We hit a few snags, needless to say. The City's been there a long time, and you never quite know what you'll run into when you start digging. At one point, we came up against stonework, some old building or other; marble, so it must've been quite grand in its day: they haven't built here in marble for six hundred years. But the sledgehammers dealt with all that quickly enough. Later I found out that we'd stumbled across the long-lost tomb of the First Emperor. It was supposed to be heaped up knee-deep in golden chalices, but we didn't find anything like that. My guess is, scholars and antiquaries from Poor Town had been there and discovered the site some time ago, but for some reason neglected to publish their results.

By the time we connected up with the main pipe we were

worn out and filthy. The sun had come out, caking the mud into the cloth, and, for once in my life, a casual observer might have mistaken me for a Robur. The hell with the dignity of labour, I thought. Nobody was watching, so I sloped off.

Victory Park – you probably know it as Bakers' Fields – is one of my favourite places in the City. Not many people go there during the day (don't go there at night, whatever you do) and you can wander along the avenues of poplars and almost forget you're in the heart of the capital of the world. I sat down on a stone block left over from some old building and tried to make sense of what I'd done, but it was all too confusing. I tried not to think of the poor devils – milkfaces – who'd been down there in the sap when the water broke through. It would've been quick; nobody can outrun a torrent of angry water, inside a tube, fifty feet under the ground. They'd have been scrambling, tripping, shoving and clawing at each other, but not for very long. We used to use the same method to deal with rats under the hay-barn; the lions of the Earth against the worms.

I looked at my hands; they were caked with mud, practically black. For some reason, that made me laugh out loud – if you can't beat them, and all that. But it was wrong of me to presume to an honour I could never achieve, so I wandered over to the fountain. It wasn't running, which puzzled me, until I remembered: no water, not until someone pulls up the manhole, climbs down into a hole, primes the fountain with a dozen or so strokes of the pump. So I did that; and, behold, water.

It's pretty stuff, and useful as well. I stood and watched it, tumbling and frothing. It can kill you, but there's no living without it. Ambiguous, you see, like pretty much bloody everything.

I remembered why I was there, and set to washing the mud off my face and hands. When I'd done that, I realised how thirsty I was, so I cupped my hands for a drink. At which point, a Parks and Gardens man came up. He wouldn't have recognised me, all scruffy and horrible.

"You," he said. "Yes, you. What do you think you're doing? Can't you read?"

He was pointing. There was a sign, a brass plate with white lettering; *Robur only*.

I opened my hands and let the water drop through them as though it was burning me.

"I'm so sorry," I said. "I promise, it won't happen again."

29

"Haven't seen you for a few days," she said.

She was looking better; different, but better. Something like that's bound to change you, even if everything still works the way it's supposed to. Henceforth her face would always be thinner, her chin narrower, her eyes deeper in her head. She didn't look quite so much like her mother any more.

"Been busy," I said.

"*Well?*" She looked round, lowered her voice. "When's it going to happen?"

"Already has," I told her.

She listened, without interrupting. Then, "You idiot," she said.

I shrugged. I wasn't in the mood.

"You bloody fool. What in God's name possessed you? Of all the stupid, thoughtless, *selfish* things to do—"

"Selfish."

"Too bloody right, selfish. You put your stupid morality ahead of saving my life. And the others, your friends. And it's all pointless. You said so yourself."

"Maybe," I said mildly.

"What's that supposed to mean?"

"I reckon I've improved our chances considerably," I said. "We've now got water, a secure supply, as much as we need. I killed God knows how many of their engineers, so they won't be in a position to start sapping for quite some time. So, not quite such a foregone conclusion as it might have been."

"Bullshit," she said. "You've just put it off, that's all. And you've pissed off your friend, so bang goes any chance of him telling his people to let us alone when the City falls. How could you do something like that? Don't you give a damn about anyone except yourself?"

30

"You've got to come right now."

I was getting sick of hearing that, ten or twenty times a day. But there was always the chance that it might really be something important, so I went. "This had better be good," I said.

The clerk looked at me. "It's a ship," he said.

Running isn't my thing, to be honest with you, though I imagine it could be if I was ever in a battle. But a ship— "Wait for me," I heard the clerk wailing behind me. Screw him, I thought. I ran.

Sure enough: an actual ship. It had been a long time since we'd seen one of those. It looked very strange and lonely out there on the North Quay, half a mile long, poking aggressively out into the Bay like a pointing finger.

I don't know spit about ships, but the harbourmaster told me it was a cog: a round, podgy sort of a ship, like half a walnut shell, with a single tall mast. "Not a warship," he explained, "a trader. This quay used to be crammed with them."

The crew were standing about on the quay, surrounded by Watch. I pushed my way through. "Who's in charge?" I said.

One man, no different from the rest, raised his hand. I gave him my big smile and a handshake. "Who the hell are you?" I asked. "And how did you get here?"

His name was Teldo, and he was from the island republic of Selroq, about twenty miles offshore from the Echmen border. The Selroq people aren't Echmen; they're too dark for milk-faces and too pale for Robur and nobody knows where they came from originally or how they ended up where they are now; nobody cares much, either. Their function in the great scheme of things is to be neutral, so that when the Robur and the Echmen are at war, which is nearly all the time, there's a safe, legal conduit for Echmen silks, copper and spices to be exchanged for Robur wine, olive oil, iron and dried stockfish. Selroq is tiny and nothing grows there; I believe there's one freshwater well on the island, which is plenty because everybody drinks wine. The whole island is covered with houses, shipyards and warehouses. Under normal circumstances we see a lot of the Selroquois, though we know so little about them. They bring us nice things we couldn't otherwise get, and they keep themselves to themselves. Whether a Selroq would be allowed to drink from the fountain in Victory Park is a moot point. I don't suppose one has ever tried. He'd have more sense.

"We didn't plan on coming here," Teldo said, wiping his lips with his sleeve. I poured him another drink. "The blockade, you see. Nobody's been able to get past it for weeks."

"There's a blockade," I said. "Well, we guessed it was something like that."

"There was a blockade," Teldo said. "But we got caught out in a freak storm out of the north-east, which blew us right down here – we were headed for Psammetica – and by the time we'd got control of the ship, we could see the Five Fingers. We were terrified."

The Five Fingers are a bunch of rocks about ten miles outside the Bay. You can't see them from here, because the south headland is in the way. "Go on."

"That's where the blockade's supposed to be," he said. "Forty Sherden galleasses, they've been stopping and sinking every merchantman that's tried to get in here. But they weren't there."

I frowned. "You mean you managed to slip past them."

He shook his head. "They weren't there. I don't know if the storm scattered them, or they've been recalled, or someone came and chased them away. It's not a case of slipping past them, if they'd been there it couldn't be done. Right now, for the time being at least, there is no blockade. Anybody who wants to can come and go as they please."

Artavasdus, who was duty officer, had given express orders to keep the arrival of the ship deathly quiet. In this town, not a hope. About an hour after I got there, the docks were crowded so you couldn't move; men and women and kids and handcarts. Artavasdus shut the gates and put a double cordon of Parks and Gardens men round them; a bit of a nuisance, because although they did a bang-up job of keeping people from getting in, it meant I couldn't get out. We made an announcement; there is no ship, go home. The crowd started to drift away around sunset.

The ship was fully laden, a hundred and twenty tons of cargo; bales of silk, barrels of cinnamon, pepper and nutmeg, crates of distilled essence of rosewater, exquisite pale blue eggshell-thin porcelain, jasmine tea, boxes and boxes of chessboards and ivory-backed mirrors and the world-famous and justly celebrated Echmen pornographic wall-hangings. Would you care to make me an offer for the lot, Teldo asked. No, I said. We don't want it. What we want is wheat, dried fish, bacon, cooking oil, lamp oil, hemp rope and arrows. Sorry, haven't got anything like that.

"Fine," I said. "Go away and get some, and I guarantee I'll make you rich. Same goes for all your friends and relations. It's the chance of a lifetime."

"But suppose the Sherden come back."

"Quite," I said. "If I were you, I'd go now. How soon can you go home, load up and get back here?"

"I'm not sure I want to."

"I quite understand," I said. "Your choice. But in that case, I'll impound your ship."

"You can't do that."

Which made me want to laugh. You can't do that, it can't be done. "I'm sorry," I said. "I don't like it myself. But compared to some of the truly appalling things I've done lately, stealing your ship barely registers."

I'd lost a friend. Story of my life. "In that case," he said, "we'll do as you say. We can be back here in five days, if we're lucky with the wind."

"Actually," I said, "you won't be going. You'll be staying here. That way, I can be sure your shipmates will do what you've just agreed to. They will, won't they?"

He shuddered. "Yes," he said. "Most of them are my family. They're decent people."

"They wouldn't like it here, then," I said, and poured him another drink.

*

"There could be all sorts of explanations," Nico said. He has an exceptional flair for the unhelpful remark. "We daren't make any assumptions."

Also, he's got a loud voice, and that precise, clipped Imperial blue-blood diction that means you can hear everything he says perfectly clearly half a mile away in a thunderstorm. "Not so loud," I told him. He looked puzzled, then guilty. It's a problem his sort have – the mighty, born-to-rule Great Families, I mean. All their lives, wherever they are – in the street, at home, probably squatting for a shit or screwing their wives, for all I know – they're constantly waited on and surrounded by a legion of servants. You couldn't live like that unless you taught yourself to believe that the lower classes are stone deaf. They aren't, of course; and yet Nico's lot never cease to be amazed that they can't keep a secret.

I wanted him to keep it down because we were standing on a scaffolding platform up against the wall in Canonsgate, watching fifty Greens and forty Blues pouring a mixture of water, quicklime, sand and pumice (you want to know the exact proportions? In your dreams) into a hole in the ground. To explain: the hole we were filling was the one Ogus's sappers had made, before I flooded them out. The weird mix is a recipe I came across in Tomae, right up in the frozen, godforsaken north; it's a sort of mortar, except that you can cast it, like bronze, to make slabs and pillars and whole floors – you make a wooden box out of planks and boards and fill it with the gloop, and when it goes off it sets hard as stone, even – now here's a miracle, if you like – underwater. I can only assume it's never caught on because you need pumice, which most people haven't got in any useful quantity. But we have; there's a vein of the stuff running right down the middle of North Hill, under Hill Street and out into

Old Castle. If ever I get out of the military, I'll make my fortune with the stuff. You could build whole cities out of it, and never have to shape another stone block or lay another brick.

Secrecy – sorry, I got sidetracked there – because the rumours about a ship suddenly appearing out of nowhere had spread across town like the plague, and people were getting excited. Ships meant a way out of the City before the savages broke in, and I still had a double guard posted outside the docks gate, which was still firmly closed and bolted. Ships were therefore not something I could be heard talking about in public, especially not with ninety-odd Themesmen straining to catch every word I said.

"You must have some idea," Nico went on, in what he thought was a whisper. "You talked to the man. What did he say?"

"I told you," I said. "His ship got blown off course, and where he expected to find the blockade, there was nothing. That's all I know."

"Makes no sense," Nico said. "Mind you, it begs the question. If they've got ships for a blockade, why haven't they tried to attack us by sea?"

You think you know people. He said it like it had only just occurred to him. I'd been losing sleep over it since about Day Two of the siege. I'd assumed he'd thought of it, too, and we hadn't discussed it because it was too depressing. Still; good question.

31

"It's obvious," she said. She was feeling a lot better. They'd propped her up with about a million cushions in a gold-leaf chaise longue that used to belong to the Empress Theophano. I didn't tell her that, of course; it'd have given her the horrors. "How many Sherden ships did you say you saw at Classis?"

"Seventy odd."

"Well, then. That's probably how many ships they've got. Plenty for a blockade of the Bay, if you stand out beyond the Five Fingers, and of course you wouldn't dare come in any closer because of the evening currents—"

I had no idea what she was talking about. Sailor stuff, of which I know nothing. "Of course," I said.

"But hopeless for an invasion," she went on regardless. "Seventy ships carrying twenty marines, that's fourteen hundred men. To capture and hold the whole of the docks. That'll be why."

That was roughly what I'd come up with on Day Three, hence my ability to get at least some sleep. "I'd figured there must be a blockade," I said, "because of no ships coming in, and I guessed we couldn't see them because it's too dangerous to hang about in the Bay itself. I don't know why, but I gather it just is."

"It's all to do with the rip tide and the undertow off Start Point, which means that when the tide turns mid-morning coming in from the west—"

"Yes," I said. "Quite probably. And I thought, sooner or later they'll have repaired that bloody lighthouse, and the Fleet will be able to get back here, and – well, I didn't bother thinking past that, because as soon as the Fleet gets here, I hand over command to whoever's in charge of it, I'm off the hook and none of it's my problem any more. But time's gone on, and no Fleet."

She frowned. "If I was them," she said. "Sorry, if I was your pal Ogus, the first thing I'd do is get hold of that lighthouse and make bloody sure it's out of action and beyond repair."

I nodded. "I think we can assume he did that. And likewise, it's a certainty the Fleet's been trying to take it back. I've never been there so I don't know the geography, but I'm guessing the Imperials built it there precisely because it was safe from an attack from the sea." I looked at her. "Which doesn't shed any light on anything really, does it?"

She doesn't give up that easily. "Possibility," she said. "The Fleet's broken through, and the Sherden have been called off the blockade to stop them."

"No chance," I told her. "The Sherden against the Fleet? They wouldn't do it. And if they did, they wouldn't last five minutes, the Fleet would be here by now. Stand-up fighting against a superior enemy isn't the Sherden way. Or an inferior enemy, come to that."

"All right," she said. "Possibility. The blockaders got messed up by the same storm that blew those traders off course."

I nodded. "That's a good one," I said. "And, as we all know, I don't know sailor stuff from a hole in the ground. Even so. If a nasty big wind blew the Selroqois off their line into the Bay, wouldn't it also have blown the blockaders in here, too? Or can a storm have two nasty big winds blowing in two opposite directions at once? I honestly don't know, it's too technical for me."

She glared at me. "Good point," she said. "All right, possibility. The Sherden are the only ships Ogus has, and he needed them for something somewhere else."

"Distinct possibility," I said. "Such as?"

"It could be anything." She scowled at me. "If you'd had half a brain, you'd have asked him when you had the chance."

32

As a matter of fact—

I hadn't told her about that part of the conversation. I've been making arrangements for a big push, he said, on the off-chance you wouldn't listen to reason. But I won't have to bother with all that now.

Big push?

He nodded. We just cleared the blueskins out of Leuctra Opuntis, so that's another thirty thousand men available. Also, we had a stroke of luck there.

That was all he said. But I'm in the trade; I know that Leuctra Opuntis is where they store most of the siege equipment captured from the Echmen in the last war, or the war before that. You'll have grasped the significance. All government-issued equipment has to go through Classis. But stuff looted from the enemy isn't our-government issue. A canny provincial general would therefore make damn sure he got hold of it and kept it safe, to be sure of having it to hand if he ever had need of it, rather than going through channels. And the Echmen; they're rotten soldiers or we wouldn't keep beating them, but they're a long way ahead of us – don't tell anyone I said this – when it comes to making things. Trebuchets, a case in point. It stood to reason, therefore, that Ogus's stroke of luck was a cache of state-of-the-art siege equipment, which some fool had neglected to soak in lamp oil and set light to when the savages started coming over the wall. From what I'd heard about the stores squirreled away in Leuctra, seventy Sherden ships would need to make several journeys to shift it all. Something to look forward to.

That, in my experience, is the way life works. Things tend to come in linked pairs of opposites. Thus, a heaven-sent chance to stock up on supplies, hand in hand with the prospect of heavy plant and equipment which would kill us all.

Faced with something like that, the sensible man thinks at right angles. Ships, or at any rate, a ship comes to the City laden with wheat. It unloads, and is empty. Of rather more interest, in the wider scheme of things, is not what the ship can bring into the City but what it could take out of it. Me, for instance. Or, if I'm hell-bent on being noble, the people I care for.

Then I stop and think a bit more. Aichma; who else? Nico and Faustinus and Artavasdus; for a start, they probably wouldn't go. Question: my friends? Define friend. And any meaningful definition of friend, applied in my case, probably wouldn't include them, but would definitely apply to Ogus; my old friend, my mate, my pal. And if I'd wanted to save my friends, or, to be more accurate, my friend's daughter and my colleagues, I had a splendid opportunity, which I pissed on. The difference being, in order to save my pals by taking up Ogus's offer, I'd have had to betray the City. Putting them on a ship to Selroq wouldn't have the same unpalatable consequences.

I was still agonising over that when the ship came back: alone, just the one ship, but riding dangerously low in the water because of its weight of cargo.

"Of course," I said, as they unloaded, "you'll want paying for all this."

Teldo, a much-enduring man I'd treated very badly, gave me a sour look. "You don't have to," he said. "You could just take our stuff and not pay for it, just like you kidnapped me."

"I'm sorry you see it that way," I said. "and of course you'll get paid." I glanced down at the manifest. It was short and to the point. One hundred and fifty tons of wheat, in sacks. If his brothers and cousins had paid more than six hundred stamena for it, they didn't deserve to survive in business. "Five thousand stamena, " I said. "Fair?"

He opened his mouth, then closed it again. Amazing how simple arithmetic can change your world view. "All right," he said.

"Of course," I went on, "we can't give you actual coins."

"What?"

"Sadly, no. But instead I'll give you a letter of credit guaranteed by the Imperial treasury and bearing the Great Seal. Every bit as good as gold, if not better."

He looked as though I'd just pulled out his front teeth. "Fine," he said. "That'll have to do, then."

"Alternatively—"

It's how I do things. First, despair. Then hope.

I took him for a tour round the Palace – the ground-floor rooms and the library – followed by the Council Chamber, the Golden Chapel of the Blue Feather monastery, the Scriveners' Guildhall, a few other places like that. City people see these places every day. If they even notice the icons, the triptychs, the altarpieces, the tapestries, the incunabula, the iconostases, all they see is a vague, familiar blur of gold and bright colours; they don't stop and think, just how much is all that lot *worth*?, because of course it's not for sale. Nobody bothers stealing it, because who in his right mind would buy it? We have tons, literally tons, of the stuff; painted wood, mostly, you can't melt it down or hammer it into sheets. But in Echmen, where the Selroqois do so much of their business, or further east still, where the silk and the jade come from, giving evidence of great and prosperous realms governed by men of exquisite taste – and entirely legal, with a bill of sale and a provenance, and each piece guaranteed unique . . .

Worth risking a blockade for, even.

He looked at me, wild-eyed. "You're sure," he said, "this stuff is yours to sell."

"Absolutely," I said. "I hold the Great Seal. I can do what I damn well like."

So much better than gold, which is heavy; the most a little Selroqois cog could carry would be a hundred and twenty, hundred-thirty tons. But the Ascension of the Golden House – egg tempera on lime boards, thirty-one inches by twenty-seven, weight one pound nine ounces; plenty more where that came from . . .

"And all you want is wheat," he said.

"Wheat and arrows. A few thousand bowstaves would be nice."

He looked at me the way the male spider gazes at his beloved. He knows he's going to get eaten afterwards, but it'll be worth it. "Deal," he said.

*

"You can't," Faustinus said. He was almost in tears. "You can't do it. It's unthinkable."

"Don't tell me what I can and can't think," I said.

"You can't do it, Orhan. No, listen." He was beside himself with fury. "Those paintings are the soul of this city. Let them go and you may as well burn the place to the ground."

"I beg to differ," I said. "I think the soul of the City is the people who live here. But they won't live much longer with nothing to eat. No, you listen. Have you been to the stores lately? It may be all right now, just about, but fairly soon it'll be pretty desperate. And people aren't fools. They know as well as you and I do, what we had stored before the enemy came won't last forever. Do you really want corn riots, on top of everything else?"

Usually you can shut him up with stuff like that. He's terrified of the common people, afraid he'll wake up one morning and find them standing over his bed, ready to eat him. But not this time. "I don't give a damn," he said. "Your precious Blues and Greens aren't the empire, they just live here. In a hundred years' time nobody will remember their names. But the Golden House Ascension is probably the supreme achievement of the human race, and it belongs here. And if you think—"

I looked at him, and he trailed off. "Actually," I said, "I agree with you. Which is why, if the Selroqois didn't want to trade wheat for it, I'd beg them to take it for nothing."

"You what? Are you mad?"

"No, you are. You'd leave it, and all the other really precious stuff, for the savages to smash up and burn. They won't care about *art*, Faustinus. As far as they're concerned, it's Robur, so they'll kill it. Which is why it's got to go somewhere safe."

That shut him up.

"And, if we survive this," I went on, "we'll save up our pennies for a hundred years and we'll buy it all back. But it'll still be there, even if we aren't. It won't have gone up in smoke. What do you take me for, Faustinus, a barbarian?"

Simple as that.

33

Three days later, there were seventeen Selroqois cogs in the Bay.

No point trying to keep it a secret. I had all the Watch and the Parks and Gardens guarding the docks gate, but they weren't much use. For one thing, I had a lot of difficulty trusting them not to leave their posts, charge the quay, steal the ships and sail away in them. But the crowd of desperate would-be refugees outside the docks was huge and dangerous. People were getting trampled to death. It wouldn't be long before they figured out that the Watch wouldn't use their weapons if they made a concerted attack on the gate with a battering ram. You've got to do something, Faustinus said, useful and resourceful as ever.

I knew what I had to do. But I was damned if I was prepared to do it.

But they didn't know that. So I gave orders for five of the catapults on the dockyard watchtowers to be turned round to face the crowd.

It takes a while to turn a catapult. You run a pair of long levers into iron hoops driven into the sides of the carriage. Then, of course, you've got to chock up the back end to get the reverse elevation. Enough people had relatives and friends who did shifts on the wall to recognise what was going on. It didn't take long for the noise to die away. Instead, there was the most appalling silence. But they weren't moving.

It was going to be an absolute disaster as and when they did move, of course. Ever seen a really big crowd break up in a panic? It's not like they're trying to hurt each other, they simply don't have a choice. Someone pushes, someone else overbalances, falls against someone else; now there's people on the ground, people tripping over them, boots landing on faces, bodies piling up, weight beyond the tensile strength of arms and ribs and skulls. Query whether the catapults could do significantly more damage, or even as much. I realised I'd just made a catastrophic mistake. Just as well there was time to undo it.

"Turn the bloody things back again," I yelled.

I think the crews were only too happy to oblige. And then it occurred to me that I might just have done a clever thing by accident. Sheer fluke; but I'd managed to shut them up, which meant I'd be able to make myself heard.

I don't have a loud voice and I don't like shouting. This, though, wasn't something I could delegate.

"Ladies and gentlemen," I yelled, and remembered to pause, give the words time to get there. "God knows you've tried my patience, but I've decided not to shoot you after all. But what I will do, if you don't disperse quietly and sensibly, is give the order to those catapults to sink the ships in the Bay. We haven't unloaded all the food yet, so most of it'll be wasted, but please understand this. If we can't all go, nobody goes. And if anybody so much as leans on this gate, so help me I'll scuttle those ships so fast it'll make your head swim. Thank you for listening."

I've done some bloody stupid things in my time, but I reckon that has to be the prize exhibit in the collection. If one voice had shouted or one hand had thrown a stone, I don't believe the entire Imperial army, at full strength in its glorious heyday, could've kept them from sweeping away the gates and crushing my soldiers underfoot like snails. What can I say? I got away with it, and it worked. When the crowd had thinned out by about four-fifths, I sent out stretcher parties to pick up the poor devils who'd got trodden on. There wasn't a lot we could do for most of them. Just think of what could have happened, and judge me accordingly.

I was still shaking like a leaf, but I had to get those ships unloaded and on their way quickly, before my fellow citizens realised they'd been tricked and came back to tell me what they thought about that. Maybe presumptuously, I'd had half the public buildings in the City surreptitiously looted of their moveable artwork; we had it all stacked up in a big warehouse on Quay Six, and thank God there wasn't a fire. I'd have liked to take my time showing those Selroqois round and screwing them to the wall for the best possible deal. As it was, we more or less shovelled artworks into their outstretched arms until they couldn't carry any more, then sent them on their way. As it was they missed the evening tide, but I insisted they stand out to sea so that at least they were out of sight from anywhere in the City. And please come back, I added, as quickly as you can.

"Sure," said one of them. "If you think you can handle the trouble that'll cause. Were you actually prepared to launch stones at your own people?"

"No, of course not."

"Mpm," he nodded. "How about us? Would you have sunk us, like you said?"

"Don't be ridiculous," I told him. "I need you."

Not long afterwards, Artavasdus asked me the same two questions. I answered yes to both. I'm not good with the truth. I guess I just want people to like me.

The next ship that sailed into the Bay wasn't Selroqois, and it wasn't bringing wheat. It was Sherden, and they unloaded their cargo into a small boat, which they cast adrift so that the early morning tide could bring it ashore. I was sent for.

Inside the boat, packed in wicker hampers, was a considerable number of human heads. Some of them I recognised: they were the Selroq merchants I'd talked to the last time, and members of their crew; most likely their brothers and nephews and cousins, trade being a family business on Selroq. Others were new to me. I imagine they were other members of the mercantile community, eager to cash in on a very good thing while it lasted.

Pinned to one hamper was a note. Nobody could read it; hardly surprising, since it was in Alauzet, written in Jazygite script. *We ought to talk.* Ah, I thought.

Goes without saying, nobody had any paper, or ink, or a pen. Someone found me a thin bit of charcoal from a brazier. I scrawled on the back of the note, then called for a volunteer; five stamena for anyone who'll row out to that ship and give them a letter.

I had my pick of three. Never ceases to amaze me, the insane things people will do for money.

It had been good while it lasted. The granary wasn't exactly full, but at least we couldn't see those distressing patches of bare floor any more. We'd also picked up a quarter of a million arrows, which really isn't that many when you come to think of it.

You have to pay for everything in this life, however, and the food and the arrows cost me any popularity I may have had in the City, even with the Themes. Arrasc and Bronellus were still talking to me, though they insisted on having witnesses present, and the work was still getting done. But Lysimachus – he still liked me, and I was still terrified of him – lost no opportunity of warning me not to go here or there where I'd felt safe walking alone all my life, because I'd be bound to be recognised and torn to pieces by the mob. The Watch and the Parks and Gardens were livid with me because I'd nearly put them in the position of having to launch bouncing stone balls into a street packed solid with women and children. The Engineers were still on my side, though they reckoned I'd lost the plot recently. The sections of society who'd always hated me – the House, the civil service, the mercantile and commercial sectors – hated me more than ever. I tried not to let it bother me, with indifferent success.

So what? We still had the wall, and superior artillery (for the time being), and plenty of good water and a certain amount of food – enough to last the rest of our lives, if I was right about the captured Echmen siege machines, but we'll come to that in a minute. My Engineers had been renamed the First Imperial Regiment of Archers; we'd kept the bows and arrows for ourselves, on the grounds that archers are further away from the enemy than other troops, and we wanted to put as much distance between ourselves and those murderous bastards as we possibly could. And, being engineers, they'd figured out how to use a bow, practised, tried a few modifications to bracing height and fletching configuration, added a few new skills to their repertoire. They weren't good archers, but they were competent, and an overwhelming improvement on what we'd had before, which was nothing at all. Meanwhile, there were basins and buckets on every street corner. True, the general public used them for purposes other than those intended, but since that tended to increase rather than decrease the amount of fluid the containers contained, why the hell not?

I'd found an interesting book in the military science section of the abbot's library at the Blue Spire monastery. It was very old and very depressing; *Notes on Siegecraft*, it was called, and chapter thirty-six was about how you capture an otherwise impregnable city by undermining the walls.

Hardly catapult science; but you need an awful lot of men, materials and time. You start to dig well beyond the maximum range of the defenders' best artillery. For most of the distance between your lines and the wall, you needn't go down terribly far; an open trench about ten feet deep will do just fine, but you don't drive it straight at your objective, because a skilled artilleryman could drop a shot into the trench, squash your sappers and probably collapse a section of the works. No, you follow a zigzag line, and you pile up the spoil you've just dug out on the side facing the wall. Your soft, crumbly earth stops projectiles rather better than stonework or brick, which are stiff and fragile and prone to shatter into clouds of flying splinters. A stone hitting a bank of earth is cushioned, it sinks into the soft bank, maybe scatters it a little, but causes relatively little incidental damage by way of shrapnel. If you can be bothered (and Ogus undoubtedly could) you line the outside your bank with big wicker baskets filled with sand, to keep the heaped-up dirt from sliding down and leaking out if it takes a hit, or if it rains. To speed the digging there are a number of handy mechanical aids, most of them Echmen in origin. There's a giant screw mounted on a frame like a battering ram, for boring through heavy clay. There's cranes for shifting the spoil and carts that run on rails, hauled back down the trench by a relay of winches, to save you having to lug the stuff about in baskets. There's a thing like a colossal bellows on wheels, for blasting a jet of hot flame – if you run into solid rock, you heat it up real hot with the bellows gadget, then douse it down with cold water or (for some reason, not explained) vinegar; the rock splits, and you can get in there with crowbars and big hammers and break it up small enough to shift. When you're two hundred yards or so from the wall – that is, still comfortably outside arrowshot – you start to dig deep. Ideally you want to go down as far as the wall is high. When you reckon you're directly under it, you dig a big chamber, which you stuff full of dry brushwood. This you soak with oil and set alight. The fire burns through the pit props supporting the tunnel; the tunnel collapses; the earth on top of the tunnel is displaced and falls down to fill the chamber, displacing the ground above it, on which rests the heavy, rigid wall. Result: the wall cracks up and subsides into the hole, leaving a sprawling heap of rubble, over which your shock troops can climb into the city. Simple as that.

Chapter thirty-seven is much shorter. It tells you what you can do to defend your city from sappers. You need to figure out or find by trial and error where the enemy tunnels are; then you dig tunnels of your own to undermine or intercept them. If you can bring the roof down before they reach your wall, splendid. If you can break into their tunnel, from the sides or above, you can send in your soldiers, or light fires of damp hay, so that the backdraught will suck the smoke down into the enemy's working, or – and here, I think, the author was letting himself get carried away – you can turn loose wolves or bears or even lob in a couple of dozen beehives, then seal up the breach as fast as you can. But mostly what you can do, and are advised to do, is surrender. The trick is to time your capitulation just right. Not too early, or he'll know you're scared and strike a viciously hard bargain. Not too late, or by that stage he's nearly there, so why bother to negotiate. But time it perfectly, and he'll give you good terms rather than waste time, lives and money. He may let you leave with what you can carry, or leave but empty-handed, or let the civilians out with a few possessions but the soldiers stay, or maybe he'll kill the soldiers but sell the civilians; it all depends on the circumstances of the case, the skill of the negotiators, the level of malice so far generated and the timing of the offer. There's even a handy chart, to help you do the calculations. One thing, however, always happens, regardless of the other terms of surrender. The defending king, general, governor or garrison commander is handed over and slowly executed. That's a given, and non-negotiable.

Thanks ever so much for that, I thought, and put the book back where I'd found it.

I lent Nico the book. He read it and gave it back to me. "Well?" I said.

"Well," he replied, "obviously we haven't got any wolves or bears. Under normal circumstances we could get some from Garia or somewhere like that, like we do for the Spring Games, but if the blockade's back, that's out of the question. But what we could do is round up a load of stray dogs and not feed them for a week, and then turn them loose. What do you reckon?"

Ye gods. Sometimes I think he lives in a world of his own.

34

I was racking my brains trying to figure out how Ogus would get a message to me, replying to mine saying, yes, let's meet. His spy's carrier pigeons had long since gone in the pot (not bad, actually; a bit stringy, perhaps) and he hadn't mentioned any other resources of his inside the walls. I needn't have worried. My trouble is, I think sly and furtive, which comes of having a fundamentally dishonest nature. Ogus thinks on a grand scale, as befits a conqueror.

He sent an ambassador: a pleasant enough old boy, dressed in monks' habit, complete with hood and cowl. His arrival puzzled me, because I knew for a fact there was nothing to talk about; and so it proved. We had him in and sat him down in the throne room of the Palace; me, Faustinus, Nico, the Theme bosses. I was waiting for him to slip me a message on a scrap of paper, and hoping to God he wouldn't be too obvious about it. Given my disastrous slump in esteem, the last thing I wanted was for anyone to suspect that I was in secret communication with the enemy; difficult, since I wanted to be just that. But no, nothing of that sort. We sat on one side of a big rosewood and ivory table, he sat on the other. He demanded our unconditional surrender. We said no. He rephrased it. We said no, again. This went on for a bit – that man had a remarkable gift for saying the same thing in different ways – and then it was obvious we weren't getting anywhere, and he got up to leave. As he did so, his hood, which he'd kept up all the time we'd been talking, slipped sideways, while he was facing me but not the others. Then he put the hood back up again, thanked us politely for our time, and left.

That's what I mean about doing things in the grand manner. On the old boy's tonsured head were tattooed – not just written on, but actually pricked and inked into the skin – a few well-chosen words, written in Alauzet using the Jazygite script. Anyone seeing them – almost anyone seeing them – would've taken them for some of the weird stuff monks get decorated with if they've been particularly good or clever; mystic runes and cabalistic sigils and whatever.

That's the difference, I guess, between my old pal and me. I would never be able to bring myself to believe that any scheme of mine was important enough to justify some poor innocent going around for the rest of his life with the words *Lead a sortie against the ram and get captured, your safe return guaranteed* indelibly carved into his scalp. For Ogus, I feel sure, it was just a chance to get his message across and show off at the same time.

What ram? Oh, that ram.

It was a beauty. The moment I saw it, I wanted one. The next moment, my blood ran cold. It was a magnificent piece of engineering and construction, but it was headed directly for my gate, and if it got there we wouldn't stand a chance. Then I remembered, it wasn't supposed to.

Indulge me, though, and let me tell you about it. When the Echmen – nobody else could have designed or made something like that – built it, they'd addressed all the problems I'd thought of and reckoned to be insuperable and brushed them away like flies. Direct hit from a catapult? Surround it with a stout frame covered with stitched-together hides and padded like a cushion. Same principle as the dirt banks; don't resist the impact, dissipate it. Brilliant. The sixty-strong team of oxen needed to move the thing vulnerable to arrows? Padded jackets for them, too – covered from nose to tail, I kid you not, in quilted armour of a quality the Imperial guard never aspired to. All right, what about a direct hit on the oxen with a catapult stone, squashing them flat and shattering the yoke boom? Simple; have ten more teams of oxen standing by, plus a quick-release connection so you can uncouple the smashed yoke and couple up the new one faster than you could say it – the spare teams protected, of course, by huge wooden pavises the size of warship sails, mounted on wheeled limbers. The pavises alone would be enough to give you nightmares; they'd stop arrows and almost certainly slow down my horrible bouncing stone balls. The ram itself was a straight oak trunk about fifteen yards long, with a bulbous tip that was almost certainly bronze filled with lead. There was a marvellous-looking winch arrangement on the back, so that a relatively small crew protected by shielding could wind the thing up and let it go without being exposed to arrows from the ramparts. I couldn't begin to tell you how much the whole thing must have cost; more than my entire Engineers' budget for a decade, and then some. If ever I get the chance, I'm definitely going to go and work for the Echmen. Those people must really appreciate fine engineering.

Even if I hadn't seen the writing on the ambassador's head,

I'd have ordered a sortie; it was the only way of stopping the monster. Trust Ogus to make it all delightfully plausible for me. His note hadn't said whether we'd be allowed to stop and destroy his wonderful gadget; the implication was that, yes, we had his permission, because if we didn't it'd complete its mission and crunch the gate into kindling. Typical Ogus. He always was generous with his toys.

"What we need to do," Nico said beside me, and his voice wasn't as steady as it might be, "is dig a sap, quick, right in front of the gate. Then, when that thing rolls on top of it, its own weight will cave in the sap and it'll fall through and break its back."

I was impressed. Hadn't thought of that. "Don't be stupid," I said, "there isn't time."

He gave me a sad look. "You're quite right," he said. "Sorry."

"Put our lads on the wall with their bows," I said, "and get me the hundred best Blues. We're going to have to go out there and smash it."

"A sortie? But that's—"

"Yes," I said. "But your idea's stupid and I can't think of anything. What does that leave?"

He nodded, the minimum movement to convey agreement. "I'll go," he said.

"Like hell you will. I need you here. I'll go."

"With respect—"

"Quiet." I hadn't meant to yell at him. "Stopping it and killing the crew won't be enough, we've got to pull it down and break it. Engineering. You stay here and be a soldier, like you always wanted."

I'd hurt his feelings. "Of course," he said, and ran off to organise the sortie. But naturally I couldn't let him go, he'd never come back, and neither would most of the poor bastard Blues. And if they did supremely well and proved themselves true heroes and killed the monster, it really wouldn't signify worth a damn, since the whole performance was just an irrelevance, a show put on because Ogus couldn't trust me to have myself lowered over the wall in a laundry basket at midnight without getting caught. I reckon the way you go about doing things says a lot about the sort of man you are. I'd never have thought up something like that in a million years. Which explains why Ogus, not me, was leading the great crusade against the forces of darkness, and why I was trying to stop him.

35

It was a shambles. My fault. We came running out in a sort of shield-wall configuration – running isn't my thing, as I think I may have mentioned – but they'd got about a hundred archers tucked away behind those bloody pavises, and we ended up kneeling in the dirt behind our shields, pinned down and not daring to move. Which would probably have worked out fine in the end – we could have surrendered, thereby achieving the object of the exercise while avoiding all the mess and bloodshed – except that bloody Lysimachus suddenly jumped up and led a charge, howling at the top of his voice. Lysimachus is a Green and the rest of them were Blues, so by rights they should have stayed put and let him get shot to bits; I don't know. Maybe it was the shame of being outmachoed by a Green, there's no accounting for idiotic heroics when you're dealing with Theme fighters. Anyway, there was a terrific yell and off went all five hundred of the fools, leaving me kneeling there in the dust all on my own.

About seventy of them didn't make it; the rest covered the

distance to the ram in an amazingly short time, followed not that much later by me, gasping for breath and thinking I was about to die. Lysimachus was already halfway up the side of the ram, running up it like a rat up a curtain. Whoever those poor devils were on the ram, it was clear they hadn't signed on to face dangerous lunatics like Lysimachus. They shot at him until he got close, then they scrambled down a convenient ladder and scampered away like rabbits. I think he managed to catch two, but the rest got away. Still, you can't have everything in this life.

A second or so later, fifty-odd Blues were swarming all over the ram, making ropes fast to beams and throwing the ends down. The ram itself sheltered them from the archers behind the pavises, and we still had enough manpower to haul on the ropes and topple the ram; which we did. For a moment I thought the padding would keep it from breaking up when it fell, but the leverage was too good. The thing was twice as tall as it was wide; its own weight tore the tenons out of the mortices, and it came apart like a stack of firewood. Victory, in the face of insuperable odds, and I hadn't been captured. Don't you hate it when that happens.

Time was running out. I looked round for some way of separating myself from the rampantly triumphant Blues without being obvious about it or getting shot, but I couldn't see anything. The Blues were drenching the trashed woodwork with oil; someone yelled at me, "Time to go". He was grinning happily. This is ridiculous, I thought. Then the pavises in front of me slid aside, and out came a half-company of heavy infantry, running straight at me.

I heard the Blues shouting; then something dashed past me and knocked me off my feet. By the time I'd scrambled to my knees, Lysimachus had hurled himself at the locked shields of the advancing heavies. He leapt into the air, kicking hard with his left foot and battering down a couple of shields; then he was through, the line was broken. The snatch squad surged on past him as though he didn't matter. Then he broke through them from behind, scattered their line, stumbled, fell forward onto his face. A spear stuck up between his shoulders like the mast of a ship.

Someone grabbed me and pulled me up. I took no notice. I was staring at Lysimachus, dead on the ground, being trodden on. They dragged me towards him, over him, my foot on his head; I think I turned my ankle on it. Loads of yelling behind me, fighting noises; two men were frogmarching me toward the pavises, we passed them, they slid together behind us. There was a single riderless horse; they helped me up onto it. Nobody spoke. Someone gave the horse a slap, and it started forward. I nearly fell off but hands pushed me upright in the saddle. Then it was off at a brisk canter, with a man either side of me, running flat out, hanging onto the stirrup leathers. One of the men looked up at me, grinning. He said: "That was close. Who was that lunatic?"

I didn't answer. I hate people who can talk and run at the same time.

The first time I visited Ogus's tent, it was magnificent. Since then, he'd smartened the place up a bit. I don't know anything about art, so I couldn't say for sure, but I think the stunning altarpiece he'd set up behind his favourite chair was the Chrysostoma Transfiguration, which I seem to remember being the pride and joy of the abbots of Shasida, up in the frozen north-east. The three-quarter-size ivory figure of Our Lady in her aspect of the New Moon was definitely the one that used to stand in the atrium of the governor's mansion at Molan, because I saw it there ten years ago. The tapestries looked remarkably like the set I once saw on the walls of the Marshal's court at Spendone, way down south on the border. My guess is, they were trophies, like stags' heads. I don't think Ogus had them there because he liked looking at them.

"Hello, Orhan," he said.

I wanted to laugh. He was wearing the full outfit: the purple floor-length robe that only the emperor can wear, the criss-cross gold-embroidered sash, heavy as armour and to my mind unspeakably vulgar, the ermine cape and a really very good replica of the Triple Crown, except that the egg-sized uncut ruby in the middle of the central fleuret was, if anything, a mite too big. "Aren't you hot in all that lot?" I said.

He grinned. "A bit," he replied. "Beats me how your man can spend all day in this get-up. It's an hour's work to take a pee." He moved his fingers very slightly, communicating perfectly that I was allowed to sit. Never seen it done better, to tell you the truth. I stayed put.

"You promised," I said. "When we're done here, I can go back."

"Fuck you, Orhan." He scowled at me. "What, d'you think I'd break my word?"

I shrugged. "I did."

"Yes, well. Oh, sit down, for God's sake. Please?"

I sat down. The chair was four elephant tusks, with a seat of gold wire. Not, however, very comfortable. "Would you like me to say I'm sorry?" I said.

"Yes, but you aren't. Are you?"

"Actually, I am," I said. "I'm sorry because instead of just saying no, I'm not interested, I tricked you into sacrificing your best sappers and doing a job I needed doing that I couldn't do. That was dishonest."

"You're dishonest. I knew that."

"Did you think I'd betray you?"

He shrugged. "It was a distinct possibility," he said. "Let's say it didn't come as a total surprise."

"But you sent all those men to their deaths—"

"It was worth the risk," he said, and his face didn't move. "I knew I was asking a lot of you. I thought maybe what I'd said was enough to win you over. For that, I apologise. I should've known, you're too smart to be taken in by fine words."

"They weren't bad," I said. "Most of them I agree with."

He smiled. "I cheated," he said. "I hired a lawyer – well, half a dozen of them, actually, from Sozamen, you have no idea how much those vultures charge. I told them to prepare the case, then put it into my own words. You don't mind that, do you?"

"Why should I?"

"It struck me as a bit – well, you know. Getting other people to polish up my arguments for me. Making me look cleverer than I am."

"Did you use much of what they gave you?"

"Some of it. Didn't work, though, did it?"

I shook my head. "I'm not a court of law," I said. "I'm not bound to do what's just, or what's right, or what's in the interests of the human race. If I was, you'd be warming your hands by a nice big fire right now. But I'm not. And I reserve the right to be wrong, if I choose to be."

He laughed. "When this is over," he said, "I want us to be together again. You can be joint emperor. You can rule the east, and I'll have the west."

"You mean, after you've burned down the City and killed all the Robur."

"That's right. By then you'll have made your point and I'll have made mine. I'd really like that."

"This is after I've opened the gates, like I promised you the last time."

"No." He waggled one fingertip, meaning serve the wine. But for me it was my favourite tea. "I can see now, I was wrong. Stupid of me. I should've known, I can't make you do what you don't want to. I shouldn't have tried. It wasn't the act of a friend. No, you crack on, make the best defence you can, I know how much it means to you to do your very best." They poured the tea. Just the smell of it was heaven. "On the way here, we passed that bridge you built, about eight years ago, over Hoar Water. I didn't know at the time it was one of yours, but soon as I saw it, I knew, Orhan built that. It was like meeting an old friend."

I couldn't remember which one he meant. I've bridged Hoar Water at least four times, but the bloody thing keeps flooding. "That's what I do," I said.

"Of course it is," said Ogus. "Well, there's ever such a lot of rivers in the world, needing bridges. Or cities. Ever fancied building one?"

"You're doing it again," I said.

"Sorry. But seriously, have you? I'll be needing a city, when all this is over. Will you build me one? Anywhere you like."

"Here?"

He looked at me. "If you insist."

"I'll think about it," I said. "What did you want to see me about?"

He sighed. "Just to tell you no hard feelings, I guess. It's been on my mind. Please build me a city. I've destroyed so many lately, it'd be nice to put something back."

"No hard feelings? Are you serious?"

"Of course. You're my oldest friend." He said it as though it didn't need saying. "The people in that city aren't your friends, Orhan. Which reminds me, did you sort out those bastards who were going to kill you?"

"Yes. Thank you."

"They weren't your friends, Orhan. But what the hell. I know you, you hate it when someone lets you win. It was always like that when we were kids, you'd sulk and be miserable all day. You need to know you actually won, or it's all spoilt for you."

Perfectly true. Of course, I never beat Ogus at anything, unless I cheated. Which I did, whenever I could. I figure, winning is winning. Cheating is just one of many ways of prevailing; just happens to be the way I'm best at.

"Like I said," he went on, "give it your best shot. Do it the hard way. Only, please don't get yourself killed. There's only so much I can do to protect you. And I will, of course. But don't make that hard for me, too."

"I won't, trust me," I said. "I'm a coward."

He laughed. "You're sensible. Not the same thing at all. Anyhow, the hell with this. How about a game of checkers with your old pal?"

We used to play checkers, with a set we'd made ourselves. I carved the pieces out of wood and bone. There had been times when I'd won. Guess how. "I should be getting back," I said.

"Don't be stupid. You've got to stay here a while. No, really, otherwise it's going to look pretty odd."

True. "How am I getting out of here, by the way?"

"Ah. You escape, naturally."

I scowled at him. "Talk sense."

"No, honest. Well, you're rescued."

"You what?"

He smiled at me. "By that pet ape of yours, Lysimachus."

"He's dead."

"Oh no he isn't. Strong as a bull. And that glued-cloth breastplate saved him. Never seen anything like it. Your idea, naturally."

Something I'd read in an old book. "Yes," I said.

"Brilliant. Anyway, we pulled him out and patched him up, he'll be a bit sore for a while but nothing serious. He's being guarded by a bunch of drunks who carelessly leave weapons lying about, and who happened to mention where you're being held. I think we can leave the rest to him, don't you? I mean, what's the point of having a hero if you don't make use of him?"

Lysimachus was alive, at any rate. "He nearly died."

"He'll be a hero, he'll like that. The girls'll be all over him."

"He doesn't like girls."

"Robur," he said, and clicked his tongue. "Ah well. Anyway, it's going to take him a while to get loose, so in the meantime we can stop talking business and act like human beings for a change. For a start, I'd really like you to meet someone."

I like to think I know what the person I'm talking to is going to say next. Not this time. "Who?"

"My wife."

Some things you just don't see coming. "Wife?"

"Yes, you idiot, my wife. My better half, the love of my life," he grinned. "I'm not exaggerating. I can't wait for you to meet her. She's gorgeous."

*

Other people's wives. The wife, for example, of my good, dear friend Aichmalotus, who died in the arena. I can't wait for you to meet her, he said.

I remember, all too clearly. She seemed like a nice woman; short, younger than he was, rather quiet and serious. We talked awkwardly for a while and then Aichmalotus was called away and there was one of those fraught silences. You feel uncomfortable alone with your best friend's wife, You want to be friendly, but you're on your guard; a man doesn't know what to say to a woman under those circumstances. Some men are like the good dog, that knows its job is to chase sheep but not these sheep, for some reason. I'm not a great chaser at the best of times. This is hardly surprising. I've spent most of my life as a milkface among Robur. First, it's illegal. Second, it's highly unlikely. Robur are taller, stronger, more muscular, finely built and toned. Even Faustinus is stronger than me. I'm used to thinking of myself as ugly, comical, misshapen, appropriate for other purposes but not *that*. Hard to get out of that way of thinking, even with a half-milkface woman who's shorter than me.

Anyway, after a while we had to start talking, before the silence set harder than mortar. We talked about being milkfaces in the City, about where we were from originally, about Aichmalotus – turned out she didn't actually like him very much (she didn't say that), but she'd married him because it was so much better than the alternative; why he was crazy about her she really had no idea, but he was, and so that was all right; most women, Robur women who'd had choices in their lives, at least at some stage, are put up with rather than loved; being loved, she said, made things easier, it was one of those irrational advantages, like being born rich or pretty, it meant life wasn't quite such a struggle, all the damned time. I wouldn't know, I said, then wished I hadn't. She looked at me, then said; no, I suppose not. Count yourself lucky, she said.

I wasn't quite sure what to make of that. You just said yourself, I said, it makes things easier.

True, she conceded, it does. But it's such a responsibility.

I confessed I'd never thought of it in that light. Like I said, she replied, you're lucky. By being loved, you're under an obligation. You've undertaken to still be there, tomorrow and the next day. When things get to the point where it's just plain stupid to carry on, you can't simply drink hemlock or open a vein. You're stuck. The ship's sailed away without you on it.

Strange conversation, I thought. I've never considered not carrying on, I told her.

You're very lucky, then, aren't you, she rebuked me, gently but firmly. Of course, you're a man, you get so many more choices and options than a woman does. You need to be a woman to understand the true meaning of being totally and hopelessly stuck. The closest you'd ever come would be if you got locked up in a cell for forty years.

I nodded slowly. And being loved is the gaoler, I said.

Probably just as well that Aichmalotus came back at that point. He was cheerful and smiling, having just been paid some money he'd never expected to see. I remember he brought her an apple.

So Ogus introduced me to his wife.

You've heard about trophy wives. She was more a triumphal arch; a monument, I guess, to how far Ogus had come and how far he still intended to go. Beautiful isn't the word. A few centuries back, when it was time for the emperor to choose a wife, they sent emissaries all through the empire rounding up girls, by the thousand, by the tens of thousands. These were sent on to regional centres, who weeded out the dross and referred the cream to Area Command, who sent up the top ten per cent to the provincial governor, who chose the best ten, who went on to Division headquarters; eventually, about five hundred made the trip to the City, where a House committee pared them down to two hundred, who were passed on to Special Commissioners, who selected seventy-five for the consideration of the Chamberlain's office, who picked out forty for the emperor to choose from. Ogus's wife would have sailed through to at least the Special Commission, unsightly skin condition nothwithstanding, and quite probably the Chamberlain.

I can't say I care much for beautiful people. I think I resent them. Beauty rather more so than other kinds of outrageous privilege. I've known a number of very rich men, and nine out of ten of them were bastards, but some of them had earned their wealth, which is supposed to make it better, and all of them could've lost it in a matter of hours. I've known rather more rich men's sons, and they're harder to take – but Nico's all right and so's Artavasdus, and when you get to know them you can learn to ignore the differences and focus on the things you have in common. Outrageously clever people are worse, but quite a few of them mean well, and often they tend to have disadvantages (of appearance, manner, social skill) that allow you to forgive them. Beautiful people, though, I struggle with. Unless you keep your eyes shut or look the other way, you can't help but have the awful fact ground into you, like the wheel of a heavy wagon running over your neck, that here is someone divided from you by a vast, unbridgeable gap, and they've done absolutely nothing to deserve it. Ogus's wife – her name was Sichelgaita – was that level of beauty. I won't even try to describe her, because they don't make words that could take the strain. You felt ashamed to look at her.

"So you're Orhan," she said. "I've heard ever such a lot about you."

Aichmalotus was a good friend to me. He passed the word along; this man may wear a uniform, but he's not one of them, he's one of us. Suddenly my life got easier. Things stopped disappearing from my stores. Civilian contractors finished early and under budget. I met interesting peeople at Aichmalotus's place, the sort of people who helped me turn government gold into useful and plentiful silver, who could get me stuff I couldn't get elsewhere, at a price I could afford. Suddenly, there were people in the City who didn't seem to mind the fact that I didn't look right. As a direct result, I was able to get things done; getting things done got me promoted; I became the colonel of the regiment. I spent a lot of time at Aichmalotus's place. Whenever I was in the City, he insisted I stayed with him, wouldn't hear of me lodging at an inn or guest quarters at the barracks. His work called him away, and I was left at home with his wife. She was a pleasant enough woman and I think she liked to have company.

Sometimes, she told me, I have this dream. I'm watching him fight in the Hippodrome. And then suddenly I'm down there and I'm the one fighting him. And I try and explain, I'm not a gladiator, I'm a woman, women don't fight, but I'm wearing this helmet that muffles my voice and nobody can hear me. So I try and tell him, it's me in here, it's me, but he can't hear me either. And he keeps stabbing and slashing at me, and somehow I manage to block him but I know it's only a matter of time. And also I'm up in the stands, cheering him on. I want him to win, even though I know perfectly well who's under that helmet. And then he drops his guard for a split second and I can see a gap, and I draw back my hand to stab him, even though I know that if he dies, I die, too.

And? I asked.

That's when I wake up, she said. And then I lie there, listening to him breathe, and gradually the dream fades away, but I feel like I've done something really bad, something horrible.

I seem to remember saying something, I have no idea what. I hate him, she said, I wish he was dead. You don't mean that, I told her. He's not a bad man really, he's my friend. You sleep with him then, she said.

Is that the problem, I asked. Not that it's any of my business. Part of it, she said. He makes my skin crawl, like a spider on your face.

Ogus's Sichelgaita wasn't just a pretty face. I'd done my old pal an injustice, assuming he'd picked her for her looks. She was smart, shrewd, sharp, bright, cheerful, funny, and when she cupped her face in her hands and listened to you, only then did you realise just how wise and brave you actually were. I seem to recall talking a lot about building bridges, and I swear she was hanging on my every word.

But that was all right because Ogus was there, and I was happy to be his little friend, his pet monkey; we weren't talking business and I knew she was being polite. Fine, until someone in a shiny breastplate pushed aside the tent flap and told Ogus he was needed for something. Won't be a moment, he said, and there I was, alone with my best friend's wife.

She was still and quiet for about ten seconds. Then she leaned forward and lowered her voice.

"You're his friend," she said. "Can't you talk some sense into him?"

*

"You're his wife," I remember saying to her. "Can't you talk some sense into him?"

She looked at me. "Why should I want to?"

(Aichmalotus had just got himself carved up in the arena. The other guy, of course, was carried out on a door, but Aichmalotus nearly died, too. It's time you called it a day, I told him as he lay there in the hospital, you've got nothing left to prove. He just grinned at me. It's what I like doing, he told me. How could you, I asked, how could anyone enjoy killing? And he grinned some more and said, the man who's tired of killing is tired of life.)

"I can't wait," she said, "for them to come from the arena, looking all solemn, and break the news. I'll probably scream and sob and tear my hair out, because you're supposed to, aren't you, but when they've gone I'll dance round the room singing. The thought of it's the only thing that keeps me going."

"You don't mean that," I said.

No reply.

"He's my friend," I said.

She nodded. "You're very loyal," she said. "He's your friend, so you're on his side, no matter what. That's a wonderful way to be. I envy you."

Third evening that week that I'd stayed and sat with her while Aichmalotus was in the hospital. Look after her for me while I'm laid up, he'd said, there's a pal; and then, you're a true friend, Orhan. Indeed. But that wasn't really why I was there. Other men's wives. A true friend would've made an excuse and set off for Olbia.

I fell in love for the first time at the age of thirty-four. It's like other childhood ailments. If you catch it when you're a kid, it doesn't do much harm, and then you're basically immune. But if you get it when you're grown up, it can be very serious indeed.

So, that evening, while my best friend was in the Guild hospital, his wife and I put our heads together and figured out how to get rid of him, for good. Murder, we decided, wasn't our style; too risky, neither of us could live with the worry of getting found out; besides, there really was no need, given Aichmalotus's line of work. All I had to do was find the Greens a new champion, someone really good. How hard could that be?

It took me eight months. His name was Bestialis (I kid you not) and I met him for the first time when his sergeant brought him up on charges: fighting; grievous bodily harm to a fellow soldier, to wit, biting off one ear; assaulting an officer. Son, I said to him, you're just not cut out for an engineer, but have you ever considered a career in the arena? His eyes lit up. It's all I ever wanted, he said, but I never got the breaks, you need to know people, you need contacts. Funny you should say that, I told him.

Bestialis had the most meteoric career in the history of the Hippodrome, rising from unknown newbie to Green champion in an incredible twelve weeks; fought thirty-six, won thirty-six, all clean kills. When he fought Aichmalotus, there wasn't a seat to be had for any money – they'd been queuing all night to get in, and the lines went right back to the South Gate. I wasn't there. I don't like watching that stuff.

By that time, she was dead, in childbirth; the father wasn't Aichmalotus, though my dear friend didn't know that. I remember him saying to me, before he went to the arena for that fight, the biggest of his career; if anything happens to me, you'll look after little Aichma, won't you? She means everything to me. And then, you're a pal, Orhan. I know I can rely on you.

Bestialis lasted about two minutes. Aichmalotus came out of it without a scratch. He told me afterwards, it's a great help in the arena if you really don't give a damn if you make it or not.

He lasted another twenty-six fights, and then he turned his ankle over in the middle of a stupidly flamboyant *volta* – I think that's the technical name for it – and that was the end of him. Showing off, because the crowd loved it. They cheered him to the echo when he pulled off stunts like that, and they cheered the man who killed him. Say what you like about the Hippodrome crowd, they don't let favouritism get in the way of their appreciation of true skill.

I hated them all that day. If there'd been an enemy laying siege to the City, I'd have opened the gates, because while my friend lay dying they were cheering for his killer. Well, there you are. Bestialis was no great loss, but he's on my conscience. So is she, the only woman I ever loved, and the fact that I killed her with my dick rather than a knife is neither here nor there.

"You're his friend," Sichelgaita said. "Can't you talk some sense into him?"

It took me a moment to recover from that. "If he won't listen to you," I said, "what chance have I got?"

She looked at me as if I was stupid. "You don't get it, do you?" she said. "You mean everything to him. You're all that's left of what was taken from him. As far as he's concerned, there was a disaster and only two survivors, you and him. Everybody else doesn't matter, they don't count, not real people. I thought maybe if you really talked to him—"

I was too stunned to think straight. "I tried," I said. "But it's hard. I agree with him. That makes it really difficult."

I wasn't winning many points with her. "Then open the stupid gates and let him win," she said. "You know he will sooner or later. At least it'll be over quicker, and then perhaps we can put all this behind us. The way it is now, I don't know how much more I can take."

"I'm sorry," I said. "I don't think I can do that."

She sighed. "In that case," she said, "we'll just have to kill him."

Other men's wives. "Why would I want to do that?" I said.

I really wasn't making a good impression. "Oh, I don't know," she said. "End the war at a stroke and save your stupid city from annihilation? It's the only way. You know that, don't you?"

"He's my friend," I said. Of course, she didn't know I'd said that before.

"Well, you're just going to have to sort your priorities out, aren't you? One or the other, because you can't have both. Sorry, but it's a hard world."

I looked at her. A tiny, stupidly unrealistic part of me was clinging to the hope that this was all a trap, to see if I'd betray my friend for a pretty face and the salvation of a city. But she meant it. Superb communication skills, on top of everything else. You always knew exactly what she wanted. "Why don't you leave him," I said, "if he's such a misery to live with?"

She laughed at me. "You can't just leave someone like that," she said. "I wouldn't last five minutes. Don't get me wrong," she went on, "I'm used to men like him and most of the time we get along just fine. But ever since we came here, it's all been different. He's obsessed, and I can't stand it. Have you ever tried living with a lunatic? It's slowly killing me, I feel like I can't breathe. So, either the city's got to go or he has. I'd rather it was the city – actually, I'd rather he gave the whole thing up, he's got the rest of the world, this is just ridiculous, but he won't give up, it's not in his nature."

She was fascinating. Listening to her, I'd stopped noticing what she looked like. "It's only a matter of time," I told her, "you said so yourself. Can't you hang on and tough it out till the City falls? That's got to be better than murdering your husband."

Her face said, I should've known better than to expect sympathy from the likes of you. "Frankly, no," she said. "I know him. He wants to give you a chance. Chances. If he's got to fight you, it's got to be with one hand tied behind his back. So it'll take months, and I simply haven't got that much patience left. Come on, I made you an offer. You won't get an opportunity like that anywhere else."

"Let me think about it," I said.

"Oh, for crying out loud," she said. "What's there to think about?"

Not long after that, Ogus came back. I've never been so glad to see anyone in my entire life.

The more people try and impress me, the more nervous I get, so I didn't like the guest tent much. The silk sheets made me itch, and the scented pillow turned my stomach. I lay on my back, waiting for that idiot Lysimachus, and worried.

One thing that didn't worry me; it was all right that she'd opened up to me like that, because a woman that beautiful would never for one moment imagine that a man would betray her confidence; besides, she expected I'd take her up on her offer without a moment's thought. I worried a bit that at that moment she was telling Ogus a plausible story and showing him her torn dress, but, no, she was too shrewd for that. Ogus knows me too well.

I worried because I didn't want to take her up on her offer. She was right, of course. The siege would be over, the City would be saved, I'd have won and Ogus was an obsessive, a menace, he had to be put down. Ogus was right, too, about the empire. It was an abominable thing, intolerable. How could any sane man want to protect it? My duty was to stamp on its head until it stopped twitching.

I'm an engineer, I told myself. People bring me problems, and I fix them. I'm an engineer; my answer to any and every problem is a gadget, a trick, a device. I don't consider the politics or the ethics. If a bridge needs to be built, I rig something up with logs and ropes. If the system is so hopelessly fucked up that I can't get pay or supplies for my men, I manufacture coins and seals. If the City is threatened with a fate it richly deserves, I modify and improve catapults, improvise armour out of bedlinen, manufacture, sorry, forge (both senses of the word) new communities – fake ones, naturally, authorised by a fake seal. I fix broken people with things, with stuff; with tricks, lies, *devices*. I'm resourceful and ingenious. I don't confront, I avoid; and one of the things I do my best to avoid is justice, and another one is death.

People don't fix easily, and neither does the world they live in. If I'd been the Creator, we'd have ten months, each month ten days long, each day ten hours, each hour a hundred minutes, each minute a hundred seconds; it'd work so much better, it'd be *efficient*, it'd be *convenient*, and everyone would know what was going on, and why. It would be sunny all day and rainy all night, and the snow would fall on time in the right places, and everyone would get on with everyone else, and there would be no more love—

Where did that suddenly come from? Best not to ask.

Sichelgaita had been rather helpful, though she didn't know

that. In order to convince me of the hopelessness of our position, she'd told me that Ogus had ordered to be built fifty enormous barges – he'd had to capture the dockyards at Phyle intact in order to do it – on which he could mount trebuchets, catapults and cranes. These barges, escorted by the Sherden pirates, would sail into the Bay and bombard the docks to cover a fleet of landing craft, bringing in fifty thousand soldiers. There was absolutely nothing I'd be able to do about it. The barges were already on their way, they'd be here in a week or so.

Thank you, I said. Forewarned is forearmed. She laughed. You idiot, she said, don't you get it? Fifty barges, fifty thousand men. You can't bounce stone balls across water. You haven't got a chance.

Ah, I told her, but I do. I happen to have it on very good authority that the Fleet is on its way. No disrespect to your people, but they're the ones with no chance, not against a squadron of Imperial warships.

She looked at me. Don't know where you got that from, she said, but it's bullshit. Your fleet's still holed up the wrong side of the lighthouse. It's cost Ogus fifteen thousand men to hold that promontory against your precious marines, but, guess what, we're still there and you're nowhere. So, sorry, no fleet. Think again.

So; thanks to her I now knew two things I hadn't known before. I knew the nature and timing of the grand assault, and I knew we were still on our own. When you know all the relevant facts, all you have to do then is figure out the solution.

36

Bloody Lysimachus didn't come that night; too busy lolling in bed, the idle turd. So, next morning, breakfast in the Commander's tent with my old pal, dressed today in an old tunic and hobnail boots, with the lovely Sichelgaita reclining next to him on a gold and ivory couch and asking if she could tempt me to another honeycake. Then Ogus had to go and see to something, and we were alone together. Again.

"Well?" she said.

"I've thought about it."

"And?"

"What do you need me for?" I said. "If you want to kill him, kill him. A pillow over the face, or funny mushrooms in his soup. It's hardly catapult science."

"I need you," she said, "to take command, the moment he stops breathing. Otherwise all hell's going to break loose, with all the contingent and regional commanders tearing each other to bits over who takes his place."

"I don't follow," I said. "What am I supposed to do?"

"Ogus will have made a will," she said, "naming you as his heir. His best friend, and all that. They raise you on a shield, you pardon them for mutiny, they go back to their provinces, everything's how it was. I know where he keeps his seal," she said. "And it's common knowledge, you being his friend from back home."

You can warm to people. That's what I'd have done, in her shoes. "You don't need me," I said. "Write him a will naming you as heir. You're his wife."

Scornful look. "You've been away too long," she said. "That lot aren't going to accept a woman. It has to be a man, and you're the only one I can trust."

"Wouldn't do that if I were you," I told her.

"Because our interests coincide exactly," she said. "All right, I'll make it easy for you. I'm going to kill him anyway, whether we make a deal or not. So; do you take advantage of the situation to save your blueskin city, or do you waste it and wait for those barges to sail into the Bay, albeit under the command of someone else? You're not the sharpest arrow in the quiver, Orhan, but even you should be able to figure out that one."

Wait for those barges to sail into the Bay – that rang a bell at the back of my mind. Then, quite suddenly, I knew how I could defeat the barges and the seaborne invasion. Brilliant; only I had to wrench my mind away from it and deal with her instead. Some people have lousy timing.

"It occurs to me," I said, "that the soldiers probably won't accept you just because you're his widow, and they may not accept me just because I'm his friend and the heir in his will. But if I was his friend and heir, and married to his widow—" And I let it hang in the air, like a worm with a hook inside it.

She kept a straight face, which showed strength of character if nothing else. "That'd do the trick."

"I think so," I said. " And, anyway, it's time there was something in this for me. If I've got to betray my friend, I ought to get something out of it, wouldn't you say?"

She nodded sagely. "Perfectly fair."

"And a reasonable result for you," I went on. "You'd go on being queen or chieftainess or empress, that's got to be worth something." I grinned at her. "I'll try not to be too much of a pest. How about it?"

"I like powerful men," she said. The ghastly thing was, I think she probably meant it.

We sealed our bargain. Not my finest hour, though she was very polite and long-suffering. But it had been a long time and, besides, my mind was on other things; winches, lifting gear, the reliability of Polynices' *Histories*, the effective range of trebuchets and the drying time of my special pumice mortar. Not even my not-finest hour. More like fifteen minutes.

37

It was a long day, what with one thing and another. I was tired and went to bed. I'd just dropped off to sleep when this idiot woke me.

His hand was over my mouth. I couldn't breathe.

"It's me," he said.

I remembered, just in time, that the last time I saw Lysimachus he was dead. He relaxed his fingers. "You're alive," I whispered. "I thought—"

"Shh." There's gratitude for you. "We're getting out of here."

Yes, I know. About bloody time, too. "How can we? There's guards everywhere."

I couldn't see his face in the dark but I bet he was smirking. "I brought a hostage."

Oh God. Well, he would, of course. The sort of man who's never properly dressed without one. I peered into the gloom but I couldn't see a damn thing. "I'll just get my shoes," I said.

He hissed something uncouth about my shoes, so I left them. Getting soft, is my trouble. I didn't wear shoes till

I was seven, but now I can't go a few yards barefoot without hobbling.

Outside the tent, in the moonlight, I could see who his hostage was. He'd stuffed a gag in her mouth and tied her wrists, but the moon glinted on her golden hair. Terrific. "You're insane," I hissed at him. "They'll crucify both of us."

"This way."

Later I found out it was just fool's luck, or hero's luck, same difference. The first tent he came to happened to be Sichelgaita's private latrine. He didn't know she was Ogus's wife; just figured a pretty lady would make a dandy hostage. How can anyone doubt the existence of God when evidence of His sense of humour surrounds us on all sides?

We got halfway across the parade ground before the sentries spotted us; and then Lysimachus was in his element. Naturally he'd got hold of a knife, a whacking great big one; he's like a magnet, sharp instruments just seem to sidle up to him and beg him to take them with him. He made a big show of prodding her under the ear until she squealed. I've never been so embarrassed in all my life.

Lysimachus being Lysimachus, it never occurred to him to be suspicious about the ease with which we got out of there. It was easy, he doubtless told himself, because he was such a superlatively excellent hero. In fact there were half a dozen times at least when a half-competent archer could've picked him off as easily as a popinjay in a low tree. But pretty soon we were outside the light of the watchfires and running like hell; let her go, I panted, she's slowing us down. Which wasn't actually true, because he was towing her along by the hair, on account of which she was making pretty good time, but just for once he did as he was told and let go. I heard a few arrows swishing past us, well over our heads, and voices baying behind us. How we were going to get back inside the City was another matter entirely. As I think I mentioned, opening the gates was no casual matter. That genius Lysimachus hadn't thought about that, of course.

So, not long afterwards, there we were under the North Gate. I knew for a fact there'd be nobody chasing us, but of course I couldn't tell him that. "Watch my back," I told him, then I craned my neck back and started hollering: it's me, Orhan, throw down a rope for God's sake.

Praise be, it was Bronellus's shift on the North Gate tower, and he recognised my voice. They hauled us up like grain sacks. One damn thing after another.

"What the hell—?" Nico started, but I cut him off short. "First," I said, "sort something out about Lysimachus. Grand procession down Longacre, then standing ovation in the Hippodrome, and finish off with presenting him with the Bronze Crown. He'll like that, and it'll give people something to cheer about."

He never makes notes, he just remembers it all, like a barmaid. "Right," he said. "Good idea. What *happened* to you? We thought—"

"Next," I said, "I need to write a letter. Now."

Orhan to Ogus, greetings.

One good turn deserves another. Your wife is going to kill you. I'm supposed to take your place. She's got a mole on the inside of her left thigh about two inches down from her crack. If you stroke it, she hisses like a kettle. Take care of yourself.

That ought to cover it, I thought. I wrote it in Alauset using the Jazygite alphabet. I wrote OGUS on the back in ordinary letters, put it in a silver-gilt reliquary and had them leave it on the ground a hundred yards from East Gate under flag of truce. Either the right thing for the wrong reason or the wrong thing for the right reason. What are friends for?

"Right," I said, to Faustinus, because by now Nico was busy. "I need divers. At least fifty. Right away."

"Divers? Orhan, are you feeling all right?"

"Divers," I said. "Matter of life and death. *Go.*"

Nobody bothers with history any more. How many people walk past the stone blockhouses at either end of the Long Quay and know what they were built for? Maybe one person in ten will tell you, weren't they something to do with Jovian's Necklace? And when you ask them what that was, they just shrug.

Two hundred and forty years ago, give or take a decade, Jovian V lost a great sea battle against the Echmen. It wasn't the end of the world; he'd lost two of his four fleets, but the enemy weren't going to come sailing into the Bay quite yet. But Jovian – let's skip the pretence – Jovian was a halfwit who only cared about breeding pedigree wolfhounds, but his City Prefect Martialis was a very smart man, though maybe a tad overcautious. What if the other two fleets were to go the same way? So Martialis and his colonel of engineers put their heads together, and the result was Jovian's Necklace.

They made an enormous bronze chain, each link as thick as a man's waist, long enough to stretch all the way from one side of the Bay to the other. Most of the time, it lay underwater, deep enough so that all classes of ship could sail over the top of it. But the moment the enemy were sighted, the chain could be raised, blocking the entrance completely. It was, I can categorically state, the biggest and most effective project ever undertaken by the Engineers. It was delivered on time, on budget, and it worked; at least, it would have worked if an enemy fleet had ever tried to sail into the Bay. But that never happened. Jovian was assassinated, not before time, and his successor Pacatian started off his reign with a string of dazzling victories over the Echmen that gave the Robur control of the sea for two generations. The Necklace wasn't needed any more. It became something of a joke – read Galba's *Satires*, he's very witty about it – and they stopped holding chain-raising drills and greasing the winch; the chain itself was bronze but the winch-chains were iron, and they rusted. One night, they quietly and unobtrusively gave way, and the Necklace sank to the bottom of the Bay. Eusebius II sold it to a consortium of scrap metal dealers, who tried very hard to raise it until their money ran out. That was ninety years ago. Received wisdom is that there's no point trying to do anything about it now, since its precise location has been lost and forgotten. Besides, bronze is much cheaper now than it was, thanks to the new mines in Thouria. Even if you could find the damn thing, it would cost more to salvage it than the metal is worth.

Regimental archives – we never throw anything away if we can possibly help it – gave me the designs for the winch, which of course we'd have to build from scratch. I nearly burst into tears when I saw them. Still, as we say in the Corps, if it was made once, it can be made again. I put Genseric on it; matter of life and death, I told him, and for crying out loud be nice to the Greens and Blues, the regiment hasn't got the manpower to do it all ourselves.

Finding the bloody thing; Polynices Simocatta, the dreariest poet ever to set pen to paper, wrote a triumphal ode to celebrate the completion of the project, for which Jovian paid him good money, God knows why. It's hard going, believe me (I've read it, so you don't have to), but there's a bit where he compares the chain to a rainbow, stretching 'from Sidera's porch to Actis' shimmering fane'. Generations of scholars have dismissed this as Polynices being his usual tiresome self. For one thing, they point out, a rainbow is a great big arch, while a stretched chain is flat and level. Sidera's porch and Actis' fane they take to mean sunset and sunrise; Sidera, the evening star, Actis, the morning star, fair comment. No help there, then. But take the trouble to read round it a bit and you'll find that in Jovian's time there were temples to Sidera and Actis in the City; really read deep and you'll discover that they were at either end of the Quay. In which case, Polynices was doing one of his trademark hideously laboured double conceits. The rainbow stretches from one end of the earth to the other – evening and morning, understood in poetic convention to stand for the west and the east – while the actual chain is anchored in two places: the temple of Sidera, at one end of the Quay, and the temple of Actis, at the other.

If you think I'm being brilliant and displaying my encyclopaedic knowledge of the minor Robur poets, think again. I got all that out of a report compiled by some unknown freelance for the scrap metal boys – not the ones who went bust, another outfit a century later, who thought about salvaging the necklace, did some research and then decided against it. I have this document because some fool gave it to me in the hopes of interesting me in yet another salvage venture; I pointed out the change in bronze prices, he gave up and went away. The whole thing only lodged in my mind because I happened to know where the temple of Sidera used to be; because the Engineers did some work at that end of the quay and stumbled on stone slabs inscribed with religious texts, and we had the devil of a fuss with the ecclesiastical authorities before we were finally allowed to crack on and finish our job. But, no doubt whatsoever in my mind. Sidera's temple used to stand where the new slipways for the Class Four warships stand now. And, if the unknown scholar and that moron Polynices could be relied on, somewhere very close by, but under a lot of water and probably a lot of mud, was one end of the mighty bronze chain that might just save all our lives. And, guess what, it's a chain. You really only need to find one end. The chain itself will find the other end for you.

"That was two hundred and thirty years ago," Nico said, trying to keep his temper. "It'll be nothing but rust and slime by now."

"It was *bronze*," I told him. "Bronze doesn't rust, it just goes green. It's still down there, I know it. Nobody's salvaged it, it's too big and heavy for anyone to have stolen it, it won't have squiggled away on its own like a great big snake. All we've got to do is find it."

One of the things I like about the City is the unbelievable range of skills lurking inside its walls, just waiting to be needed. Water diviners? Put out a sign saying water diviners wanted, they'll be lined up round the block. Snake charmers? Offer the right money and get yourself a big stick to fight them off with. Pearl-divers? No problem. The Blues and Greens found me a hundred and sixty-two experienced pearl-divers in a matter of hours.

It works like this. Out in the far reaches of the empire, there are places where people have learned and practised esoteric specialist skills for generations. Then the empire comes along. Realising there's money to be made from water divining, snake charming, pearl diving, whatever, the new Robur governor and his staff turn that particular field of endeavour into a government monopoly, grant the right to carry on doing what they've done for generations to a favoured few (in return for a modest fifty per cent of the take) and drive out the competition to fend for themselves as field labourers or beggars. They – doubtless because, having had a taste of the advantages that contact with a superior culture brings, they yearn to immerse themselves in the fountainhead, so to speak – gravitate to the City, where there's bound to be a shanty town full to bursting with their compatriots, and a skilled pearl-diver can earn good money (compared with what he was used to getting in the old country) gutting fish or loading the shit barges. Naturally, the first thing they do on arrival is join a Theme (in return for a modest twenty per cent). So; one hundred and sixty-two pearl-divers, just like that. God bless the empire, I say.

I thought that for men and women used to fishing out tiny oysters from the bottom of the sea, finding a stupid great big chain in the Bay would be a piece of cake. I was wrong about that. It took them three days, during which time I kept scanning the horizon for the characteristic brown-and white-striped sails the Sherden use, and by the time they found it, there were one hundred and forty-seven trained pearl-divers in the City rather than a hundred and sixty-two. I remember thinking, that's a nuisance, we'll need divers to get the damn thing linked up; a nuisance, just listen to yourself. Imperial thinking, omelettes and eggs. Clearly, therefore, Ogus is right and the empire has got to go. But Ogus spends lives like a rich man who's just bought a house in the country spends money. I wish things would make sense, but they don't.

Meanwhile, the winch – you don't want to hear about the winch. I could get very boring very easily telling you about the winch, which had triple-locking ratchets and a gear train so beautiful it nearly made me cry. To work the original, they harnessed teams of a hundred oxen to the capstan. We didn't have a hundred oxen, so we had to make do with people, which meant a fundamental rethink, something I'd have loved to do myself but had to delegate to Artavasdus because I was too busy. He moaned like hell because he had so much work on his plate he barely had time to breathe. I think I may have lost my temper with him when he told me that. In the end, I think a young lance corporal did the actual design, which was simple and brilliant and much better than anything I could've come up with, after too little sleep and too much trying to make myself heard at meetings. I used to be an engineer, but that was a lifetime ago.

After all that, they told me it couldn't be done, because I'd specified bronze chains to connect the necklace to the winches, and there wasn't that much bronze left in the City. I was ready for that. We were in the Small Audience Room at the Palace at the time, so I was able to lead – I forget who – to the window and point at the colossal equestrian statue of Quietus II down in the courtyard below. Look, I said, bronze; use that. Then, a minute or so later when they'd yelled themselves hoarse, I said; fine, we'll call in all the bronze coins in the City and melt them down instead, starting with your regiment and your Theme.

It's a big statue, *was* a big statue. We had eighty-five pounds of good bronze left over, which I sent to the Mint.

38

But it was all taking too much time. Two weeks, according to Sichelgaita, quite possibly less, and the barges would be here; and a construction project, as anyone in my line of work will tell you, proceeds at the pace of the slowest contractor. In this case – and, dear God, could you blame them? – the divers. It was their job to join the new winch-chains to the two ends of the Necklace, tie the other end of each rope to the new chains, then pass the rope through the end links of the old one. I make it sound simple. Not really. The Necklace was down there all right, down at the very limit a human being can reach before having to return to the surface. Add to that the fiddly job of manipulating the end of a heavy, waterlogged rope, and you're four, maybe five seconds outside the capacity of mere flesh and bone. So, what happens? Silly question. You have two options. You try and you give up, or you stay down there, try a bit harder, and drown. Mostly, my divers took the first option, then went back and tried again. Some of them reckoned there was a third option, and that was the last anyone saw of them. I'd have cried my eyes out except for the little voice in my head saying, these people, can't they do anything right?

Finally, when we were all at our wits' end, who should save the day but that insufferable pest Lysimachus, now fully healed of his wound and bouncing around the place looking for further and better deeds of exceptional valour. No, he'd never been a pearl-diver, but he could swim, and hold his breath; how hard could it be? I'm ashamed to say I agreed, in the pious hope that he'd drown and I'd be shot of him.

By now he had a regular fan club numbering in the thousands, all of whom turned out to watch him, naked as a baby and smeared all over with olive oil, diving magnificently off the West Quay with a rope's end clenched in his shining white teeth. He sliced into the water like a smug dolphin, and then everything went quiet. We waited, counting under our breath. No way can any mortal man hold his breath for more than six minutes; six sixties is three hundred and sixty. Round about two-ninety we were starting to worry. At three-thirty, you could've heard a mouse squeak. At three-seventy I could distinctly hear sobbing. Damn, I thought. The fool's gone and drowned himself, and it'll all be my fault. Some people have no consideration.

I'd given up counting by then, but I'm reliably informed he broke the surface after four hundred and nine seconds, with the rope still in his teeth, punching the air with both hands as the crowd bayed for pure joy. Someone rowed out in a little boat to pick him up but he was fine, no ill effects whatsoever. So I ordered him another public triumph and the Order of the Bronze Chain, first class; silly fool had won all the existing honours so I had to invent him a new one. I never could abide a show-off. Still, it got the job done.

"A hero is no bad thing," Faustinus assured me, while I

sulked all the way back to the Palace. "People need a figurehead, someone to put their faith in. This Lysicrates—"

"Lysimachus."

"He's just the man for the job. Typifies all the Robur virtues. He's strong, brave, loyal, altruistic, dedicated to the service of his superiors—"

"The right colour."

He gave me a nasty look. "That, too. People need heroes, just like they need legends. Probably in a thousand years it'll be Lysimachus who defended the City and saved us all, and you and I will just be a footnote."

"You think this lot'll still be here in a thousand years?" I said to him. "Get real."

After that, it went like a dream. I don't suppose I'll ever forget the first time I heard the winch. There was this deep ringing sound, like a bell, which tells you that the iron is strong and true, with no cracks or flaws, no cold shuts or inclusions in the welds, and then the most amazing soft, sharp clicking as the ratchet hand engaged with the detents and dropped exactly into place – click, click, click, and it was telling you, everything's fine, the strain's being taken, you're in safe hands now. I swear, there's nothing in this world as satisfying as the sound of a beautifully made machine working perfectly. And I thought: I caused that to be, I'm responsible for its being called into existence, that beautiful piece of work. And I thought: I didn't make it, someone else did, while I was having meetings and doing the paperwork. Ah well.

We were having trouble finding enough bodies to work the capstans. Then Nico, who very occasionally shows signs of starting to think like me, suggested that Lysimachus might like to go down to the Market Square and call for volunteers. I gather several people were quite badly hurt in the crush, but we got our winch crews, one shift on and another standing by.

("Lysimachus," I said, "how would you like to be the new City Prefect? Faustinus won't mind, I'll promote him to Lord Chancellor or something. People really like you. It'd be a great help to me."

He looked at me. "I can't," he said.

"Don't worry about that," I said. "We've got loads of clerks to read stuff out to you and take dictation, and I'll have them make up a stencil so you can sign things."

He shook his head. "My place is at your side," he said.

Shit. Still, it was worth a try.)

Five of my best smiths from the regiment on each end of the chain, welding shut the ends of the connecting chains, which is harder than you think with bronze. You need a localised heat, so they'd rigged up bellows with long, thin nozzles, like the blowpipes people use for getting a fire going. Soon as they'd finished, the winches took up the weight until the chains were taut; we were ready to go. Part of me really didn't want to give the signal, because what if it didn't work? What if the Necklace was corroded through, somewhere out at the bottom of the middle of the Bay, or maybe the connecting chains wouldn't stand the strain, or the winches bent or snapped, or simply weren't powerful enough? I could see all these contingencies as clearly as if they'd already happened, they were memories rather than fears, part of me was already saying, he should've known better, calls himself an engineer? Shut up, I told them, and gave the signal.

Lots of clicking, as several hundred yards of shining golden chain wound itself round the winch spools. Then someone gave a great shout. Out in the distance, on the other side of the Bay, something broke water, like a dolphin or an enormous seal. A second later, the same on our side; then, it was as though God had drawn a straight line across the water with His fingertip, and there was this low, slow rumbling, a bit like the noise the incoming tide makes when it rolls the pebbles together. It looked like a wrong-way-up bridge, or – God help me, I thought of that clown Polynices and forgave him, and was properly ashamed of myself – an upside-down rainbow, the reflection of a green rainbow in dead calm water; and still the winches clicked softly, no grunting or straining because they were machines, and machines can be perfected, unlike their makers; and then they stopped, because there was no more slack, and the Necklace was raised. Three feet clear of the water at either end, just dipping under the surface in the middle; an amazing, extraordinary thing. I stared at it, and I realised, my mind was too small to take in what I was looking at. It was as though the Gods had dropped something – a comb, a hairpin, a needle – and it had fallen down to earth; unimaginably huge and incomprehensibly magnificent, made of celestial materials by a divine craftsman, too big and too beautiful to have any place in our world, utterly incongruous, a numbing statement of the difference between Them and us—

Excuse me. It was an impressive sight. It was a very nice chain. And I was damned if I could see how any ship, from a cockle boat to a quinquireme, was going to get past it. Job done.

Job almost done. The most vulnerable point – sorry, the only vulnerable point – was the winch housings. So we built hollow moulds out of planks and poured in the magic pumice mortar; two instant castles, walls eight feet thick, fitted with iron doors we'd borrowed from the strongrooms of the Imperial treasury (where they were redundant these days, since we'd spent all the money). Then, because we'd learned a thing or two, we buried both castles in soft sand and earth, to take the impact out of trebuchet stones.

From start to finish, twelve days. Not bad.

I was fast asleep. I'd had a long, hard day. In a siege, sleep is the only luxury you have left.

"Wake up," some idiot was shouting in my ear. I told him to go away, or words to that effect. He was shaking me by the shoulder.

"You've got to come right now." Not a he, a she. "Something's happening."

"Sawdust." She can't stand being called that. "You lunatic. What the hell do you think you're doing?"

"*Now*," she said.

Sawdust isn't one of those loud, assertive women, and she never shouts. Something was wrong. "What's going on?"

"We don't know. You've got to come now. *Please*."

Dark night, no moon. Some fool had put out all the lights on the wall. "That was me," she hissed.

She'd been up there fine-tuning the catapults (in the middle of the night, because she hadn't had time during the day; for Sawdust, sleep is something that happens to other people). But everyone (she blushed when she got to this part) needs to pee sometimes, and in the pitch dark, over the side of the wall's as good a place as any and better than most. So she was squatting there, pissing into space with one hand on the crenellation to stop her falling over, and out of the corner of her eye, at the extreme edge of her peripheral vision, she saw something move.

"But you can't have," I said. "It's dark as a bag out there."

She explained that working late on the wall had done marvels for her night vision. She'd seen something move, out there in the space between the wall and Ogus's watchfires. So she'd come running and woken me up.

"You stupid bloody woman," I said. "If you saw anything, which I doubt, it was a fox or a stray dog or something. But you didn't see anything, because it's too dark."

She'd seen something, she said. And when a quiet, shy woman tells you something three times, even though she's been shouted at and called a stupid bloody woman, you start asking yourself: *did* she see something? And then you worry.

"Besides," I said, "even if you're right, what am I supposed to do about it? It's the middle of the night."

"Actually," she said.

She hadn't told me, she explained, because she didn't want to mention it until she was sure it would work; but it had occurred to her that if you filled a narrow-necked pot with palm oil, stuck a bit of rag in the neck and lit it, and then shot it out of a catapult on a high trajectory, when it landed it'd burst into flames and give you quite a bit of light. It's been tried, I said, loads of times, it can't be done. Yes, she said, but I've been thinking—

Just so happened she had a stack of suitable jars handy, modified to her specifications, and a barrel of oil. I helped her load a jar into the spoon of a catapult, and we jacked up the ratchet to forty-five degrees. This won't work, I told her, and it's dangerous. Probably it'll shatter on the spoon and we'll get spattered all over with burning oil.

It made the most amazing whistling noise as it sailed through the air, and when it pitched it split open in a fountain of blazing slops. There was a split second when the flames roared up into the sky, and then they died right down. And in that split second, we saw—

"The bastard!" I yelled. I'd forgotten she was there. "Fucking shitty bastard, he lied to me."

We saw pavises, huge hide-covered pavises as tall as a house moving forward in a line across the empty plain. Which meant she'd lied to me, he'd lied to me through her. The attack wasn't coming from the sea, there weren't any trebuchet barges, he'd blindsided me, used that bitch to make a fool of me, tricked me, his friend; I wanted to circle his throat with my hands and squeeze. How could he do something like that?

"It's all right," she was saying – stupid woman, of course it wasn't all right, my best friend – "We need all the catapults, now."

What? Oh, that. I tried to remember who was duty officer, but the name escaped me. "Duty officer!" I yelled, so loud I scared myself. "All crews to stations, now."

It was the Blues' night on shift. I reckon it was no more than four minutes before they were in their places, hauling the levers to span the catapults. Four minutes; how far had the pavises moved in four everlasting minutes? "Let's have another of your firebaskets," I said.

We hadn't moved the windage or elevation. The jar went splat against a pavise. Something to aim at. "Line ready," someone yelled. "Loose," I yelled back. The thudding of catapult arms against frames made the parapet shake.

"And get those bloody trebuchets going," I shouted. "Wake up, you idiots. Have I got to think of every damn thing?"

The trebuchet crews had been on station at the same time as the catapult boys, but their machines take three times as long to span. They went off while the catapults were still winding up. A trebuchet shot hisses as it flies – swish, swish, swish, very fast. Even if you can't see a damn thing, you get a pretty good idea of what it's hit by the noise. A stone pitching idly in the dirt is a dull, soft thump. A hit on any form of structure is a crash, like an accident, a pile of bricks falling over. No fluke; in a matter of seconds, they'd taken a mark on the brief yellow flare and shot a spread at fifty-minute intervals on either side. Amazing work; the Echmen royal artillery couldn't have done better.

I suddenly thought: whose job is it to call out the garrison? Mine, probably. "Keep going," I snapped at Sawdust, one of those entirely redundant orders I seem to specialise in, and groped my way along the wall to the tower.

On the stairs, which shuddered like a fly-bitten horse under the shock of the pounding artillery, I tried to draw myself the bigger picture. We had artillery and they didn't; we had lots of very good artillery, enough to carpet the plain with smashed bones and crushed bodies. They had pavises. A pavise is a shield the size of a ship's sail, on a wooden trolley. Hit it high up and it falls over; hit it low down and you smash the frame. Directly behind it you'll generally find between ten and fifty men, pushing. They're meant to protect against arrows, not monstrous balls and blocks of very fast stone. Hit the pavise, it's inconceivable that you won't hit, kill, crush double figures of men pushing it or crouching behind it. The bloody fool, I thought; bloody bastard cheat, bloody fool.

I reached the bottom of the stair, where the answer lit up in my mind like a lamp in the darkness. Pavises are a liability for men crossing open ground against artillery, but essential when you bring heavy machinery within arrowshot of a wall. Therefore, it wasn't men, or just men, behind those things, it was engines. Ogus was making his big push. He'd done it at night, hoping to get across the plain without being cut to bits but not really all that fussed if it cost him a thousand, five thousand, ten thousand dead. He was bringing up his brightest, best, most beautiful weapons, his pearls of great price from the treasures stolen from the Echmen; that would be the worms, which screw into wooden gates and crumple them up like a bit of paper or a dry leaf.

Across the empty space, where the Bailiffs' Market used to be (but I'd cleared all that; streets and blocks of wooden buildings just begging to go up in flames, and we needed the timber). I thought, he knows I'll have undermined the approaches to the gates, so that anything heavier than a haywain will break the frail underprops and go crashing down twenty feet. So he'll have wagons of big rocks, our catapult and trebuchet shot, most like, to fill in our mines and make hard standing for the worms. Does he seriously imagine enough of his pavises will make it across the plain to shield his engineers while they're doing all that? Answer? Not bothered, one way or the other. Omelettes and eggs. I know Ogus fairly well, and one thing he's not is penny wise and pound foolish.

Thank God Nico was where he was meant to be, asleep in his own bed in the prefecture. All I had to say was, they're here, they're coming, and he knew what I meant. I told him what I was expecting while he scrambled into his armour – aketon and cuirass next to the skin, he didn't bother with clothes, no time – then I scuttled away, yelling for someone to take a message to the Miners' Guild.

Ogus, I figured as I ran back towards the wall through streets that were rapidly clogging up with suddenly mobilised, sleepy, terrified people – Ogus didn't know me quite as well as I knew him. He figured I'd take artillery off the wall to defend the harbour against his mythical fleet. I hadn't done that. I'd built new engines; because the machines on the wall had been modified to throw the bouncing balls, and we'd have had to modify them back to use against ships, quicker and easier to build new ones from scratch. No, fair play to him, only an engineer would've realised that. Therefore he was anticipating maybe a third less firepower on the wall; losses horrifying but not catastrophic, therefore a reasonable price to pay, acceptable, omelettes and eggs. I could imagine him being annoyed to find he'd missed a trick. Serve the bastard right.

The Miners' rep was at the tower gate waiting for me. I knew him slightly, a Green, quiet sort of a man, seemed dependable. I explained: you know those saps you dug under the gates? Well, they're bringing up heavy gear, and when they get here they'll collapse them and start filling them up with stones. What I want you to do is open the saps up from our end, go down there, start fishing out the stones as fast as they drop them in. Can you do that? He gave me a look that told me I'd asked a stupid question. Ten minutes, he told me. Thanks, I said.

Artavasdus was in charge of assault drills and procedures: where the hell was he? Actually he was up there already – I asked myself, when did we get so good at all this, when did we turn into *professionals*? – and I could hear him, shouting orders in that rather too high, slightly annoying voice that shows he's in control but only just. Moving his men into position, and if I could hear him, so could the enemy. Not that it mattered, but I clicked my tongue. Maybe not so professional after all.

Back up the stairs, onto the wall; I realised, nobody knows where I am, this is very bad. People will need to be able to find me, I'm supposed to be in charge. Then Faustinus, in a yellow silk dressing gown and slippers . . . They told me you'd be here, he said. Then, this is terrible, what are we going to do?

The tower I was in became command headquarters for the entire defence, simply because I was in it and I was so busy with people running in wanting decisions that I didn't have time to move somewhere more sensible. Needless to say we couldn't hear ourselves think, with that damned racket of catapults going on outside, and the walls and floor shaking; no table, no chairs, nothing to write on or with (but then a Green turned up with a fat sheaf of paper, a horn of ink and a whole box of pens; God knows who sent him, but he saved the City; people were actually thinking without me having to tell them to). Genseric stumbled in from time to time to let us know roughly how far the enemy had got. They were having a devil of a job; smashed pavises all over the place, unsmashed pavises blundering into them and getting stuck, then a direct hit on the blockage cleared the bottleneck, only for it to re-form a dozen yards further on. I kept asking, how are we doing for ammunition, are we going to run out? And when they said, no, we're fine, we can keep this up for hours, I didn't believe them. How could it be possible, the rate we were getting through it? And then someone would remind me, we saw to all that, we've had thousands of men and women working round the clock for weeks, we've got enough stone balls, honestly. Also, I kept asking what time it was, and they said about five minutes since you asked the last time. That made no sense. I was sure we'd been in that horrible shuddering room for days, maybe weeks, and here were people telling me it was just minutes, lying to me, men I thought were my friends.

At some point, it dawned on me. I'd long since passed the point where I was having good ideas or making any sense, and it didn't seem to matter. Other people were coping. All those hours and days we'd spent, thinking out drills, figuring out what we'd do about this and that, as and when the time came.

I remember saying, we need to change shifts on the catapults, those boys must be fit to drop. And someone looked at me like I was senile and said, we're changing shifts every quarter of an hour. Who told you to do that? You did, they said, about three weeks ago. We do actually listen, you know.

And I kept hearing this loud, booming voice, somewhere up on the roof of the tower we were in, so that it echoed down the stairwell, and not even the thump of the trebuchet arms could drown it out. Lysimachus, of course, cheering the men on – what I should've been doing, except that's not me, not one bit. For God's sake make him shut up, I said, he's giving me a headache. Genseric pointed out that he was doing a great job and the men were working like lunatics for him, but if I really wanted him to stop, I could send him a direct order. Then he changed the subject.

I remember really, really needing to take a pee, but being too busy.

And then the thumping and the shaking stopped. What the hell's going on, I shouted, and they told me: the enemy had closed the range, too close now for artillery to be effective. They're here.

Then the tower really shook. I was sure we'd been hit, but apparently not; walls, ceiling and floor still in one piece, men getting up off the floor, still alive. Someone put his head round the door. That, he explained, was the saps under the gate thresholds giving way.

Everyone left the room in a hurry, except me. They were needed on the wall, every pair of hands that could draw a bowstring or throw a brick or hold a shield. Not me, though. You stay here, they all said to me, where it's safe.

So there I was, alone in the dark, because the only light we'd had was one lantern, which someone had taken with him. Don't know how long I was there on my own. My head was splitting, though I hadn't been aware of it before. I stood up and pissed against the wall, floods, which helped a lot. I couldn't think. I sat back down on the floor with my back to the wall, suddenly, horribly aware that I'd done everything I was capable of doing and was now completely useless. And did I trust those brave, clever, brilliant people, my friends, who'd just been proving how well they could do and how far they'd come, to carry on the defence without me? Like hell. I closed my eyes, not that it made much difference. The noise was very loud, and I'd lost the ability to analyse it or understand it, tell bowstrings from catapult sliders or orders from yells of pain.

I'd never been useless before. I didn't enjoy it.

"Are you all right?"

The last thing I'd expected to hear was a woman's voice. Made no sense, until I remembered there was one woman up on the wall. "Sawdust?"

She hates being called that. "Why are you sitting in the dark?"

"Some bugger stole my lamp."

"Ah."

"What's happening?"

"They've reached the wall. The catapults aren't doing any good, so we've been stood down. I sent the men to get spears and swords, but—"

Quite. Sawdust and me, useless on the wall among all those rough men. I could see the logic. She, being a woman, and I, being a coward, would be no use there. Further, we'd be a danger to others, because we'd get in trouble and some poor fool would have to save us, probably get cut up or killed in the process.

Have you noticed, by the way, that women don't fight? Even on those rare occasions when they scrap with each other, it's all slaps and scratches, they don't try to maim or kill. And as for soldier-fighting, sharp weapons, blunt trauma, chops and cuts and slices, butcher's work; they don't do that. It's not in their nature. This is frequently offered as proof that men are better than women. Me, I think it means the exact opposite.

"How are we doing?" I said.

"I don't know. It's still dark." She paused, realised that she was making a report to the supreme commander. "Basically, the archers are shooting at shapes and noises. I think you're right and those engines they've brought up are worms, because they're all jammed up together headed for the gates. They may have siege towers, but they'd have to be pretty tall, and I didn't see any big black shapes against the skyline. There were a lot of rumbling noises, like rocks being tipped off carts."

"I sent sappers to clear the stones out from our end," I said.

She nodded. "I think Artavasdus has got men standing by at the top of the saps, in case they try and come through that way."

I hadn't thought of that.

"We used up all the fire jars," she went on, "but we only had a few. They worked quite well."

"Get some more made," I said. If we're still alive in the morning, I didn't say. "How did you stop them from breaking in the spoon?"

"Wire," she said. "Pressed into the clay before it's fired."

Hadn't thought of that either. It came as a shock to me, that I hadn't thought of everything, that I didn't have to. "Smart," I said. She grinned, then went all serious again. Still reporting. "General Nicephorus stopped the trebuchets, because he couldn't tell if we were hitting anything or not. He says he'll start them up again as soon as it's light. Colonel Artavasdus wanted to lead a sortie round the back of the attackers, but the general thought not, in case we needed the men inside."

"Just as well I wasn't there," I said. "I'd probably have gone for the sortie, and it'd probably have been a mistake."

She wasn't sure what to make of that. "That's about it, really," she said. "Oh, and Prefect Faustinus has ordered a general curfew. Everyone not needed on duty stays home till further notice. That's everyone not fighting or working in the masons' or the armouries."

I nodded. Very sensible. Good old Faustinus. A second later, I was on my feet, blundering for the door, tripping over Sawdust's legs.

"What's the matter?" she said.

"All your bombardiers," I said, "down at the harbour, now. Don't just sit there, move."

She jumped up, bumped into me, bounced off. My head was agony, as though my brain had swollen to three times its normal size, and there was this awful throbbing. "What?" she said.

I have a feeling I haven't been lied to, I didn't say.

Because he wouldn't; not Ogus. Come to think of it, I can't ever remember him telling a lie, except to protect someone else; well, me.

In which case, there was a fleet of trebuchet barges, and it was on its way, and it must be very close, or else why would Ogus throw away so many lives and so much fine equipment on a futile attack, unless as a diversion? And, right now, all my trained artillerymen were off shift and resting, when they should be at their stations at the docks. And the chain was down.

*

I'm woefully ignorant about sailing stuff, so we were halfway across town before I realised. Ogus's fleet wouldn't be sailing into the Bay until there was enough light for them to see by. Without leading lights to steer by, they wouldn't know where to go, or where the rocks were.

I glanced up at the sky, which was starting to show blue, just a little.

Sawdust's bombardiers were mostly Blues, because they're traditionally strong in carpentry, masonry and allied trades, but she had at least seventy-five Greens – remarkable thought, if you'd spent all your life in the sure and certain knowledge that the only connection members of opposite Themes were ever likely to make would be along the length of a knife. They reached the docks ahead of me, goes without saying. I can't help it. I have short legs.

I tried to remember how many men she had, all told, but my head was jammed full of numbers, so I couldn't. Enough to man the capstans, turn the winches and raise the chain? No idea. Behind me, somewhere in the darkness, thousands and thousands of men were fighting and dying in a battle – arrow-wounds, bones crushed, flesh torn, bleeding external and internal – and I was hurrying in the other direction, because what they were doing wasn't actually very important. All that mattered now was a fine point of engineering, the sort of thing better expressed in numbers than words; how many men of physical capacity x does it take to operate a winch of specification y to create a force capable of lifting a mass m? It should have been all right – I'm an engineer, for crying out loud – but my head hurt and I was scared and useless, and at some point during the last hour I'd lost the ability to think. But that was all right, because I had a shy little milkface girl to do my thinking for me. If my brain hadn't been trying to squeeze out through my ears, I'd have laughed like a drain.

There was a crowd outside the docks: men, women, kids. I thought, volunteers rushing down to help with raising the chain, that's good. Then I remembered: I hadn't sent out for volunteers.

I got closer, and saw Sawdust, with a load of her bombardiers bunched up round her, yelling bloody murder right in the face of some man I recognised but couldn't quite place. I'd never seen her so angry, didn't think she was capable of it. But she was howling at the top of her voice; how can you be so stupid, how can you be so unreasonable? And the man said, piss off, milkface. We don't want your sort round here.

I'm a coward, and I hate physical confrontations. A moment later I'd somehow got through the densely packed crowd, and someone was holding my arms behind my back, to stop me killing the man Sawdust had been talking to. And she was saying, it's all right, it doesn't matter, which is what I usually say in these situations. What's going on, I asked her. Who are these people?

Actually, as I was asking the question I'd figured out part of the answer. The man I'd wanted to kill, I now remembered, was a ward manager for the Greens, and all the people with him were Greens too. And they weren't here to help; I didn't need to be told that.

"This man," Sawdust said, making *man* the deadliest insult in the history of semantics, "thinks there's a Selroqois fleet on the way to evacuate you and your friends. I've told him, he couldn't be more wrong, but he won't listen."

I wriggled my arms loose – there's a knack to it, which you eventually pick up when you've had your arms pinned as often as

I have. "You moron," I said to him. "Yes, there's a fleet coming. No, it's not Selroqois, it's Sherden. That's what we raised the Necklace for. Or maybe you haven't been following the news."

"Bullshit," he said. "That's all just bullshit, to distract us. You knew the attack was coming, and you fixed it with your Selroq pals to come and pick you up, soon as it starts getting hot. Well, fuck you. We're getting on those boats. You can stay here with your Blue buddies and fry."

I stared at him. I kid myself that I understand people, that I can predict what stupid, pathetic thing they're going to do next. I think God sees me doing it, and decides to teach me a lesson in humility. "That's not true," I said. "For crying out loud, you halfwit, if I wanted ships to get into the Bay, why the hell did we just bust our guts raising the fucking chain?"

"Smokescreen," he said, and I swear he believed it. And faced with belief, what can you do? And we had so little time.

I took a long step back. "I hold you directly responsible," I said, in a loud voice. "This is all going to be your fault."

Because while we'd been talking, a lantern shadow had fallen across my face, and there's only one man in this city tall enough to cast a shadow at that angle. "Lysimachus," I said.

"Here, boss."

"Get these idiots out of my way."

He has his faults, but he does what he's told. He slid past me like an eel, reached out with those long arms of his, one hand on the top of the fool's head, one round his chin; then a movement so quick I didn't really catch it, and a click, no louder than that, and the Green ward manager fell to the ground like a coat dropped on the floor. Then I saw metal flash – the shadow had passed over me – and then there was just Lysimachus, doing what he loves to do. That, for about five seconds; he can get a lot done in five seconds. Then Sawdust's Blue bombardiers raised a horrible yell, realising that it was suddenly all right to murder Greens. They were wildly outnumbered, but they had weapons, and for months they'd had to pretend that these people were their friends. We had no trouble getting to the gates after that.

39

Of the people, by the people, for the people. I can't remember offhand where that quote comes from; it was something to do with some bunch of wild-eyed idealists overthrowing the tyrant so they could become tyrants themselves. No good will have come of it, you can be sure. The people; God help us.

You look – at least, I do, or I did – at the emperor and the nobility, lording it over the people while they starve and suffer, and you say to yourself, something's got to be done about all this. This can't be right. The lions of the earth must not destroy the worms any more. And then you do something about it, and what do you discover? The people turn out to be – well, people; a collective noun for all those individual men and women, none of them perfect, some of them downright vicious, most of them monumentally stupid. As stupid as the emperor, the great hereditary lords, the priestly hierarchs, the General Staff and the Lords of the Admiralty, the merchant princes and the organised crime barons. When push comes to shove, thick as bricks, the lot of them. You wouldn't trust any of them with the helm of a ship, or the regimental welfare fund, or your dog if you were going away for a few days, or anything sharp.

I speak as a member of the people. I've done some colossally stupid things in my time. I never asked to be placed in a position of authority. Most of the time I've done my best, and it's never been good enough. Just dumb, I guess.

In my time I've met three, maybe four genuinely smart men and women. One of them was Ogus, my old pal, who for some reason always had a high opinion of me. I think that says it all, really.

40

Soon as Sawdust and I were inside, I called out, "Lysimachus, get those Blues in here, right now." I didn't expect him to obey, it'd be like whistling to a dog once it's on the scent of a deer, but obey he did, herding the bombardiers inside the gate, none too gently, with the flat of his sword. We got the gates closed and then the Green mob outside nearly sprung them, by sheer weight of numbers. But Lysimachus got the bars up, and the bars held. That problem solved, for now.

I sent a man up to the top of the lookout tower. What am I supposed to look out for, he said, it's dark, I can't see squat.

I'd made sure there were plenty of lanterns in the winch-houses. The levers were already in the slots in the capstan barrels, secured by wedges. I'd already split up the available manpower into two teams, me in one winch-house, Sawdust in the other. This is going to work, I told myself. I gave the order, and threw my weight against the lever. We couldn't budge it. Not an inch.

"We need more men," some genius told me. "There's just not enough of us."

Outside the gate, doing their best to stove it in with benches from the nearest inn, were more men – the people, on whose behalf I was fighting this desperately difficult war. A few dozen of them, with their strong arms and broad shoulders, would have those capstans turning in no time flat. Beyond that impenetrable cordon, a whole city full of the people, whose survival depended on the turning of those capstans, but we couldn't reach them or get a message to them. I'd done my bit. I'd made and salvaged the hardware, dealt with the things, devised and executed the cunning tricks; what I hadn't done, apparently, was take the people along with me; neglected to win their hearts and tiny, tiny minds. And so the capstans weren't turning, the chain wasn't going to lift, it had all been a complete waste of time, and I'd betrayed my friend, the last of my people, all for fucking nothing. There's an old saying, isn't there, about leading a horse to water. Well. You can lead the people to water, but you can't make them think. Nobody, it seems, can do that.

Someone was yelling at me: sails, sails. For a moment, I didn't understand what he was talking about. What did sails have to do with getting the capstans to turn? Then I figured it out. Oh, I thought. Oh shit.

I left them to it, heroically straining every sinew against the levers of capstans that wouldn't bloody turn, and wandered out into the soft red light of dawn. The newly risen sun blazed on the water, exquisitely beautiful. I couldn't see anything. No, belay that. I could see the sails of ships, hundreds of them, beating up the Bay with the morning tide.

Well, I thought, we nearly did it. We nearly saved the City, we nearly kept all these tiresome people from being slaughtered,

334 K. J. Parker

we nearly prevailed against insuperable odds. We built the winches, we hooked up the chain, we actually got it lifted and in position; just not at the right time. Great hardware, but the people let us down. Pity about that.

Never mind, I reassured myself. Ogus, my pal, had given explicit orders that I wasn't to be harmed, on pain of death. All I'd have to do was walk up to the first enemy officer who set foot on the quay and tell him who I was, and a fast dinghy would carry me safely out of harm's way. I'd known that, ever since that first meeting, and don't for one moment imagine that it hadn't factored heavily in my decision-making. There's some freak cult somewhere that believes that the king of the gods sent his eldest son down to earth to die for the sins of the people; they arrested him and strung him up and stretched his neck for him, and he died; and on the third day he rose again from the dead, and that was supposed to prove something, though I'm not sure what. The hell with that. The eldest son knew perfectly well that he'd rise again, unlike his temporarily fellow mortals, so it really didn't matter, just a brief inconvenience. I assume that's why the cult never caught on, because any fool can see the gaping hole in the logic. Anyhow; that was me. Everyone else is mortal, but I can't be touched. Screw it. Eventually, no matter how hard you wriggle and squirm, there comes a time when you've got to admit that you're beat and the game is over.

"Lysimachus," I said.

"Boss?"

"Stay here," I said. "I expressly forbid you to set foot on the quay as long as I'm alive. Stay back here and organise the defence."

He looked at me. He was in agony. For some utterly

incomprehensible reason, that vicious bastard loved me, or what in his poor addled mind I stood for.

"Please," I said.

There were tears in his eyes. "Sure," he said. I turned my back on him and walked away.

There was nobody on the Quay. Everybody was in the winch-houses, straining at the capstans. I had the place to myself. Ideal. There'd be nobody to see me walk up to the enemy soldiers, raise my hands above my head and call out, "Don't hurt me, I'm Orhan, Ogus's friend." Everybody would assume that I'd died fighting, in a final act of heroic stupidity. How little they know me. I may be dumb, but not that dumb.

Ashamed? A little, though the failure wasn't really my fault. I'd done my best. It was nearly good enough. Mostly, though, I just felt very, very tired.

I watched the ships grow, from little white flecks of sail into recognisable shapes. They were Imperial warships; clearly, Ogus had managed to capture one of the fleets, along with all those armies and all that gear. I counted the ships and did some mental arithmetic, number of marines per ship. At least ten thousand men. Even if every man in the City capable of bearing arms hadn't been tied up defending the wall against Ogus's horribly bloody diversion, we'd never have stood a chance – not against ten thousand soldiers arriving suddenly at the docks, with the whole City wide open in front of them. I imagine we'd have held the docks gate for an hour or so; Lysimachus would've loved that, his moment of apotheosis. Nico would almost certainly have fought and died at his side, for the honour of his noble family; he'd have felt justified, redeemed. I really wish I could've made that possible, it would've meant so much to him. Screw them both. If there's one truth in this life, it's that you simply can't win. The most you can achieve is to make a nuisance of yourself, for a very short time.

I stood on the quay and watched the ships come in, going through in my mind the list of people I was going to do my best to save. Aichma, and Sawdust, and Artavasdus if he'd allow me, and Arrasc and Bronellus, though at that precise moment I wasn't too kindly inclined toward the Themes; mustn't forget poor Faustinus, who'd always done his best to be my friend, though his best, like mine, really wasn't worth dogshit. I thought some more, but those were all the names I could come up with. Probably I'd forgotten someone, like I always do, and I'd kick myself later, when they were dead. What I should've done, of course, was write a list. Too late for that now. Ah well.

The front rank of ships, twelve of them, had passed the line where the chain would have been, if we'd managed to raise the bloody thing. Even if there was some miracle and the stupid thing suddenly came soaring up out of the water like an angry dragon, there were enough marines on those twelve ships to clear out the winch-houses and slaughter everyone inside them. It was over. God forgive me, I felt relieved.

The rumble of anchor chains. Splashes as boats hit the water. I fixed my eyes on the nearest boat, which would be the first one to land. Of course, the oarsmen had their backs to me. I rehearsed my speech; please, don't hurt me, my name is Orhan, I'm Ogus's friend. I said it to myself under my breath, over and over again.

41

You'll probably have guessed by now that large parts of this narrative are unreliable. You'll have figured out that I come across as rather too heroic, too eloquent, too self-assured, too much in command of the situation to be credible, knowing what you've learned of my character. It's probably struck you as improbable that I should've always been ready with the smart idea, the right words.

The hell with it. This is my story, and if I choose to make myself look as good as I think I can get away with, why not? In a hundred years, or a thousand, who's going to know any different? I did my best, and nobody gave me much credit for it at the time. I've been to all the trouble and effort of making a record, so that the deeds and sufferings etcetera. The labourer is worthy of his hire.

But even I'm not so brazen as to try and kid you into thinking any better of me at that particular moment, when the ships crossed the invisible line and I knew I'd failed, it had all been a waste of time, all the people in the City were going to be killed and all my clever devices had nearly worked, but not nearly enough. Consider me on the quay, alone, waiting to betray my people in return for my own worthless skin – and please, whatever you do, don't you dare feel sorry for me.

42

The boat drew up next to the stone steps. A man in a red cloak and a shiny helmet clambered out. I stared at him. He was a blueskin.

He looked round, then walked up to me. "Where is everybody?" he said. "Who the hell are you?"

"I'm Orhan," I said. "Who are you?"

He sighed. "Get me whoever's in charge," he said.

"That would be me."

A look of deep contempt from a tired, busy man. "I want to talk to the man in charge," he said, slowly. "Do you understand?"

"I'm Orhan," I said. "Colonel of the Imperial Regiment of Engineers. Who the hell are you?"

He opened his mouth, then closed it again. I guess he'd remembered; now he came to think of it, yes, the commander of the Engineers was some milkface, and what's the world coming to? "Admiral Auxinus, Sixth Fleet. Oh, for God's sake, man, pull yourself together. What's the matter with you?"

43

Floods of tears, God help me. I gave him my report, phrased in proper military language, with tears gushing out of my eyes and rolling down my cheeks. Eventually I ran out of things to say and just stood there.

He stared at me. "You've got the Great Seal," he said.

I fished about in my sleeve, pulled it out and reached out my hand to give it to him. He sort of shied away, as if it smelled bad.

"Dear God," he said. Then I guess he remembered that he was an admiral in the Imperial navy. "The City is under attack," he said.

I nodded.

"Right now. There are enemy forces trying to break in."

Another nod. I could see him struggling to make up his mind whether to believe me or not. "I've got nine thousand marines on my ships," he said. Slight pause. Then, "Do you want them, or don't you?"

Me? Then I remembered. I was in command. "Yes," I said.

"Right." Immediately he transformed, the way gods do in

legends; instead of a weary middle-aged man in a red cloak, he was a pillar of fire or a whirlwind. He shouted, and junior staff officers materialised at his elbow. He barked orders; they turned and ran. Behind him, I could see ships drawing up at the quays. Suddenly and unexpectedly, a grown-up was in charge. I turned to leave.

"Where do you think you're going?"

Strange. "You don't need me," I said.

"You're in command here," he roared at me. "Isn't that what you just told me?" You stupid little monkey, he thought but didn't add.

Ah, I thought. "You're the senior officer," I said. "They're your men."

"It doesn't work like that." He was a feather's breadth away from losing his temper. "Don't you understand the chain of command?"

Too much for one day. "No," I said. "I build bridges."

I walked away. He yelled at me. I kept going.

44

It was, they tell me, a close-run thing. Auxinus's marines turned the tide and saved the day, but not before the enemy undermined a fifty-yard section of the north Wall, broke through into Foregate and seized control of nearly a quarter of Old Town. The Greens just managed to keep them out of Haymarket, but the Blues broke and ran; the Greens were outflanked and would have been wiped out to the last man if Auxinus hadn't counterattacked just in time and driven the enemy into the Hippodrome. Once they were kettled up there, he had his men jam the gates shut from the outside, then set fire to the whole complex. They'd been saying for years, the Hippodrome is a death trap, a disaster waiting to happen; all those wooden benches and beams and floors, canvas awnings, jerry-built stands only held up by bent nails, frayed ropes and force of habit. In the event, more enemy soldiers were trampled to death than burned alive. A couple of hundred survived and tried to surrender, but were massacred by the Greens before Auxinus's men could stop them.

Needless to say, I kept well away from the fighting, though

Auxinus insisted that I show my face. He needed me to tell Nico who he was; orderly transfer of command, he called it, and I can see his point. Nico was pleased to see him; that's a slight understatement. The look of joy on Nico's face, as though he'd been carried up to heaven in a fiery chariot and dumped down at the right hand of God; a real soldier, finally. I left them to it and sneaked away, out through Bell Yard, down the alleys, then a short dash across Lower Foregate in the direction of Poor Town. And it was there that the stupid arrow hit me.

45

Sheer bad luck, was the general verdict. Probably a stray shot from the scrimmage on the wall by the North Gate tower, where we'd nearly finished mopping up the last of the enemy raiding party. But it hit me in the guts and went right through into my stomach. There's a medical word for it, which means blood poisoning. People have been known to survive and recover, they assure me, and while there's life there's hope.

46

By the time I came round, the assault was over. Auxinus had me woken up. He needed the Seal, and a signature on a bit of paper, to confirm his authority. They had to lift my hand by the wrist and guide it across the paper.

It hurts. To take my mind off it hurting, I've spent the last couple of days dictating this. People have been trying to get in and see me, but I've got Lysimachus on the door, keeping them away. I don't want to see any of them, not knowing it'll be for the last time. Not Aichma – she made a scene, hysterical, demanding to see me. Lysimachus slapped her face and threw her out. I'm a coward. Dying is bad enough. I can't face stuff like that.

A letter came for me, and a present; from Ogus. I guess he hadn't heard about me getting shot. We've actually managed to keep it a secret, so far at least, which is a miracle in this man's town.

The present was a book, in a rather unusual binding. At first I thought it was just ordinary leather but with the hair still on. But the hair – about a quarter-inch long, thick and stubbly – was golden yellow. I stared at it, once I'd figured out what it was; a human scalp, with the hair shaved. The book, incidentally, was Planginus's *Manual of Siegecraft*, which I've always wanted to read, but copies are rare as hens' teeth.

Ogus to Orhan, greetings.

Thanks for the warning. You were quite right about the plot to murder me. You saved my life. Here's a little token of my gratitude, to remember my wife by.

You'll have gathered by now that your Sixth Fleet managed to smash through our blockade and sink the assault barges. Annoying, but makes no difference in the long run. Yes, I know; in the short term, you'll be able to bring in food from outside, mercenaries to help man the walls, tribute from the few bits of the empire that haven't fallen yet. Quite possibly you may be able to keep going for a year or two. If you think prolonging the agony is a good thing, please accept my congratulations.

You're my oldest friend, and you saved my life. But you can be a real pain in the arse sometimes.

Look after yourself.

47

This story is ending abruptly. So is my life, so you'll have to forgive me if I can't tie up the loose ends, tell you what became of who, say a proper goodbye to the men and women whose adventures you've been following. Sorry, but I can't help you. If by some miracle the City survives, maybe so will the official records, and you can look up the registers of marriages and deaths. Otherwise, what the hell. The most someone like me can do is strike a light in the darkness. As soon as it burns my hand, I have to let go. Besides, I'm not really a historian, only an engineer.

The poor, long-suffering clerk is sick to death of the sound of my voice, so I'll keep it short. These are the unsatisfactory histories of Orhan son of Siyyah Doctus Felix Praeclarissimus, written down so that the deeds and sufferings of great men may never be forgotten; which is why, Ogus, I'm sending them to you. After all, once you've finished the job, there won't be any Robur left to read them, or make copies. Once the worms have inherited the earth, they may like to be reminded of the last dying whimper of the lions. And besides, after all the trouble I've caused you, I guess I owe you a keepsake. I'm sorry to say, this is all I've got left. I apologise for getting in your way, hindering you, being a nuisance. Not a friendly way to behave, and I am, though you may find it hard to believe, your friend. I'm sorry for getting myself killed. It was careless of me.

I think that more or less covers everything.

Translator's Note

The authenticity and authorship of the *Commentaries* has been fiercely debated for over a thousand years, and there is no point in rehearsing the convoluted and inconclusive arguments of the opposing academic factions. Almost anything is possible. It could be a contemporary record written by the man who conducted the defence of the City. It could equally plausibly be a Restoration forgery, designed to further the agenda of the Foundation and give legitimacy to the counter-revolutionary coalition. It could even be, as Kember so ingeniously suggests, a metaphysical and alchemical allegory, with no foundation whatsoever in historical fact.

There are many serious problems with the text as it stands: the notorious inconsistencies; the distinct possibility that substantial and significant parts of the book are missing; above all, the problem of the narrator. Recently, scholars have attempted to establish a link between the Orhan of the *Commentaries* with a military engineer, Orianus Peregrinus, attested from a badly worn inscription from Nobe Bhaskoe, which they would like to see as the 'bridge in the middle of nowhere'. However, it seems increasingly likely that the Nobe Bhaskoe inscription will be proved, on epigraphical grounds, to date from the mid-seventh century, a hundred and fifty years earlier than the events purportedly described in the *Commentaries*; in which case, there is no external evidence that any part of Orhan's version of events is true, or that he ever existed.

Regrettably, therefore, we have no option but to let the narrator speak for himself. It is enormously frustrating that our only witness to such momentous events should be so unsatisfactory; unreliable, self-serving and barely literate. But, bearing in mind the almost miraculous survival of the manuscript (saved first from the sack of Perimadeia and then the destruction of the Library of Mezentia; presumed lost for six hundred years and eventually rediscovered during the confiscation of the met'Oc family library, among a pile of discarded manuscripts scheduled to be cut up and used for bookbindings), we must be grateful for what little we have.

extras

about the author

K. J. Parker is a pseudonym for Tom Holt. He was born in London in 1961. At Oxford he studied bar billiards, ancient Greek agriculture and the care and feeding of small, temperamental Japanese motorcycle engines. These interests led him, perhaps inevitably, to qualify as a solicitor and emigrate to Somerset, where he specialised in death and taxes for seven years before going straight in 1995. He lives in Chard, Somerset, with his wife and daughter.

For a comprehensive guide to the unreliable world of K. J. Parker, go to http://parkerland.wikia.com.

Find out more about K. J. Parker and other Orbit authors by registering for the free monthly newsletter at: www.orbitbooks.net.

if you enjoyed

SIXTEEN WAYS TO DEFEND A WALLED CITY

look out for

THE WINTER ROAD

by

Adrian Selby

*THE GREATEST EMPIRE OF THEM
ALL BEGAN WITH A ROAD.*

*The Circle – a thousand miles of perilous forests and
warring clans. No one has ever tamed such treacherous
territory before, but ex-soldier Teyr Amondsen,
veteran of a hundred battles, is determined to try.*

*With a merchant caravan protected by a crew of skilled
mercenaries, Amondsen embarks on a dangerous mission to forge
a road across the untamed wilderness that was once her home.
But a warlord rises in the wilds of the Circle, uniting its clans
and terrorising its people. Teyr's battles may not be over yet . . .*

All roads lead back to war.

Chapter 1

You will fail, Teyr Amondsen.

My eyes open. The truth wakes me.

You will fail.

I had slept against a tree to keep the weight off my arm, off my face. My tongue runs over the abscesses in my mouth, the many holes there. My left eye is swollen shut, my cheek broken again, three days ago, falling from a narrow trail after a deer I'd stuck with my only spear.

I close my eyes and listen, desperate to confirm my solitude. A river, quick and throaty over rocks and stones. A grebe's whinnying screech.

I take off one of the boots I'd stolen, see again the face of the man who'd worn them as I strangled him. I feel my toes, my soles, assess the damage. Numb, blisters weeping. My toes are swelling like my fingers, burning like my face. I need a fire, cicely root, fireweed. I have to be grateful my nose was broken clean. A smashed-up nose is a death sentence in the hinterlands.

If you can't sniff for plant you're a bag of fresh walking meat. You need plant to heal, plant to kill.

If I keep on after this river I can maybe steal a knife, some plant and warmer clothes. These are Carlessen clan

lands, the coast is beyond them. I'm going to live there, get Aude's screaming out of my head, the horns of the whiteboys, the whisperings of the Oskoro who would not, despite a thousand fuck offs and thrown stones in the black forests and blue frozen mountains, let be their debt to me.

The grebe screeches again. Eggs!

I pull on the boot with my right arm, my left strapped against me and healing, itself broken again in my fall.

I pick up my spade and the small sack that I'd put Mosa's shirt in, the spade something of a walking stick to help me along the mossy banks and wretched tracks. Snow was making a last stand among the roots of birch trees, a few weeks yet from thawing out. A few handfuls ease my gums.

The sky is violet and pink ahead of the sun, the woods and banks blue black, snow and earth. I stumble towards the river, a chance to wash my wounds once I've found some nests and broken a few branches for a fire.

The grebes screech at me as I crack their eggs and drink the yolks. I find five in all and they ease my hunger. If a grebe gets close enough I'll eat well. The sun edges over the hills to the east and I am glad to see better, through my one good eye. The river is strong up here, my ears will miss much.

I drop the deerskins I use for a cloak and unbutton my shirt. I didn't have to kill the man I stole that from. I loosen the threads to the discreet pockets that are sewn shut and take a pinch of snuff from one. It's good plant, good for sniffing out what I need. Feels like I've jammed two shards of ice into my nose and I gasp like I'm drowning, cry a bit and then press another pinch to my tongue, pulling the thread on the pocket tight after. Now the scents and smells of the world are as clear to me as my seeing it. For a short while I can sniff plant like a wolf smells prey.

I forget my pains. Now I'm back in woodland I have to find some cicely. The sharp aniseed smell leads me to it, as I'd hoped. I dig some up, chopping around the roots with the spade to protect them. Around me a leaden, tarry smell of birch trees, moss warming on stones, but also wild onion, birch belets. Food for another day or so.

I wash the cicely roots and I'm packing my mouth with them when I hear bells and the throaty grunts of reindeer. Herders. The river had obscured the sounds, and on the bank I have no cover to hide myself in. I cuss and fight to keep some control of myself. No good comes of people out here.

The reindeer come out through the trees and towards the river. Four men, walking. Nokes – by which I mean their skin is clear and free of the colours that mark out soldiers who use the gifts of plant heavily, the strong and dangerous fightbrews. Three have spears, whips for the deer, one bowman. There's a dog led by one of them, gets a nose of me and starts barking to be let free. Man holding him's smoking a pipe, and a golden beard thick and long as a scarf can't hide a smirk as he measures me up. The herd start fanning out on the bank. Forty feet. Thirty feet.

"Hail!" I shout, spitting out my cicely roots to do it. My broken cheek and swelling make it hard for me to form the greeting. I try to stand a bit more upright, to not look like I need the spade to support my weight.

"Hail. Ir vuttu nask mae?" Carlessen lingo. I don't know it.

I shake my head, speaking Abra lingo. "Auksen clan. Have

you got woollens to spare? I'm frostbitten." I hold up my good hand, my fingertips silver grey.

He speaks to the others. There's some laughter. I recognise a word amid their own tongue, they're talking about my colour, for I was a soldier once, my skin coloured to an iron rust and grey veins from years of fightbrews. One of them isn't so sure, knowing I must know how to fight, but I reckon the rest of me isn't exactly putting them off thoughts of some games. Colour alone isn't going to settle it. Shit. I reach inside my shirt for some of the small white amony flowers I'd picked in the passes above us to the north.

"No no no. Drop." He gestures for me to drop the spade and the amony. He lets a little of the dog's lead go as well. The bowman unshoulders his bow.

At least the stakes are clear, and I feel calmer for it. He has to be fucked if he thinks I'm going to do a word he says, let alone think his dog could hurt me.

He has nothing that can hurt me, only kill me.

"No, no, no," I says, mimicking him before swallowing a mouthful of the amony and lifting the spade up from the ground to get a grip closer to its middle. I edge back to the river, feeling best I can for some solid flat earth among the pebbles and reeds.

He smiles and nods to the bowman, like this is the way he was hoping it would go, but that isn't true. The bowman looses an arrow. Fool could've stepped forward twenty feet and made sure of me but I throw myself forward. Not quick enough, the amony hadn't got going. Arrow hits my left shoulder. It stops me a moment, the shock of it. He's readying another arrow, so I scream and run at the reindeer that strayed near me, the one with the bell, the one they all follow. It startles and leaps away, heading downstream, the herd give chase.

Time and again I made ready to die these last nine months. I'm ready now, and glad to take some rapists with me. I run forward while they're distracted by how much harder their day is now going to be chasing down the herd. The one with the pipe swears and lets his dog go at me while one of the spears fumbles in his pockets for a whistle to call the herd, running off after them.

Dogs are predictable. It runs up, makes ready to leap and I catch it hard with the spade. It falls, howling, and I get the edge of the spade deep into its neck. I look at the three men left before me.

"Reindeer! You'll lose them, you sad fuckers!" They'll understand "reindeer" at least.

The pipe smoker draws a sword, just as my amony beats its drum. I don't know how much I took but it hits me like a horse just then. I shudder, lose control of myself, my piss running down my legs as my teeth start grinding. I gasp for air, the sun peeling open my eyes, rays bleaching my bones. My new strength is giddying, the amony fills me with fire.

He moves in and swings. He's not very good at this. The flat of my spade sends his thrust past me and I flip it to a reverse grip and drive it hard into his head, opening his mouth both sides back to his ears. I kick him out of my way and run at the bowman behind him. He looses an arrow, and it shears the skin from my skull as it flies past, almost pulling my good eyeball out with it, the blood blinding me instantly. He doesn't know how to fight close, but I'm blind in both eyes now and I'm relying on the sense the amony gives me, half my training done blind all my life for moments like this. I kick him in the gut, drop the spade and put my fist into his head, my hearing, smell exquisite in detail. He falls and I get down on his chest and my good hand seeks his face, shoving it into the earth to stop its writhing, drive my one good thumb through an eye far as it'll go. A shout behind me, I twist to jump clear but the spear goes through me. Out my front it comes, clean out of my guts. I hold the shaft at my belly and spin about, ripping the spear out of his hands, his grip no doubt weakened a moment with the flush of his success. I hear him backing away, jabbering in his lingo "Ildesmur! Ildesmur!" I know this name well enough, he speaks of the ghostly mothers of vengeance, the tale of the War Crows. I scream, a high, foul scritching that sends him running into the trees.

My blood rolls down my belly into my leggings. There's too much of it. Killed by a bunch of fucking nokes. No more than I deserve. I fall to my knees as I realise, fully, that it's over. The river sounds close, an arm's length away maybe. I fall forward, put my arm out, but it gives and I push both the spearhead and the end of the arrow that's in my shoulder back through me a bit. A freezing spike of pain. My senses lighten to wisps, I fall away from the ground, my chest fit to burst, my blood warming my belly and the dirt under me. Why am I angry that it's all over? The sun keeps climbing, the pebbles rattle and hum as the song of the earth runs through me – beating hooves, distant cries, roots of trees stretching and drinking. I hum to quieten the pain. It's my part in the song but I was always part of the song, I just haven't been listening. The birch trees shush me. Snowy peaks crack like thunder in the distance. The sky is blue like his eyes, fathomless.

"I'm coming," I says. He knows I'm coming. I just have to hold out my hand.

Chapter 2

A Year Before

"You will fail, Teyr Amondsen."

"I will not. I cannot."

I was standing before the chief of Citadel Hillfast, Chief Othbutter. We was in his chamber of justice. He has a simple wooden chair up on a modest dais he believes gives his people the right impression of his priorities. His gut and the jewels braided into his beard speak otherwise. The jug of wine, red as his fat spud of a nose, also speaks otherwise.

Stood next to him his high cleark, Tobber, a beech-coloured broom brought to life, long narrow face and smooth bald head. Tobber has told me I will fail. He stood as a master of an academy would stand before his class, for he had an audience, mostly the merchants that make up my competition along with representatives of Othbutter's favoured clans. A king and courtiers in all but name, crowding the room so it was hot and thick with the smoke of pipes and whispers.

"I think she's far more prepared than you think, Tob," said Othbutter. "She takes my captain, an escort of my best men, she has employed an excellent drudha to mix her plant and your most capable cleark, she takes my brother here as well, to do my justice. Our clans in the Circle need our support from the bandits that terrorise them. Master Amondsen presents us with an interesting solution." Othbutter had a table to his left, on which stood his jug and a plate, from which he picked and folded two big slices of beef into his mouth.

"She has not the trust of any of the clans who live in the Circle," said the high cleark to the room. Othbutter's brother Crogan muttered a "Hear, hear."

"One of Khiedsen's sons, Samma Khiese, now terrorises the Sedgeway and the Gospeaks and claims himself lord of the Circle and all its clans, including her clan, the one she abandoned. Steel, not tribute or errant daughters, is what they require."

Chief Othbutter looked at me, expecting me to continue the rebuttal, defend my honour.

"We will clear out whatever bandits we find," I said. "I've done it all my life as a soldier. But this expedition isn't just signing some contracts and trading plant, it's about spending profit, my profit, towards strengthening our rule of law. It's about reconnecting the Circle to all of us, so that my clan and all the clans there have good reason to bury those enmities that lead them now to blood. The routes through to Elder Hill, before even we reach the Sedgeway and the Circle beyond, are difficult if not impossible half the year for want of work to drain land or build cord roads and rip raps and keep them. I aim to forge a proper road beyond Elder Hill, right across the Circle as far as Stockson and the busy markets your fathers will no doubt have fondly remembered to you. Citadel Hillfast might then rekindle the good relations with Citadel Forontir that we once enjoyed."

Tob paused for effect as my words were met with murmurings of disbelief. "Yes, Amondsen, I hear that you will build forts from your own chests of gold, drive out bandits, keep hundreds of miles of road maintained from here to Stockson and yet charge nothing for it. You would do what our chief it seems cannot, with but a handful of men and a few wagons. Maybe somebody here not already hired by you or sleeping with you would offer a wager as to your success?"

Before a silence could burnish his point I spoke. "The chief has many more responsibilities than I, problems up north with the Larchlands and Kreigh Moors biggest among them. I'll set an example to all the merchants." I cursed myself the moment I spoke these words, for they did me no favours with those assembled, for all that I spoke true. "The merchants of Hillfast have responsibilities other than filling our purses and lining our cloaks with fur and silk. These forts, this road that my people are building, will further my own prosperity, you can bet on that, but they will help the people of the Circle, grow the common purse through taxes and in so doing raise us all up."

A peal of laughter then that Tobber allowed before saying, "I look forward to seeing all our beggars and slaves bedecked in the silk and ermine that will fall behind your bountiful wagons!" This made the nokes laugh harder and even Othbutter smiled, though in looking on me his eyes pleaded innocence.

"A man as travelled as yourself, Cleark Tobber," I continued, the irony of that sending further ripples of laughter through the crowd, "would have seen Farlsgrad's Post Houses for himself and seen what service they do for the people, easily triple the distance walked or ridden in a day." Fuck him, he'd get seasick crossing a stream and he knew it. "And tell me,

Tobber, what else should I do with my coin if not empower Hillfast in its trade? Do you know any good whores I should go piss it all on?"

That got a lot more laughs, and it infuriated that sad old prick for we all knew enough what his pleasure was with girls. I could never weave words as well as others though, that's as good as it got from me. I'm more used to giving orders than winning people over.

I looked behind me to Aude. He smiled and winked. He was still worried there might be some move to stop this dream of mine at the final hour, but the chief had signed and sealed commendations and proposals for the clan chiefs, giving my caravan his authority.

Then Tobber started up again. "Did you know, Chief Othbutter, that she means to take this caravan to the Almet, the dark forest at the heart of the Circle? She means to get the monsters living there, the Oskoro, to swear fealty to your staff. Is that right, Amondsen? But will you recognise them amid the other trees? Will you get within a mile of them before their spores put you to sleep and they feast on your flesh?"

"It's pig shit, Chief. All my years there we never had anything bad from these people. Tributes have always been paid to them and they've saved lives in return, my own for one. Until we forge a friendship, the Almet won't be the common ground it used to be, a neutral place where we can meet the clans, a place of peace and not blood, made so by the Oskoro and respected by all who live in those lands."

"Well well, Amondsen, if you could harness their drudhaic power, I'm sure our troubles in the Circle would soon be over. I won't fault her for trying, Tobber," said Othbutter.

The Oskoro would not be used, but they would be in my debt

from the gift I had for them, though what that could mean for us was as hard to fathom as they were.

"Cleark Tobber," said Othbutter, "you have spoken well in favour of your chief's interests, as always. However, I will not leave these merchants to fend for themselves in the Circle when they are doing much to fill our coffers, not least by giving your clearks an ease of passage. We are done, masters. Amondsen, I wish your path swift and dry." He stood to signal the gathering was ended. The high cleark bowed and walked past me without a nod or a word. We locked arms for a farewell, me and the chief, and I took Aude's arm and led him out of the chamber into the main avenue that runs parallel to the dockside the far side of Othbutter's court.

"That might have gone better," I said. "They think it's a ruse, a way of getting one over on them and nothing more."

"You upset the merchants gathered there to be sure, but there's none there that don't already despise your success. Too proud to be part of it and all."

"I saw pity for an amusing child."

"Who, except Chalky Knossen, who's coming with you, has even a slip of your ambition? You show them their sorry limits." He leaned in to kiss my head as we walked.

"Aye, perhaps. Can we walk back to the house? Might be the last bit of time we get to ourselves for a while."

We wound our way up through the carts and children, plant-addicted droopers and hawkers of the streets of Hillfast, edging the slums and the merchant's store sheds. Those guarding them I knew well enough to ask after, teasing word of their masters out of habit, for I would not be back in Hillfast for a year. Then it was up through the steep cobbled lanes of the farmers' huts onto the Crackmore path, a hill that led up to our house amid the cliffs.

"How are you?" he said once we'd crested the hill and turned to look back over Hillfast, as we always did on this climb. I guessed he was meaning how I was since we'd argued the previous day. Knowing we might meet resistance on the road, I had tried a day brew, a dayer as we called it, something a bit less than the fightbrews I took to enhance my skills as a mercenary all those years ago. I lost control of the dayer, it being the first time since then I was putting my body back through it. My cleark Thornsen had taken our son Mosa out for the day while I tried it, but it didn't go so well for Aude, who had stayed with me, and I had hurt him during the rise, when my body was fighting with the hard, violent thrill the dayer caused.

"I'm excited to be getting going at last. I've gone over our tactics with Othbutter's captain, Eirin, Thad as well, but I have a duty for you too, and Mosa won't be back for a while." I give him a wink but he didn't return it and it stung.

He was a slender, beautiful man, ropes of black hair swept to one side which I kept wanting to tuck behind his ear framing the sharp ridge of his cheek. Today the cheek was bruised.

"Well, some instruction on getting our son to eat fish would be welcome. He tried bilt too, rabbit and reindeer. It didn't go well, seems he can only eat their meat fresh," he said.

"I'm sure he'll take to bilt with no other choice." I took his hand in mine for the rest of the walk and let the breeze and the gulls fill our silence as we approached our house because I didn't know how better to fill it.

Near the gate was our two wagons and the packhorses. We'd got some boys from the shed up to help us. Thad, my drudha, was there too, overseeing the plant we were looking to trade or gift.

"Teyr! Did you get Othbutter's scribble on our scrolls?" he asked.

"I did. We ride out tomorrow." "Purses for our mercs?"

"Yes, those and all. Sanger, Yalle and her crew, all paid retainers." He nodded and turned back to the chests that he'd packed the jars and bottles of prepped plant in.

"I'm going to cook us all some eggs and pitties," said Aude. He put his hands on my shoulders then.

"I'm sorry, bluebell," I said, wanting to reach out and touch his cheek but not daring to try.

"No, Teyr, you told me how it would be, that you might lose yourself. I didn't think . . . well, I don't know."

"I would say there's no excuse, but it took hold of me, I couldn't stone it. I . . . "

He kissed me, the gentle crackle of his whiskers compressed to the softness of his lips. He always closed his eyes. I mostly closed mine, except that day, and when I saw his eyes open, I felt the hint of a smile in his mouth that cradled all else we felt.

"We've a lot to do if we're going to prove that dusty cinch Tobber wrong." With that remark he gated off what we could not speak of to protect what his kiss reaffirmed. I watched as he walked away against the sun, his familiar off-kilter stride, shoulder slightly higher on the right, back straight up as a plank of wood, all from a twist in his left foot from his being born that would never right.

I had a well of confidence when I first courted him. My asking around after him got back to Tarrigsen, who he worked for. Tarry was a merchant, had been like a father to me when I'd returned from soldiering with a fortune for savage work done for the armies of Jua and Marola. Aude had started with Tarrigsen a while after I served an apprenticeship there. Wine and fucking had lost their appeal quite quickly after I'd landed in Hillfast. I was a curiosity, a bet even, a barren woman with the strength of two men cold – by cold I mean without a brew – but a little too old, so I began to hear. I had thought, for all the years I was taking purses, that I just needed enough to pay out and sit on my arse getting soaked on good wine, stilling out on kannab and eating fine beef twice a day. And while I was doing that I knew I was only trying to chase out what was gnawing at my guts, that I couldn't settle with the idea that all I did with my life was kill people for coin and then drink myself to death. So I had begun to use my knowledge of the world and give it the weight of my coin. I became a merchant and was developing a "concern", as the other merchants would say, and they might have meant both senses of the word in saying it. Tarrigsen the merchant had also travelled far and wide, and when, one day, he took a seat at my side in the Mash Fist tavern down on the south quay he explained to me exactly what I was feeling, finding the heart of my thoughts so quickly I almost choked on my rum.

"There's the look of a seaman, Teyr, staring at a horizon while sat in a tavern. You in't the first soldier to nurse her cup and wonder if she could go about the world killing and getting rich and be happy coming back home. But you also in't the first to realise, now all the killing's done, that a life smithing at the same forge for twenty year or keeping tally of an old ass's coin don't make a man poor in his spit and spirit."

"Well said, Master Tarrigsen. And you mentioning the work of a cleark is a bit of what brings you in your finery here among the deckhands, carters and soaks, I imagine."

He laughed, clacked my cup with his and drained it, putting it down heavy on the table to get old Geary to hear it and splash us out a couple more from a bottle kept put away for me.

"He's my best cleark is Aude, and you in't the only merchant's got his scent in their nose. Much as I love you, I won't be fucked with by any merchant of Hillfast, whether she paid the colour or not."

"Well, it's not really his letters or his tallying I've discovered an interest in, Tarry."

He raised an eyebrow. "Good, well, along with the merchants I'm having to slap away, there's also one or two women that have an eye for him as you do. I recall now I sent him over to get your scribble on the Shares. Had his boy with him I believe, Mosa."

It had been a week before. Aude had earnest, gentle blue eyes that I very much liked looking at and he sang rhymes to the boy on his shoulders amid our pleasantries. Mosa was playing with the piece of amber his father had on a necklace. I must have apologised for my appearance, for I'd spent the morning shifting sacks in my shed, and he'd said to that only that I looked fine.

"You know his keep, Mosa's mother, she . . . "

"Yes Tarry, Thornsen told me a bit about it, you know how the clearks go, tight like a virgin's cinch with each other."

"Ahh Thornsen, an excellent cleark, you're lucky to have him, but yes, they spill more of our secrets than they do their own ale when they finish their day, I'll bet," he said. "But her dying giving birth to the lad is well known. It snuffed the drink out of him rightly. Caring for a dut'll do that when there's nobody else, I guess."

"I need a reason to see him. Can you give me one?"

He laughed again at that. "How many men have you led into war, how many killed, and you're after me cooking up some story so you can give him that look you women give us." And he made to flick his hair about and look at me sort of side on.

"Ha! Any women you didn't have to pay for ever look at you

like that, Tarry? I bet these others after him got proper long hair though, not a head like this, no axe blades giving their lips an extra curl either."

"There's few got your brains and your means. We both know there's a bit of chatter about you around the quays, more than a few merchants got their cocks in a twist because they won't be half the trader you'll be, and the gangers can't put up any muscle worth a shit to take a slice of what you'll make, you having paid the colour. You want to go courting Aude to keep you warm at night, I'll be happy for both of you. Poach him as cleark and you won't find a ship'll take your interest or your cargo from Hillfast to Northspur, not while I'm breathing."

"I'll never do that to you, Tarry. There's my word." "And I'll take it. Now don't wear him out."

I've harpooned whales, been holed up in blizzards in the Sathanti Peaks surrounded but unseen by a hundred enemies. I've been a castellan, I helped the great Khasgal found his own throne, wedding the most inspirational and powerful woman I'd ever met, the only other woman he loved. You would think then that I wouldn't be short of things to talk about when I called on Aude to go riding for an afternoon. Tarrigsen had Mosa, saying he was going to get him helping make us all some supper. Tarry loved this man and his boy, that was clear.

On that ride I learned Aude was naturally quiet. We must have done a couple of leagues before I managed to speak, saying I was a bit surprised he would agree to a ride with someone Tarrigsen was having to keep a backeye out for when it come to trade. And he rode on for a few moments, smiling to himself and just said, "But you're beautiful." I wasn't expecting that of course, I know I'm not a painting, not after my life, and he'd have seen me blush if it wasn't for the colouring over my face from the years of the skin rubs and how the fightbrews had changed it. Nazz'd wet himself, and Ruifsen, if they could have seen me shy like a young lass, having known what I was like on campaign with them when I was a few years younger.

Aude took a keen interest in plant, more than anyone I knew that wasn't a soldier, and we'd stop when we saw this or that, and it filled up most of what we talked of. There was a run of chestnut trees flowering, and we climbed a couple to get us a few handfuls of their teardrop leaves and some hunks of bark. He said he knew a good infusion for coughs and breathing troubles that I used to get a lot of when taking the brews, and that Mosa would get from time to time. He didn't make a fuss either like some men had when I, having been a soldier and also a deck-hand, flew up a tree faster than he did. Even asked me to lend him a hand up. I liked that he had no idea how to work up to a kiss, and it quieted him enough when I took the initiative that I realised I might have been the first he'd kissed since his keep, Mosa's mother, had died.

Of Mosa he couldn't speak enough, two summers old and a handful by all accounts, having found his feet and now pulling on anything left near the edge of tables, including a bottle of ink, which, even with cleaning, left him looking like he'd soldiered and paid the colour down in Jua. They sat me next to Mosa that night after our ride out. I tried eating my stew and helping Mosa with his, but not without getting the odd spoonful in the face from his bursts of excitement or frustration. I sang a few songs I knew and pulled some faces, which got the boy laughing, and it felt nice, filled my heart up.

Before the end of summer Aude had moved with Mosa up to my house, which pleased my kitchen girls and everyone else besides, it seems. By winter the boy called me Ma. I looked up at Aude the moment Mosa said it, for it made me tearful. He said, "That's right, she's Ma to you and her crew, I think. Isn't that right, Ma?"

He was smiling too, and much moved, I think, and he give Mosa a kiss. That was the happiest I've been.

Enter the monthly

Orbit sweepstakes at

www.orbitloot.com

With a different prize every month,
from advance copies of books by
your favourite authors to exclusive
merchandise packs,
**we think you'll find something
you love.**

facebook.com/OrbitBooksUK

@OrbitBooks

www.orbitbooks.net